The Hourglass Factory

Lucy Ribchester

**SIMON &
SCHUSTER**

London · New York · Sydney · Toronto · New Delhi

A CBS COMPANY

First published in Great Britain by Simon & Schuster UK Ltd, 2015
A CBS COMPANY
Copyright © Lucy Ribchester 2015

1 3 5 7 9 10 8 6 4 2

Simon & Schuster UK Ltd
1st Floor
222 Gray's Inn Road
London WC1X 8HB

www.simonandschuster.co.uk

Simon & Schuster Australia, Sydney
Simon & Schuster India, New Delhi

A CIP catalogue record for this book is available from the British Library

PB ISBN: 978-1-47113-930-7
EBOOK ISBN: 978-1-47113-931-4

Typeset by Hewer Text UK Ltd, Edinburgh
Printed and bound in Great Britain by CPI Group (UK) Ltd, Croydon, CR0 4YY

Lucy Ribchester was born in Edinburgh in 1982. She studied English at the University of St Andrews and Shakespearean Studies at Kings College London. In 2013 she received a Scottish Book Trust New Writers Award for the opening chapters of *The Hourglass Factory*. Her short fiction has been published in journals in the UK and US, and she writes about dance and circus for several magazines and websites including *The List*, *Fest* and *Dance Tabs*. *The Hourglass Factory* is her first novel.

For Alex

'The days are past for rioting and we do not need to have recourse to bloodshed or violence to carry on our schemes of progress and reform, because we have a fairly good franchise which is an assurance that the will of the people must prevail in these democratic days.'

Sir Rufus Isaacs, Solicitor-General, 1910

In the UK in 1912, women could not vote.

Prologue

At 10 p.m. on Stonecutter Street the Reuters wires begin to tick.

Nobby has his head slumped on Mr Stark's desk and he jumps at the noise, the heavy morse code girding, the out-of-joint military march. The glass on top of the Reuters machine always shakes because of a loose nut or perhaps the uneven floorboards beneath the desk. He cuts the ticker tape sharp the way Mr Stark likes it, no tears or rough edges.

And then he blinks.

Half an hour earlier, The Royal Albert Hall, London

Ebony Diamond had waited in the dark, her wrists bound tight as shoelaces. Her fingers had numbed to blue; the pearls of sweat on her palms were turning the mixture of flour and *poudre d'amour* to paste. Behind her, Annie Evans was busy tucking into two neat sacks the crowbar, ropes and chains they had used to split the roof tiles and slink down through the cold rafters. As she packed she sang gently, 'The Daring Young Man on the Flying Trapeze', singing 'lass' instead of 'man'.

'How's he getting on?' Annie's eyes were soft, but her smile was frozen with nerves.

Ebony didn't answer. She was watching the meeting going on beneath them, the Prime Minister working himself up into his speech. Down below, the moving sea of bowler hats in the auditorium looked like iron filings in a fish bowl.

'Legs together or legs akimbo don't matter,' Ebony's mother had always told her. 'But for God's sake keep your arms in or you'll lose one of them.' There were rumours that once at the Crystal Palace a trapeze artist had landed so sharply on a falling jolt that part of his brain seeped out through his nose.

Annie wriggled back into a squat under the low beams. She would hold out here as long as she could, but they would find her too. She hoped she and Ebony would make the same prison van.

Ebony checked the binding on her legs, squeezed a handful of flesh into a more comfortable position, ran a thumb over the sailor's knots she had tied, and wedged the wooden bar of the trapeze between the hollows of her feet. Annie passed her the banner and she bit its silk, and grimaced as its slippery perfume coated her teeth. She had done higher leaps than this and she had felt sick before each of them too. But this time they both had Holloway to look forward to. The hunger-strike, the force-feeding. Ebony had heard tell

2

that they didn't clean the tube. She pushed away the thought, gave Annie a last look, climbed alone onto the wooden lip of the hole. And she jumped.

Nobby watches the details judder in: dribs, drabs, sketches, the colour of lace in the woman's bodice, the look on her face as she flew through the air. He crams a jellied pork pie into his mouth as he scans and scans the never-ending tape. It is better than a story in *Strand* magazine.

The facts change. The Prime Minister is dead. The Prime Minister is alive. The woman is a gypsy. The woman is a Londoner. The woman had a famous mother. And as they change, the activity in the office also changes. Reporters dig out obituaries, men are being dispatched to Bow Street police station and the Albert Hall. And all the time the tape ticks and slaps and stamps as if it will never exhaust itself. By the time midnight comes round, the first galley proof is drawn and Nobby is growing bored. The pie is heavy in his stomach and he thinks he might sneak a swallow from Stark's whisky bottle in the top drawer of his desk while the night editor is out of the room. But then the tape starts up again, and this time when he looks at it he doesn't just blink, he cries out.

15 April 1912, Clement's Inn, Women's Social
and Political Union Headquarters, London

'Did you get the newspapers? Did you get them all? Is she in it? Tell me she's on the front page. Tell me the *London Illustrated* have dug out a snap.'

The woman's arms are outstretched and the sleeves of her blouse hang away from her. On her wrist a flash of emeralds, amethysts and fresh pearls catches the sunlight through the window.

Her friend doesn't smile and this rings a little warning bell.

The newspapers slap down onto the oak table, spilling left and right, slipping from their covers. Mrs Pankhurst and a few of the others have entered the press room, drawn by the rush of excitement. Murmurs are circulating, questions being asked.

'Did she get a clean swing?'

'She didn't hurt herself?'

Heads are craning for a better look. 'If she did it,' one woman says, 'I'll lead a deputation to Asquith myself, holding out them front pages like a banner in his face.'

'They can't ignore it, that's for sure.'

The merriment is tight and restless. Some of them were there last night; others on the blacklist for Liberal rallies who couldn't get in have heard the stories already. They know she 'flew like a bullet', they know she 'eyeballed Asquith like he was the devil'. They know about the banner saying 'Votes for Women'. They know the crowd shouted, 'Cut her down', 'Hang her from her own rope'.

But what they didn't know, what none of them could have known, was what was staring at them from seven different front covers. Tawdry rags, fine-printed sheets. All black-edged. '*Titanic* Sinks – 1500 Die', the *London Evening Gazette*'s choice of words.

Hush settles round the room. Some of the women look at Mrs Pankhurst as if she should say something, but her silvery blue eyes are fixed on the table. After a few moments of creaking and shifting, one woman coughs and asks, 'Is she not in it at all? Not any of them?'

'What do you think?' another snaps, and runs from the room.

The silence hangs a few more minutes.

'Will she get second division, do you think?'

No one speaks.

Then Mrs Pankhurst pushes her thumb smoothly behind the cover of one of the papers and begins to leaf through it, nodding occasionally, catching her breath, and as she does so the rest of the women move forward too, and gradually the papers are distributed between silent hands and eyes.

'Rotten luck,' says a quiet voice from the corner of the room nearest the window. Mrs Pankhurst's head snaps up. But someone else beats her to speak first.

'For whom?'

SIX MONTHS LATER

One

1 November 1912

The sun was beating down as Frankie George cycled along Fleet Street, trying to stop her notebook and calling cards from flapping out of her lower pockets, and her pencils from stabbing her in the chest.

She had been distrustful of the warm weather when she'd got up at noon to receive her editor's telegram summoning her to the Stonecutter Street offices. Now, as she dodged boys on motorcycles puffing out violet smoke, piles of horse muck and steaming horses dragging full omnibuses, she regretted her choice of clothing; a fetching pale brown tweed trouser suit, practical for bicycling, autumnal-hued and insulating as upholstery. The Fleet Street traffic was foul with noxious vapour and it felt like cycling through hot soup. A cart full of meat pies came wobbling towards her and she thought for a second about reaching out to pinch one, but changed her mind when she saw the horse on the wagon behind breathing over the crusts. She veered off onto Shoe Lane, dodging smashed jack-o'-lanterns left over from Hallowe'en the night before and it was only then that she remembered it was All Saints' Day. And so hot. What next? Summer Punch on Guy Fawkes night?

Stonecutter Street was mainly made up of magazine offices, all there for the cheaper rent. For the *London Evening Gazette*, that meant being crammed into a tall rambling half-townhouse, six times as high as it was wide, leaving only enough space for one room per floor. The brickwork was poor and there were always new leaks and splits in the wall, new buckets strategically placed, new wads of stuffing filling a whistling gap. Frankie leant the bicycle against the railings outside, where she'd last borrowed it from, and hopped up the steps.

The office was buzzing with its usual hysteria. Bundles of the early edition were being cut open, men in shirtsleeves and braces were flying up and down the stairs brandishing tissue-thin pieces of paper. Shouts of 'copy' came loud and fast from each of the floors, along with wafts of Turkish tobacco and occasionally the sound of a boy being boxed on the ears.

Frankie fished in her pocket for the telegram and gave it to the man on the front desk.

'Know what he wants?' The man cupped his ear for her response above the din.

Frankie looked down at the note. It read, 'STONE-CUTTER STREET STARK'. She shrugged. The man shrugged back and waved her towards the stairs.

The higher up the building, the more important the resident was. In the cellar, printers were operated by men in aprons who had grown so deaf from the noise of machinery that they bellowed at each other even when they were sat across the same table in the Olde Cheshire Cheese. One floor up in the basement, skilled men with fingers as fine as a pianist's sat at linotype machines, setting the letters in neat little rows.

The ground floor belonged to the sports reporters and the staffers, who could be dispatched to any part of London at a second's notice to weasel out a story from the police, morgues, the divorce courts, loose-tongued pub landladies and vengeful servants. The obituary writers, the political correspondents and the features editor occupied the office above; theirs had the privilege of a red velvet couch that threw up dust whenever it was sat upon. Up again, the sub-editors worked at desks covered in blue pencils, bottles of paste and scissors, chopping and rearranging the text given to them by the office boys. And then, at the top sat Mr Stark himself, Editor-in-Chief, with a rickety wooden floor and a great oak desk covered in rival newspapers, scraps of flimsy, and a whisky glass with a permanent crust of the previous drink left fossilising in it.

Stark also had the prestige of housing the Reuters machine, four pillars topped by a glass box; a tangle of electromagnetic wires that ticked and tapped out a mile a day of news. Horse-race results, parliamentary speeches, overseas events, shipping news, all came spilling out onto a thin strip of paper which

Nobby, Stark's office boy, would cut with a pair of shears and pass for Stark's perusal. Most of Nobby's offerings ended up in the waste-paper basket under the desk. On her first visit to Stark, Frankie had eyed the basket warily, wondering how many lovingly typed and hand-addressed journalists' efforts had been screwed up into a ball and tossed into it like old orange peel.

Just before she hit the landing on Stark's floor she heard a voice calling out, 'Oi, Georgie.'

'It's Frankie,' she began to say, turning. She recognised Teddy Hawkins straight away; one of the reporters who had his own desk in the downstairs newsroom. He had a badly formed mouth, like it had been squashed at some point and never found its proper shape again. In his hands he carried a stack of news clippings. 'Did you get our telegram?'

'I got Mr Stark's.'

Hawkins brushed the remark out of the air. 'He wants you to do a portrait piece. Half, no three-quarter page.' He grinned.

Frankie's pulse sped up a little.

'There's a suffragette performing at the Coliseum tomorrow night, an acrobat. Ebony Diamond. Know her?'

Instantly the little drizzle of excitement was replaced by a prickle of annoyance. She was on the verge of opening her mouth to say, 'Now why would I know her?' but Hawkins didn't give her the chance.

'None of us have a damned clue who she is. That's why he wanted you in.' He skimmed a glance down her trouser suit.

'You'll know a thing or two about suffragettes, won't you? Anyway, deadline's tomorrow. He'll tell you the rest.' He barged ahead of her into Stark's office, leaving a reek of stale smoke in his wake.

Frankie heard a rustle of quick conversation then Hawkins re-emerged, winked at Frankie – a gesture that made her feel slightly soiled – and jogged back down the stairs. She was gratified to see, as he disappeared, that a long streamer of flimsy from the Reuters wires was flapping off his shoe.

She gave her suit a quick brush down and went in. Stark's huge body was craning over a galley proof, with a single eyeglass wedged in his eye and a blue pencil behind his ear. He was an oval-shaped man, pointed at the top like an egg, with colossal features; ears, nose, blue bulging eyes that looked as if they had been stuck on with editing paste, and matched his unwieldy manner with words. He liked to call the lady journalists 'treacle', 'pudding' or sometimes 'treacle pudding'.

He didn't look up. Frankie walked closer, so that her shoes were within his eyeline.

'Ebony Diamond,' he said, still poring down the long piece of print. 'Know her?'

Frankie shook her head, then realised he was waiting for her to speak. 'No.' She cleared her throat.

'She's a suffragette.'

'I don't know her,' Frankie said, trying to keep her voice even.

'Well, I want you to get to know her. She's been in

Holloway twice now so make it sharp. Get her to tell you about the matrons and force-feeding.'

She watched his head slide back and forth along the line of text while she waited for more. After a few seconds, he paused. 'Still here?'

'Well, it's just that . . . Mr Stark, I'm not sure a suffragette piece, given my background. I mean there are some news stories I could think of to . . .'

'This or quoits on Wimbledon Common. You want to cover the quoits on Wimbledon Common?'

Frankie made a quick calculation of the distance to Wimbledon in her head. It was almost worth it. 'No, sir, thank you,' she said.

'Nobby's got some notes for you, don't you Nobby?'

Stark's boy, who had been lurking in the corner, staring at the ticking Reuters machine, leant across the table and handed her a piece of paper. On the top was written in blue waxy editing pencil in Stark's florid hand, 'Olivier Smythe, Corsetier, 125 New Bond Street.' The rest of the notes were Nobby's uneven scrawl.

Frankie creased her brow. 'I'm sorry, I'm not sure I understand. This is the address of a Bond Street corset shop.'

'Yes.'

Frankie hesitated.

'Does her costumes, doesn't he?' Stark said as if the whole thing should have been quite plain. He went back to scrutinising his galley proof and Nobby shrugged at her and turned back to the Reuters machine. Frankie sighed, folded up the piece of paper and stuffed it in her pocket before heading back out into the hallway.

She was halfway down the stairs when a man in a brown factory coat came dashing out from one of the side rooms. 'Hold it, hold it.' She stopped in her tracks as he thrust towards her a leather cube. His fingers were grubby with ink and he stank of chemicals. 'Make sure you get a good one. Get her waist in. Nice and close, mid-body, don't let her close her eyes. Plates are already in, quarter plates.' He pointed to a tube, half a triangular pipe tucked in the back. 'Lose this and he'll have your fingers for potted shrimp. If you need it, you can buy the powder at a chemist's. Get the Muller's stuff.'

It was only then that it dawned on her what the box was. 'I have taken a photograph before, you know,' she said. She hadn't, but she had had her photograph taken, which was near enough the same thing. She carefully lifted the camera out of its box and stared at it. It had stiff red bellows and shiny brass tracks and a yellow enamel circle that said, 'J. Lizars Challenge. Glasgow, London, Edinburgh'.

She tucked it away and slid the cracked leather strap of the case over her shoulder, then stepped back into the sunshine, letting the heat soak onto her face. She was trying to sedate the little prickle that had risen in her outside Stark's office when Teddy Hawkins told her why she had been offered the job. Of course Teddy Hawkins didn't interview suffragettes; he topped up peelers' ale cups and greased politicians' hands in the Savage Club.

Suffragette. She'd give him a suffragette. One look at her trousers and everyone just assumed she was a bloody suffragette. It wasn't even a real word anyway, it was a name someone at the *Daily Mail* had made up to distinguish Mrs Pankhurst's hammer-throwers from Mrs Fawcett's tea-drinkers. There were suffragists and suffragettes and Nusses and Spankers and Wasps, and they all looked the same in their blouses and tailor-mades, hawking pamphlets on street corners in taxidermy hats.

And now she was supposed to just pirouette along to a corset shop on the look-out for a suffragette acrobat she had never set eyes on before. It was all a big joke to them, with their oiled hair and their Turkish tobacco. She pictured them all gathered in the newsroom, laughing like monkeys into their coffee cups.

She swallowed and lifted her chin up. It was work, extra work. And portraits were a step up from the column she did with Twinkle, and her odds and sods cartoons. Besides, Audrey Woodford's *Journalism for Women* said you never turned down work. She ran her fingers through her tufty brown hair, tucking it tightly down behind her ears, hoiked the camera case tighter over her shoulder, and headed towards the railings. She arrived at them just in time to see a newspaper boy, still crammed between the wooden leaves of his sandwich board, swinging his legs over the bicycle and wobbling off down the street.

'Oi!'

The boy picked up speed, knocking his knees against the

board as he pedalled. Frankie sighed and drew her grand-father's old pocket-watch out of her jacket. Quarter past three already. Bond Street was miles away, the centre of town clogged. If she took the underground, she might just make it.

The tube train was crowded but not unbearable, and Frankie found a bit of standing space against the shaking wall. As the tube skated though pitch-black tunnels its windows became a mirror, allowing her to see what she looked like for the first time that day, for as usual she hadn't bothered to check before leaving the house. Her paisley neckerchief was crooked, her brown eyes shiny round the sockets. The olive oil her mother had given her to cook with was working a treat to keep her hair in check. Her hair had been short ever since her first day as a compositor's apprentice at the *Tottenham Evening News*, when the head compositor had taken a pair of shears and without warning sliced off her pigtails. Did her cheeks look chubbier than normal? She had always taken pride in being lean, but lately her waistband had been feeling tighter. Too many gin sessions with the old girl Twinkle, cooking up the weekly column, and too much ale in the Cheshire Cheese.

She slunk back against the window wondering how long it would take to find the shop or if this suffragette would even be there. If she could do a good job of the piece, it mightn't be the last interview Mr Stark sent her on. It was true, for weeks now she had been pestering him to give her something more than the Twinkle column, something juicier. At the *Tottenham Evening News* she had covered for staff reporters on sick days, and been sent to court hearings and occasionally the morgue. But it didn't seem to be the Fleet Street way to let women loose anywhere other than the opening of tailors' houses, the launch of debutantes, or sensational exposés inside laundry rooms.

By the time the lift operator at Bond Street underground station had cranked her up to street level, the sun was already beginning to sink. The sky had darkened, giving way to a tea-brown fog blowing in from the Thames.

Frankie pulled the lapels of her jacket in tight, glad of her tweeds for the first time that day. There were a few trams lined up along the junction with Oxford Street while further down New Bond Street horse-drawn broughams idled. Gas and electric lights shone from inside the shops, glowing veils of silver and gold around the goods in the windows. Shoppers huddled along, dashing to make their purchases before the weather turned.

She checked her pocket-watch – quarter to four, still in good time – and took a fat Matinee cigarette and a box of matches from a case inside her jacket. Let herself warm up to it first. She lit the cigarette and trampled on the match.

Taking the smoke in slowly, Frankie walked between the row of cabs up for hire and the shop fronts. She was halfway between a tall hansom and a snuffmonger's when a shape in the next cab window along caught her eye. She walked up to it and leaned closer. At first it looked like a dismembered body, shrunk to dizzyingly small proportions, perching on a shelf inside the cab. She blinked, then realised what she was looking at and turned around. Behind her, silhouetted by golden gas lamps, hung a mauve silken bodice in a curved shop window. As she moved towards it, peculiar repetitions of the form began to emerge in the window's milky light, dangling from the ceiling, poised on wood figurines. She looked up at the sign. 'Olivier Smythe; Parisian Corsetier.' Below it a Royal Crest was lacquered in gold and black relief.

So this was where Miss Ebony Diamond sourced her smalls. Frankie hadn't known the music halls paid so nicely. Relieved she hadn't been sent on a goose chase, she peered through the window. There was a man behind the counter and a tall elderly woman in a pastel flowered hat making shapes in the air with her hands.

How did journalists approach such matters anyway? Audrey Woodford had conveniently forgotten to say. She sucked the last bitter hit of the cigarette then pulled out her notebook and chanced a glimpse at the leaf of notes Stark's boy had given her. 'Acrobat, suffragette, tiger-tamer. Attacked Asquith, April. Works at Jojo's Cocoa Bar, Soho. Coliseum, Friday. Wouldn't pick a fight with her.' The latter was underlined in blue. She raised an eyebrow.

The customer smiled and accepted her boxed purchase, then glided back out into the street, tinkling the shop's bell, bundling her furs at her throat. Frankie watched the man, whom she took to be Mr Smythe, straighten the garments on display in the window. There was something odd about him that she couldn't put her finger on, a delicacy in the way he held himself. Buttoning up her jacket, she tried her best to look smart, lamenting the way her shirt never seemed to tuck evenly into her waistband. As she strode towards the shop door, a boy with a large cap tugged low over fiery ginger hair stepped out of the shadows and pulled it open. Frankie rummaged in her pocket in search of a penny for him, but she could only find one sticky shilling that she wanted to keep hold of for her tube fare, so she pulled her palm back out empty and smiled instead.

The bell's jangle set her nerves going. She crossed into the dark panelled sweet-smelling chamber and calmly set about flicking through the racks of fabric, as if shopping for a corset was the most natural thing in the world. The truth was it all made her feel a little nauseous: the liquid satin, the rough-textured lace. Something about the place reminded her of an effete butcher's shop, a slightly creepy hairdressing salon, somewhere Miss Havisham and Sweeney Todd might have set up business together. She had in her hands a cream and caramel number – a colour combination that reminded her of straitjackets – when she heard footsteps behind her.

'Can I help?'

Frankie turned and it was then that she realised what was so odd about the man. He was corseted to a gruesome size; fourteen and a half, fifteen inches. She tried not to stare, concentrating instead on his face. His cheeks were sharp, like they had been cut by tailor's scissors, his round brown eyes large and curious.

She cleared her throat. Could she ask outright for Ebony Diamond? She hesitated. 'I'd like to buy a corset.'

Mr Smythe couldn't conceal his amusement as his gaze roved her trouser suit. 'Really?'

'Yes, I have a wedding to attend. On Saturday,' she added curtly, thinking that corset shoppers were most probably curt. She was in the process of dreaming up some monstrous dress to tell him about, the kind her mother might have made her wear if she did indeed have a wedding to go to, when she spied a shadow springing into shape on the side wall of the shop. Smythe seemed to notice it too for he stepped in front of her, trying to block her view and began rambling loudly about the extraordinary weather and whether an autumn wedding was something he would prefer, or a spring one. But Frankie had already seen the silhouette. Now, all of a sudden it dawned on her what the photographer man at the *Gazette* had meant when he said 'get her waist'.

It was Ebony Diamond. It had to be. She could have been cut from a Victorian novel, swooping into full view now from beyond the curtain covering the rear of the shop. A black old-fashioned gown was sculpted around her, curving up to her neck and down in pleats and layers to trail along the ground behind her as she rushed. But it was her waist that caught Frankie's eye. She was corseted to a size every bit as tight as the shop's proprietor. It made Frankie want to belch imagining how tightly squeezed the food and organs were in there. Frankie had only ever worn stays for a week when she was thirteen – the nuns called them 'stays', 'corsets' were for the Mary Magdalenes of the world – but the pain from being birched for not wearing them was outweighed by the pain from wearing them so she had given up.

The woman's hands were coated in tiny black gloves and struck ahead, keeping her balance as she ran into the shop crashing into racks of carefully spaced bodices, knocking them over, tripping over her skirts. She dashed past Frankie, leaving a pleasing sweet smell drifting behind her, *poudre d'amour* and gin. Suddenly her ankle became tangled in the serpentine straps of a corset that had fallen and she stopped for breath.

Smythe coloured from the neck up, and made a weak attempt to direct Frankie towards the fitting room with his hand to her back. She nimbly slipped his grasp.

'Excuse me,' he muttered, and edged past her, picking up a couple of fallen garments as he went. 'Ebony,' he hissed. Frankie was surprised at his use of her first name. 'What has got into you? You're trembling like a kicked dog.'

The woman in the black dress spun to face him. 'She's up there, isn't she?'

'Who?'

'You know perfectly well. And if you know what's good for you, you'll come with me and not come back.'

'Now is not the time.'

With a shaking hand Ebony reached down inside her lacy bosom and pulled something out. 'You want to ask her –' she gestured with her head towards the ceiling of the shop where scuffling, workshop sounds were rumbling away, '– where she got this from.' Holding the thing up to the light, Frankie saw it was a brooch, a large silver one, with a winking, glinting, gold pattern carved onto its surface. ''Cos it didn't fall off a tailor's dummy.' Ebony tipped her arm back, pausing for a second, then hurled the thing forcefully at Smythe. He ducked, cowering his hands to his head, and it went plummeting into the green velvet drape covering the back of the shop, then hit the floor with a bullet's whack.

'Ebony!'

Ebony stared at him. Her black eyes burned. For a second Frankie thought she might be about to start weeping. Then her gaze hardened again. 'Ask her,' she said, tipping her chin towards the ceiling once more. She flung another rack of clothing out of the way, swung open the door of the shop, making the bell jerk, and slammed it shut.

So that was Ebony Diamond, Frankie thought. The Notorious Madame Suffragette. Striking face, somewhat tempestuous, but then Stark's boy had said not to pick a fight with her.

Suddenly Frankie remembered the camera still slung across her back.

'Wait!' She reached round her shoulder, unclipping the latch on the box. The brass tracks slipped out so fast she nearly dropped it. She wriggled the strap over her head and let the case fall to the floor. 'I need a photograph.' Tripping over the spilled clothing she raced towards the door.

Frankie could see Ebony Diamond moving quickly along the street, her black hourglass figure melting into the fog. She yanked open the door, letting in a rush of cool damp air. 'Wait!' she cried. 'I'm a journalist! Wait! Miss Diamond!'

Ebony began picking up speed, her swift walk becoming a jog, then a run, her skirts skating out behind her like raven wings. Frankie gritted her teeth and ran after her, feeling the tightness of her trousers catching, regretting the amount of ale she had drunk over the past few weeks.

Up ahead at the crossroads with Brook Street, Ebony had to stop as a chain of trams went sliding past tinkling their bells. A Fenwick's shopwoman in an apron approached Frankie brandishing a bottle of the latest Guerlain Eau de Parfum. 'Musk!' she barked. 'Musk direct from the Musk Ox!' Frankie dodged her spraying hand and dipped round in front of Ebony Diamond.

'Miss Diamond.'

It took a second for Ebony's black eyes to latch onto her. Her face was white as the moon with a short upturned nose and a wide scarlet mouth. 'Are you following me?' she spat.

Frankie was out of breath but managed to pant, 'I just want to ask you a few quick questions. About Holloway prison. For the portrait page. The newspaper. How does that sound?' She stuck her hand into her pocket and pulled out one of her calling cards.

Miss Diamond looked startled for a second, then took the card and ran her finger absently over the embossed surface. She studied the letters slowly. 'Francesca George, Contributor, *London Evening Gazette*.' The lines on her face straightened out; she looked like she might have something on the tip of her tongue. 'A journalist, you say?'

'That's right,' Frankie was beginning to line up the camera.

If she could just keep her in one place for a few seconds. Truth be told, she could probably make the rest up. Facts were fairly sticky at the *London Evening Gazette*. And that tiff at the shop was a winner whether it was about tax or pink knickerbockers.

Suddenly Ebony rammed the card back towards her, sending the camera stabbing into Frankie's face. 'You've got some nerve, giving this to me.'

Frankie stumbled backwards. 'I don't know what you mean. I just need to ask you a few questions. About the force-feeding.'

'Force-feeding my eye.' She jabbed the corner of the card at Frankie. 'You're the one drew that cartoon for *Punch*, aren't you – "Take it up the nose Maud I will, pass the tea".'

Frankie's stomach sank. She had known this was going to happen as soon as Teddy Hawkins mentioned the word 'suffragette'. It was why they had chosen her, she was certain. They'd all be in the Cheshire Cheese by now, knocking back pints of porter, sharing pork scratchings and smirking.

The cartoon in question had been drawn by Frankie several months ago, and had been intended for *Punch*. Frankie had been trying for years to have a piece printed there and was always told that her drawings weren't satirical enough, except this one which the boy on the *Punch* reception desk, who didn't look old enough to be in long trousers, had coughed at before handing back. After *Punch* rejected it, it had floated down the murky Fleet Street food chain, before landing at the door of the *London Evening Gazette*, a rag with circus-style lettering for its title, and the strapline, 'The Greatest Newspaper on Earth'. The cartoon was perfect *Evening Gazette* material, Mr Stark had said. A group of women poised over cakes and scones – her figurines were 'superb', he said, 'just like *Punch*' – while one was busy fixing to the teapot a long tube of the kind used in Holloway Gaol to force-feed women on the hunger strike. Ebony Diamond had misquoted her. The caption was, 'No Mildred, I think I'll take it through the nose this time'.

Mr Stark himself had called her into his office the Monday after it was published, shook her hand – the only time he had looked her in the eye – and offered her a Friday column which he billed as a 'guide to society' with Twinkle, an ageing 'lady about town'.

'Look, I just need one photograph. You don't have to say anything. But if I turn up without a picture, my editor'll hang my guts for a laundry line.'

'Get that thing out of my face.' Ebony's black skirts rustled as she pushed past Frankie. The traffic had cleared, creating an opening. Frankie ducked in her way, raising the camera to face height.

Suddenly Ebony lunged. As Frankie snapped the shutter, the full force of Ebony Diamond's right hook whipped her jaw round. Ebony was as nimble as she was strong and her hands danced over Frankie's until she had a firm purchase on the camera. In one sharp movement she had ripped it away and was striding back towards the Fenwick's woman.

'It's not mine. Give it back.'

'You should have thought about that.' Ebony tossed the camera to the ground and for one terrifying moment Frankie thought she might be about to stand on it.

'It's not mine, for pity's sake!'

Ebony took a step back, then reached across to the Fenwick's woman and snatched the bottle of musk perfume out of her hand.

'Have you gone mad?' Frankie realised with a strike of horror what she was up to and could only watch as Ebony cracked the atomiser off the top of the bottle with the side of her hand and poured perfume all over the camera. She reached into her dress pocket, pulled out a match, struck it off the sole of her boot and dropped it.

Shoppers and clerks sprang back as blue-gold flames washed up the sides of the leather. The protective gloss began to sizzle and burn.

Frankie scrambled forwards. 'What d'you do that for? Off your onion, you are! You're madder than a sack of cats.' The heat scorched her hands as she tried to smother the flames. Looking around her desperately she saw a hurdy-gurdy man with a tin cup of foul-coloured beer. She swooped on it, snatching it up, ignoring his protests, and tossed it quickly onto the fire.

Leathered smoke hissed into the air. The flames flattened then vanished. Frankie tentatively touched one of the brass tracks, and whipped her finger back as it scalded. Bits of the metal along the sides had melted out of shape. She would have to take it to one of the clockmaker's on Gray's Inn Road before handing it back.

She looked up and around her but there was no sign of Ebony. The London crowds had folded back into order. If she hadn't been swallowed by the mob of people she had dissolved into the thickening mist. Sitting back on her haunches on the cold ground, Frankie let out a long groan.

This was just about the worst day she could remember since Mr Rodgers from the *Tottenham Evening News* made her hang around Southwark morgue for six hours waiting to catch a glimpse of a man who had been savaged by a pig. She wished bitterly that she had taken the quoits tournament, or a divorce hearing, or stayed in bed and settled for no work. Anything but this mad, savage suffragette.

She climbed back to her feet and picked up the sodden, scorched malty-smelling camera. Traffic was careering along wildly, bodies began to push against her in their eagerness to get past. The Fenwick's woman was exclaiming 'dear me, dear me.'

With a heavy feeling she started off in the direction of the nearest tube station. She had gone a few paces when a colour caught her eye in the grimy mist. Somewhere along the road a flash of bright copper was bobbing up and down, at first gently, then slowly breaking into a more vigorous bounce, swerving through the traffic and pedestrians.

The boy with the ginger hair, the boy who had let her into the shop. Frankie stopped to watch him as he ducked behind a parked cart, looked ahead, then dashed out again, light as a tomcat on his feet.

Probably a pickpocket, she thought. Just as well she hadn't given him that shilling, thank heavens for small mercies. Then with another audible groan – this one drawing looks of horror from the Bond Street crowds – she realised she had left the camera case back at the corset shop.

Two

At the same time, three and a half miles away on Shoe Lane, Emmeline Pankhurst, leader of the Women's Social and Political Union – The Suffragettes – walked into an ironmonger's. She was familiar with the smell of creosote, the various sizes of nails and washers that sat in the glass cabinet behind the counter. Carefully minding her skirts against hooks and joints of wood protruding from the shelves, she sallied up the small aisle in the centre of the shop and idly fingered a row of small rubber mallets. Through a bead curtain a man appeared. He was in his fifties, ruddy in the face with a neat white beard like Father Christmas. 'May I help?'

Mrs Pankhurst looked up artfully as if stirred from a deep thought. 'Oh yes, I'm looking for twenty-five hammers.'

The man didn't bat an eyelid. Schoolteacher, he was thinking, by the look of her. The fine stern nose and Worcester porcelain eyes. And that dress, a thick brown wool creation pinned right up proper despite the sunshine. School marm of a boys' school. And a well-spoken one at that.

'Well, it depends what you're after. If it's for woodwork, the basic craft one will do. Under normal circumstances you'd pay a shilling each, but if you want twenty-five I'll do the lot for twenty shillings.'

Mrs Pankhurst mulled it over. 'That does sound rather fair.'

The man began to fumble under the counter, and at length emerged with a very sleek looking hammer, painted green at the handle, its bulb in burnished steel.

'Oh that looks lovely.' She took it into her hands. 'It has to be able to smash glass you see. Efficiently.'

The man gave her a brisk nod. 'That's your one.'

'Lovely.'

'Trouble is,' he scratched his head, 'I think I only have eighteen of them in the back. Could get them by next week.'

'Well, you see it's rather urgent. We do need them tonight,' she hesitated. 'I mean tomorrow morning. First thing.'

The man shook his head. 'Afraid it's all I can do. They're shilling and six but if you take all eighteen I'll do them a shilling each.'

Mrs Pankhurst ceased fingering the painted green stem and looked up brightly. 'Well, I think that sounds splendid. Some of them will just have to share.'

'Indeed they will Madam,' said the shopkeeper as she delved into her purse. 'Indeed they will.'

* * *

Further north, Mrs Deacon of 72 Popham Drive had also just walked into an ironmonger's on Cricklewood High Street.

The owner, a stout, shabby man with tufty whiskers, was taken aback to see a woman so delicately dressed in dark green velvet approach his grubby counter. He thought to himself, her maid must be sick. She must be running an errand for the household.

What she said next surprised him. 'Excuse me, I'm looking to purchase a number of hammers. Twenty-five to be exact.'

The shop owner gave her a startled look. Then he realised. School marm, he thought to himself. A boy's school, no doubt. And it all made perfect sense.

By the time Frankie returned to 125 New Bond Street, Mr Smythe had turned the gaslights in the window off and was on his knees, picking up wooden hangers and stacking his corsets back onto the racks. Beside him, a girl in a brown linen dress and pinny, with glossy black hair, stood brushing down the garments and straightening the laces as he passed them to her. Frankie gently pushed open the door. The bell knocked a soft sing-song, but the two figures didn't look across. In the air still hung the faint lingering smell of *poudre d'amour* that Ebony had left in her wake.

Frankie muttered her 'excuse me's' and crept past them, trying to eavesdrop on their quiet conversation. Noises from the upper floor, where she assumed the workshop must be, churned through the ceiling, so she only picked up on a few hushed words: 'lace' and 'feather piping' on a costume the girl had been making for Ebony, and her lament that Miss Diamond had not stayed to try it on. As she made her way discreetly to the rear of the shop where the camera case lay, Frankie heard Smythe mutter, 'I'll try it myself, and if it doesn't fit when she comes to pick it up it will be her own fault.'

Startled by the suggestion, she snuck a glance again at Smythe's waist and came to the conclusion that he probably was corseted to about the same size as Ebony Diamond. She felt a nicotine gurgle creep up her throat just thinking about it.

The case was lying by the fitting room, kicked into a corner out of the way. She slid the damp camera back inside, then reached for the strap. It had got itself half-tucked under the green drape running along the chamber's back wall. As she began to tug it, she felt resistance. Thinking it was caught on something, she rippled the drape, searching for the edge. Workshop noises from beyond gradually swelled, metal softly chinking, along with quiet regular wooden clicks. She found the parting, peeled back the curtain, and jumped.

At first the woman – at least Frankie thought she was a woman from the little she could see of her – was bent down picking with curiosity at the loop of the strap, but on seeing Frankie she stood up sharply, too sharply for Frankie to stop a short gasp escaping. Her grimed brow was skimmed by the lace of an old-maid's bonnet, the eyes beneath it rheumy. The rest of her face was obscured by folds of dirty cream linen wrapping the bridge of her nose, concealing her mouth, bundled down underneath her chin and secured tightly in a knot. She spoke, and her voice sounded like she was chewing wads of cotton.

'Get out, private property.' She shooed Frankie with her hands.

It then dawned on Frankie what was wrong with her. She had heard of women of her mother's generation with phossy jaw from the match factories, but she had never seen one. Most of them hadn't survived. It was a horrible disease, swelling the jaw, attacking the bones and leaving the victim with no option but to have part of their chin removed. There was a lady at the end of her street the locals said suffered from it. Frankie looked away, ashamed to find that she had been staring.

'There, take it.' The woman flicked the strap. Picking up the case, Frankie dodged back out into the chamber of the shop where she bumped straight into the squeezed waist of Mr Smythe.

His voice was soft but cold. 'That part of the shop is off limits. Perhaps it isn't clear from the signage.' He quickly ruffled the drape shut, blocking sight of the woman with phossy jaw.

'My apologies,' Frankie mumbled, 'I was picking up my camera bag.'

Smythe hesitated before standing aside.

'Incidentally,' he said as Frankie brushed past his cotton shirt, 'if you really are a journalist, you only had to say. We've received quite a lot of positive press in the past. We advertise too. In *The Times*, the *Pall Mall Gazette*. Which paper was it you wrote for?'

'The *London Evening Gazette*.'

His silence drifted towards her. She could practically hear the wrinkling of his nose. She thought she might as well chance her luck anyway.

'Actually while I'm here, d'you happen to know where I might find Miss Ebony Diamond? Usually? Of an evening?'

His gaze chilled.

'Right,' Frankie said. 'Shall I leave a card? Just in case?'

'If you like,' he said politely, then took it from her at a pained distance. All of his irritation had been carefully swallowed by the time he held the door open. Just before she passed through it she felt a pinch on her hips. She was on the verge of howling when she caught the eye of the seamstress girl with the black hair and brown dress, standing right behind her. The girl flashed wide her dark eyes. Frankie closed her mouth.

'You want to try Jojo's in Soho,' she whispered. 'If she's not here, she'll be there.'

Frankie nodded a silent thank you and was relieved to hear the final jangle of the bell as Mr Smythe snapped shut the door.

Out in the street, she rubbed her hands together and breathed a long steaming puff of air into the darkening fog. She checked her pocket-watch. It would take just twenty minutes perhaps to get to Twinkle's flat on foot. Was there time before then for a jaunt to Soho? Probably not. On the other hand, arriving early at Twinkle's could be hazardous; she might be made to eat all manner of unspeakable diet foods.

As she moved away in the rough direction of Soho she caught sight of the saloon doors of a public house on the corner of the street. The Maid in the Moon. She knew the landlord of that one, Tommy Dawber, a Tottenham man she used to see at the Spurs matches with her father when she was little. He'd done well for himself, with three or four gaffs now in the centre of town. She paused, looking again towards Soho, then back at the public house. Through the steamy windows she could see clutches of workers gathered around small tables, an old gin queen up at the bar with rouge on her cheeks and powder spilling from her hair. Tommy was behind the steel-topped counter, his head thrown back, spitting while he laughed. The foamy stout coming out of the pumps as he pulled them looked tasty. She could probably get him to tap her one for a favour too, if she mentioned the Spurs. The wetness of the camera was beginning to leak through the case and into her back.

She took one last look along to the end of the street, then jogged across the road, letting thoughts of Ebony Diamond spill away as she pulled open the door of the Maid in the Moon.

Three

Dusk had given way to brownish night by the time Frankie drained the bitter dregs of her stout and made a move back towards the public house's swinging doors. She pulled out her grandfather's old pocket-watch and took a look at the time. Twinkle would be expecting her. Her heart grew sluggish. Reaching into her pocket, she took out a Matinee, sparking it up on her way out of the door. A hackney drove past and the driver slurred at her, something about women smoking. She tossed the spent match in his wake.

The streets were almost empty now, except for a few men with briefcases scurrying towards the underground station and shopgirls with hands clutched to their throats, holding shut their coats against the cold. I was right all along, Frankie told herself. Sunshine never lasts in November. Fools the lot of you, she thought, snuggling into her tweeds.

A few puffs into the cigarette she set off in the direction of

Marble Arch. She had only gone a few paces when a noise distracted her.

It was horses' hooves but not the usual kind, the cab nags. This was a tidy clop, a fine dressage trot. A memory stirred of military processions along the Mall. Something made her turn.

Out of the foggy street a lone carriage appeared, a four-wheeler, richly decorated with red touches on black, the kind that would pull up at Covent Garden for the opera or Westminster on Coronation day. Two black horses lurched to a halt and tossed their shiny heads, stopping parallel to the shop. The cabbie wore a cloak and top hat and paused for no more than a second before pulling off again and disappearing into the mist, tucking the horses' heads in on a tight martingale rein.

Frankie hid the glow of her cigarette with one hand and looked back towards the shop. Where the pavement had been empty, a pair of long black legs had now appeared. The silhouette of a man in a top hat, carrying a strong black cane, was now outlined by the gas lamps, his face lost in the murk. He straightened his coat and walked quickly to the opening of Lancashire Court, the alley that ran down the side of Smythe's. His shoes cracked the silence; in a second or two he was gone.

From the recesses of her grubby pocket she withdrew her watch again. She knew she should be on her way. He might not even have been going in to Smythe's. There could be another apartment further down; the area was fairly well-to-do with hotels and museums.

Suddenly, a slice of light cleaved the middle of the first floor window above the shop. It vanished as quickly as it came, the twitch of a thick curtain folding it back into the room.

Cold was closing in and Frankie breathed into her hands, feeling the hot moisture turn quickly to a chill wet film. She had just straightened herself to be on her way again when the second carriage arrived.

Like an apparition drawn by a ghost horse it stopped as discreetly as the last. Down stepped a man in a brushed topper. His cloak reached the ground; a flash of pewter revealed the tip of a cane. If he hadn't coughed, Frankie might have thought she was hallucinating. The carriage melted back into the fog, the man disappeared down Lancashire Court. The next thing she heard was the tap of pewter on glass. Three times. What, was he going in the window? She hardly had time to answer herself before a motor cab crept furtively to the kerb side, spouting blue smoke as it crawled up to the gutter. Its passenger got out. Top hat, cane.

Suddenly the car thrust its engine to full force and sped past her, sending a gust of petroleum vapour straight up her nose. She choked on her cigarette smoke and went for the handkerchief in her top pocket. By the time she looked back up the car was gone. But it wasn't long before the fourth and the fifth vehicles arrived, and the sixth cab. Like a penny cinema screen with a skipping reel on loop the spectacle repeated itself until she had counted thirteen top hats all in all into the darkness of Lancashire Court.

Four

Night was falling by the time Detective Inspector Frederick Primrose gathered his belongings, packed his notepad into his leather briefcase and turned down his shirtsleeves. Just before he reached for his desk-lamp switch he took one last look out the window. His office was on the third floor of New Scotland Yard's headquarter building and he could see all the way over Victoria Embankment to the river. A barrow-man was loading his unsold vegetables into a small wooden boat. Beside him, a little girl with a red ribbon in her hair sat on the boat's prow still trying to hawk the last of the day's shrimps. 'Half pound for sixpence. Get 'em fresh!' Even in the din of omnibuses, electric trams and horse-hooves, her voice cut through. It all seemed so vivid outside the office, compared to the dull quiet buzz within.

When had it begun, this fug of apathy about his work, this consuming melancholy? Before the move to Scotland Yard? Or after the move into the suffragette squad? When he had first arrived at the Metropolitan Police, a fresh-skinned farm boy, Frederick Primrose the second had been bounced from division to division, from clerical work to the beat, his frustrated superiors wondering why a lad so practical, so quietly intelligent had not the literacy to be able to file reports or write up casework, wondering if he was a lost cause destined to sniff out pickpockets in Charing Cross station for the rest of his days. An opening for a Detective Inspector in the sixteen-strong branch allocated to deal with suffragettes had arisen several weeks ago, and someone unknown to him had recommended him for the post.

Perhaps they thought it was a joke. That would explain the newspaper that was left on his desk this morning, its front page showing Mrs Billinghurst grinning in her wheelchair. May Billinghurst had been part of the Black Friday demonstrations in November 1910, the worst violence yet in the women's movement. Primrose, one of the hundreds of uniformed sergeants drafted in that cold afternoon, had found her abandoned in an alleyway with the wheels ripped off her wicker bath chair, and kindly escorted her home in a police car. Only afterwards his Super had told him she had been ramming the lines of police horses with her chair, making them rear. 'A vicious piece of dynamite,' the Super had said, 'who would endanger lives as readily as she would butter toast.' The wheels had been removed by another officer. And now there she was, on the front page of the *Daily Mirror*, newly freed after two months in second division for throwing acid in pillar boxes. Whoever had left the paper on his desk had drawn a big loveheart in red ink round the grainy photograph. Of course it was a joke. If he had been marked out as a suffragette sympathiser how on earth could he have been given the special branch post? But the anonymity of the gesture – its silent, private positioning on his desk, rather than in the main office in front of everyone – had been dogging him all day.

A sharp scuffle at the door made him look up. With a nasty scrape the wood shuffled back against the parquet and the grinning faces of Inspector Barnes and Sergeant Wilson dangled in.

'Fred-boy!' Barnes chirped. 'Look lively! Quick one in the Hat and Feathers?'

Both men's cheeks and noses were ruddy and already bore the cheer of drink. Primrose looked at his wall clock. It was well after working hours; there was no reason he shouldn't. On the other hand Clara would be waiting at home and it was the third night this week he had been late for his tea.

'Come on Freddie, cheer up, they put away over a hundred at Bow Street today.' Wilson looked pleased as a fox.

'One by one, the suffragettes are gone,' Barnes wheezed leaning further into the room. 'Holloway's chock-full. Word is they'll be sending them to the Tower next.'

'Really? Not a bad idea,' said Wilson.

'It's a joke,' Barnes sneered over his shoulder at the Sergeant. 'Come on, Fredboy, what do you say? Hat and Feathers? Drink up an appetite. My wife makes chops on a Wednesday.' He rubbed his hands together.

Primrose sighed then looked back out of the window at the costermonger's girl. Her eager little spirit was making him glum. 'Not today, I'm afraid. Have to wade through this lot at home.'

'It'll be here in the morning.' Barnes waited, his luxurious moustache twitching in anticipation. After a second, he slapped his hands down against his hips, defeated. 'Your choice.'

Primrose nodded graciously.

The detective bustled backwards into the corridor, pushing Wilson along with him, and let the door fall shut. Primrose ran his gaze around the room. It fell on the closed copy of *Vincent's Police Code* which he kept lying in the corner like a sneaky eye. 'You must when on duty allow nothing but duty to occupy your thoughts.'

That was all very well, but the suffragettes had changed everything at New Scotland Yard. Now it was the criminals who wore the reproachful looks as they were arrested, cried 'shame' at the officers when standing in the dock. The lines of right and wrong were blurred and morals seemed bent all over the place. And what was the role of the police if not a moral one?

He packed a few case files into his briefcase to look over at home. A woman charged with pouring acid on golf courses, another two arson cases, both park bandstands, and a handful of suffragettes who had breached the terms of their prison release.

As he stood up to leave, his eyes briefly came to rest on the board on the right hand wall of the office, where the smiling portraits of the Pankhurst women were pinned; soft focus family shots Special Branch had somehow obtained. They looked like music-hall stars; Mrs Pankhurst and her wise eyes; a tall elegant woman in muted silks – that was Sylvia Pankhurst; and the bright, sharp gaze of Christabel, alongside a copy of her arrest warrant, issued by the Yard when she disappeared six months ago.

Out in the main office he handed a pile of typing to the night secretary, filed some reports in the tray for the Chief Inspector and went back to lock up his office. He was just about to slide his key in when a slow collection of voices creeping through the corridor made him pause. Junior detectives began hauling their coats from the backs of chairs and carefully taking revolvers from locked desk drawers. A uniformed man strode towards him and stopped sharp. Primrose recognised him as Sergeant Price from Westminster division, based down the road, and wondered briefly what he was doing at Scotland Yard. He didn't have to wonder long.

'Sir, window smash going on right now,' the Sergeant barked. 'Length of Bond Street. Chief Constable wants as many men as possible.' He slowed down and said carefully, 'To avoid the kind of happening of . . .'

'Black Friday,' Primrose sighed heavily. He clicked back open the lock of his door, dumped his briefcase inside and locked it again. It was beyond his hopes that they would leave him alone tonight, just leave him to get on with his paperwork and his supper.

'Chief wants us to get our skates on, so if you don't mind I'll jump in the Daimler with you.'

'No, I don't mind,' Primrose said quietly. He kept his eye on the crowd of officers gathering along the hallway, looking out for Wilson or Barnes. He wondered if they had made it out of the building yet and were on their merry way to the Hat and Feathers.

'Were you there on Black Friday?' Sergeant Price asked as they strode towards the stairs.

Primrose paused before nodding, half-relieved that there was still someone in the Metropolitan Police who didn't know about his heroics with Mrs Billinghurst and her bath chair.

'Super said it was grim. I heard two died.'

'Something like that.' He wished the young sergeant would shut up.

'Still, if that's the game Winston Churchill wants to play. It was Churchill who ordered the beatings, wasn't it?'

Primrose looked at his curious face. 'Where did you hear that?' He tried to keep his voice flat but there was an edge to it.

'I thought it was common knowledge. Since Churchill wouldn't allow an enquiry they never got to the bottom of it. Men like that don't just rally themselves by accident . . .' His voice faded as Primrose stopped walking. He took the sergeant by the elbow and dropped his voice.

'A word of warning, a friendly one. You ought to watch your words with senior officers. You might not find the next one you say such things to so lenient.'

They became caught in a throng of policemen piling down onto the street and Primrose felt his breath suck in. Moments like this convinced him he was still more comfortable in a scrum of animals than people, heaving around the Lancashire heifers on his uncle's dairy farm rather than rubbing shoulders with fellow men.

Out in the yard a uniformed constable was already climbing behind the wheel of the Daimler. Officers were piling into the Black Maria arrest vans; more inside were checking the locks on the wire cubicles. Primrose slid into the front seat while Price and another two plain clothes officers jumped in the back. The clod of hooves and the roar of engines folded into one as each vehicle set off in turn for Bond Street.

Five

Twinkle, Frankie's writing partner whose name was printed significantly larger than hers on their shared column, lived just off the Edgware Road. The rich strawberry red of her building meant that the turn off was always easy to find. Street lamps snaked clouds of electric light up against the walls, gleaming off the lacquer. As Frankie walked, she let her fingers strum the glossy black railings lining the gardens. She was still puzzling over the sight of the carriages outside Smythe's. Perhaps there was another exit to Lancashire Court. Perhaps they weren't going into the shop at all. There were plenty of clubs down that way; it could have been nothing but a dull meeting of politicos.

Twinkle's block lay halfway down the row of Oxford and Cambridge mansions. A whiskered porter let Frankie into the hydraulic lift and she rose with a jerk. In the safety of the metal cage she sniffed herself. She had the whiff of public house on her, tobacco and beer. Twinkle would probably try to attack her with the eau de toilette. She wrinkled her nose. So long as it wasn't violets.

The lift cranked to a halt on the top floor, glowing in dainty yellow light. There was no one about. Frankie had never seen anyone coming or going in her visits to Twinkle. The whole place had an eerie quiet to it, nothing like her own lodgings on Percy Circus where there was always a noisy communist meeting going on upstairs, or an Italian family shouting at each other in the street. She straightened her shirt and knocked on the door.

In her day Twinkle had apparently been quite something to talk about; the last of the great Courtesans, so it was said. Books were dedicated to her, paintings made of her in the classical style, and hung in Mayfair drawing rooms under the guise of art. Legend had it that a poet once threw himself into the Thames over her, though he had then thought better of it and swum ashore, only to die of cholera weeks later. She had been an icon of fashion, seen at Ascot, at the Savoy, riding along Rotten Row with an entourage of copycats. The papers never called her by her real name, which Frankie didn't know, and not even by her nickname, which she had earned, so she claimed, for being 'the little star of our times'. She had always just been 'fair anonyma' or 'the muse'. Rumours flew round society circles like flies in a dirty cake shop about who her clients were or had been. Names that read like a roll call of the House of Lords were bandied about as blackmail currency.

Boredom had settled on her like dust in recent years. Itchy

to dip her toes back into the limelight she had been on at Mr Stark about a column. The trouble was, he said, she was a little 'balmy on the crumpet' these days; she would need a helping hand to make sure her ideas were fit for the public to consume. So four months ago, on the 30th of June, the Ladies' Page Friday column 'Conversations from the Boudoir' was born and suddenly Frankie found that every Saturday on her doorstep, a little cheque for one pound and one shilling would appear. She couldn't say that she had ever had pride over the work. But it was bread, it was a pot-boiler, as Audrey Woodford would say, and pot-boilers were never to be sniffed at.

She waited minutes before the parlourmaid answered the door, a pale-cheeked girl with ginger freckles. Frankie didn't recognise her. Twinkle went through parlourmaids like most women went through handkerchiefs.

'Sorry to keep you, Ma'am,' she dipped at Frankie.

'It's all right. I'm late anyway.' Won't last a week, thought Frankie as she stepped inside. There was a strong sweet-savoury smell in the air, wafts of stew on the boil coming from the kitchen, gravy, beef and onions. Her stomach rumbled. The stout had made her hungry and she hadn't eaten since breakfast.

'She's in the boudoir.' The maid led the way down the hall with fragile steps, towards a pair of lavishly etched glass doors. From beyond, a muffled voice trilled, 'Is that you, Puss?'

Frankie winced at the nickname. The maid paused to pick up a tray of tea from a Japanese sideboard and pushed open the doors with her hips.

At first Frankie wasn't quite sure what she was looking at. Twinkle's body seemed concealed inside a box, the kind magicians used when they wanted to cut women in half. Except this one was upright and only her head poked out of the top, her plentiful grey hair whipped into a turban like cream on a trifle. She must have been sitting down or crouching because the box was wide and squat and was making streams of perspiration tumble down her face. Above her, leaning precariously, a contraption had been rigged; a tilting hat-stand held in place by a pulley roped to the legs of the enormous bedframe. Attached to it, two ribbons had been looped through the upper corners of a newspaper, holding the pages apart. Twinkle's face was half-covered by a thick rubber band circumnavigating her head, strapping a pair of horn opera glasses in place to magnify the paper's text. She turned slowly towards Frankie until she had her in the sights, looking for all the world like a terrifying mechanical owl.

'What the devil . . . ?'

The maid whispered, 'It's a gem–wood cabinet. Turkish bath.'

Twinkle's head snapped round. 'Page. Quickly girl, I'll lose the train of thought. Hello, Puss.' The maid scurried over to the cabinet and ran the next page along the ribbon.

'You're not going to make me get in that.'

'And why not? You could do with one.' Twinkle looked at the maid. 'No, dear, not tea, I said gin. We want gin, don't we, Puss? But first you're going to eat. I can't of course, I'm fasting.'

'You can drink gin on a fast?'

'Pardon?'

'Nothing.' Frankie sniffed the meaty air again. 'What are you making?'

Twinkle twitched and made little grunts as the parlour-maid struggled to unstrap the goggles. 'That's better. Give me a kiss, Puss.' Reluctantly Frankie walked over and kissed Twinkle's red cheek. Her skin felt like hot wet paper. 'Gracie's made oysters, haven't you?'

The maid blushed.

'Doesn't smell like oysters.'

'The prairie kind.'

Frankie stifled a retch. 'Aw, I'd love to but I'm stuffed. Had cockles and chips on the way over,' she lied. She should have known; last week Twinkle had surreptitiously fed her goat pizzle disguised in a heavy paprika sauce. Dr Freud and his followers, Frankie fancied, would have a field day with Twinkle. There was a purple velveteen chair perched between the window and the bed and she sat down at a safe distance. Gracie was still standing awkwardly by the door.

'What are you waiting for? Gin, girl, I said. 'Now, where was I? Ah yes, you'll never guess what that piss-pot Mr Fox-Pitt from the *Pall Mall Gazette* has said now. Where is it, I can't see without those damned glasses? Listen to this.'

Frankie took her notebook from her pocket and licked the tip of a pencil.

'"You cannot call a fashionable French or English woman well dressed, but you might describe her as expensively upholstered. Dressmakers," he thunders, "appear to have lost sight of the fact that the primary object of clothing is to keep the body warm . . ." Well, I might say to him that a woodland is exceedingly plain without its flowers. Flowers also serve that other essential purpose.'

'Decorating cakes?'

'Pollination.' She looked accusingly at Frankie. 'Of course, if you can make the plain look work. But . . . I can't help thinking that if women were encouraged to dress like you the birth rate would slow.'

Frankie bit her tongue and looked around the room. Across the bed lay a tangle of furs with heads, paws and tails flopping in every direction. 'Are you going to get out of there? You look as cooked as a Christmas goose.'

'What do you think about Mr Fox-Pitt? I think we should get our revenge. I have the idea to recommend that men wear purple.'

'Purple? Why purple?'

'I would like to see women arriving at the theatre, and being shocked to find a man sitting next to them who clashes with their dress. And purple clashes with quite a lot of things. Like your suit, Puss.' She glanced at Frankie's trousers against the chair, and continued to ramble. 'Purple has a sort of ecclesiastical feel to it, and that would make things feel very naughty at jollifications, don't you think?'

To Frankie's relief Gracie came back with a bottle of Old Tom and a couple of crystal sherry glasses. With a weary heart she knocked back a couple of swallows. Twinkle had

Gracie pour the gin straight into her mouth. The sight reminded Frankie of the Holloway feeding tube. She suddenly sat up straighter.

'Twinkle, do you know a trapeze girl?'

Twinkle's eyes had gone glossy with the hit of alcohol. 'I know a dozen. Gracie, I think it's time to get out, turn around, Puss.'

'But do you know one called Ebony Diamond?'

'Name rings a bell,' she grunted. 'No, not that way, I'll never get my feet through that hole. Are you simple?' Frankie realised she could still see Twinkle in the mirror, heaving herself into a pink satinette robe with Gracie fuddling over the ties.

'She's a suffragette.'

'Well they've all got bats in the belfry if you ask me. Who wants a vote anyway? Next they'll be expecting us to sit in that dull parliament, stinking of men. Now,' she wriggled her arms down into the sleeves. Gracie gave a yelp. 'That's what you get for having fists like ham hocks.'

Frankie closed her eyes for slightly longer than a blink. 'She's a gypsy. You'd know her if you saw her.'

When Frankie opened her eyes she saw Twinkle had turned to face her. Her gaze was cold. 'Why do you want to know, Puss?' She batted a hand at Gracie. 'No, leave my hair, just fetch the cold cream will you?'

'It's Mr Stark; he wants me to do a portrait of her.'

'Really?' There was a sour note in Twinkle's tone. 'How strange.'

'Well she's on at the Coliseum tomorrow. And –' she broke off, seeing the hard bright smile on Twinkle's face and felt herself treading on thin ice. 'Do you mind if I . . . ?' She reached for the Old Tom bottle.

Twinkle smiled, deliberately wide. 'Not at all, Puss. Pour me one too, there's a dear.'

Twinkle sat at her dressing table and began rubbing grease into her face. Gracie had scarpered. Frankie passed across a glass, then knocked back her own and poured another. It was hot, herbal, pleasant. She felt it swimming up to her brain. 'She's interesting. She wears these black corsets.'

Twinkle turned on her stool and stared again at Frankie. 'Really, these Sapphic obsessions of yours are so dull.' Her eyes, though sunk amid folds of skin, had a ball-bearing of steel to their core.

'Right,' Frankie slunk back in her seat. 'Dinner party topics?'

'Well, now you mention it, I do think I know her. Quite the Gibson girl, as I recall.' She sucked in her cheekbones and put her hands round her waist. 'Out of fashion now, of course. It's all thick waists and skinny hips these days. But she must have had a fun time in Holloway. Hunger striking would be positively up her strada.' Suddenly Twinkle spun round, her face lit up like the moon. 'That's it, Puss. That's the dinner party topic. Starvation fashion. I love it, it's brilliant, you're a genius, Puss.' She threw her hands in the air and for a second Frankie was worried she was about to be assaulted by a squashing embrace. But Twinkle only made for the bed instead and flung herself backwards, groaning as her back hit the furs. A noxious cloud of violet eau de toilette flew up from her.

'Hold on a minute.'

'No, it's perfect, write it down. Will hunger striking ever catch on as a fashion trend? It's perfect. It's so wonderfully now. It's delicioso. It's deevie, Puss. Get the suffragette waif look without setting foot in Holloway.'

'Twinkle, you know how much trouble I'd be in. It's taken long enough to get them off my back after the cartoon. It's my name goes on the column too. You know that.'

'Mr Stark will love it.'

'Twinkle, please.'

'Well what? Have you got any better ideas? Next you're going to be suggesting we write about Lloyd George's budget or national pensions. How about the death of the House of Lords or the rise of trade unionism?' She reached for her gin glass. 'Come on, they're all bats. What do you care?'

'But Ebony . . .' she tailed off.

'Yes?'

'She'll kill me.'

'Since when was Frankie George frightened of a suffragette? Do you remember that day we dressed up my cockatoo to look like Christabel Pankhurst?'

'It's different, that didn't offend anyone.'

'Well why do you care?'

Frankie fiddled with her pencil.

'Come on, spit it out, or you shan't have any more gin.'

Frankie sighed. 'Ebony Diamond. She had this huge argument today with the man who makes her costumes. Right in front of me, got proper violent. I'm not sure what about, but she's big in the suffragettes and I just, I don't know. If I can get her trust I might be onto something. You know how desperate I am to get into reporting. Proper . . .' She suddenly stopped herself.

'Proper reporting,' Twinkle said dryly.

'I don't mean like that. I mean—'

'Puss, you want to watch that mouth of yours. It's going to get you in trouble one of these days.' Her hand roamed the covers until she found the head of a dead mink to fondle. 'You know you're not really a woman of independent means yet and let me tell you it takes a lot of hard work and quite a bit of doing things you don't like very much to get there. Greasing men's beards. Massaging gouty knees.' She smiled an eerie, indulgent smile. 'Do you think I bought all this by only working jobs I felt like?'

'I was only hoping . . .'

'You think that because you don't dress like the rest of us you are above all this froth and nonsense.'

'Don't think that at all,' Frankie muttered.

'The roaring girls were trussed up like that three hundred years before you. You sound as snotty-nosed as those self-righteous suffragettes you're so eager to stick up for.'

They sat in silence for a few minutes. Frankie sipped the dregs of her gin glass. She didn't dare pour another.

'Purple then?' she said after a few moments.

Twinkle was still in a sulk. Her gnarled pink hand fingered the rim of her glass.

'Twinkle, you know I only brought it up because I thought you'd know a thing or two about her. You know all the society girls.'

Twinkle smiled weakly at the flattery. Newspapergirls, Frankie thought, were nursemaids as much as anything else. 'And,' she continued, 'I thought if anyone would know what men in toppers were doing going into a corset shop after hours it would be you as well.' She tossed it out like fish bait. Twinkle suddenly looked sharply at her. Frankie couldn't be certain but she thought she saw a frown momentarily crease her forehead. Encouraged, she went on. 'Oh, crazy it was. I thought I was seeing things. You must know Smythe's, Bond Street. I'll bet you've got a couple of his in that wardrobe.'

Twinkle's eyes had fogged over again with the gin. At length she said slowly, 'If I were you, I wouldn't go digging around either that girl or any goings-on at Smythe's. You might find yourself learning things you rather wish you had left alone.'

Frankie sat up. 'So you do know the shop I mean?'

'Olivier Smythe's? Any woman worth her flesh knows that shop.'

'So why is it so special?' She inched forward. 'What do you know about it?'

Twinkle was silent for a moment, then looked at her coldly. 'Nothing I would dream of sharing with you.'

Frankie felt her organs beginning to boil.

Twinkle went on, 'You know I really do feel better after that Turkish bath. I think there's still enough fuel in the spirit lamp for you to have one too. You don't mind going after me, no of course you don't. Perhaps we'll write about it after all.'

Six

The wind beat Inspector Primrose's face as the constable drove, dodging horses and carts and electric trams and white-gloved policemen directing traffic along the Mall. The Westminster sergeant, Price, tried absurdly hard to keep up a shrieked conversation from the back seat. They approached Old Bond Street from Piccadilly where two vans were parked blocking the turn off. The constable reared the car up onto the pavement; a group of onlookers dashed for cover as it grunted to a halt next to the Royal Arcade. Primrose clung to the dashboard, slamming into the side of the door. On the opposite side of the road, the Fenwick's side, a line of gaping shattered windows ran as far as the eye could see. The hundreds of police seemed equal to the number of women, voices and catcalls pierced now and then by a single scream.

'It's like dominoes the way they do it,' Price was saying to the other officers. 'I've seen them. They line themselves up. One goes first, then the next.' They climbed out of the car, walking apace. Price demonstrated in the air the movement of a hammer on glass. 'That way they only get fined one window each.'

The doors of the Black Marias across the street were open and Primrose saw that already there was a cuffed woman in each cubicle, shouting through the wires.

'I pay taxes, I pay your wages, you criminals!'

'This is the work of that devil Asquith, let him draw our blood, you'll never make us stop.'

'Finger your wife with those hands, do you, sergeant? She's an unlucky lady.'

In the cubicle nearest the door a woman was weeping. Another reached a hand though the wire towards her. 'Hold on in there, lovie, don't worry, they might smell like dogs but their bark's worse than their bite.'

Primrose shuddered, watching Price wade into the scene as if it were nothing more than unruly traffic. In the distance towards Oxford Street a breakaway group had pulled out hatchets and rocks in stockings and were attacking a police car. Other suffragettes were trying to hold them back, calling for just the windows of shops to be smashed, while a group of women with Freedom League posters were demonstrating, calling for an end to the vandalism. It was all a gigantic mess, Primrose thought, and in the middle of it, green coppers fresh from Peel House were grabbing the arms of women older and more respectable than their own mothers. All of a sudden Price was behind him again, snapping his fingers. 'Inspector, Inspector. Look.'

Primrose turned back to where the sergeant was pointing. At first he only saw a woman in a suffragette sash blowing a kiss to her friends as she was led off, cuffed. It was a scene being repeated the length of the street, ladies in furs calmly being arrested. But beyond the woman a crowd was growing. Bodies were moving in a scrum towards one of the shattered shop windows.

'Something's not right there. Why aren't they on it?' Price gestured to a couple of constables up the road, whispering and turning a blind eye to the fight. A chant was creeping steadily from the core of the group, but with all the knotted bodies tangling for the centre it was hard to tell what they were shouting. Primrose pushed forward, Price behind him. Feathering the group's edges, small tussles were breaking out, men on men. They were working men, not police, by the look of their neckerchiefs and flat caps, their brown jackets and shirts open at the neck. Primrose wondered who had alerted them to the smash. Two were at loggerheads, clutching one another by the shoulders, rutting like stags. 'Call them off,' the smaller, stockier one was shouting while the other man grunted and sweated and wrenched him to the street.

'Here, watch it!' a tea girl in a pinny cried, as Primrose dug into the clutch of bodies, parting the crowd like a bread roll.

'Scotland Yard,' he snapped back.

Her eyes flamed. 'Well get in there and call off your dogs!'

He heaved his way into the mess leaving Price hovering at the edges. There were some shopkeepers nearby, still in their aprons and overalls. Fists were being thrown towards the centre, people were shouting. The light was so dim it was hard to see where bodies ended and shadows began.

'Mercy! Mercy!' one woman cried. A suffragette in a sash tried to fling in her hammer. Primrose caught her arm just as it flew at him. A flat-capped man turned and snarled in his face, 'Get out of here. On police orders.'

'I am the police.'

The punches were still beating inwards. Something was desperately not right at the centre of the commotion and the crowd outside it was growing larger. As bodies knocked against each other, people lost their balance and dragged others to the ground by their knees. Primrose flung a boy out of the way and he landed in the stomach of the tea girl, sending her backwards. She screamed. All of a sudden with the sweat and the bodies bashing against each other he was finding it hard to breathe. Then he saw the legs.

Two white-stockinged pins lay like birch saplings across the pavement. One had lost its boot and been stabbed in the foot with a shard of glass. A little streak of blood ran down the white silk. Primrose rammed the final few men out of the way, until he saw the rest of the figure lying in a heap.

In front of him two men were pinning her to the ground. From the shape of her body she looked barely older than a teenager, though he couldn't see her face, obscured as it was by mounds of shredded petticoats lifted high over her head. She was clinging desperately to a suffragette sash as if it would protect her, screaming blind, her arms held fast above her head. The two men bent about her were tickling her stomach, pinching her thighs, laughing hysterically. Suddenly a jolt in his back threw Primrose toppling into the girl, sending the two men sideways off their haunches onto the pavement.

'Watch it,' one snarled, turning.

Primrose froze. He knew the voice. But it couldn't possibly be. He squinted in the dim light, until he was able to focus on the two faces. The crowd suddenly simmered to a hush, interested now in the men in the centre squaring up to one another.

'Make up your mind,' a woman cried scornfully, 'Either kill us or protect us, don't pretend you can do both.'

In front of Primrose, smiling sheepishly, as if they had been caught with their fingers in the jam jar, were Wilson and Barnes. Barnes's lips curled underneath his thick moustache, not a bit embarrassed, while Wilson looked at his scuffed shoes. 'Advice we got was to be a bit rough with them, Inspector, make an example.'

Primrose stayed immobile for a second. Then his reason found him and he rushed to cover the girl's bleeding legs, pulling her skirts back into place.

'Inspector.'

'I don't want to know. This woman needs a doctor.' Two suffragettes came forward and helped her sit up. Her face was swollen from crying. With her shoulders slumped forward and her legs sticking straight out she looked horribly young.

Barnes swayed on his feet. 'There is hysteria bacillus in

every case of suffragitis. Think of us as doctors, Freddie-boy.'

He looked Barnes in the eye. 'Chops, was it? On a Wednesday?'

Barnes looked confused. Then a noise in the middle of the road distracted them. The crowd, already dispersing, were turning their attention back to the street.

'It's her. Mrs Haverfield,' whispered one of the suffragettes on the ground.

Primrose turned to watch. With the majority of the window-smashers rounded up, the centre of the road was now clear and was being patrolled by three constables on horseback. As the onlookers stared, the three horses tentatively stopped, then stepped backwards, swayed, arched their necks, and slumped full force to their knees. The officers on top clutched the reins and their helmets, kicking the horses with the spurs on their boots, trying desperately to regain control over the animals, who were suddenly behaving as if they were spellbound.

'What is it?' Primrose murmured. Barnes nodded towards a woman straight ahead of the horses, kneeling on the dirty, glass-flecked street before them. She wore a top hat and black velvet-collared coat, a long tweed skirt spread around her on the ground. The horses lowered their heads as if bowing to her, paying homage to the smile on her face. All around had hushed. In the queer twilight breaths were frozen. Even the police officers had stopped short, prisoners still attached to them by the cuffs.

Barnes leaned closer and Primrose could smell stale beer on him like old garlic. 'That's Mrs Haverfield. She charms police horses. It's witchcraft, pure and simple, that's what it is, Freddie. And if we don't put a stop to it, right now, tonight, who knows what they'll do next?'

Seven

A gust of air greeted Frankie as she opened the door onto the street, cold as buried bones, but a welcome relief. She drank it in. After being stewed in the gem-wood cabinet, she had been scrubbed with boiled almond bran, rinsed in orange-scented vinegar and doused by Gracie in the bathroom with borax water. The wretched machine had been about as comfortable as sitting in a coal scuttle. Twinkle of course wanted it lauded as the greatest invention since buttered toast, along with purple suits and starvation fashion.

Frankie shook out her arms and legs and gathered the broken camera back onto her shoulder. Anger and disappointment tugged viciously at her, her stomach raged with hunger. She hadn't eaten since breakfast, except for a few claggy sickly rose creams Twinkle had popped in her mouth while she was in the cabinet. Her blood was starting to feel weak. She fought against it. This was what she had chosen, and she always knew it was going to be harder than fitting machines up in that stinking composition room. She pulled out her pocket-watch. Half past eleven. There was one last thing she could try before the day was spent. Bending down, she poked a finger into the side of her brogues and sure enough there was the spare half crown that always lived there in case of emergencies or pickpockets, something her father had shown her when she was a little girl, the place he kept his winnings when he had been at the bookies.

Soho would be alive at this hour.

She doubled back on herself until she came to a junction where omnibuses were still roaring about the empty roads, their golden lamps lighting up the faces of the passengers inside: evening workers, waiters in white shirts, warehouse men in factory aprons. She thought about taking a motor bus but settled instead for a pirate horse-drawn for the cheaper fare, hopped on the back and paid her penny. For the first time that day her limbs gave way to the rattling, comforting movement of the bus, the solitude it gave its passengers, all soaked in their own private worlds.

Some still said Soho was the devil's haunt. The City Council's twenty-year crusade against 'disorderly houses' had cleaned up some of it, cleared out the slums and set a programme of eviction on the brothel madams that saw them shift their business down Piccadilly to congregate round the little statue of the Angel of Christian Charity (now nicknamed Eros). But there were still some landlords that preferred the rent a red-light worker could pay, compared to a family of tailors or cobblers. It was its own enclave, a village where the children were smart, and the shadowy figures of illegal bookies talking in unfamiliar tongues could be taken for menace. Frankie's father, who had been born and bred in Tottenham, couldn't wait to drag her Italian mother out of Soho. Visiting it always had the uncomfortable feeling for Frankie of going somewhere she felt she ought to know but didn't. Whenever she saw Wardour Street she would think of her grandfather Lucchese's funeral, the blurred memory of a gun cart, an open coffin and black horses with sinister plumes.

She hopped off the bus at Leicester Square and made her way up Greek Street, where the markets were still going, auctioneers selling off the last of their antiques, costermongers tossing half-rotten veg to children with wicker baskets. French laundresses walked the streets with panniers of pressed linen bound to their hips. The public houses spilled out onto the streets, and the steamed windows of French bistros and Hungarian restaurants were full of well-dressed men being served rich-smelling stews. There were men and women of all hair and skin colours bustling about, speaking a mixture of languages, that seemed to shift with each street corner you turned. Tailors' houses and patisseries of sweets and cakes had closed their doors for the night. A man in a chef's hat was smoking in the doorway of a trattoria. Frankie asked him in broken Italian if he knew Jojo's Cocoa Bar. He gestured down the street, pointing away from Soho Square towards Duck Lane.

Several slick-dressed men were smoking clove cigarettes and laughing on the corner of the junction, and because of them she

almost missed it. They were standing in front of a painted sign
with an arrow pointing down the lane. Beyond them, a curved
staircase led down to a basement door, open just a chink, where
warm red light spilled up, deep and inviting, A glazed poster
flapped against the railings in the night breeze, showing a carni-
val of harlequins, tumblers, exotic barely-clothed people,
bearded ladies and a woman with two heads, all clustered
around one figure hanging in the centre, as if her trapeze strings
were being held up by the clouds: Ebony Diamond.

A sweep of wind pushed the basement door open and
Frankie blinked as two figures standing beside the poster
were suddenly lit up. She recognised the shape and stance of
one of them, an older woman, and her mind cast back to the
previous summer. She had seen her outside the Palace
Theatre. Lady Thorne, leader of the National Vigilance
Association, notorious for causing fuss outside theatres with
her pamphlets. She wore a long blue cloak with a fur-trimmed
hood, showing off her sharp little features. She was waving a
bunch of papers in the other woman's face.

The other woman, as Frankie clocked her, was slight and
young, shiny with greasepaint and shockingly, or so it
appeared from the back, wearing nothing at all on her top
half. Frankie did not consider herself a prude and knew that
strange things went on in Soho – she had once seen a gentleman in a shirt and morning coat and nothing else running
down the street howling for his breeches – but she blushed
and looked at her feet as soon as she clapped eyes on the
muscles of the girl's back. As the girl shifted, Frankie saw that

in fact a looped bunch of shells and coins was just about protecting her modesty. Her hair was covered by a velvet turban. The girl launched a hand for Lady Thorne's face, making the shells on her top hiss. The old lady darted backwards with impressive speed. Now the men who had been lounging at the sidelines were taking an interest.

'Will you leave us be? People will think you've escaped from St Barnabas.' The younger woman tried to grab Lady Thorne's cloak but instead ended up with a fistful of the pamphlets. A sea of papers fell over the cobbled street like giant confetti.

'Jezebel!' the woman cried. 'Sharper than a serpent's tooth!'

The girl looked ready to launch another attack, but then she put her face in her hands and took a deep breath. 'François, call one of the cabbies over.'

A man in a bowler hat took his cigarette out of his mouth long enough to whistle and in a few seconds a bony horse appeared, leading a hackney into the yard. Frankie darted back as the horse passed her. The girl had her arm on the old woman's cloak and with a surprising strength managed to manhandle her into the cab, but not before the old lady had grappled up a few of her pamphlets from the mucky ground. Her shoulders were hunched now; she looked as if she had woken from a bad dream and was willing herself to vanish. The young woman in the turban muttered something in the driver's ear. He frowned, and asked if she was sure.

'Don't worry, she'll pay.'

Frankie leaned out of the way as the cabbie lashed his horse and the vehicle lumbered off back into Soho.

The young woman leaned against the railings and wiped a hand across her face. When she took it away a trail of smeared make-up had been left in its wake, black kohl and green eye paint. Frankie only realised she was staring when the girl looked across at her. She ran her eyes up Frankie's body, from the dark brogues on her feet to her trousers, jacket and short hair. 'Haven't I seen you in the halls?' She had a cool educated voice.

Frankie shook her head. 'No, I'm . . .' she hesitated. 'I'm a reporter.'

The girl's eyes rolled back in her head. Her face was familiar-looking; the large cold features. 'How did you find out?'

'I'm sorry? I'm looking for Ebony Diamond.'

She paused, then something like relief flooded her face. 'She didn't turn up tonight. Matter of fact I'm doing the finale.'

'Any idea when she'll next be on?'

The girl nodded towards the entrance. 'Ask Lizzy. She's the dwarf. Does the rotas. I've no idea.'

'What do you mean?'

The girl shrugged. 'You're a reporter. You should know.'

Frankie shrugged back.

The girl sighed. 'She's been in and out of prison. She's never here. I'm surprised Jojo keeps her on.' Shivering, she gathered her arms round her shoulders. Something in her pockets moved. She dipped a hand into the fabric and to Frankie's horror produced a heavy curled pink snake. Struck by the mawkishness of what she thought must be an automaton, Frankie peered closer. The snake flicked its tongue and she jumped back. It began to travel round the girl's hands in a slow dance.

She didn't seem to notice Frankie's revulsion. 'Look, you can come in and watch the finale if you want. It's tuppence tonight, and for sixpence more you get devilled kidneys and potatoes.' The snake licked the air again.

Frankie shuddered. Another wasted trip. She glanced at the covering of pamphlets sticking to the ground and bent to pick one up. In black dripping letters it read, 'This way to the Pit of Hell'. Below were listed the dangers of going to the theatre. There was a grotesque drawing of a group of prostitutes lurking like cats behind the Alhambra in Leicester Square.

'That woman. That was Lady Thorne, wasn't it?'

'I have no idea who she is. Will you excuse me.' The woman moved away from the railings, stroking the head of her snake as she went.

'Wait. Can you tell me anything else about Ebony Diamond? When was the last time you saw her?'

She stopped and turned. 'I don't remember. Last week probably.'

'But I thought . . .' Frankie's gaze shifted to the poster where Ebony Diamond was the centrepiece.

'Things change, don't they?'

'What's your name?'

She hesitated. 'Salome. My name is Salome.' With a seashell rattle she disappeared down the stairs into the gaping red door.

Frankie stood thinking for a few seconds. Did she want to part with eight pence? It would cost her at least that to fix the camera. There were still two more days before Saturday's cheque. And her bed was beckoning.

What would the girls on the society pages do? They would go in, of course. Teddy Hawkins would. But then none of them had just spent two hours having their skin purged by Twinkle and being offered bull testicles for refreshment. She peered closely at the poster, still flapping against the railings. There were a few names on it: 'Eloise, the two-headed chanteuse', 'Jojo the wolf-man', 'The Black Diamond'. And there was the other woman tucked behind a pair of conjoined twins, 'Salome Snake dancer, Princess of Egypt'. Frankie stared for a second, then turned her nose up. That well-spoken girl with her hair all piled up in a Paul Poiret turban had never set a foot near Egypt, she would bet all the riches in Mayfair on it. She began to skulk back towards the main street and was almost there when a child ran up to her, blocking her path. 'Tuppence for a Lady Thorne doll.' From behind his back he thrust out a hand, full of half-inflated balloons with eyes and mouths sketched on in feathery traces. 'Look,' he put on a hoity-toity voice, '"This way to the pit of hell!" Look at her faint in the face of the demons.' He let the air out of the balloon and it farted to a flop.

'Enterprising bag of little shits, aren't you?' She prised the boy out of the way and disappeared off down Greek Street, heading back on foot towards Clerkenwell.

Eight

Primrose was helping two junior constables book in a couple of suffragettes when his Chief appeared, brandishing a telegram. Bow Street Police Station raged with the noise of furious women and hoarse constables. Behind the front throng, queues of prisoners were lining up waiting to be registered; conversations were breaking out between bored policemen and the well-dressed ladies attached to them by the wrist.

Chief Inspector Stuttlegate was Primrose's immediate superior in the suffragette branch, and had been in the role as long as the unit existed. At five foot seven he was just under the regulation height for new recruits. Common folklore had it that his wits had got him through the training rather than his brawn, but those who knew him suspected 'wits' was a generous word for brass neck. He had a pointy nose like a sniffer dog and wiry ginger hair twisting from his head in separate threads. He pulled Primrose's elbow.

'This,' he held out a crumpled piece of paper, 'just came in from Dover.' There was a shifting of attention among the officers behind the desk. One of the constables turned his head. 'Did I ask you to join this conversation? Look there's a woman there wants booking, get on with it, fingerprints.'

The woman standing before the counter fixed the Chief with a stubborn look. 'I shan't give fingerprints.'

'You'll bloody do as you're told or it'll be third division and no porridge.'

'I'm not obliged to give fingerprints unless I'm convicted of a crime. We may be women, but we're not stupid.'

The Chief's face coloured from the neck up. 'Now you listen to me!'

Primrose pointed to the telegram. 'What does it say, Chief?'

Stuttlegate released his fix on the woman and gestured to Primrose to move further down the bench. 'Out of that bitch's hearing.'

'What's happened?'

He sighed tersely. 'She's only gone and been here, under our bloody noses, cavorting like a sparrow, probably there tonight with this lot.'

'Who?'

'Who do you think, the cat's mother? Wake up, Primrose. Christabel Pankhurst.'

Primrose, in his weary state, smarted from the admonishment. His gaze drifted to the clock on the wall. He was bleary-eyed and it took a moment to focus on the time. A headache had begun brewing behind one of his eyes.

'She was spotted on the Paddington train, transferring to the ferry to Calais.' He rapped his fist on the bench. 'If they'd been a second sooner we'd have had her.' He gritted his teeth but didn't sound convinced by his words.

'She was here tonight?'

'Yes tonight, Freddie. Suffragette leader, the one in hiding, here. Tonight. Do you have somewhere you need to be? You keep looking at that clock.'

Primrose swallowed, 'No, sir.' He cleared his throat and tried to demonstrate that he was paying attention. 'Why didn't they just arrest her when they spotted her?'

'Because it wasn't our bloody man who clocked her. It was a solicitor travelling with her on the train. Says he couldn't be sure till he got a look at her in the light. He pulled the guard in just before the ferry left. They tried to find her, but I don't know, she was in the tea room or the ladies' room or wherever they go to polish up their broomsticks. If you ask me he's one of them.'

'A suffragette?' Primrose's brow creased.

'You do get them, Primrose, men's league for women's whatever it is.' He puffed out his cheeks and released his breath. 'Seems a bit of a coincidence that he kept mum all that time on the train because he couldn't be sure, then soon as that ferry's on its way, that's when he's bloody sure.' He looked at Primrose with his pinprick eyes. 'They're laughing at us, Freddie. They brought her over here under our noses.'

Primrose said nothing. He sensed the Chief was testing him, willing him to agree.

Stuttlegate smoothed out the telegram on the counter. 'Look, I'm at the end of my tether here. Don't mind telling you this is driving me into the ground.'

'You and me both,' Primrose said quietly. The headache was starting to spread out to his ears. He thought of Clara. He hadn't had time to send her word or even telephone her yet to say he would be late.

The Chief rubbed his head. 'I've got to get out of here. My wife's raising merry hell. Says the children have forgotten what their father looks like.'

Primrose raised a weak smile. He knew what was coming.

'You don't mind, do you, Freddie? Just need to get the statement from the man logged, write up a quick report tonight and we'll file an investigation tomorrow. It's just if I leave something this big . . .'

Primrose nodded. He hadn't realised until now quite how hungry he was. Perhaps the hot potato stand at Covent Garden would still be open, he could pass by it on his way back to the Embankment office.

The Chief slapped his back. 'Knew you'd come good. Next time, we'll nail her. Then we'll both be heroes.' He gave a wink and strode off past the two constables on his way out, knocking into the shoulder of one of the suffragettes. 'Pardon me,' he called, and made to tip his hat.

Primrose looked at the grubby telegram from the Dover Customs office with its brusque capital letter account of the sighting of Miss Pankhurst. It was marked twenty past ten. He elbowed past the desk constables until he reached the station telephone. Picking up the receiver, he asked the operator for Clapham two-seven-five.

Clara answered almost immediately. Sitting near the telephone meant she was worried.

'My love?'

She was silent.

'Suffragettes,' he said. 'Again.' He tried to smile. He imagined her nod. 'Didn't you fancy a smash and a jolly to Bow Street yourself?' Either she didn't understand the joke or she didn't find it amusing.

There was a short silence. 'I'll leave the stove on. There's stew and potatoes. I'm going to bed mind.'

'That's ok, I'll . . .' He wanted to say 'I'll be home as quick as I can' but he didn't dare.

'I'll see you in the morning,' she said. The line went dead.

Primrose made it to Covent Garden just in time to see the hot potato seller emptying a pile of cold ash into the market rubbish heap. He looked to see if the toffee apple stalls were still out, or if anyone was selling whelks but the market was deserted, the food smells muted. On the other side of the square, a man in a filthy apron was hawking brown paper bags of sliced pigs' ears from a greasy basket. Deciding he had no choice Primrose grudgingly parted with a ha'penny.

They were brined to bursting, then fried to a crisp so that little remained of them but scraps of salty leather. He took a couple of mouthfuls before depositing the rest into the hands of a beggar on the Strand. The wind was blowing up foul gusts from the Thames as he approached New Scotland Yard's building on the Embankment. He had hoped the walk might have woken him up a little but as he hopped up the steps and tried to focus on the clock in the deserted lobby of the building he could feel his eyes fuzz with fatigue. It was past midnight but there were a few lights on in the downstairs offices and he could hear the Remington typewriters slamming away under weary fingers. Someone had recently boiled coffee. It lingered in the cold lobby air.

He had heaved himself up half a staircase towards his office when he heard his name called by one of the clerks downstairs. He didn't know the boy, so he hesitated. The boy called again.

'Yes?'

'You are Primrose, aren't you? Sorry, Inspector Primrose?'

'Yes.'

'Primrose from Special Branch?'

Primrose pinched the upper bridge of his nose where the headache hurt most. 'How many Primroses are there in Central Office?'

The boy, who could only have been twenty or so, looked put out. 'Telephone call from Bow Street. They said you would be on duty, and they need someone from Special.'

Primrose stifled the simmering of rage that came from hearing that phrase 'on duty', the image of Stuttlegate kissing his children goodnight hovering close to his mind.

'What's happened?'

The boy consulted a yellow notebook in his hand covered

in messy ink. 'There's been a girl murdered up Tottenham Court Road. Sorry, Inspector, Bow Street said you would be on duty.'

Primrose felt briefly ashamed to think the boy had noted his sourness.

'Any other details?'

'They're saying her throat was cut.'

He couldn't stop a little groan coming out from between his lips but quelled it when he saw the boy's face. 'No chance this is a late Hallowe'en prank is there?'

The boy's face told him there was not.

A thought suddenly occurred to him. 'Why Special Branch?' He asked. 'Murders go to the divisional detectives.'

The boy shifted. 'No one's allowed to pass this on but . . .'

'Well, what is it then?' Primrose asked, scratching the bridge of his nose.

When the boy opened his mouth again Primrose almost wished he hadn't asked. 'Suffragette, sir. Victim was a suffragette. She's not been identified formally yet, but the local landlord will swear on his life the girl's name is Ebony Diamond.'

Nine

Frankie slept restlessly through the night. The window pane in her bedroom had a crack near the bottom that sent cold gusts wheezing in every now and then. There had been no coal in the scuttle when she arrived home and the measly fire Mrs Gibbons had lit was barely more than embers. With the blankets curled round her body she tossed and turned, half-dreaming about Ebony Diamond, snakes and coal boxes.

When she awoke, light was cutting a shard across the dusty floor, illuminating her desk with its scattered papers, the Blickensderfer typewriter part-hidden under newspapers and notebooks. The room was otherwise empty apart from a washstand, a rusty mirror, a stiff-backed chair covered with shirts, trousers and braces from the day before, a pile of books on a small shelf, and a tin of Colman's mustard – invaluable ammunition for her landlady Mrs Gibbons's cooking.

As she prised her head up from under the covers, a little wash of gin crept up her throat. She reached down for the jug of water she kept on the floor by the bed but it was empty.

While she fumbled for a glass there was a knock at the door. Before she could cry, 'Who is it?' it swung open and Mrs Gibbons appeared, a bucket of lightly steaming water braced against her hip. She marched across the room and sloshed it into the washstand, slopping great drips onto the floor.

'My mother always said there were only two reasons for being in bed beyond eleven o'clock,' she said briskly. 'The one's childbirth.'

Frankie nodded, letting her eyes focus. Mrs Gibbons now stood with both hands on her hips, the pail dangling off her wrist. She was stiff as ever in a brown tweed skirt that skimmed the floor, and a starched but grimy white blouse. Frothy brown hair framed her crooked face.

'What's the other?' Frankie rubbed her eyes.

'Bone idleness.' She marched out of the room slamming the door.

'I was working last night . . .' Frankie trailed off as the footsteps echoed down the stairs. She could hear shuffling from along the corridor. If Piggot was up it must indeed be late. Mr Piggot was a sub-editor who worked afternoons and nights. She reached across the floor for her waistcoat and extracted her pocket-watch, but she had forgotten to wind it again and it said three o'clock. Feeling heavy in the belly at the thought of having to pick her Blickensderfer out from the messy desk and write up the Twinkle column, she heaved herself out of bed, washed quickly in the water, which was only just warmer than the air in the room, and put on the same clothes as yesterday. Her comb was nowhere to be seen so she smoothed her hair down with her fingers and made her way downstairs.

On the parlour table sat a rack of toast, slowly curling in on itself. Alongside it was a pot of Mrs Gibbons's famously tart marmalade that she boasted could both kill a rat and bring a dead man back to life. Frankie heaped a spoonful of it onto a piece of soggy toast and reached for the coffee pot. It was cold and empty. Mrs Gibbons bustled through, shunting open the door with her rump, and made a show of surprise at seeing Frankie up. 'Miss George, breakfasting before noon, what will the other citizens say?' She called all her lodgers 'citizens' as if she was the despot of some boarding-house empire.

Piggot prised open the door and snorted as he heaved himself into a chair at the head of the table. Frankie ignored them both and concentrated on not wincing as the marmalade went down. She watched Mrs Gibbons place coffee and a boiled egg in front of Mr Piggot then stand staring for a few seconds with her hands clamped to her hips. Frankie became gradually aware that she was spoiling for a fight and wasn't about to move until she had one.

'I'll thank you to eat like a lady under my roof and use a plate so you don't spill crumbs on the tablecloth.' She swiped a claw at the oilskin cloth. A spray of crumbs hit Frankie's lap.

Frankie swallowed the mouthful of toast and imagined it curdling in her stomach with the gin. 'Is something the matter?'

Mrs Gibbons stopped assaulting the tablecloth and stared at Frankie. Her cheeks were puffed with an angry shine; she had fury in her brown eyes. Piggot, Frankie noticed, was concentrating harder than ever on his egg. She took a pile of newspapers from the side table and slapped them down on the oilskin. 'That's what's the matter. Fenwick's.'

Frankie looked puzzled for a second, then bent over the wrinkled copy of the *Daily Mail*. 'Suffragettes Smash Bond Street.' Piggot sneakily reached across, extracted a copy of *The Times* from under the pile and spread it out across half the table.

Mrs Gibbons went on, 'They're the only ones do the lavender pillows I like. I used my last one last night. Now there's no chance of sleep until those bloody insufferables are dealt with.'

A smirk tickled the corners of Frankie's mouth but she bit it back and reached instead for the fresh coffee pot.

'Well,' she said slowly pouring a cup, 'it is important. I for one am grateful to the women of the WSPU. I couldn't survive Holloway. I'm glad someone can.' She stretched a lazy arm behind her head.

Mrs Gibbons narrowed her eyes. 'You've changed your tune.'

'Beg your pardon? I don't know what you mean.'

'Thought Miss George was too busy and important to

trouble herself with suffragettes. She don't need to. She got a job with the menfolk.'

Mr Piggot looked up. 'Yes, there was something I recall, wasn't it a cartoon?'

'Oh, don't go bringing that up now.' Frankie put down her toast and wiped her fingers on a fresh napkin.

'I recall when you first came here,' Mrs Gibbons said, 'wasn't there an incident with one of them?'

Frankie concentrated on the newspaper. 'Says there were over two hundred arrested.'

'That's right,' Mrs Gibbons went on, as her pointy fingers began folding the napkins. 'Didn't you want to write for that paper they sell about votes but they said your English weren't good enough?'

'It wasn't anything like that,' Frankie snapped. 'Why would I write for them for nothing when I can earn a perfectly good living on Fleet Street? Oh, of course I'd love to afford to support the cause but some of us have rent to pay.'

'Speaking of rent, it was due yesterday.'

'I get my cheque on Saturdays, you know that.'

'Just as long as it comes in. More than a week late and I'll have to charge interest. Got a living to make myself.'

Suddenly Frankie sat up straight. She looked back down at the newspaper. 'Over two hundred suffragettes arrested.' Frantically she read down the thin columns until she found it. 'Due to be sentenced at Bow Street Court.' She checked the carriage clock on the mantelpiece. It was quarter to twelve. A suffragette window smash? Ebony had to have been on that.

She would be in court today for certain. Perhaps that was why she was so agitated yesterday at the corset shop.

'Have to dash, Mrs Gibbons, breakfast was a treat, thank you.'

Mrs Gibbons looked like she had been slapped with a fish. She watched speechless as Frankie sank her coffee and ran out of the door leaving it open behind her. 'Cheek,' she spat.

'Sorry,' Frankie called over her shoulder, 'but I'm a working woman.'

The Black Marias were pulling up thick and fast. Van after van drew to a halt outside Bow Street Police Court where a thin line of constables in dark wool tunics struggled to contain the crowd. The horses leading the vehicles were growing restless, hoofing the ground, tossing their heads. Someone threw a stone at one of the vans, scoring a dent into the metal. If there was a cry that came from inside, no one heard it above the din of the protests.

Frankie didn't have a press card but used her elbows to barge her way to the front of the public gallery queue. On her way she passed placard holders, jeering women and the shopkeepers who had divided themselves into those allied to the cause and those against it. Some of the placards said, 'Send 'em to second division,' while others declared, 'Let the Government pay for my broken windows.'

Inside, bodies were squeezed into every inch of the court's dark wood galleries: women in hats, families and children in their Sunday best, newspapermen with yellow notebooks on their laps, lady journalists in slender skirts. The air was close and stifling with a stew of fragrances. From beyond the dock a rattling of metal from the cell passage filtered through.

Frankie wedged into a seat between a woman with a pair of seagulls taxidermied to her hat, and a father with two children. The younger, a little boy in a brown suit, was staring through the wooden bars at the magistrate.

Frankie followed the little boy's gaze to a plump man wearing pince-nez and a wig that had yellowed at the fringes with tobacco stains. She had seen him on the bench before, but he looked dog-tired today. On the way in, two laywers had been discussing a rumour that he had a police escort now – constables on bicycles following him to and from court – owing to the number of threats he had received from the WSPU.

She looked round the court for Ebony but couldn't see her. Women were being brought up in groups of ten, squashed into the dock looking like they had spent a rough night in the cells; young women, old women, women in torn silk and dirty-looking fine-cut clothes, women in jute and linen and ill-fitting jackets. They were all in high spirits, laughing and linking arms as if they hadn't a care for what was coming to them. As Frankie watched she felt a growing sense of bewilderment and a strange envy.

Mrs Gibbons had tweaked a nerve. It was true a sharp-tongued woman at the WSPU had told her a few years ago that if she wanted to write for *Votes for Women* she would need to find something to say. But it wasn't the reason she hadn't joined the suffragettes. It was the righteousness that unsettled her, the knowing look they had in their eyes. It made her uncomfortable and she didn't quite know why. They knew what they wanted and they knew they were right.

The first two groups were sentenced to two weeks each in second division, after being offered a fine to pay and refusing. As the magistrate's gavel slammed down someone in the gallery cried, 'Well done, duckies, you'll get your Holloway degrees!'

When the third group was led in, the little boy beside Frankie leapt out of his seat and plunged his arms through the gallery bars. His father and sister quickly moved to grab him, prising his fists from where they were clutched round the wood.

'It's all right. Mamma's going on holiday again. Mamma's very brave and so must you be. Brave boy. Home by Christmas.' The father rocked the boy back and forth.

The yellow-wigged magistrate looked put out to have been interrupted, then turned to his clerk who read out the charges. 'Breaching both Section 12 and Section 51 of the Malicious Damage to Property Act 1861, by smashing glass windows on Old Bond Street. In doing so you did create tumultuous assembly. Three among you, Mary Clune, Florence Jackson and Edith Craggs, did also breach an order, allowing you release from prison for recuperation from hunger-striking, on the condition you engage in no further acts of vandalism.'

'I never signed no order saying I'd not keep protesting,' a large woman in a crumpled tweed jacket called out.

The magistrate removed his pince-nez. 'Your sentences will of course be commuted if you are willing to pledge not to engage in further acts of vandalism, you do all realise that?'

He was met with cries of 'Shame!' and 'No surrender!'

'It is an insolence of your worship,' the mother of the little boy spoke up, 'to expect us to put up with torture in that prison, and then to be asked to behave ourselves when we're set free. All we want to do is to be treated as equal citizens. Instead we are treated like animals. Your worship.' Two Holloway wardresses on the edge of the dock exchanged a glance.

'Over one hundred doctors,' she continued, 'have signed a petition against force-feeding. I dare this magistrate to swallow vomit, take a slap across the face and not feel bitterness with the whole country . . .'

'Quiet!' the magistrate slapped his gavel down.

'That's it, duckie, go on, have your say,' a woman leaned over the gallery rails close to Frankie. Frankie looked at her hands. They were gripping the bar, shaking.

Then a voice cut through, deep and male. 'Let the lady have her say. She has a degree in law. Allow her to use it.'

An uneasy silence spread through the court. Some of the police on the benches turned round to look for the source. Frankie frowned and scanned the gallery before realising with a start that the man who had spoken was in the middle of the group in the dock. He was squashed between two women, both of whom looked old enough to be his mother. His thick straw-coloured hair was ruffled like a bird's nest. He looked less than thirty and had a clean handsome face, a sharp nose and large blue eyes with tired purple rings spreading round them.

The magistrate squinted at him. 'Who are you?'

'William Reynolds,' the man said loudly. 'Suffragette.'

There was a snigger, then a timid round of applause, as if the gentleman had just played a fine hit in a tennis match. Some of the policemen coughed uncomfortably.

'What on earth are you doing in the dock?' the magistrate asked.

The gallery responded, hooting and hissing.

The man straightened his black wool jacket and stood up to his full short height. He had a confident note in his voice with a hint of an accent Frankie couldn't quite place. North perhaps, or Bristol. There was a roguish look in his eye; he was enjoying himself. 'If it weren't for women you wouldn't have a home to go to at the end of a day's work. None of us would. In fact, you'd probably be sitting there naked as the day you were born. I'm willing to wager a woman wove the cotton for your gown. Your worship.'

'I'll have you held in contempt of court.'

'Just let the lady finish.'

Frankie craned forward. Chattering from the galleries and scratching from the press pencils had stopped.

The magistrate cleared his throat and scanned his notes. 'You've been arrested before, haven't you? Attacking a

Cabinet Minister with a horse whip.' He replaced his pince-nez to get a better look at the man, as if his face would reveal his character or provide an explanation for why on earth he had chosen to fight for such a cause.

'That's right, sir. And I'd do it again.'

'You're a member of the Men's League for Women's Rights or something?'

Someone cut in from the gallery, 'The only woman's right is a man's left.' Some of the policemen sniggered.

The magistrate chewed his tongue. Then he said three words: 'Pentonville. Six weeks.'

There was a woman's gasp from further back in the gallery.

William Reynolds raised his hand and bowed his head gently. 'I would expect no less.'

As he was bundled away with the rest of his group down to the cells, the clerk announced 'Mrs Rosemary Muskett,' and the wardresses led in a woman in brown sackcloth printed with black arrows, the Holloway Gaol uniform. A pile of thick grey hair was heaped on her head like straw, which she scratched with thin fingers every now and then.

'Ah, we've seen you before,' said the magistrate.

'That's right, sir, I've been here six times and I'm ready to come another sixty. What is the point of a country like ours if—'

'You'll get to make your point. Swear the arresting officer in.'

Constable Tipple 675A was brought to the witness box and testified that he had arrested the woman on Oxford Street after she had broken three windows with a hammer concealed in a black stocking. According to the young man she had hit him and left him with a bruise. Finally the magistrate turned to Mrs Muskett. 'Your turn now, my dear. Have you anything to say?'

She stiffened, swallowed a couple of times, looked as proud as she could in her sack cloth and made sure the room was silent. 'I stand here before you as a mother of four children, two boys, two girls, who will be raised as equals. Our tax-paying women are working in worse conditions than the miners. You only have one point of view and that's the man's, but this country is made up of men and women. We have been driven to this, and we'll be driven further, mark my words. That's all I have to say on the matter.'

The magistrate leaned forward on the bar, his eyes tiny under huge hoods of skin. 'Are you threatening me, Mrs Muskett? Driven further? There is no question of doubt that you recognise the law, you recognise you are doing wilful damage and each of you tells me you intend to go on with it. But you have brought London into a state which cannot continue. A seventh offence, Mrs Muskett? I have no choice but to sentence you to two months' hard labour in third division.'

She wasn't quick enough to stifle the cry that escaped. Second division was one thing, but hard labour in third? Third meant straw mattresses with things living in them, cold, damp, pickpockets, madwomen. Composing herself, she drew three or four breaths and looked up to the galleries.

She was met with a stunned silence. She dropped her head

again and stared at her hands, gripping the cold square metal bar of the dock.

'Take her away,' the magistrate nodded to the two wardresses. As they moved forward, Mrs Muskett's fingers curled faster round the bar. One wardress looked at the other. Lawyers on the counsel benches stopped perusing their papers and looked up. One of the wardresses ran her hand gently down Mrs Muskett's arm.

Then the storm broke.

Cries of 'Shame!' pelted from the galleries. Fists banged wooden posts; feet thundered the floor. Someone threw an egg at the bar and the magistrate ducked. It smashed against the wall sending a backsplash of yolk into the face of his clerk. The next missile was a boot with a spiked heel. Frankie flinched as it went flying over her head into the press gallery.

Mrs Muskett was trying to beat off the wardresses who were aiming rubber clubs at her face, while the prosecution counsel joined in, wrestling her arms under control. Screams and cries of 'Votes for women!' mingled with the racket.

The magistrate slammed his gavel on the bar, shouting at the constables 'Clear the court, clear the court!' There was a rush from the back of the gallery as families tried to whisk their children to safety above the clamour of police hands fighting to grab suffragette arms.

Eventually the scrapping died down into a hazy aftershock of panting and grunting. The magistrate stared them all down with the yellow-whites of his eyes, then said coolly, 'Clear the court.'

Frankie sighed as she heaved herself to her feet. She gave another sweep of the room with her eyes, but there was no sign of Ebony Diamond, and if she was in custody, there was no saying now when she would be sentenced. The hearings could spread over until late afternoon or even the next day.

At the door, she passed the magistrate's clerk who was wiping egg from his face with a handkerchief. His eyes looked crestfallen. He was busy saying to the duty constable, 'I don't know why they threw the egg at me. I love ladies, everyone knows I love the ladies. Fat ones, thin ones, posh ones, common ones. All of them.'

Back in the yard outside, Frankie withdrew a cigarette from her jacket pocket and felt around for her box of matches. Sighing, she remembered she had left them on her desk at home. She looked around for a likely candidate to scrounge from. Standing over by a Black Maria, a well-dressed woman in a neat crimson tailor-made was sucking nervously on a long thin white cigarette, fiddling with her hair in between draws.

Frankie trotted up to her. 'Don't suppose you have a match?' The woman looked up suddenly. 'Sorry, I didn't mean to startle you.'

She breathed out. 'No, it's just I expected you were going to come and tell me to put it out. Women smoking in public. I don't normally you see, but . . .' She reached into a lean clutch bag and pulled out a small box of Vestas.

'Much obliged.' Frankie took one and struck it off the stone wall of the building.

The woman replaced them with a shaky hand.

'We lady smokers stick together, don't we?' Frankie let the cigarette hang from the corner of her mouth, enjoying the taste of the paper. 'I mean, watching that in there, why shouldn't we enjoy a little smoke or a glass of brandy? Only time you ever get given brandy as a woman is if you're a toff or you're sick.'

The woman gave a slight laugh. 'To be honest, I wouldn't mind a brandy myself. My husband has just been sent to prison.' She laughed nervously again and Frankie realised she was the woman who had gasped when the magistrate said 'Pentonville'.

'That was him was it? Handsome fellow.'

'It should be me really,' she said quickly. 'Silly, I know. But I'm not quite brave enough.' She shrugged. 'Don't know what possessed him; my family would be quite embarrassed if they saw him up there. Still, they won't know, will they? I'll tell them we're off to Bath or something.' She gave a fragile smile. 'My husband loves women, you see. In the most incredible way.' There was more to her than nerves. There was a wateriness in her dark eyes and a bitterness in her voice. Frankie watched her carefully for a few seconds. Then she remembered why she was there in the first place.

'I'm actually looking for someone in particular.'

'Oh yes?' The woman looked at her.

'Yes. She's a sort of stunt woman.'

The lady turned her face away and went back to sucking on her cigarette. 'That wouldn't be Ebony Diamond would it?'

'That's right. Know her, do you?'

She rolled her eyes. 'Who doesn't? She was the talk of the suffragettes once upon a time. So I hear.' She looked at Frankie and there it was again, that distance in her eyes. 'He actually bought us tickets to see her at the Coliseum tonight.' She nodded towards the court. 'That's why she's not in there. Not stupid enough to go getting herself arrested.'

Frankie remembered with a weary feeling and a jab of self-reproach that the Coliseum was the very reason Stark had wanted her to portrait Miss Diamond in the first place.

The woman smiled a scornful smile. Frankie was starting to dislike her. She wasn't worried about her husband, she was bitter about him. 'It's hot ticket of the night.' She blew out her smoke. 'I think it's the Coliseum, or maybe the Palace Theatre.' The lady looked up but Frankie was nowhere to be seen.

Something had struck Frankie's memory from the day before. 'If it doesn't fit,' Smythe had said, 'by the time she comes to pick it up . . .' If she really had missed the smash because of her Coliseum performance, there was one place she would have to be.

Ten

Frankie was ten feet away from Smythe's corset shop when she spotted Teddy Hawkins idling outside the Maid in the Moon, and couldn't stop her nose from crinkling in distaste. He was smoking a cigarette with a look of intense concentration on his face. She followed his gaze across the road to see, to her fright, Ebony Diamond stretched backwards on the lap of a police constable, her lips a ghastly shade of blue, her chest heaving like a fish pulled from the water. Her head was thrown back, her eyes were rolling. A shocking shade of teacup-white had spread over her face.

Over near a black police car, a small crowd of policemen and journalists had gathered. Some of them were pointing at the corset shop door, talking in whispers. Deals were being struck. Money and favours were changing hands, secrets exchanged for exclusives. Frankie looked back at Ebony. She shifted position and Frankie saw, underneath her full underskirts, a newspaper flapping in the gentle breeze.

'Cut the laces, quick,' the man holding her was saying. His own cheeks were puce, his black boiled egg hat pushed back on his forehead.

'I don't have a knife,' a young officer standing above them said.

'Use a key, man, do you want a repeat of what happened in there?' The beetroot constable pointed at the door of the corset shop, then snapped his fingers at his young colleague. The young man's hands trembled as he reached underneath Ebony's waist.

'Use a match, damn it, just burn them loose.'

Frankie watched Teddy Hawkins step coolly forward, reach into his pocket and toss them a cigarette lighter. The red-faced constable struggled to light it in his clammy hand, then held it gingerly to the small of Ebony's back, waving the little flame back and forth. The laces crackled as they singed down to threads.

Suddenly Ebony came to, lashed out with the back of her hand and caught him on the nose. The cigarette lighter skidded into the street; the constable caught his bruised face in his hand. 'Damned vanity,' he hissed. 'You see how dangerous those things are.'

Ebony looked around wildly.

'Teddy,' Frankie whispered.

Hawkins turned round, saw who it was, frowned and went back to writing in his notebook. She crept closer. 'Mr Hawkins,' she said a little louder.

He looked up and made a point of focusing as if he had just

noticed her. 'Ah, Georgie.' His lips bulged, giving him a cruel look. He touched the brim of his hat and continued scribbling.

'It's Frankie,' she sighed. 'What's happening?' She pointed at Ebony.

'Surprised to see you up and about. All those late-night social gatherings, portraiting openings of envelopes and such haven't taken their toll.'

'I don't know what you're talking about. What's the matter with her?'

He snapped shut his notebook. 'There's been a nasty accident.'

Frankie pointed at the shop. 'In there?'

He nodded. 'Um-hum.'

'Well, can you tell me any more? Who was it? Him that wears the corsets?'

Teddy Hawkins turned to her, taking in her face very carefully. His eyes were dark-rimmed like a beagle's and he wore a doggish expression that made him look both simple and dangerous. 'Look, Miss George, it's really not the kind of thing a woman would be interested in. I assume you've been sent to cover the suffragette damage. That's further down, beyond Fenwick's.' He nodded his head towards the end of the street.

'Why do you lot all think I . . .' she began to growl. 'I mean, what are you doing? Are you on a news piece?'

'Georgie, I don't have time for this.' He began tucking his pencil back into his pocket.

'Oh, I know, you don't have time for this. You're on every blooming story in London.'

He shoved his notebook in his breast pocket. 'As a matter of fact, I do have somewhere else to be.'

Frankie could feel dignity slipping from her as the jealousy rose. She tried to push it back down. 'Where?'

Teddy's lips twitched into a furtive smile. 'You'll see in the five o'clock special. Copy deadline's in an hour so I'd better . . .' He made to move.

'Well, why don't you let me cover this one? Take the pressure off.'

'Really, Miss George?' his soft lips splurged at her.

'But that's two stories. Go on, Teddy, let me cover this one.' She was about to protest that she already had quotes from Ebony Diamond that might help with a news piece, when Hawkins moved her gently out of his way by the shoulders.

'That's not the way the world works and that's not what Mr Stark wants, is it? You do the bits and bobs for the Ladies' pages, I do the hard news for the front pages. Mr Stark wants a hard news piece, doesn't he? You should think yourself lucky those suffragettes are giving you something to write about besides bran baths and parlourmaid-taming. Now, excuse me.' He tipped his hat and made to move off.

'Well, you could at least tell me what the story is; it's not as if I'm going to swipe it.' She glanced over to where Ebony was bent double over the pavement, looking as if she might be sick onto the policeman's shoes. Someone had, perhaps ill advisedly, passed her a brandy bottle.

Teddy Hawkins must have felt a little penitent at his smugness for he stopped and turned. 'It's nothing terribly exciting. Just a showgirl murdered off Tottenham Court Road. It'll most likely turn out to be an ex-lover or a landlord and the whole thing will have dropped by tomorrow. As for him, it's page seven stuff. Titbits.' He smiled unconvincingly, 'I'm sure the suffragette damage will get far more inches.'

Frankie tossed her head. 'Who was the showgirl? Anyone famous?'

He checked his notebook. 'Says here the *Pall Mall Gazette* named her as Ebony Diamond. Isn't that the one you were portraiting? Oh well, I suppose he'll want that dropped now. Mind, if you have any quotes you could leave them at the news desk.' He paused. 'Wasn't she the suffragette threw herself at Asquith in March?'

'April,' Frankie corrected him instinctively, for a split-second feeling it on the tip of her tongue to tell him that Ebony Diamond couldn't be murdered because she was over there, dribbling sick onto a police constable's navy blue trousers. She turned briefly to stare at the woman on the pavement, to check that it was Ebony. There was absolutely no doubt – the black eyes, the lips; even her scent was pervading the air. Then Frankie remembered the other girl who had stood in the shop, with the glossy black hair and the linen dress. A thought crossed her mind. Vindictively she decided to say nothing. Let him get the wrong name, serve him right.

Hawkins's face had resumed its pitying pout. 'I'll see you

in the Cheese, shall I? Thursday night?' He wrinkled his lips into a grin.

'Yeah, Thursday.' She wanted to slap him but the satisfaction of hoping he might file a goose of a story temporarily quelled the urge.

His lean bouncing form made earnestly for the tube station and Frankie turned back to Ebony. The policeman had sat her up and confiscated the brandy. It was only when she looked up that Frankie saw her ravaged face, her drained cheeks streaked with tears. Ebony raised a gloveless pale hand and pressed her finger and thumb into her eyes as if she might staunch her crying.

Frankie took a couple of breaths and walked over. 'Miss Diamond.'

The policemen with her exchanged a glance. 'Do you know this woman?'

Ebony shook her head.

Frankie dropped to her haunches feeling the fabric of her trousers strain uncomfortably. She tried to look beyond Ebony through the glass of the shop window but two police officers, one in uniform, one plain-clothed, were chatting closely, blocking the view. 'What happened in there? Is Mr Smythe all right?'

The question set Ebony shaking and Frankie rose to her feet with an involuntary groan for her calf muscles. She took a few steps towards the shop.

'Oi, hold it there,' the policeman beside Ebony cried. 'Where do you think you're going?'

'Press,' Frankie muttered at him and kept walking.

'No, hang on, you need to show a card.'

She cursed herself for forgetting her card. Although thinking carefully about it she wasn't sure she had ever had one for the *Evening Gazette* to begin with, and her *Tottenham Evening News* one rarely held much currency. She walked on.

'Hold it, miss, mister, whatever you are.'

Frankie felt the blood rising in her as she nudged past the two officers with their backs to her. What she saw stopped her dead.

Smythe, the man she had spoken to yesterday in the shop, was spread out across the floor. Across his legs a rack of peach corsets had spilled to the ground framing him with frilly patterns. His shoulders were bare, and bloomed a rich livid. Deep indigo ringed his eyes, mouth and the crest of his Adam's apple. He looked peaceful and unreal, painted in crude colours like a drawing by a child. Frankie's eyes moved down his body to his chest and she stifled a dry gag. He was wearing a black corset, shiny, with a trim of magpie feathers in black and white, laced grotesquely tight, so that the little fat he had was pushed out over the top along with the skin-covered lump of one of his skewed rib bones. His flesh had swelled outside the corset, making him look even more freakishly minuscule at the waist.

She felt a hand on the small of her back and jumped. 'I think I should be moving you along.'

Instinctively, she slapped out, but in doing so lost her balance and toppled precariously close to the corpse. The smell hit her and made her retch as she steadied herself. The policeman didn't have to ask her to leave again. She pegged it out of the shop, gulping fresh air.

Ebony was still on the pavement.

Frankie stared at her until she had her gaze. 'Mr Smythe . . .' she began, but couldn't bring herself to say it. Ebony looked white as a fish belly, her eyes bloodshot. What she said next made Frankie's flesh go cold.

'I must be a cat. I must have nine lives.'

'What do you mean?'

Ebony shook her head at the ground.

'What do you mean? Do you know what happened to Mr Smythe?'

'Ollie . . .' She looked towards the door of the corset shop, then with a sudden movement clutched Frankie's wrist like she would crush it. 'Will you meet me somewhere? I could tell you things. I want folk to know I'm on the right side.'

'Right side of what?' Her eyes were wild, the whites showing. Frankie tried to extricate her hand gently, but Ebony kept hold of it. She picked up the newspaper flapping underneath her and pressed its crumpled grey pages between Frankie's fingers. Frankie saw it was the *Pall Mall Gazette*.

'Third page. Look at it.'

'What? Of course I'll meet you. I could take you somewhere now.' Frankie looked round at the Maid in the Moon where the landlord, Tommy Dawber, was keeping a crafty eye on the police and journalists through the window. He gave her a quick salute. She was about to turn back to Ebony and suggest they go in there, but Ebony sprang to her feet and began fleeing down the street, stumbling as she ran.

'Miss Diamond, where are you going? Wait . . .'

'Outside the Coliseum,' Ebony called out behind her. 'Afterwards. Meet me there.'

'After what? Your show? Miss Diamond, wait!' Frankie gave chase for a few more steps but Ebony was in the back-streets quick as a fox and no more than a dart of black in the shadows. Frankie bent down to catch her breath. She was still grasping the newspaper, the loose pages threatening to flutter out of her hand and all over the street. The headline was about a Lord who had committed suicide over increased death duties. Carefully she turned the crumpled pages one by one. On page three she spotted a small headline: 'Is Jack back?'

Her eyes took less than a second to fall on the illustration of the victim and she felt her gnawing unease turn into shock. Nine lives or no, looking at the clothing the girl had been wearing she was beginning to get a very good idea of why Ebony Diamond was so terrified.

Later that day Frankie sat at her desk in Percy Circus. She had slipped in without Mrs Gibbons noticing and filched a couple of rock cakes from the afternoon tea tray. They lay on the desk beside a pile of crumbs covering her notebook. She was trying to put off eating them for as long as possible so that they could serve as her supper.

The Blickensderfer stared up at her. Twelve pounds it had

cost, on a weekly plan, and she still wasn't finished paying it off. But these were risks a newspaper girl had to take. Her pocket-watch said half past two. Forty-five minutes until copy deadline, two hours until the afternoon edition would be on the streets.

She let her hands spread across the keyboard feeling the lovely smooth circles of the keys press against each fingertip. She loved the noise of typing, the smell of the ink. She had three options; write up the column and drop the portrait, as Teddy Hawkins had suggested; fudge a quick portrait and dash off the column; or the third option. Without thinking about it, she began to press out the usual heading, 'Conversations from the Boudoir.' Then she tore the sheet of paper from the machine, tossed it into the fireplace and loaded a fresh one. This time she typed, 'Conversations from the Suffragette's Lair: Is Ebony Diamond's life in danger?'

Eleven

Outside the London Coliseum a thin drizzle of rain was misting to the ground in silver sheets. Frankie had no umbrella and the brim of her bowler hat wasn't wide enough to keep the drips off her cigarette. She flicked the soggy stub onto the ground where it was quickly scavenged by a tramp in a wool coat. She hadn't seen the paper yet. She had bought a copy from a paperboy on Gray's Inn Road then promptly thrown it into a bonfire on Clerkenwell Green without even opening it. She didn't want to know what had been done with her copy. She had done it now. That was all there was to it. She would catch Ebony Diamond at the stage door afterwards and pin her down until she told Frankie everything there was to know about that cursed corset shop and the people who worked in it. If all went well Mr Stark would want a follow-up piece.

On top of the theatre, Frank Matcham's giant revolving globe beaconed in the theatregoers who drew up in whining tramcars and four-wheelers. The pavements were full of women dripping furs off their shoulders, casting shadows a yard wide with their huge hats, and men in dress jackets anywhere between tailcoats and scrubby tweed patched at the elbows. Pulled together from all corners of London, they moved like a colourful soup, tinkling with laughter through the lobby. Over on one corner of the street with a skivvy holding an umbrella over her head, Lady Thorne was enthusiastically handing out pamphlets with pictures of the devil on them.

Frankie tipped her head one way, then the next, to drip off the rainwater that had pooled in her hat brim, then slid into the crowd making for the entrance.

It was like walking into the gilded stomach of a goddess. The lobby, with velvet and chandeliers, palms, frenzies of stucco sprawled across the ceiling, swallowed everyone who entered her. There were confectionery stalls for sweets and a row of box office kiosks worked by men in bell-hop uniforms, gold thread on red cotton and hats to match. Staircases rose into Fullers Tea Rooms on the vestibules above, concierges ran amok with messages from the newly installed telegram service, set up so patrons could never be out of touch, even while at the theatre. Oswald Stoll had spared no expense when it was built; other theatres may have had more scandal or class, but the Coliseum topped them all for sheer size. Frankie made for the ticket booth with the smallest queue but was intercepted by a man in a broad collared suit, too big for him at the shoulders. 'Miss George?'

She puzzled at his recognition of her and looked at his face to see if she knew him. His skin was the colour of an unbaked pie, with little boy's features. His figure, Frankie thought, was rather unfortunate for someone who couldn't afford proper tailoring, narrow at the shoulders, broad at the hips. She racked her brains but couldn't place him.

He smiled, child-like, and asked again. 'Miss George, *Evening Gazette*?'

His hand prodded towards her. 'James Parsons. I'm Mr Stoll's clerk. Mr Stoll apologises that he couldn't meet you in person but . . .' It seemed he couldn't think of a good enough excuse for the proprietor's absence, so let the sentence hang. Frankie met his soft handshake during which he passed her, not very slickly, a ticket, moist from his palm.

'I saw your name on the box office list. We've arranged for you to have a guided tour before the show. How is Miss Twinkle anyway?'

Frankie shuddered to think that people actually read her column. She forced herself to smile. 'Very well, thank you. Testing the latest technology in thermal . . .' she trailed off.

'Well, I look forward to reading what she has to say tonight, after the show. I have a copy in my office. My weekly treat.' Frankie felt her stomach drop, then snuck a glance down at her ticket and noticed it was in the third row of the gods. Can't have been that impressed, little liar, she thought.

He flourished his hand into a display of chivalry and guided her by the small of her back away from the crowds and into the hub of the foyer. 'Drink, glass of champagne as we tour?'

'No thank you. Don't drink and write,' she lied, and reluctantly followed him into the throng.

To her annoyance Frankie was not offered another drink and, finishing Mr Parsons' tour, found herself with nothing but a heavy brain and a sticky patch on her back where his hand had rested for much of the tour. Resentful at the sight of people sipping port in the tea rooms she went directly up to her seat. The growing crowd on the top floor was hot as a farmyard market, scents of women's perfumes and men's cologne stifling the air. Fur and silk had given way to tweed and cotton. Frankie's chair was hard and wooden with no upholstery, and she could only see the top of the stage if she craned her neck to an uncomfortable angle. 'Weekly treat, my eye,' she murmured.

Down below, stiff bottoms were making their way onto velvet seats while violent discussions arose in the stalls about the size of ladies' hats. Those who had paid for their tickets wanted to see, and those who had paid for their hats wanted to be seen. Scanning her eyes round the hall she frowned. Two women in brown were leaning forward discussing something earnestly. Were those two faces she had seen before? She racked her brains for a few moments, then the memory popped up. They had been in the gallery at the suffragette sentencing. One of them had on the same taxidermied seagull hat.

The bang of the auditorium doors closing made her jump and as her eyes settled, she found her face had lit on a box below, not the closest to the stage but the next in. She had always had good long-distance eyesight so it didn't take her long to realise that the girl sitting in the box was the snake girl from the other night. Now however, she looked different. Her long blonde hair was pinned up, a faux hairpiece creating curls round her face. She wore a perfectly fitting turquoise gown with exquisite beadwork spidering her fine shoulders, and yet she seemed strangely uptight with discomfort. She glanced up and caught Frankie's eye. Startled, Frankie looked away, finding anywhere else to plant her gaze. When she tentatively looked back, the girl was staring at the stage.

Frankie didn't have time to think on it because once the lights dimmed, the rumbling of bodies hushed, and the curtain whipped up sharply.

The first half of the show rambled slowly. There was Xandra Beagle, a muscular woman who belted out Wagner from a plasterboard crescent moon; the Boston twins who played ragtime and danced a two-step; a bizarre German imitation of the Ballets Russes in silk harem pants and dirndls, and a pack of bulldogs dressed as can-can girls who slobbered violently making treacherous piles of slime on the stage. In between each act the Chairman emerged with his gavel, hurling jokes into the audience like grenades – 'What's the difference between a motor taxi and a hansom cab? One's got acetylene lamps, the other a set o'lean horses!' Frankie had begun to grow anxious, not just about Ebony's act but for the day's article. She wished she hadn't thrown the paper away. She pictured it curling in the fire and wished she'd had the guts just to open it and see if they printed it. She wondered if she had time at the interval to go out and buy a copy, then remembered that she only had one shilling left in her pockets to last until tomorrow.

The Great Foucaud was up next. The Chairman's red bald pate nearly burst in excitement. The interval nigh, Frankie could smell wafts of sugary buns and eclairs through the auditorium doors.

The stage lights dimmed until the footlights were just a glowing hiss. Then came a sound she had heard backstage on Parsons' tour, an irate roar; a narked catty beast, hot under stage lights, pacing back and forth. Stripes became visible one by one until the whole back corner of the stage was lit and out of the gloom materialised the striding form of a tiger, its slow hulking gait rippling behind the bars of a shining cage. Any doubts there might have been about the authenticity of the Great Foucaud's impending trick evaporated. The crowd shifted quietly.

After letting the sight of the big cat soak in, a jungle drum began to murmur in the pit and a woman in white tripped across the stage, screaming politely. Minutes later, men in tiger loincloths followed, their bodies greased dark and streaky by some kind of varnish. The woman swayed this way, then that; the drums echoed her movements. Upstage, The Great Foucaud himself appeared in a mawkish burlesque of savagery, feathers and bones, leather and teeth, little plaster of Paris monkey skulls rattling from him. He snarled and joined the mob until they had the woman pinned on her back and were lifting her by her wrists and ankles towards the tiger's cage.

Frankie sat forward. They weren't going to . . .

They pressed her spine against the bars, one man on each limb, the Great Foucaud casting gigantic spells with his arms around her. A gentleman behind Frankie cleared his throat. The drums beat louder and faster. Foucaud's conjuring grew wilder. His men thumped their feet and bent their knees. The woman thrashed her head. The man behind Frankie coughed and she jerked her neck back at him until he stopped.

Foucaud paused, his hand on the cage. The tiger was crouched at one end, licking its fangs with a slippery pink tongue. Then, without flourish, Foucaud swiftly opened the cage and shoved the woman inside. He snapped the door shut. She pinned herself to the back bars. Something about her posture said that she wasn't entirely confident about Foucaud's magical powers. The lavish play-acting stopped. She took a couple of steps to the left. The tribal dance picked up and the men ran around the tiger cage, pressing their hands to their mouths and shrieking, waving their arms in the air.

Frankie leaned closer. The woman inched one way, then the other. The tiger swayed, following the pattern of her pacing. She clutched the bars behind her. It meandered forward, hunched and skulked, then pressed itself backwards as if it would spring. Suddenly, it took both front paws from the ground. Someone screamed prematurely. But instead of lunging, it raised its paws to its head as if something was bothering it about its face. Frankie watched intently as the tiger scratched away, eventually managing to tug its own head off, and standing there in the cage, dressed from head to toe in tiger skin was the Great Foucaud, who even now had seized the hand of the woman and was dragging her out of the cage, spreading his body, wide and cruciform into the centre of the stage for a huge showman's bow, his arms up, his head proud, the tiger mask tossed aside.

The stalls were on their feet applauding. The Great Foucaud luxuriated in the approval, bowing first to one side, then the other, then a special twist of the wrist and a flop double at the Royal Box. Frankie found to her irritation that her heart was racing wildly. She didn't like to be tricked.

She blew her breath up into her hair. Most children loved the thrill of deception; a coin disappearing behind an ear, a queen of spades turning into a jack. She had always wished she were quick enough to yank the hand free, see where it was concealing the coin, prise open the folded card. Once or twice she'd had a go, before being hauled out of the magic tent by her mother.

The interval was brief and the show began again, but Frankie found herself unable to concentrate on any of the acts. The two suffragettes in front of her seemed to be having the same problem, whispering so loudly to each other that a woman with a necklace of taxidermied mice round her throat to rival the seagull hat leaned forward and hissed at them.

And then she was announced. The last act. Ebony Diamond: The circus girl who had spent her childhood in a travelling wagon had made it to the London Coliseum. Peachy footlights slammed to black. A communal fidgeting rustled round the space, then halted as the scenery began to shift.

From the top of the proscenium arch a trickle of stars rained down, tiny firefly lanterns held on wires, drifting to the floor. They came to rest a foot short of it stretching from the footlights all the way to the back wall. And in this pitch Milky Way, lowered from the heavens of the theatre with a slow mechanical crank, down she came like a raven, every inch of her skin except her face sheathed in black stocking, silk or lace, her figure almost disappearing against the twilight. It was as if she knew, in this replica of the galaxy, inside the replica of the world itself, here was a place she could vanish safely and become just a reflection, a spectre of herself. She looked incredibly calm, the horror on her face that Frankie had seen earlier in the street all washed away. Frankie held her breath.

The orchestra played the opening of a melancholy waltz. After a few bars she recognised the tune. 'Once I was happy, but now I'm forlorn . . .'

Ebony Diamond began to swing gently, back and forth, catching the melody's three-beat circle at the peak of each swing. When the trapeze was in full motion, she twisted her legs to a stop several feet up the rope and held herself there, using gravity to fly for a split-second before she plunged, catching the bar upside down with the tops of her feet.

There was a gust of applause. The tune faded to the end of its first run, and Ebony hung among the stars.

A rush of strings, and it whipped itself up to a fiercer volume, repeating the chorus. Some people in the stalls had begun to sing along. 'She flies through the air with the greatest of ease . . .'

Ebony twisted and her hands caught the bar before she took off again, swinging and catching, swinging and catching, knees, ankles, then elbow joint, using the thick ropes to snake round her thighs that strained through their bloomers, then flipping again, catching the bar only with her fingers, hoisting herself up, spinning with the wood nestled in the crook of her pelvis, somersaulting, somersaulting among the stars, as the trapeze whipped faster back and forth. In the crowd, the voices fell silent. There was only the pitch of the maddening waltz. '. . . And my love she purloined away . . .'

Her body became a twirling ball, a shooting star, a Milky Way of its own. She was joined to the trapeze like another limb, a lover she could charm and entwine. She spun for minutes and minutes, and as the second run of the song came to an end, she dropped suddenly and hung from her neck, facing the crowd while the whole of the stalls stood to applaud.

The ovation lasted a full minute and she hung there, not moving a muscle.

Then came the third verse. This time more slowly, statelier, while she slipped her ankle round one of the ropes and swung upside down. The music continued and she pulled herself upright, waiting patiently as a leather hoop on a chain slid down the rope towards her. She clipped it to the middle of the bar. Frankie's stomach jumped. She had heard of acrobats holding on by their mouths before but never seen it.

'. . . The daring young lass on the flying trapeze. Her movements were graceful, all the world she could please . . .'

She began to swing again. The orchestra sped up the dizzy waltz. Her swing grew wilder. The strings of tiny lights flickered back and forth in the current, and soon were moving at different paces at different times, a black sky shimmering with diamonds.

Frankie could barely keep her heart from her throat as Ebony swung faster. The final round of the chorus was coming to an end; the audience could hear it in the violins, pelting out against the wall of trumpets and brass. 'Her movements were graceful, all the world she could please . . .' She leapt into the air like a jackdaw, spreading her arms. There was a giant wave of exclamation. And Ebony disappeared.

It looked at first in the silver gauze of the footlights as if she was falling fast. But if she was, she never made it as far as the ground. There was no thump, no body to see. The stage was nothing but an empty black sea, sprinkled with the firefly lamps. No smoke, no mirrors, no changes in the light. Just a swinging trapeze and a woman who was somersaulting one minute and gone the next.

There was a collective holding of breath, then a few people began to applaud. The idea began to cotton on that this was it, the end of a brilliant act. The leather strap had been a ruse, she had no intention of catching it. The applause grew until it was louder than the Great Foucaud's. People began jumping to their feet. The stalls turned into a garden of swaying colourful hats. The vigour of the clapping grew overwhelming. Young men put their fingers in their mouths and whistled.

Frankie's hands stayed on her lap. Looking down she saw that she was trembling slightly. She waited and waited for Ebony to appear. The stage stayed black, the lanterns still swinging with the current of the trapeze that was flinging itself back and forth as if a ghost rode it now. People began to clap in rhythm, demanding her, summoning her. The rhythm swelled, fell into a beat, one, two, three, four. Voices joined in, cheering for 'The Black Diamond'.

A movement at the back of the stage caught Frankie's eye. She breathed out in relief, for a second struck dumb by her own stupidity, realising she had been tricked again. But it didn't draw any closer. At least not at first. And gradually it sunk in, sickly and slowly, that it was not the movement of a woman striding out to take her bow. It was the inching of something prowling left to right along the backcloth of the stage, stripes catching the footlights every now and then. It didn't waste much time before it made towards the crowd, a thin, slinking predatory lope; a tiger heading straight for the centre aisle. And Frankie was glad for the first time that evening that she had been given a seat in the gods.

Twelve

The tiger stumbled as it snaked down the side steps into the stalls. Men and women jumped on their seats, grabbed umbrellas and canes. One man made a valiant attempt to clasp his wife to him before swooning back into a faint, toppling into the next row. A stampede began towards the back doors of the auditorium. Frankie knew for certain it was no trick when the ushers threw their trays of cigarettes and ices into the air and joined the crush.

The tiger was busy licking one of its heavy paws, idling on the front aisle that ran along the orchestra pit, blithely unaware of the chaos it had caused. It sniffed the footlights and turned its nose away then stared down the aisle at the screaming swarm. It pulled back its shoulders, stretched its front paws and bowed like a kitten, twisting its head, enjoying the strain on its muscles. A thought crossed Frankie's mind, and reaching for her notebook she began to move, not towards the fire escape, but down through the empty red corridor that led to the stalls.

She took the steps two at a time, but when she got to the grand circle her nerve faltered. It wouldn't be prudent to get too close. She squeezed back into the auditorium against the grain of a fur-perfumed crowd heading reluctantly for their own fire escape. 'Most drama we've had all week,' one lady laden down with gemstones lamented to her companion.

Frankie reached the lip of the gilded balcony just in time to see a curl of gold-black tail lingering in the left fire exit, beside the pit. Two stagehands in brown aprons were waggling sand buckets at the cat's rear, creeping closer, until one took courage enough to reach out and grab the fire door behind it, then slam it shut with a crash.

Some of the crowd turned tentatively to look. Word quickly spread and screams turned into sighs, shrieks to weeping. Men breathed out, and put back down their canes; some women took off their hats to look for signs of damage in the crush. The auditorium seemed to relax its huge belly.

Frankie exhaled slowly and was annoyed to find that she too was now shaking. People continued to make their way out but at a slower pace now, aware that the one place the tiger was not prowling was the auditorium. Frankie pushed back into the corridor and continued down to the stalls.

As she nudged her way in, she tried to scribble down snippets of conversation. For once Teddy Hawkins was nowhere to be seen, though she could be certain he would be dispatched to the Coliseum like a fusty old bloodhound the second the wires tapped into Stark's office. She touched a man on his elbow. 'Excuse me.' He turned, and after a second, frowned at her trousers. 'Sir, were you sitting close to the stage when the tiger came out?'

'What?'

'I'm from the *London Evening Gazette*. Did you see . . . ?'

Frankie tailed off as the man smirked, turning back to his wife.

She cursed him under her breath. A cane patted her shoulder. 'You the press, are you?' She twisted her head to see a short man with military medals pinned to his blazer. 'I did, I saw the tiger. Captain John Barnes. I saw it open its mouth, teeth big as a walrus. He was a hungry beast. I was in the second row.'

There was a tug on her sleeve. 'Miss Mildred Gibson. I saw it too. It came right at me. I had goosebumps all down my spine, thought I was a goner I did. Never seen anything like it.'

'Excuse me, mister,' a poke in her back, 'you write this down for your paper. That beast nearly had my wife. James Horlicks, Stroud Green Road. It looked right at us, I had to lift my cane to stop it leaping across the seats . . .'

Suddenly the throng was upon Frankie. Names were flung at her, wild claims thrust at her notebook. She peeled slender clammy fingers off her elbows and dodged the tap of heavy hands on her shoulders. Everyone had valiantly fended off the tiger, single-handedly, everyone had been in grave danger. It had licked its lips; it was furious; it was three times the size of a circus beast; they didn't know what Mr Stoll thought he

121

was doing letting it loose in a theatre; he was lucky no children had been eaten.

Frankie made a show of scribbling it down, then politely ducked under a cane at the moment it was raised to tap her shoulder, and picked her way into the auditorium. The front twenty rows were clear, the back still jammed with people trying to force their way free. Some folk had given up and were fanning themselves, complaining of dizziness.

That was when Frankie looked up and saw the tiger was back.

Without fuss or noise it paced a quick path onto the stage from the rear. The footlights were now at full blast and caught the blazing colours of its fur. But there was something different now about its appearance. It seemed agitated where before it had been languorous. The stage manager staggered on, brandishing a chair, the Great Foucaud behind him, half-dressed and sweating profusely, his braces bashing his knees. And then the big cat opened its mouth and let out a roar that sent ice into Frankie's blood.

Pandemonium re-erupted. The few who had sat back down leapt to their feet and the pushing began again. This time blows were thrown and people emerged from the crowd with red smarts and dark scratches on their faces and hands. Frankie stood frozen as the safety curtain began to crank down. 'Faster, man,' called one of the stagehands. 'It's as fast as it will go,' came the cry back from the wings.

The stage manager had the tiger cornered against the back wall but it was beginning to growl and pace. Foucaud was fiddling with a bottle of something in his hands. A slab of dripping meat flew at him from backstage and he caught it, splashing his shirt, then soused it in liquid from the bottle and threw it to the tiger. The tiger arched its neck and locked the meat in its teeth, smacking the sinews apart. Everyone watched and waited. It wavered, moved forward. The stage manager dodged back.

'Just wait,' snapped Foucaud.

The tiger's shoulders rocked and faltered. Frankie could have sworn she saw a glint of betrayal in its amber eyes as it looked first at the stage manager, then at its sweating owner, then collapsed in a bleary-eyed thump that made the ground shudder.

She took a step closer. The iron curtain was still cranking down, but there was a gap of a few feet, which, if she was quick, she could make it through. Fighting her instincts to run in the other direction, she dashed into the orchestra pit, scaled the bars and burnt her hand on a hot footlight as she hauled herself onto the stage. A few more seconds and the metal curtain slammed to rest on the wood.

Lit by the stage lights, technicians and stagehands had started to approach the sleeping tiger. 'Is it dead?' one of them asked.

'Dead?' said Foucaud. 'Do you know how much one of those costs?'

'Laudanum,' the stage manager said.

The stagehand backed off.

'Don't worry,' Foucaud said, 'he'll be out for a good hour

with that dose. But I'll need your men to help get him back in the cage.' The men all suddenly found fascination with their boots or bits of the stage curtains. Then one of them clocked Frankie.

'Hey, who are you?'

'Francesca George, *London Evening Gazette*.' She patted her pocket for a press card to flash and in the end settled for waving her notebook aloft.

'No, no, no,' the stage manager said. 'We run a respectable theatre here. We have it under control. I'm afraid you'll have to leave.'

He started towards her. Suddenly the tiger snorted and everyone jumped. All eyes watched it as silence settled again, muffled by the iron curtain. Finally, the Great Foucaud pulled himself to his senses and fetched a rope from the wings. With a weariness that suggested he had done it all before, he began binding the beast's twitching legs.

The stage manager looked up and down at Frankie. 'Out.'

'Hold on, hold on,' Frankie dodged his manhandling. 'I don't care about your bloody tiger. What I want to know is: hasn't anybody bothered to ask where Ebony Diamond is?'

She watched each of their faces carefully for traces of something. Reassurance, contempt, knowledge that it was a trick and she had been duped. Instead there came an uneasy shifting of eyes. A passage of alarm passed from the lighting technician in his brown coat, down to the stagehands holding a tarpaulin over the heaving belly of the cat, to the stage manager, who swallowed twice. 'She's bound to be somewhere.'

'Did you know about the end of her act?'

He made a show of scoffing. 'Damn gypsies never tell you anything. These circus folk are always trying to get one up on us. Think they can . . . you know . . .' He tipped his chin to one of the young stagehands, a Chinese boy in overalls too large for him with the sleeves and trousers rolled up. 'Check her dressing room. And clear off you.' He nodded at Frankie then turned round to supervise his men from a distance as they dragged the glossy body of the tiger onto the tarpaulin by its bound paws and tail. It was as sorry a sight as Frankie had seen, sedated, its shining teeth rendered useless by a stupefied brain. It somehow reminded her of Ebony the day before, vomiting and wailing on the pavement kerb.

Suddenly the ground shook under her feet as the tiger dozily struggled in its tarpaulin swaddle. Six men leapt in fright. 'Can we get it through the trapdoor?' one of them shouted.

'Too heavy. It'll break a bone if it falls from that height. Are you still here? I said bugger off.'

Frankie dodged as the convoy of men heaved past her, uttering blue curses at the weight of the cat.

'You sure we can't just toss it down?'

'I said no.' The Great Foucaud, who had a surprising Black Country flavour to his accent the more he spoke, began directing the men into the wings. 'If you lift, it'll be easier.'

'You're having a laugh, you lift it, sunshine.' Their voices trailed off and Frankie took the opportunity to slip into the shadows and have a nose about the stage. It was at least fifty foot across, shiny and black with white chalk markings ghosted here and there to identify where the different sets should be placed. The air, as well as carrying the scent of tiger, smelled of sweet greasepaint and burnt electrics. She paced the length of the front before moving back into the centre directly below the trapeze. Looking down at the floor she found that she was standing in the middle of a large square cut into the wood. It was about six feet across and would have been all but hidden except for the light catching the very slight darkening of the groove, and a pattern of chevrons in the dust to suggest it had been recently disturbed. She knelt again, bracing a crick in her knees. Running a hand along the edge, she came upon a flap on a hinge, a small, flimsy bit of veneer that concealed a larger clasp, pressed shut but not locked. She checked around her. The men were still busy trying to heave the tiger through a door backstage. Swiftly, she clicked open the clasp. The door creaked, then swung down into black. Warmth rose and a rank fog hit her; rotting meat and a cat's moist unwashed coat. Tentatively, braced just in case there should be another animal down there, she bent her head towards the gloom. It took her eyes a few seconds to adjust. She remembered with a growing unease the stage manager's words, 'It'll break a bone.' Looking back up she saw the trapeze still dawdling in an unseen draught of air above. She looked back down. It was impossible. But it was the only way. Unless she had gone up she could only have come down. Frankie peered back through the trapdoor, squinted into the gloom, and saw the corset.

Directly underneath the stage a large rectangular space was marked out by high steel bars, with an open gate on one side. She could make out a bucket of water in one corner and the unpleasant shadows of faeces scattered round another edge. In the centre lay a pile of shredded black fabric on top of a ragged dark pool with gnawed bones protruding here and there. She had to pull back to steady her stomach. From a careful distance she peeped again. The corset was spread open but it was distinct enough. The trim, the feathers. A swell of disorientation hit her and her head swam. What had she thought she was doing? An escape gone wrong? A sabotaged stunt? Or had someone else set it up? Could someone have been controlling the trapeze from above and the floor from below, someone inside the theatre?

Frankie sat back on the stage, her legs stretched ahead of her, trying not to breathe the foul air. Her body suddenly felt weighed down. She had known Ebony was in danger. She had broken an unspoken promise, failed an unsworn oath. If she had told Mr Stark sooner, if she had gone to his office instead of filing her copy to the newsroom. If she had gone to the police . . .

She saw movement on the stage and noticed that the young Chinese stagehand who had been sent to Ebony's dressing room was staring nervously at her from the wings. She quickly drew in her legs, dusted herself off and stood up.

'Don't you think you'd better close that?' she pointed at

the trapdoor. The boy hastily ran over and levered up the flap, securing it with the catch.

'Well, was she there?' A dying ember of hope was in Frankie's voice.

'Where did Mr Higgs go?'

'That the stage manager?'

The boy fidgeted in the pockets of his large overalls. 'He said you had to go.'

'Was Ebony Diamond there?'

He paused then shook his head.

Frankie tipped back her head, sucking in the lingering foul air. She closed her eyes and felt strain on the muscles of her neck. When she opened them again, she found herself staring straight into the leather loop hanging down off the trapeze. It took her a second to register that something was moving on it, then a drip hit her square between the eyes. She shook her head reflexively, then raised a finger to the spot and dabbed. She stared back up again. She could barely see the thing in the dim light, but she hadn't imagined that drip.

Cautiously she sniffed her fingers. It wasn't cyanide, she knew that much, from reading *Strand* magazine. Cyanide smelled of Amaretto. Chloroform, that was supposed to be mousy. Arsenic on the other hand had no smell in liquid form.

She looked across at the young stagehand then back up at the trapeze. 'Can I get up there?'

He was regarding her warily and she bitterly wished she had something to bribe him with. She was reluctant to part with her last sticky shilling and thought instead there might be sixpence in her shoe, but when she rummaged to check, there was nothing. Then she had an idea. 'How'd you like to be in the newspapers?'

His expression didn't change but a flash of pride brightened his eyes.

Frankie was halfway up the ladder when she began to regret her request. 'You're doing this for someone else,' she whispered to her fears. But it didn't stop the vertigo rushing round her, making her fancy the ladder was wobbling. The metal rails were thinner than apple branches, and by some trick of fear seemed soft and bending. She reached the top and swallowed, her mouth paper-dry, before making the final climb on a rope up to the platform. The rig was deserted, the fly-operator's post abandoned. The boy wedged round her with effortless dexterity and she followed on hands and knees, trying not to look down.

They hauled up the trapeze by its ropes, lifting on it a cloud of Ebony's scent. The fibres had a sticky silken feel to them. Frankie reached for the leather strap, then thought better of it and raised it to her nose using the wooden bar. The boy watched her curiously as she sniffed. There was no odour but leather, but it was definitely wet. Ebony hadn't caught the strap, Frankie was sure of it. So did that mean she knew something was wrong?

There were only two ways to find out what was on it, and as she didn't have access to a laboratory of potions and litmus papers, she was going to have to use the dangerous one. She swallowed, then smeared her finger along the sodden leather. Her heart was beating as she raised her moist fingertip to the tip of her tongue. She hesitated. Her tongue would make her swallow whatever it was. Better to rub it on her lip. She touched her finger very gently to her top lip. After a couple of seconds, a familiar sensation set in, one she knew well and didn't have pleasant memories of. Emboldened, she rubbed a little harder, the boy watching from the shadows. And then she knew. Not poison, but something equally deadly for a person whose nerves in their mouth kept them alive.

Now she had the distinct impression that Ebony Diamond had known exactly what she was doing when she missed that strap.

'You know her dressing room?'

The stagehand nodded.

'Take me there.'

Halfway down a paint-scented corridor, Ebony's name had been badly calligraphied onto a piece of card and stuck to a flaking door. The young stagehand held it open for Frankie. She crept inside, feeling slightly violatory, the same way she had felt going into her Nan's parlour after she had died. The smell was there; *poudre d'amour* and Old Tom gin. Frankie looked at the lamp-lined mirror expecting to see it framed in postcards from suffragette colleagues, surrounded by green, white and violet bouquets. Instead there was only one card, an old picture of a man in a strongman's leotard, holding up a baby elephant. She tweaked it from the wood frame and turned it over. The handwriting was poor, block capitals. It said, 'LOVE, PAPA.'

The mirror reflected back a rack of corsets, all black with jet beads, lace and magpie feathers. The large taffeta dress Ebony had been wearing at the corset shop was upended over a chaise longue, its petticoats splaying out into sooty petals.

'What was she wearing when she came in?'

The stagehand pointed at the dress.

'She keep clothes in here?'

'She moved a few costumes in the other day. Said she couldn't make up her mind.' Frankie turned and ran her finger along the corset rack, rough silk and slippery satin. She peeked at one of the labels. 'Olivier Smythe.'

Something moved in the mirror, a flash of bright copper, and she spun only just quick enough to see a figure in brown tweeds slipping out from behind the door and into the corridor, pulling his cap down over his red hair as he ran. It was enough. She recognised him. The ginger-haired boy from Smythe's. Frankie skidded out into the corridor and pounded the linoleum floor in chase but he was faster, and slid round a corner and out of sight. The screech of friction on his shoes split the air. She heard the handle being turned on a fire exit, a gust of cold air whipped down the corridor and a door smacked shut.

'Do you know that boy?' she shouted back at the stagehand.

There was no reply, and when she turned she saw that he

had been joined by the stage manager and three of his men, their sleeves rolled up, still panting and oily-faced. The stage manager's complexion was a chalky beige and he carried something in his hands that he quickly tried to conceal behind his back. The straps dangled out and Frankie saw it was the shredded corset from the tiger pit.

She looked both ways down the corridor. She was determined not to leave until she'd had a better look at that cage.

'Get her out of here. Police'll be here any minute. Last thing we want is press sniffing around.'

'Police?'

The stage men moved towards her. She backed up a few steps.

At that moment a noise distracted them all, braces slapping against marching legs. At the far end of the corridor, the Great Foucaud appeared, puffing, puce, his hair plastered to his face in brilliantine triangles. He threw his hands into the air. 'Gone. Priceless.'

For a second the stage manager was distracted, and turned his gaze on Foucaud who had raised a threatening finger. 'And if I find out that any of your men are involved. I'm suing this so-called theatre. You'll never open another show in London again.'

'What's gone?' Frankie asked.

'Thirteen different tailors, one of whom is now dead. One hundred and eighty-five shows. It's simply irreplaceable, and this so-called theatre . . .'

'Excuse me . . .' The stage manager held aloft the ripped

corset. His hand was shaking badly though he kept his voice steady. 'Your animal was responsible for the death of Ebony Diamond tonight. I don't give a donkey's tit what it is you've lost.'

Foucaud blew spit between his lips. 'That pile of bones in the tiger's pen is made of beef, you idiot. I checked. His food's been ransacked as well. Someone has it in for me. Someone here wants to ruin me.'

'Not you,' Frankie muttered under her breath.

The stage manager seemed torn between relief and humiliation. He looked down at the corset as if it was part of a conspiracy to trick him.

Frankie's relief was swiftly followed by confusion. If Ebony was not in the tiger's stomach, then why were her clothes in its cage, and more pressingly, where was she?

'I want this place searched, top to bottom,' Foucaud snapped. 'I bet it was that electrician's boy with the gammy eye; he saw me being tied in before the act.'

'What are you talking about?' The stage manager pressed his brow.

In a sudden blaze of anger Foucaud seized him by the throat with one of his great, card-palming, dove-squashing hands and pressed him up against the corridor wall. The stage manager began to splutter. Frankie noted that none of his men came to his aid. 'The tiger suit for God's sake,' Foucaud snarled. 'The climax of the bloody act. Someone has stolen my custom-made, mechanical limbed, six-months to replace, not to mention the cost, tiger suit. And unless you find it you will never, and I mean never work in London again.' He released his grip and ran the huge hand back through his greased hair, pressing it to his head.

The stage manager was trembling and swallowing. He lifted his finger at Frankie. 'Out.'

Three stagehands started towards her. 'All right, all right,' she held up her hands. 'But your boss, Mr Whatshisname, when he gets wind of this . . .'

'Out!'

She backed into the exit door, clipping the latch with her spine, then reluctantly pushed her way out into the cold. The rain had stopped but the air was sharp and icy. She gathered her jacket round her and muttered a curse. Looking up at the high walls of the theatre, it seemed there were no windows low enough to climb back in. She looked down at her footwear. Her days shimmying up trees and drainpipes were over anyway.

Reluctantly, she began moving towards St Martin's Lane, when the sight of an old drunk crouched up against the wall made her stop. It wasn't the scarred and ruined face of the man that made her start but the blanket he was sitting on. He stretched his arms out and Frankie walked closer until his weathered hands clutched the knees of her trousers. 'I've not got nothing.' She peeled him off. She had been right at first sight. The blanket was furry with the soft oily shine of a cat's pelt. 'Where did you get this?'

He slurred something and spat on the ground.

She reached out until her fingers touched wet animal hair. Her skin began to creep at the friction.

The man boxed her a hook but the move toppled his balance and he fell sideways onto the pavement. Frankie quickly grabbed the blanket but it was too heavy and a corner was trapped under the man's buttocks. As he scrambled to his feet, his eyes glaring for a fight, she spied what she was after, leant against the wall. It had been propping the old man's back up, an unconventional cushion but a comfortable-looking one. A tiger's gold-eyed head. She picked it up with both hands and ducked the man's blurry punch. Taking the head with her she stepped a few paces beyond his reach and examined it.

Its glass eyes stared at her uncannily. She touched her index finger to one of the fragile lids and it closed in a lazy wink. She turned it over and ran a finger along the seams. It was poorly patched on the inside. Knotted strings dangled down from the eyes and mouth like chopped ligaments. She pulled one. The eyelid closed. She pulled another. The jaw snapped shut. She thought back to the tiger licking its paw in the auditorium. She had been far away, in the gods but it had looked deathly real, as real as the tiger that had come back onstage, that Foucaud's men had caught and drugged. Was it possible Ebony had made her escape, releasing the real tiger on her way out as a diversion?

Frankie lifted the empty head closer to her face and probed her nose inside. She sniffed twice, once near the top of the mask, and once at the neck, and then she knew. The crown smelled like brilliantine, pungent and sickly, but at the neck was the light, distinctive scent of *poudre d'amour*.

Thirteen

Primrose looked up sharply at the knock on his office door.

Chief Inspector Stuttlegate didn't wait for an invite before swinging into the room. It was after ten o'clock and the office crackled with the quiet hum of electricity and the occasional burst of typewriting on the machines in the corridor. Primrose put aside the sheaf of wispy papers printed in faint blue ink he was correcting – the report on Christabel Pankhurst at Dover – and managed a smile.

The Chief sighed and scraped across a chair. He hitched up his trousers with fat fingers. His knees cracked as he sat. From his coat pocket, he pulled out a small bottle of Irish whiskey and held it up. Primrose nodded politely and reached across his desk for two dirty coffee cups. He had nothing but his handkerchief to wipe the rims with, but Stuttlegate didn't seem to notice. He poured them each a short measure. When they had chimed cups and sipped he said, 'I know what you mean, Freddie, I really do.'

Primrose looked down at his fingers. There was a stain of grime and ink settled between the wrinkles on his knuckles, and for a fleeting moment he forgot where he was and mistook it for muck from the dairy.

Stuttlegate knocked back his whiskey. 'You and me, we just want the best for King and country. You're a farm boy, I was a farm boy once. We know what's real. You understand that different men deal with pressure in different ways.'

Primrose placed his cup on the desk. 'I'm sorry if I've caused offence with my complaint.'

'Not offence, Freddie, it's just that, well, we're a team. If them outside, if they get any whiff that there's dissent within our ranks, what will it do to theirs?' He scratched his fingers through his ginger hair. A pungent odour of tobacco and spice was coming off him. 'Barnes, Wilson, never going to rise above the rank of Inspector, I don't mind telling you. But filing complaints against other officers, it's just not done, Freddie. It might have been done in other branches, but here we have to play things a little tighter.' He brushed his whiskers with a finger.

Primrose coughed weakly. 'That tightness is undermined when people see us taking liberties. You didn't see the state of that girl. Unfairness,' he let his eye slide to the copy of the Police Code in the corner, 'is sure to bring discredit on those who are guilty of it, sir.'

'I know, I understand, Freddie, and a rogue police officer's just about as bad as a mouldy bit of cheese in my book. But,' he followed Primrose's eyes to the Police Code book, 'a zealous officer who is desiring only to call attention to himself is liable to fall into a habit of exaggeration. Page nine, I think you'll find.'

He let the words settle on the desk.

Primrose couldn't meet his superior's eye. 'You have to understand, Freddie,' Stuttlegate sniffed and his nose turned for a second into an awful snout, 'that these are not ordinary women we're dealing with. They're rotten eggs, these window breakers, and I'm not afraid to say it. I'm thinking of the reputation of my wife as much as anything when I'm on this type of work. These women, if you can call them that, are common criminals, not ladies. If a bit of rough and tumble goes hand in hand with an arrest, well, that's the way of it.' He sighed slowly. 'I'll have a word with Barnes myself, but no more filed complaints, eh?'

Primrose said nothing. The Chief sensed the mood thicken and rubbed his hands together, self-consciously relaxed again. 'All right, where are you now with the arson; did they ever get their hearing?'

Primrose flicked through a pile of brown card folders stacked on the corner of his desk. 'They did. Today, in fact. Pleaded guilty to attempting to start a fire but claimed it was only the summer house they were after, not the main one.'

Stuttlegate nodded. 'In that case you have a window while they prepare trial.'

Primrose felt his stomach tense up. He wanted to look at the clock but knew it would be bad form. The dark outside the window and shady sounds of the night from the street below already told him how late it was.

'There's a call come in from the West End. Strange business. Acrobat disappeared from a theatre. They've looked everywhere but no sign of a body. Stage manager thinks there's something fishy, her equipment might have been tampered with. We've been called to that theatre before. They've had some pretty rotten accidents in the past, animals getting loose, girls committing suicide.'

Primrose nodded.

He paused. 'I don't think I need to tell you who the girl was mixed up with and why I'm passing it to you.'

Primrose worked to keep his voice level. 'Suffragette?'

'Suffragette indeed. Ebony Diamond.'

Primrose frowned.

'No, I know what you're going to say. That girl they found yesterday on Tottenham Court Road. It wasn't her. Guaranteed. I read the report. Landlord misidentified the body, although he swears the clothes belonged to Miss Diamond. And this,' he foraged in his pocket and pulled out a small sharp object, then tossed it to Primrose.

Primrose recognised it instantly. A tiny portcullis, the size of a tuppence piece, made of black iron. He had seen them hundreds of times over, even before joining the suffragette squad. 'Found on the body?'

Stuttlegate nodded. 'Divisional detectives had it until now. The first constable on the scene took it away with him. Now I don't know if there's a connection but listen to this.' He retrieved a notebook from his breast pocket and flattened out the creases where it had taken the shape of his chest.

'One of our officers says he saw Ebony Diamond yesterday outside the shop of that corset maker who strangled himself, did you read about that in the evening paper? Nasty business, grade A deviant. Don't know yet if it was an accident and frankly don't care.' He gave a shudder.

Primrose brushed his fingers through his thick hair and rubbed a spot on his forehead. 'I'm not sure I'm quite clear. The murdered girl on Tottenham Court Road and the corset maker on Bond Street: you believe there's a connection between them and this Ebony Diamond going missing tonight?'

Stuttlegate held up a finger. 'There might be a connection.'

'But if it's murder why hasn't it gone to Central Office? Why Special Branch, and why—'

'Suffragettes.' Stuttlegate held his eye. 'You see, this is one I would have given to Barnes. But I don't know about him, Freddie. After what you said. Especially since Miss Diamond was such a well-known suffragette. Twice in Holloway. Don't know if it's wise to pass this his way, after, you know . . .'

Primrose felt his jaw go tight. A flush of bitterness rose in him. So this was his punishment for being a rat, was it? Sending Barnes's cases his way, a bit of overwork would show him not to challenge his comrades. His stubbornness quickly countered his resentment and he sat up straighter, his shoulders flexed.

'Certainly, sir.' He cleared his throat. 'I'll have a team assembled by tomorrow. We'll start with the stage equipment.'

'Good. The stage manager thinks it might have been tampered with. Poison registers in local chemists might be a good start. Oh and one other thing, I thought you and Wilson worked so well together on that arson case, so I've assigned him to you on this. Don't have a problem with that do you, Freddie?'

Primrose swallowed then managed his most pleasant smile of the evening. 'Not at all, Chief. Not at all.'

Fourteen

Frankie still had her hands on the tiger's head when she heard the sharp toppling of a dustbin lid on the pavement at the end of the lane leading to the stage door. She snapped her head up to see the ginger-haired boy dodging out onto the main street, one hand clinging to his cap. Tossing the head back towards the old drunk she tore after him. 'Oi!'

A horse skittered backwards, showing the whites of its eyes as Frankie ran across St Martin's Lane. ''Ere, watch it! My mare could have had you!' She ignored the cries of the Victoria driver and his lady passengers, and scrambled onto the opposite pavement, looking right and left. A flash of red up ahead cut across towards Charing Cross Road. The boy pushed past late-night booksellers' stalls and rammed men carrying umbrellas out of his way. Frankie had to give it to him. He could dart like a tomcat. The only tag on him was that brush of hair lighting up his head like a fox's tail.

On Charing Cross Road he headed directly for Leicester

Square underground station. Frankie paid for her ticket with the last sticky shilling she had in her pocket, not bothering to wait for her change and skidded into the iron-latticed lift moments before the door slammed.

At the bottom of the lift shaft she saw the boy head for the northbound Hampstead line and lengthened her stride to catch up, feeling a stitch brewing in her side. The platform was packed tight. Ladies in hats vied for space with working men, young women in gaudy dresses, and clerks in bowler hats. There were dogs too: greyhounds, mongrels, pekingeses, underfoot, on leashes, in ladies' arms.

As the tube rattled towards them, a mad crush swarmed; gatemen held the crowd back until the train halted. One carriage down from where Frankie was standing there came a cry, 'Hey, he hasn't got a ticket!'

She turned to see the red-haired boy flash past her towards the rear of the train. As his feet battered the platform she could have sworn he looked right at her. Oh, he knew all right what she was up to. She didn't care. She managed to squash herself inside just as the train began to shift.

The crush inside the carriage was too dense to even think about moving through it and Frankie pressed her face to the window as the train rucked and jerked through its black tunnels. At Tottenham Court Road a squeeze of people got off, easing up the breathing room. The tube had begun to shift again when a flame-coloured smudge passed by her window. Her chest suddenly seizing, she scrambled to the carriage gate.

The gate was locked.

'Miss, you can't . . .' the gateman snapped.

Outside on the platform the ginger boy was sprinting to the exit. He looked back over his shoulder, his green eyes shining at her.

The train was picking up speed again; the gateman was on Frankie's back. 'We're moving, you can't . . .'

With a sudden crack the handle gave. Her feet almost tumbled from under her as she hit the platform. She ran towards the lifts but the latticed doors were already slamming, the lifts ascending along with the pale face of the ginger boy.

'Fuck a barrel.' Frankie kicked the tiles and pain shot up her toe.

By the time she reached street level there was no sign of him. A forceful driving rain was beginning to wash sideways in the coal-scented gloom. Frankie turned a circle outside the station, looking at every avenue of escape, but the London streets were as good as quicksand for disappearing into once the crowds closed in. She wiped her moistening hair out of her face and let her breath out, feeling furious at herself. He had to be following Ebony; he must know where she was. And why the devil had Ebony not held her nerve and made good on her plea for a meeting? The anxiety in Ebony's eyes as she'd thrust the newspaper at Frankie that morning hovered in her memory.

Frankie stepped out of the way as a motor omnibus sprayed rainwater and dung-scented muck at her, then stared after its receding back window. She blinked, not quite believing what she was seeing. The bus was headed back towards Charing Cross Road, the direction they had come from. And the boy was on it.

Frankie ran, ignoring the sound of her trouser seam tearing, soaking up the pain as her too-thin shoes hammered the pavement up into her feet.

The traffic was still thick enough to keep the omnibus in sight, and she watched as it continued back on the route they had taken, then swung off right, heading for the edges of Soho. She kept a skittering pace, pausing to dodge a two-step round pedestrians coming in the other direction. The omnibus veered onto Greek Street, then stopped.

The boy hopped off, tearing at a gallop, his weedy supple legs allowing him to run high, low, hurdle over and around the market barrels and breadsellers. He chanced a glance back over his shoulder at Frankie, and that was when she knew for certain: he was trying to lose her.

She kept her eye on him as the distance between them grew, then watched with a dawning realisation as he hurtled down Duck Lane; he was headed for Jojo's Cocoa Bar.

As she approached the club doors, noises of merry-go-round music and laughter swelled up into the street. The red glow from inside the basement diluted the lane's darkness, casting half-illuminated shapes and moving shadows.

There was no sign of the boy, but as she reached the railings a man in a black cape and top hat stepped into her path. 'Sixpence if you want in.'

Frankie was out of breath. The damp air caught on her throat when she tried to speak. 'I need to see the boy. The one with the . . .' she gestured to her hair. 'You know, the ginger-haired boy. He came in here.'

The man looked over his shoulder and exchanged an eyebrow raise with a short woman in striped trousers, propping open the door and smoking an enormous cigar. She coughed and laughed.

'Sixpence,' he repeated, and held out a fleshy palm.

Frantically Frankie checked her pockets, inner and outer, and her shoes, remembering she had left her change at the tube ticket office. Nothing. 'Please, is Ebony Diamond there?'

'She's not on tonight. She's at the Coliseum.'

'She's not. She's gone. I've been there. Please, it could be life or death. I need to see the boy.'

The large man looked greatly amused. 'If you want to see a boy,' he said, nodding with a glint at Frankie's crotch, 'believe me it'll cost you a lot more than sixpence. Even round here.' He laughed, showing the huge cavern of his maw, and gestured out towards the main road where the red shadows were denser and darker. 'Now, be off with you.'

Frankie tried to peer over each of his shoulders, but both times he blocked her view. The warmth of the club was creeping through the open doors, damp and full, and she wondered whether once inside she would even have any chance of finding the ginger boy among the hive of revellers.

'I'll be back tomorrow, you mark me.' She pointed a finger towards the man's weathered face. Through drink or age

146

some of the large veins had popped on his nose, giving his skin the look of blue cheese. He flicked her finger away.

'Tell that boy . . .' she started.

'Oh, I will.' He winked salaciously.

Shivering with the cold, the wet, and her rage, Frankie retreated back down the street. She took a moment to gather her breath, then deciding there was nothing more for it, began to pick her way back through Soho, for the second time in as many nights, towards home.

Frankie's fingers were still trembling as she bent over a pail of steaming water in the bathroom and scrubbed the back of her neck. It was past midnight. Her body tingled with electricity, thoughts swam in her head. Ebony Diamond had seen her own death that evening, as surely as she had seen that tiger prowling below her. She must have loosened the trapdoor hatch herself, prepared a landing, said a prayer. Nobby's notes had said she was a tiger tamer. Animals could be predicted; animals could be trusted in a way humans could not.

The carbolic soap stung her scalp but it felt good getting rid of the dust, the tobacco smell around her and the oil in her hair. When she finished, the water was grey. She picked her clothes up off the damp floor and wrapped herself in a towel then padded back to her bedroom. The floorboards groaned as she settled at her desk, pulling the Blickensderfer towards her. She had no fresh sheets of paper left so she uncovered an article about single women's cookery she had never submitted and loaded it in back to front.

'Exclusive: Ebony Diamond Escapes Murder.' She hesitated as she typed the word 'murder'. Then her tongue ran to her missing tooth. She remembered the day it had been pulled. The darkness of the waiting room, the smell of blood, the rub of the surgeon's finger on her gums. That taste, that distinct numbing of cocaine solution. She had felt it on the leather strap, soaked through. If Ebony had caught it, it would have taken only seconds before her mouth was numbed beyond holding on. What was it she had said? 'I must be a cat; I must have nine lives'? Someone was after her and she knew it.

Frankie continued to type, not caring how much noise the keys made, not caring if she was making sense. When she finished, she whipped the paper from the machine and shut the box. Dumping the two sheets on her desk without bothering to read them through, she stumbled over to her bed and crawled between the blankets. Before she knew it, she was in a deep, nightmarish sleep.

Fifteen

3 November 1912

Frankie woke with a start, realising she hadn't closed the drapes. A dusty gold cloud of light was pouring in. She checked her pocket-watch. It was ten o'clock.

Clumsily, she pulled on a pair of tweed trousers, a shirt, neckerchief and cardigan and rushed downstairs to see if the post had arrived. On the sideboard at the bottom of the stairs a pile of letters had been tucked under one of the pot plants, to stop it from falling off as the 'citizens' dashed about.

She picked through the pile, feeling for the small brown envelope with the stamp of the *Evening Gazette* and the slender cheque inside. It wasn't there. A wave of panic passed across her, as she remembered Mrs Gibbons's demand for rent. Quickly checking again, she spotted that there was in fact something with her name on it. A folded telegram. She looked closer at the little blue print in capital letters on the

149

fragile paper and her heart dipped. It said, 'STONECUTTER STREET STARK.' On the next line was another word, three extra characters' worth of cost underlying the message's urgency; 'NOW.'

Traffic on Fleet Street was slow at this time of day and as she sat in the back of a hansom cab, with an almost comatose horse plodding through the tangle of omnibuses, Frankie cursed the newspaperboy who had sped off on the office bicycle she usually borrowed. The printing presses were spewing out first editions of the evening papers; the paper boys were gathering like geese in the distribution rooms waiting for the bundles of hot newsprint to appear all wrapped up in string. There were Reuters boys on their bicycles weaving in and out of horses and trams. Runners on dirty motorcycles were taking bundles out to the suburbs. Subs' boys were already squirrelling first editions of the rival papers back to their masters who were ready to stop the linotypes at a word and rearrange a paragraph here, an exclusive there, re-write the lower half of the page with stop presses and sports results. The smell on the street was suffocating; printer's ink and motor exhaust all but masking the subtler perfume of barber's soap, coffee stands and hops from the public houses. And the noise; it was as if all the sounds in London had been squashed into one tiny pocket of street, the roaring basement print machines, the cries of 'copy' from open windows, the sound of builders working on shiny new edifices along the Aldwych, throwing up buildings as tall as dreams.

The hansom stopped abruptly as a man ran across the street clinging to his hat. Frankie leaned forward in the cab for a closer look. On the other side of the road an old man in a raincoat was making a lewd gesture. 'That will serve you right for milking our copy, you swine.'

The cabbie hissed at them and summoned the horse on with a snap of the reins. Frankie's gut lurched as she saw the hapless young journalist still desperately clinging to his hat, pounding at the door of his own paper with his fist. No one would let him in.

'Stonecutter Street,' she directed the cabbie and he swerved them off the main road. She paid him with sixpence, taken from her emergency fund she kept in a slit in the back of the Blickensderfer case, and straightened the edges of the papers she had brought with her. With a tipping stomach she made her way up the staircase and knocked on Stark's door.

'Come,' the voice spat from inside.

She swallowed and tweaked open the door.

Stark was seated at his desk, bent over a collection of scattered papers, his wide hand fumbling in a pot of blue pencils. He looked oblivious to the clacking tape machine behind him and to the slumped form of Nobby staring at it. There was a sharpness in his eyes, which he turned now on Frankie as she approached the desk, keeping her papers neatly folded in front of her.

'Ebony Diamond.' He un-wedged the monocle from his eye with some difficulty. 'I wanted a portrait on her, didn't I?'

'Yes, sir.' Frankie kept half an eye on Nobby in the corner.

He looked into the distance. 'Force-feeding. Matrons. Suffragettes. I think those were the instructions. Tantalising tales from inside the prison. Not difficult.'

Frankie tried to stifle her nerves.

Stark seemed to read her mind. 'Do you see Nobby over there? He does the Reuters flimsy, he cuts the cable and gives me the stories he thinks are worth looking at. Do you know, Nobby's only fourteen years old, isn't that right, Nobby?'

The boy nodded, his eyes still on the ticking tape.

'Right now, Miss George, I wouldn't trust you with Nobby's job.'

Frankie took a breath. 'No sir.'

'Do you have the photograph I asked for?'

Frankie shook her head. Her fingers were beginning to sweat onto her typed copy.

'Why not?'

'Miss Diamond was not amenable to having her picture taken.'

Mr Stark's fat face cracked a nasty smile. 'Do you think many ex-convicts are?'

'I wrote up what I thought was an important story.'

Stark was shaking a finger at her. 'It wasn't what I asked for, and with forty years in the business I'll trust my own opinions on what I think's an important story. And that's another thing, where was your damn column?'

'I only had time to . . . because Ebony was at Smythe's . . . and—'

He cut her off by placing his fingertips very suddenly and

deliberately on the table between them. 'Do you know why I hired you?'

She shook her head, before realising that was the worst response possible.

'To prove a point, Miss George. To prove a point. You know W. T. Stead, God rest his soul?'

Frankie's eyes flicked to the copy of the *Pall Mall Gazette*, open on the desk in front. 'Yes, sir.' The former editor of the *Pall Mall Gazette*, famous for his exposés and political crusades had been something of a hero of Frankie's.

'Stead was a good friend of mine. He was a smug bugger and there weren't many things he was wrong about, unfortunately, but he once said to me, "Edward, never trust a mannish woman."'

Frankie shifted her weight and dared to look up at his tiny black eyes. 'With respect, sir, I know there's more to Ebony Diamond than she cared to admit. I was following my instincts.'

'It doesn't matter, Frankie, it wasn't what I asked for. That piece was supposed to be about the grime in prison, women getting held down by other women and force-fed. I'm here to sell papers, not make up fairy stories about the likeness between cons and murdered prostitutes.' His fingers furrowed around for something to play with, finding the crusty edge of the whisky glass.

'The girl on Tottenham Court Road? She wasn't a prosti– sorry, sir.'

'Anyway, whether or not our subs could extract anything

from that garbled mess of a portrait I'll never know. I wasn't so angry about that as I was about you missing a deadline on your column.'

'But Mr Stark, it was supposed to—'

He glared at her. Her stomach began to feel heavy. She couldn't begin to face the thought that there would be no cheque this week. She would have to bide her time and sneak in and out of the boarding house after dark. She had a couple of cans of corned beef in her room. She could fry them up on her gas stove, perhaps go via Exmouth Market and beg the dregs of a baker's leftovers, or an onion. She realised her mind was wandering and Stark was still talking.

'I don't think you realise the full extent of the hot water you've put me in. I only gave you half the story about Twinkle when I hired you.' He sighed and cast a glance towards Nobby, as if wondering for a second whether he could be trusted to stay. 'Twinkle was on the verge of suing this newspaper. I can't go into details but she's not a woman whose feathers we like to ruffle. You know who takes the blame whenever this paper is up in court? You know who the buck stops with?'

Frankie cleared her throat.

'That's right. You may well cough. But it's not your behind that'll be sitting in Bow Street Court, it's mine. And that's not something I can risk. As of this moment you are suspended from this newspaper.'

'Mr Stark,' Frankie cried before she could stop herself.

He held up a fat hand. 'You're damned lucky you're not out of a job. I'll have none of your protests, and don't you go grovelling to the Savage Club again; that didn't impress our publisher last time and it won't impress him again.' Frankie's eyes widened and her lips dropped open involuntarily. 'Yes, I know about that escapade, we all do.'

She suddenly found herself unable to meet his eye. Her face felt as if it were beginning to roast. He knew about the Savage Club. How could he know about her trip to the Savage Club?

'You see, Frankie, your quirks are funny when you're winning. I'd even go so far as to say they are endearing. But what I don't think you realise is that this is not a joke. You've been lucky to get where you are. You've got pluck more than talent but at some point you're going to have to understand that following instructions puts food on the table.' He took a breath and the cushions of his face seemed to soften a little. 'Do your job. You're not an editor, you don't decide what goes in and what doesn't. Do as you're told, manage your time and for God's sake learn to accept your limitations. Or next time it will be worse.'

He shoved a copy of yesterday evening's paper across to her. The paper she had been too nervous to open. The ticker machine suddenly paused for a second and the room became unbearably silent. Frankie peeled open the rag to page eight. In lieu of her column there was a three-quarter page advert for the Aeolian Orchestrion, a coin-operated pianola with drums, cymbals and glockenspiels. 'We were lucky they were ready to stump up the cash,' he said coldly.

'But the portrait? The "Ebony Diamond's life in danger" piece?'

'I binned it. I told you force-feeding and you gave me some rot about a circus girl who looked like a tom crying over a dead corset maker.'

'She wasn't a prostitute. She was a seamstress who worked for Smythe. And don't you know what happened last night?'

He scratched his balding head. 'I know very well what happened last night. Ebony Diamond fell off a rotten trapeze and Oswald Stoll's trying to cover it up. He's always been known for his cheap equipment. I hope it bites him where it hurts. Mr Hawkins is on the story already.'

'Mr Hawkins thought Ebony Diamond had been murdered yesterday. The body was misidentified and he didn't bother to check. Next night Ebony Diamond disappears. What does that tell you? Two things. Firstly that—'

Mr Stark leaned back in his chair. 'Frankie, what exactly do you want?'

'Just let me investigate. Pay me expenses only, I don't care, I just need enough for my rent and food; I know there's something going on; I know I can get to the bottom of it.'

Mr Stark's expression was now one of full condescension. 'I can't do that. You're not a reporter. You write for the ladies' page. I gave you a chance with that suffragette portrait and look what you did with it.'

'Mr Stark,' Frankie felt the nerves taut in her voice, 'a portrait is hardly a chance. Something terrible is happening, right now, something involving Ebony Diamond. I'm sorry if I disappointed you but if you take a proper chance, give me time to do my investigations, I can do as well as those men on the news desk, I swear it . . .' She swallowed. Rage was backing up behind her eyeballs and she fought it bitterly. To lose her temper in here would be more than her life was worth.

Stark shook his head and began to wedge the eyeglass back in. The clicking tape had started again, the noises from the street below filtering in. He swivelled in his chair for a few seconds. 'I'll think about reinstating you once I've heard what Twinkle has to say. Prove me right, please, Frankie. Don't make yourself an easy target. Stick to what you can do.'

Frankie didn't respond.

'What's that in your hand?'

She blushed. 'It's a report of the full story. It's what I saw last night.'

He reached out. 'Let me see.' He took it and flicked through quickly, his eyes scanning the type with practised speed. 'Our boys downstairs have spent years learning how to handle a story, how to wheedle information out of folk.'

'With respect, that's what I did at the *Tottenham Evening News*.'

'With respect, the *Tottenham Evening News* is not the *London Evening Gazette*.' He shuffled in his chair. 'What's this on the back?'

'Sorry, sir,' Frankie mumbled, 'I had no clean paper.'

He stared at the text for a few seconds. 'I'll give you ten shillings for the recipe. For the ladies' page.'

Sixteen

Frankie didn't know whether to feel devastated or furious, whether to kick the railings or her own shins. She had almost yanked the lapels of the sub-editor when he asked for the camera back.

'It's being cleaned. I'm having it cleaned.'

'What's wrong with it?'

'Nothing, I'm just a conscientious reporter, that's all.'

He snorted and because she was feeling sensitive she took his scorn to be because she had called herself a reporter. Conscious that her temper was up and liable to get her into even more trouble, she had marched out of the building as quick as possible.

She walked past a scrapheap on St Giles where a group of street children were performing a scene from *Oliver Twist* on an apple cart. When they saw Frankie's trousers one of the boys stopped his speech and shouted 'Suffragette!' They all joined in, making obscene gestures. The boy started to sing,

'*Mrs Pankhurst, with a nine-pound hammer in her hand, breaking windows down the Strand. If you catch her, lay her on a stretcher, knock her on the Robert E. Lee.*' He slapped the bottom of one of the little girls, who shrieked then turned and boxed him hard on the ear.

On the steps outside Percy Circus, she could hear the grandfather clock indoors chiming noon. As she stuck her key in the lock, a postman in a cap appeared behind her. 'Number six?' Frankie nodded. 'Letter for you.'

She took the envelope and her heart sank as she recognised the handwriting, the elaborate curls and flourishes; a letter from her mother was the last thing she wanted to see. She heaved a sigh and opened the door. There was an eerie week-end quiet about the place as if the ornaments and clocks in the hall were lazily watching her. Thankfully Mrs Gibbons was nowhere to be seen. She went upstairs and lay flat on her bed, her head swimming. The letter sat in her hand like a threat. She knew what it would say: 'When are you coming home? The butcher's son will not wait for you forever.'

Frankie tossed it onto the pillow and prised herself up. Her room was filthy with dust; Mrs Gibbons had given up sending the girl in to clean it. Dirty grey light streaked through the window, hitting the desk where her typewriter and the broken camera lay. She reached for her notebook, lying open at the page she had been reading the night before, and ran her finger down the text, smudging the lead writing. 'Corsets, costumes, top hats, carriages.'

Stark was right. It was a mess. She looked across at the

unopened letter on the bed and a shudder ran down her back. The butcher's son. Harry Tripe. It was his real name, although everyone thought it must be a joke. 'Couldn't you have gone for sirloin?' they asked, or 'It's an offal coincidence.' He was not a bad looking boy. Last time she saw him, he'd grown stocky from his work heaving carcasses onto great meat hooks. They had an uncle with a pawn shop who always lent them expensive suits left by his clients, and there was a whiff of flash about the whole family. Francesca Tripe. She rolled the words in her mouth. It made her nauseous. She picked up her notebook, swallowed her hunger and headed out again into the gloomy day.

First stop was a watchmaker's shop on Gray's Inn Road where she deposited the camera. The man behind the counter was Italian and suspicious of her, as if she might have been the sort of woman who sold dirty photographs. He took two or three short sniffs of the leather bellows before handing her a collection ticket.

She then headed on foot to Soho in drizzling rain. The sky was falling heavier and closer with each cloud that blew in. The wet road crackled as wheels passed down it; women's dresses trailed on the ground. In the golden shop windows, cakes, hams, and wines were lit up, glowing. Frankie felt a twinge of sadness as she passed by the street her grandfather used to live on. His grocer's was now a Hungarian bakery, the signage all changed. Generations passed. Would he have expected his granddaughter to write in a newspaper when he barely spoke English himself? And would she just fall back into the fate she was bred for, a costermonger by blood, destined to be a wife like every other woman in London?

But not every woman was destined to be a wife. Ebony Diamond wasn't a wife; it hadn't been in her cards. Or Twinkle's. As she walked past a suffragette handing out pamphlets for a meeting at the Caxton Hall she felt a strange combination of envy and regret. It took courage to go to Holloway for a thing that some said didn't really matter. But it did matter, and all she had done was mock them. Mock them because when she boiled it down, a tart-mouthed woman at the Clement's Inn *Votes for Women* office had told her exactly the same thing Edward Stark had just told her, that she needed to take better care with her work. The only difference was it was easier to take revenge on them; they were sitting targets. The last time she had tried to take revenge on Fleet Street . . . She shivered at the thought. Of course Edward Stark had known about the Savage Club, who wouldn't have, in a room full of journalists? She was only glad they'd had the courtesy not to print it in the papers the next day.

It was her coverage of a bicycling race down at the Camden canal that had got her noticed by *London on Sunday*, a sister paper to the *Evening Gazette* with the same publisher. She was twenty-three and proud and for a treat had bought herself the autobiography of Nellie Bly from a kiosk outside Chancery Lane tube station. Nellie was the founding mother of exposés and had gone undercover in a New York lunatic asylum. Frankie devoured the book like it was a box of Fry's chocolates and the following week invited herself along to the Cheshire Cheese on Fleet Street where the journalists congregated, and where she felt she must now belong, having had a piece printed in a real Fleet Street paper. Only there was no one there. Eventually an old soak with a blistered nose told her that Tuesday night they all went to the Savage Club. Men only.

Frankie boiled with rage and rejection for a few minutes, before putting two and two together, and beginning to see an idea that she thought Miss Bly would have been proud of. She used kohl to subtly darken the skin on her throat and chin, and purchased a sixpence false moustache from the joke-shop floor of Gamages. She would do a woman's exposé inside the Savage Club.

It could have worked beautifully. She was whisked through the door, name-dropping her editor without an eyebrow being raised, and found journalists she had seen on Fleet Street playing poker and bridge in the library. Better still, in the Lounge, decorated with statues of feathered American Indians in savage poses, she saw the publisher of the paper himself, Lord Thorne, reading *The Times*. She invited herself onto one of the Chesterfields opposite and took out a pair of wire spectacles with plain glass in the lenses, another purchase from Gamages. He nodded. She smiled. She ordered a brandy and took out a cigarette. She drank three brandies in all, smoked two cigarettes and batted a brace of sentences back and forth with the publisher.

Parched on alcohol, dizzy with brandy she took the sensible move to order some soda water, at which point a young sub-editor next to her struck up a conversation. He worked for the *Daily Mail*. They chatted about skittles and trains and the terror of child-snatchers. They talked about football and Frankie did not hold against him the fact that he supported Woolwich Arsenal.

Her bladder, by this point had begun to strain. She caught herself just in time before asking for the ladies' room, and instead requested directions to the conveniences. But she was only halfway there when she noticed to her horror that the young man was following behind. He tipped her a wink.

Inside she headed for the cubicle, flushed, harangued, fit to burst, only to find the *Daily Mail* man still following. Panicked into forgetting her disguise she shrieked an obscenity at him in her natural voice – at which point the man, stunned only for a second, saw fit to turn the indiscretion to his advantage and began hollering, 'A woman, a woman in the Savage Club! She almost foxed us but here I've tracked her down, look, here, help!'

Before he could grab her, she darted to the door, sprang down the corridor and out into the street, praying she could hold her piddle until she reached home. She only got as far as the Camden canal before she had to give in, and threw Nellie Bly's book in along with it.

Frankie never tried an exposé again. As she rounded the corner into Duck Lane, dreading seeing the man with the cape and the blue cheese nose, she thought that perhaps it was time to gather a little courage again now.

Jojo's was boarded up fast. The posters on the front had been soaked by the rain and sagged unhappily on their tie-ribbons; ink had run down Ebony's upside-down front, casting streaks across her face. There was no one around, not even a lamp lit outside.

She hopped down the steps and banged on the red door, her fist stinging with the cold. The rain was starting to pick up, drips trickling down her neck. There was a scrabbling inside, the press of footsteps, then the door opened a crack and a warm draft escaped, along with the face of the tiny woman in striped trousers she had seen smoking in the doorway the night before. She glared at Frankie with green eyes. 'We're closed,' she said in a Scottish accent. 'Can't you take a hint?' She nodded to the empty lamp and the wet posters. 'No show tonight.'

'But it's Saturday.'

The woman shrugged. Her skin was covered with a thick layer of greasepaint.

'I left my hat the other night. Thursday.' Frankie tried to peek past her into the club but the woman cottoned on and narrowed the opening of the door. There was a kitcheny smell drifting out, liver and gravy.

'We've had no hats. You'll have dropped it in the street.'

'What time are you opening next?'

'We don't know.' She pushed the door, and was an inch from shutting it when Frankie wedged her hand in the gap.

'I'm a reporter. I'm investigating the disappearance of Ebony Diamond. I knew her, I met her. If she's in there . . .' She held her breath, bracing her fingers for the pain of a slammed door. 'I think she's in danger.'

The woman paused, then opened the gap a fraction more. The liver smell grew stronger along with the stink of old red wine. A voice Frankie recognised called from the pitch black inside. 'Let her in.'

The small woman took a sharp breath, before opening the door wide. She stood in the way, making Frankie edge round her to get inside. Once they were both in, she slammed the door and shoved a great bolt across the lock. It was dark in the lobby, powerfully scented with meat residue. In the gas-lamp glow Frankie could see that the walls were painted a dark blood red, like the inside of an eyelid. She jumped as a chattering came from behind her shoulder and looked round, startled to see a monkey in a waistcoat and fez screech-ing at her. The small woman grabbed it by the haunches and bundled it up like a baby into her arms.

'He thinks it's the show. He's trained to do that. People think he's Jojo's baby.' She gave a horrible smile as if antici-pating that Frankie would be alarmed or repulsed by something she was about to see. She led the way down the corridor, past a wooden ticketing desk to a set of double doors inlaid with stained glass. Still clutching the hissing monkey, she pushed the doors open with her bottom.

The lights were at full blast inside, cruelly displaying the cracks in the red paint, stains on the wood floor. The room, no bigger than a large parlour with a stage at one end, was filled with round tables draped in yellowing white cloths, and chairs with pieces of upholstery missing. The stage curtains were a dusty turquoise fringed in gold. Curios were pinned to the wall; exotic masks, a stuffed crocodile, a print in the style of Toulouse-Lautrec, a stiff black corset with a tiny waist, signed in white chalk. The monkey struggled out of the little woman's arms and hopped up onto one of the tables, picking at a plate of leftover stew and pastry.

Frankie stopped short when she saw the trio assembled in front of her. If she hadn't known Jojo straightaway from the posters, she would have guessed him from the way he was standing, proprietorial, his shoulders back, both hands in his trouser pockets. Every inch of him was covered with a fleecy golden mane, brushed to a shine over his face. An expensively cut suit of dark green velvet followed the contours of his body, a pocket-watch chain dangled over his abdomen. Salome, the snake girl, the voice Frankie knew, was slouching on the left, wearing a loose silk robe painted with blue and gold flowers. Despite her pose, she couldn't disguise the darkness on her face, nor the sallow rings round her eyes. And in the centre, with his arms tied fast to the chair he sat on, was the ginger-haired boy.

Seventeen

Primrose cleared his throat quietly as his team settled onto thinly upholstered chairs, arranged in a circle in one of the Scotland Yard meeting rooms. He was uncomfortable without his desk in front of him. His lap felt exposed. On it he balanced a notepad with a fine sheaf of yellow lined paper, and tapped his pencil gently.

There were six of them drafted in to assist from the different threads of Special Branch. The speed and efficiency with which Stuttlegate had helped him assemble the group had unnerved Primrose slightly. It was almost as if the Chief had them sitting on alert, waiting for the right moment.

When they had settled he spoke. 'Do you know why you have been called here?'

The men nodded and shifted their eyes around, taking one another in. On the far left was Sergeant Mathers from Hammersmith, a cell breaker at the time of the Walsall anarchists. He was nearing retirement age now and looked disgruntled to have been called to headquarters on a Saturday. Next to him sat a square military type with a neat blond moustache and wire spectacles, oddly dainty on his huge pink face. That was Donaldson, the motorcyclist on loan from Westminster. Next was Bain, a photographer who specialised in prison yard surveillance. Sergeant Wilson sat directly opposite Primrose, his grasshopper legs twined round each other. His head was slouched as if he might have a hangover. Completing the circle was a slender boy who could have passed for twenty, although Primrose knew he was several years older. Robert Jenkins had been a precociously talented sapper, sent abroad with the military on various assignments before an ill-judged mine clearance landed in him in hospital for almost a year. He had since decided that the police force was a safer bet, and Special Branch had made good use of his bomb knowledge on some of the anarchist intelligence operations. He had a lean, slight physique and a delicate way of speaking.

The air in the room smelled of men who had been working since six that morning, some since the night before: cigarettes, weak coffee, shrimps scoffed from paper bags. Five sets of weary eyes watched Primrose.

'Good,' Primrose went on. 'Well, the uniforms have been doing a round of questions at the Coliseum today and by all accounts the trapeze Miss Diamond was using had been tampered with. The early suspicions are cocaine solution on the mouth strap.' He checked his notes. 'If she had caught it, Miss Diamond would likely have fallen.'

'So we're looking for someone with knowledge of old Charlie. That should be easy. Did they check B Division?' Bain, the photographer, smirked. There was a titter of laughter.

Primrose coughed. 'They are looking for someone who had knowledge of Miss Diamond's act. And obviously access backstage.'

'Would they have needed to climb the rig then, to fit the mouth strap?' asked Mathers, leaning forwards.

'No,' he replied. 'The strap was taken up by a stagehand just before the second act began, and passed to Miss Diamond midway through her performance.'

'That doesn't explain where she's gone,' Donaldson said.

Primrose nodded. 'But I think it rules out an accident and cover-up by the theatre . . .' He let the thread hang.

Wilson frowned. 'Do you think she's been kidnapped?'

'That is one possibility. The other is that she twigged someone had tampered with her equipment and managed to escape herself.'

'But how?'

Primrose opened his palms. 'One of the performers has taken some notion that she stole his tiger suit. There was an incident that night with a tiger getting loose. How feasible that is . . .' There was general derision round the room.

Primrose swallowed. His palms felt clammy holding the yellow pad. He had rehearsed this last part with Stuttlegate at the Chief's insistence. 'But the more important question is *who* might be connected to this? Miss Diamond's disappearance may be linked to one or more deaths that occurred over the past two days.'

There was silence.

'On Friday, Olivier Smythe, corset maker by appointment to Queen Alexandra and also to Ebony Diamond, was found dead on his shop floor, wearing one of his own designs. It was not unusual for him to go corseted, but this one was laced so tight it had suffocated him.'

A few of the men swallowed loudly. Donaldson, the motorcyclist, looked at his muddy boots.

Primrose went on, 'The same night, just off Tottenham Court Road, a woman was killed. We don't know who she is yet but she was wearing items of Ebony Diamond's clothing.'

'So they knew each other?' Jenkins asked.

There were a few seconds of silence. Primrose continued. 'She was attacked from behind. The killer cut her throat. There was no –' he hesitated, 'follow-up. Not like the Ripper victims.' He sighed and rubbed his brow, then fished into his pocket and held out the small portcullis badge Stuttlegate had given him. 'This was found on the body.'

'Let me see that,' Donaldson leant forward. 'Holloway Gaol badge of honour? The one they get given if they've done a stint inside for the WSPU.'

Primrose nodded.

'So the murdered girl was a suffragette?'

'It would certainly look that way. Possibly one known to the authorities.'

Bain, who had been very still up to that moment, shifted his weight and eyed the camera bag at his feet, with its telecentric lens poking out. 'The authorities? Which authorities? Do you mean to suggest that the government might be bumping off members of the WS—'

'I mean to suggest nothing. You have images of Miss Diamond?'

Bain nodded. 'I looked them out.'

'What about the people she was acquainted with? Anyone in prison at the same time as her, anyone you saw her speak to in the exercise yard?'

'Anything we did take will be in the archives.'

'So we can start from there.'

Wilson stifled a yawn.

'I need someone to look into her other contacts: the club, the circus, the landlady. Wilson, perhaps you can take charge of that this afternoon? You look good and lively.' Wilson's face turned sour but he said nothing. Primrose turned back to Bain. 'How long is the range on that camera?'

'About thirty feet. Any more than that and you lose detail in the developing.'

'And did you do the mug shots or just the yard surveillance?'

'Yard surveillance.'

'Good, so hopefully no one will recognise you. Now, rumour has it that Christabel Pankhurst was in town on Thursday night. Mathers, can you make contact with the arresting officers in the Pankhurst conspiracy trial? It was

171

April this year when Miss Christabel disappeared. She's hiding out in Paris. Keep as close an eye as possible on any movements. I assume you have contacts in Paris?'

Mathers fixed him with a contemptuous look. 'Of course.'

'Keep an eye on the paper as well: *Votes for Women*. They've just launched another one, *The Suffragette*. Find out where Miss Christabel's filing her articles from.'

Primrose turned his attention to the younger officer, who was looking slightly anxious that he hadn't yet been dished a task. 'Robert Jenkins, I have a very special job for you.' Jenkins's cheeks had a rosy flush at the best of times. But what Primrose said next turned the young man's face the colour of beet.

Eighteen

Frankie stared at Jojo, the snake woman and the copper-haired boy for some time before any of them made a move. Finally Jojo gestured to her to take a seat. She scraped one of the chairs from the cabaret tables towards her and hesitated until Jojo sat down.

The snake woman continued to lean on the chair of the tied boy. 'Do you know why I let you in?' She turned her cool eyes on Frankie.

Frankie shook her head.

'First I think we'd both like to know who she is,' Jojo said. His voice had an indefinable gruff circus timbre, with notes of Lancashire, Birmingham, London.

'She came looking for Ebony.' The snake woman slid a hand into her silk pocket and pulled out a scrap which she tossed at Frankie. Frankie caught it, recognising her own calling card.

'How did you . . . ?' Frankie looked at the tied boy. 'You were in her dressing room.'

The boy kept his lips tightly shut.

'Is she here?' Frankie watched them each in turn, their faces ruined in the harsh light. The snake woman's make-up was fierce and thick. The boy had soft young cheeks but pointed features, halfway between cherub and rat. Up close his hair had lost its shocking flame and looked greasy and festering, his forehead was puckered as if he had all manner of things on the tip of his tongue he dared not say. The glare picked out patches of skin where Jojo's fur had thinned and flecked with grey. He looked keenly back at Frankie, then his brow knotted into a frown.

'No, she's not here. I think Millicent thought *you* might be able to tell *us* where she is.'

Frankie stared at the snake woman, trying to picture her with the name Millicent. Millicent stared back, then raised both of her eyebrows rudely in defiance.

'She was backstage last night,' the boy murmured, gesturing with his chin towards Frankie. He had a Northern Irish accent, Belfast perhaps. 'I saw her.'

Millicent grabbed him by the chin and forced his gaze into hers. 'You'll speak when you're spoken to. You've done enough damage.'

His green eyes blazed. 'Do you think it's my fault she got away?'

Jojo put his hand on the boy's knee. 'No one is blaming you.'

'Then why have you fucking tied me up?'

'Don't curse in front of our guest,' he said softly. 'She'll think we're savages.'

'I watched that sulky bitch for five days. I didn't take my eyes off her. Ask her.'

Frankie nodded. 'I saw him at the corset shop.'

'And in the street. And at the theatre,' the boy protested.

'What were you doing at the corsetier's?' Jojo asked Frankie.

'Interviewing Ebony. For an article.'

'So you're a journalist?' She saw him glance briefly around his chamber, the tatty curtains and the flaking paint. 'And you were at the Coliseum?'

Frankie nodded. 'When Ebony vanished. She was there too.'

The snake girl shifted on her feet. 'I knew the second I saw that so-called tiger that it was Ebony.' She looked down at the boy who was starting to squirm in his binding, then with a sigh reached down and loosened his cords. He shook his hands free and rubbed his wrists. As he leant forward Frankie heard his neck crack.

'What's your name?' she asked.

'Liam.' His neck crunched again and he sat back.

'How do you do?' she muttered. The boy repeated the phrase without feeling. Frankie looked back at Millicent. 'How did you know it was her? She done that before?'

'Lots of times. She used to do it for the Stork brothers.'

'He stole it from her,' said Jojo. 'That . . . whatever he's calling himself. Great Foucaud. Billy Grayson. He used to travel with The Storks as a labourer. Tent peg boy. Now look at him.'

'You could see though,' the snake girl took over; 'she

hasn't quite got the hindquarter movements right. Her back is crippled from the trapeze. She's been pushed too hard.' She flashed a glance at Jojo.

'Is that how you know her?' Frankie looked at Jojo. 'From the circus?'

He coughed, as if a memory had caught him off-guard, and nodded. 'Seven years ago. We made a pact to leave together. We weren't very happy with the contracts we had been given, so a number of us broke them, ran away, set up shop in London.' He suddenly looked self-consciously at the fur on the back of his hands and murmured, 'Most people run away with the circus. We ran from it.'

'They're not nice places for people like him.' Liam sat forward with an accusatory stare, as if Frankie herself might have been a purveyor of freak shows. Jojo caught his eye and he shrank back.

'No one from that world likes to see someone who looks like me in charge of his own business,' he said softly. 'That was why Ebony was different. She could have charged the Storks triple if she'd kept doing that tiger act. Imagine, a woman tiger-tamer, who can double as aerialiste. She was prized. Almost as good an earner as a dog-faced man.'

His hairy brow suddenly turned fully towards Frankie and she found herself flicking her eyes away, embarrassed. The cogs in her brain were starting to turn. She thought back to Ebony's words yesterday: 'I want folk to know I'm on the right side'. Could it be that something from her circus past had caught up with her? A big-top impresario, unhappy that an aerialiste and a sideshow exhibit had teamed up to escape? A woman unhappy with a decision she had made seven years ago?

Jojo's sharp eyes picked up on her expression. 'If you're thinking I might have somehow cajoled her into leaving with me, you're mistaken. Ebony believed in people rather than money. She made herself my star act. She was very happy here.' He held her gaze coldly. 'Make no mistake. I will find her.'

'And then what?' asked Frankie.

'And then I'll know she's safe.' His shoulders sagged, he shook his head and his hands fell into his lap.

No one spoke for a couple of minutes. The club's damp air was making Frankie uncomfortable. She rummaged in her jacket pocket and brought out the newspaper that had lain crumpled there since the day before when Ebony had thrust it at her. 'Do you know this girl? She was a friend of Ebony's.' Frankie leant across and handed him the grey pages.

'*Was?*' Jojo unfolded them and his hand moved to his furry chin.

The illustration was good, the likeness to Ebony Diamond exaggerated by the styling of the girl's hair. The artist had given her darkened eyes, generally smartened her up, souped up her deathly glamour.

Jojo passed the paper to Millicent.

Frankie went on. 'She was murdered on Thursday night and because of the clothing, the police and press thought it was Ebony. I saw her that afternoon at the shop with Smythe, so she and Ebony obviously knew each other. Did you know her?'

Millicent and Jojo shook their heads. Liam shrugged. 'I saw her at Smythe's. Just from outside, like.'

'What about Olivier Smythe, know him?'

'Of course.' Jojo handed back the paper. 'He made all her costumes.'

'Well, he's dead too.'

There was silence.

'Don't you read the papers?'

Jojo bristled, rubbing a furred hand across his brow. 'My wife won't let me, in case we're in the theatre reviews.'

'I knew,' Millicent cut in. 'But I read it was an accident.'

Frankie shook her head. 'I'm not so sure.'

'When did you last see Ebony?' Millicent asked.

'Yesterday, after they found Smythe. When I saw you the night before, you'd said she failed to turn up here. Any idea where she was that night?'

Jojo rapped one finger at a time across his knee, looking at the floor. 'That's why I hired Liam. To keep an eye on her.'

Liam looked repentant for the first time since Frankie had set eyes on him. 'I'm sorry I lost her. Honest to God I am.'

Jojo hesitated, casting his gaze on Frankie. 'If she's run somewhere, it's because she's frightened.'

'She ran away once before. With you,' Frankie countered.

'Entirely different.' He shook his head. 'She had no reason to run from me. I didn't have her on a tight contract or a forced routine. If she'd wanted out I would have been crushed, but I would have let her, wholeheartedly.' He paused. 'I'll pay Liam to help you find her.'

'I'm doing this for my paper.'

'Nevertheless . . .' He turned his palms up.

Liam perked up in his chair, pulled the cuffs of his jacket down and gave Frankie a good sweeping look up and down. The prospect of work had seemed to sharpen his interest.

Millicent cut in. 'I knew some of her habits; I might be able to help.'

Jojo and Liam turned to stare at her. Frankie couldn't work out if Jojo was appraising her capabilities or her trust.

She shrugged sharply. 'And I'm a woman.'

'What's that got to do with it?' Liam spat. She glared at him and he immediately looked penitent.

'Woman's instinct,' she replied.

Frankie held up a palm. 'Hold on, who says I want any help? This is my story.' She turned and saw the desperation in Jojo's eyes then shook her head. 'Fine.'

The monkey hopped back onto Jojo's lap, withdrew a clay pipe from his pocket and began to chew on it. Jojo looked down with fondness, stroked its tail and swallowed. 'If it makes any difference, there were cabinet ministers came down here. They knew her. They knew where to find her.'

An image flashed through Frankie's head; top hats in the mist. 'Would the government have the nerve to try and murder a high-profile suffragette?'

'Depends what she had in store for them,' Millicent said quietly.

'Or what she had on them,' Frankie mused.

The silence returned. The air hung thick.

179

Nineteen

Frankie pulled her jacket in close as the wind whipped up a cluster of leaves round the bench. Soho Square was dark, poorly lit by four streetlamps, one in each corner, casting a murky glow on the figures huddled in the shadows conducting deals, muttering close to the bushes. From somewhere behind the buildings came the cry of squabbling cats.

She passed the penny cigar to Millicent and watched as she drew hungrily on it, letting the smoke out through her nostrils in two long stripes, the way Frankie's father used to. Liam's eyes followed the trail. Millicent noticed and lowered the cigar.

'You're not old enough to smoke.'

He shrugged and kicked the dirt. After a few seconds' foraging he picked up a discarded cigarette butt and struck a match off his shoe.

Millicent coughed and handed the cigar to Frankie, her gown flapping at the sleeve; she had hardy skin and didn't seem to feel the cold. 'When it's a toss-up between food and smoke, the latter always staves off hunger longer.'

Frankie scowled. She had wanted to spend the penny they'd cobbled together on half a meat pie or one of the curled pretzels from the Jewish bread stall.

'Well,' Millicent went on, arranging her elaborate folds of silk, 'Jojo seems to think she's run away out of fear. It wouldn't really have been like Ebony to just vanish without something spooking her first.' She looked at Frankie.

'It wasn't my fault,' Frankie started to protest. 'I tried to do her a favour . . .'

'You might have made a lucky escape yourself. If that article you wrote had actually been printed . . .'

Frankie tossed the locks of her fringe out of her eyes dismissively. 'Don't see why they would come after me.'

'Murder, Miss George.' Millicent suddenly turned on her. 'When people commit murder they don't appreciate being tracked down, do they?' The contrast of her wispy blonde hair and those hard kohl-edged eyes made Frankie sit up straighter. Shrouded in silver smoke she was like Lewis Carroll's wise caterpillar. Frankie desperately hoped there was no snake in her pocket tonight.

They sat in silence for a few minutes. Eventually Frankie said, 'Anyone ever come into Jojo's that took against Ebony? Anyone from that circus lot whose goats she and Jojo got when the pair of them ran off? What were they called, the Stork Brothers? Did she have any trapeze rivals?'

'The Storks are long gone. They moved to Germany,' said Millicent.

'And she didn't have rivals,' Liam said, flicking the cigarette butt back onto the ground where it sparked the dirt.

'She must have done.'

He shrugged. 'She wasn't famous enough to compete with the ones on at the big halls and anyone else would be too scared of Jojo. And me.'

Frankie made the mistake of smiling, more at the audacity of his boasting than the notion of his strength, but his eyes flashed angrily.

'You think that's funny?' he growled. 'I knew it as soon as I saw you. Italian, aren't you? You're all the same. Greased up with your own opinions of yourselves. You think I'm stupid, don't you, just because I'm wee?'

Frankie began to shake her head.

'Well, I wouldn't push it too far. *Va bene*?' She wanted to laugh again, this time at his terrible accent but she didn't dare. 'Look, I'm only doing this because Jojo . . .'

'Asked you to, I know. I'm only letting you because I thought you might be useful, so watch your tongue.'

Millicent's voice came quietly out of the night. 'Aren't we trying to make sure Ebony's not come to any harm?'

Frankie sat back on the bench, feeling Liam's little pinprick eyes on her. She turned to Millicent. 'How d'you get to know that lot anyway?'

Millicent laughed a high tinkle. 'Oh, it's a long story.'

Frankie waited for her to elaborate but instead she glanced

down at Frankie's arms, jittering on her lap, making the cigar between her fingers dance. 'Are you cold?'

With a stubbornness that felt comfortingly familiar, Frankie shook her head and continued to look expectant.

Millicent sighed. 'I don't see what difference it makes.'

'I need to know whether I can trust you.'

She reached for the cigar again and Frankie relinquished it after a last pull of her own. 'All right. When I came back from Cairo, I didn't know anyone, except for an art student who had a room near Barons Court. And my family, of course, but they had cut me off.' She laughed a little nervously and waved her hand again.

'I guessed you weren't born Salome.'

'Neither was Maud Allen and she danced the seven veils for the Prince of Wales. Three shillings. Her costume, not her fee.' She scrutinised Frankie's face as she said it and Frankie recognised the look. Scouting for signs of Sapphism. Tell a titillating tale and wait for the blush to come. Well, she wasn't going to give her that.

'What were you doing in Cairo?'

'Now that really is too long a story.' Millicent's lips straightened into a brittle smile. 'Anyway, Maud was doing this seven veils dance at the time I got back, stripped down to her oyster shells. And we decided, my friend and I, that with some careful plastering we could come up with something just as shocking. John the Baptist, a head on a plate. A tableau vivant. I touted it to the Cyder Cellar but they weren't inter-ested, then a couple of other gaffs round the Strand, and finally Jojo. I can dance better than Maud anyway, I learned how to copy the ghawazee girls in Cairo. I don't think she's ever set foot beyond Canada or England. And I have a pet snake.' Her smile turned lopsided and sad. 'Mind you, I can't be that great because she's performing at the Royal Opera House and I'm here.' She gestured behind her, then her gaze dropped. 'It was Ebony who told him to take me. She might have had a tongue like a whip, but she knew hunger when she saw it. So long as you were down on your luck, Ebony Diamond would be the best friend you ever had. Don't mistake me, her suffragetting wasn't for everyone, but she did a lot of good. She thought she was doing a lot of good, anyway.'

'When did all this happen?'

'About six months ago. Just before she went into prison the first time.'

'And when did you meet him?' Frankie nodded towards Liam.

'Last week.'

Liam met her eye. 'No one's supposed to know I exist.'

Frankie just about managed to hold her tongue. 'What about your family?'

Millicent's mouth tightened. 'I don't like to talk about them.'

Frankie noticed she had puffed the cigar down to an inch and a half. From the look of her she was wasting away, but she didn't have the same hunger in her eyes that people who were genuinely starving had, no matter what she said. Frankie wondered if she was one of those girls striving after the new figure, whose cupboards were full, but only ate when they fancied.

'Well, my old man's a costermonger up Tottenham and my mother takes in laundry.' She raised her eyebrows. Millicent looked away as if the very idea of modest living embarrassed her, and busied herself picking at a spot on her gown. Up close in patches it was stained a faint yellow, like tinges of tobacco or rust. Some threads were missing from the flower pattern. It wasn't as fine as it had first looked. Her slight hands reminded Frankie of white asparagus, firm skinned but limp.

'And you're sure Jojo's not got her hiding in there? Stashed?'

'Why would he?'

Frankie shrugged.

'Jojo adored Ebony. But he was telling the truth. If she'd wanted to go, I mean really wanted to, he'd have let her.' Millicent tossed the cigar butt into the dirt.

'But that night I saw you. You said she hadn't been turning up.'

'She hadn't. Ever since the last time she came out of prison, she started missing odd nights. Tuesday was traditionally her night off for suffragette meetings. Jojo was all right with her missing one night a week. He believes in the women's cause. Or his wife does anyway; Eloise, that's the two-headed chanteuse. But after a while it got more erratic. A Thursday here, a Sunday there. Fridays, Saturdays. Jojo started putting pressure on me to fill the gaps. At first I didn't mind, to be honest. I liked having the chance to close the show. In fact, half of me thought in my vanity that Ebony might be bunking off nights to give me a chance. It's the sort of thing she might do. But it got more frequent. I couldn't plan anything in case I was called in on my night off.'

'And then he brought me in to keep watch on her,' Liam chipped in.

'And what did you notice?'

Liam shrugged. 'I didn't make it inside her bedchamber.'

'I wasn't asking that. Where did she go? On these nights off?'

He chewed his lip, and looked like he was aware that for just a fraction of a second he had some wonderful power he could wield over them. 'She spent a lot of time at that corset shop. I didn't go in. But there's only two doors. I kept watch on both of them.'

'Smythe's,' Frankie said softly. She couldn't get the image of those men in their top hats out of her head. It kept returning.

Millicent leant forward on the bench. 'You know you get a feeling? Mentalists would call it a sixth sense. The past couple of weeks, there was something going on. She wasn't right in the head. She was becoming fatalistic, wouldn't tell anyone where she was going. She was always looking over her shoulder and if you came up behind her, woe betide you. I saw her scream at Lizzy – the woman who does the door – about the ears, because she told her what the suffragettes were doing was wrong. It would never help a woman like Lizzy, women who were never going to own property, or settle, or lead a normal life.' She looked Frankie square in the face, her eyes blunt. Her frame was slender, but there was a confrontational edge stacked in her. She was an odd woman who would have looked as out of place at a society dinner as she did just now, perched in Soho Square just beyond St Barnabas's house for troubled women, with her stained expensive gown waving in the breeze.

'What about the government?' Liam spoke up. 'They'd have good reason to want her out of the way.'

Frankie clocked his face again, the watery gold pallor. He had stories in there he wasn't telling either. 'That's something we have to consider.'

'You know how dangerous that could be?' Millicent asked.

Frankie couldn't work out if the question was a challenge or a warning. She suddenly became aware that their eyes were fixed on her, and felt a cold vulnerability along with a sharp surge of nerves at finding herself in charge of something.

'You say Ebony'd been missing nights at Jojo's,' she said briskly. 'Well I know she wasn't at the suffragette smash last night because she wasn't arrested. I also know she was scared – both times I saw her. Two of her friends are dead, from the same place.' She suddenly stood up and folded her lapels in towards her throat, against the breeze. She had made up her mind. 'Come on, I know someone who might be able to help us.' The bells from St Patrick's began to chime hollow and deep.

'Who?' asked Millicent.

'You'll find out. On the way I'll teach you how to hop a tube fare.'

Liam met her eye with a scornful twinkle.

'I meant her.' She nodded at Millicent.

'I already know how to do that,' Millicent said curtly, raising the silk hem of her gown above the mud.

As the pavement narrowed towards Tottenham Court Road underground station, Liam fell behind and Frankie found herself walking abreast with Millicent. She caught sight of them both in a blackened shop window and was startled for a moment by the odd burlesque of a respectable couple they made. Her suit and Millicent's dress, watery in the reflection. Millicent was rambling on. 'I suppose I'd better call you Frankie. It suits you better than Francesca and far better than Miss George.'

Frankie sniffed briskly, 'Fine by me.'

'And you can call me Milly by the way. Millicent sounds like an old cobwebbed aunt you keep in a drawer. And no one ever called me that. Except Jojo. And my mother.'

Twenty

Frankie was not surprised to see a new parlourmaid at the door to Twinkle's flat. Her worried face peeped out from under a white bonnet, framed by dark curls. From down the hall came a wailing sound, a rising and falling, like a dog singing opera.

'I'm not sure she should have guests,' the girl said. 'She's been like this since last night. Something about the papers.'

Frankie cursed under her breath. The girl's arm was poised between the door and the frame and Frankie gently took her by the slim wrist and prised a path inside.

'Please, miss,' the maid cried. 'Who should I announce?'

Frankie noticed with a cringe that as they passed Liam winked saucily at the maid.

She barged open the boudoir's frosted doors, sending them cracking into the wall. Twinkle was sitting upright in her fur-covered bed, a satin turban binding her steel curls to her head. In her fleshy hands she brandished a copy of the *Evening*

Gazette, flapping it about, only pausing to point at chunks of text here and there. Her face was coated in a glaze of cold cream like the wet finish on a ham. In the couple of days since Frankie had been there last, she had acquired a huge ginger tomcat who sat on the bed regarding the spectacle squarely with his fat face. Frankie stood appalled while Milly's eyes roamed round the paintings and sketches covering the walls. She saw Liam extend a wily hand towards the paste jewels on the bedside table and slapped him back.

'I was just looking,' he hissed.

Twinkle didn't notice. She was mid-soliloquy. 'And there will be no recompense. None. He has even had a letter printed under his name, ugly name, Fox-Pitt, pointing out the errors in the write-up of Lady Barclay's masquerade. My chance, my chance to bring him to heel, and a mockery is made. Meanwhile Polly C. sits up there on the ladies' page like daughter of the duchess, bragging about her own eau de toilette . . .' She stopped in her tracks. The muscles in her brow seized into a frown as she hooked her eyes onto Frankie. 'I ought to spank your bottom,' came her low growl. 'But something tells me your sort would like that.'

'Twinkle, I can explain everything.'

'The Aeolian Orchestrion? That's what I get, is it? Replacing my column? The Aeolian Orchestrion? Let's try wearing one of those for winter fashions, shall we? Parading Rotten Row in the latest flattering fabric of wood and piano keys. I ought to strap you into the Aeolian Orchestrion and hope it drums some sense into you.'

'I can explain.'

'No need to, that grotty Stark man paid me a visit.'

'Mr Stark? Came here?' Frankie couldn't conceal her surprise.

'He thinks I should have you back as my diarist, I don't know what you did to bribe him,' she spat. 'I know what happened. You and your deviant fantasies got the better of you over that little trapeze artist.' Frankie saw Milly out of the corner of her eye, looking at the ground.

'Twinkle, Ebony Diamond's disappeared. Vanished.'

Twinkle thrust the paper out as if it were a dagger. 'Do you think I am blind? Do you? Do you think I don't have eyes in my head, or hands to turn the page? I do read the paper. It seems either she tricked that nasty little theatre man or he tricked her, none of them can agree.' She waggled a finger. 'It makes it even worse because now she's disappeared what was the bloody point in writing a portrait piece about her in the first place? Try copying the invisible woman's outfits.'

Frankie snatched the rag off Twinkle and scrunched through the pages. Inside the cover was a long thin article with Teddy Hawkins's byline below it. 'Suffragette in Mystery Kidnapping.' She read aloud, '"Ebony Diamond, once hunger-striker of the notorious WSPU dramatically disappeared in the middle of her act at the London Coliseum on Friday night. Eye-witnesses and sources at the theatre, quoted on the grounds of strict anonymity, say that the kidnapping was a revenge attack by Coliseum impresario

Oswald Stoll, for monies she owed him, lent to purchase costumes." Is that what he thinks? Idiot.' She read on. '"This strikes a further black mark against Stoll who has already seen two showgirls perish on stage, one under the feet of an elephant, the other thrown from a horse."' Blood began to simmer in Frankie's temples. 'How dare he tell me my stories aren't properly written and then publish this?'

Twinkle shrugged, 'No secret that Stark has never liked Oswald Stoll.'

Frankie let out a grunt of frustration.

'Maybe she killed herself, and they covered it up.' Twinkle shrugged again. 'Showgirls and laudanum go together like gin and tonic.'

Frankie ignored her. 'What about the others?'

'There's a copy of *The Times* in the hall. That new maid bought it by mistake.'

Frankie left the room for a second and came back with the paper hanging open. 'Tragic accident at the Coliseum. Page two. Ebony Diamond savaged to death by tiger. Bones found.'

'*Pall Mall Gazette*'s somewhere,' Twinkle rummaged among the furs. Eventually she gave a groan and yanked it out from under her buttocks. Frankie took it and began rifling through. The pages were still warm.

'Page four. Suffragette Stunt Girl Mysteriously Disappears. Oswald Stoll looking like he's in hot water. Murdered her and hid the body. This is all wrong. None of them were there, none of them saw what I did.'

Milly leaned over her. There was a picture of Ebony in soft focus, sitting upright and smiling on her trapeze. 'That's an old one,' Milly said gently. 'Comes from the Stork Brothers days.'

Twinkle, who had not yet acknowledged the two other people in the room, now peered closely at Milly with the same scrutiny she might have given to a specimen in a glass jar. She raised her eyes up and down the loose gown, pausing on the stains, then looked into Milly's chill blue eyes. 'Who's Scheherazade?'

Milly pressed a fine-boned hand into Twinkle's gnarled one. 'Millicent Barton.' She smiled. 'Also known as Salome but only when I'm performing. Apologies for the stage get-up. I've just come from rehearsal.' The charm worked. Twinkle looked at her curiously, as if she were having some kind of hubble-bubble pipe effect.

'A showgirl? Another? Pussycat must be making a collection.' She straightened herself, breathed out calmly and smiled, as if weighing up Milly's value like jewels in a pawn shop.

'She's from Jojo's; she knew Ebony. And,' Frankie grabbed a chair from near the window, 'that's why we're here.'

As she pulled it close to the bed, Twinkle looked up, latched eyes on Liam and let out a yelp. 'A man, in my bedchamber. Get him out, shoo!'

'Hardly a man,' Frankie muttered. 'May I introduce Liam?'

Liam, who had been busy taunting the cat with a piece of ribbon, held off for enough time to open his mouth and reveal a browning grin. He took off his cap. 'Pleased to meet you, ma'am.'

It was too late. The teeth had done their work. 'Absolutely not. No. He has to go.'

His face fell. Violence looked to be bubbling beneath his skin.

'He's my assistant. He's learning phonography so I have to take him everywhere.'

Twinkle looked unconvinced. 'Couldn't Mr Stark afford to get him some new teeth? Fleet Street's full of dentists.'

Liam looked on the verge of wresting the cat's orange tail off.

'Actually he's our bodyguard,' Frankie said. 'Makes us fit in, you know, in the rougher parts of town. You said yourself Ebony Diamond was a circus girl. Can't he stay? Please.'

Twinkle sighed as if Frankie had just asked her to recite the book of Genesis. She fuddled with her bed furs and wouldn't look at Liam. 'He can sit in the parlour. Tell him to ask that maid, what's-her-name, Alice to bring him some tea. Nicely.'

Liam let out a bullish breath then tossed the ribbon to the floor and went out through the double doors.

Frankie pointed Milly to the chair and braced herself as she lowered her rear onto the furs. 'This is important, Twinkle. That night I last saw you, you remember we were talking about Smythe's?'

Twinkle scowled. 'That's funny, I thought we were talking about Turkish baths for my column but I've already been proven wrong on that.'

'Twinkle, please . . .' Frankie pulled out her pocket-watch. It was getting late. She flicked a lock of hair out of her face and went on. 'I told you I'd seen some men going in there. Men in top hats, and you said that there was something about that place, something strange.'

Twinkle held up a hand. 'I said nothing of the sort.'

'You said that I might find out something I wished I hadn't.'

'That's not to say it's anything strange.'

'I don't have time for games. That night there was a suffragette demonstration down the street. The next morning Olivier Smythe was dead. Police say it was an accident. At least we know they can't say that about the girl wearing Ebony Diamond's clothes who had her throat cut that same night, just outside the Rising Sun.'

Twinkle looked uneasy. The colour had drained from her cheeks and her eyes had hollowed. 'I read about that girl. It's a hazard of the job.' She looked around her at the paintings and fabrics, the spoils of her own career.

Frankie shook her head. 'No, Twinkle, she wasn't a punk, she worked for Smythe. I saw her in there that very day. She told me where to go looking for Ebony. She knew her. Now I want to know, and you're going to tell me, what goes on in that corset shop?'

Twinkle looked stubbornly down at her enormous cat. At last she closed one languorous eye and said, 'It's an underwear maker's, Frankie. If it's a conspiracy you're after, you're looking in the wrong place.'

'What were thirteen men doing going in there after hours? And what do you mean, conspiracy?'

'How am I to know? Perhaps they rent the room above it for bridge? If you want to know what I think . . .' she slowly trailed off. 'No, of course you don't.' She turned to Milly. 'I give Puss my opinion every time she drops by, but she very seldom listens.'

Milly made a weak effort at a smile. 'Miss . . .'

'Twinkle.' She fluttered her hand.

'Very well. Miss . . . Twinkle. I know it might seem as if Ebony Diamond has run away from a debt, or had a fight with a theatre man. That seems to be the consensus of a few people I know. She had an arrogant streak. But she was not a blackmailing, squabbling showgirl. A woman who starves herself for a cause doesn't get into petty disputes with theatre men. There's too much at stake.'

Twinkle was silent for a long time, stroking the cat.

Frankie spied out of the corner of her eye a half-drunk gin bottle on the bedside table and dragged it towards her. She fumbled in a nearby cabinet until she found three mismatching frosted glasses, then poured them each a generous round.

Twinkle knocked hers back in one. 'I'm willing to forgive,' she said huskily, 'our mutual friend's carelessness over the column I write with her. You know about that, of course.'

Milly looked confused. Frankie bit her tongue and gulped her gin. She noticed Milly was pecking at hers like a bird, just wetting her lips.

'But if I were you, I wouldn't be round at the door of . . .'

she paused, 'an old society girl asking stupid questions about corset shops. It seems to me there's a reason Teddy Hawkins is covering the big stories and you're not.'

'Oh leave it, Twinkle, he just makes it up.'

'If you watched your tongue a bit more you might get further. Maybe he makes it up better than you. You can't blame every failure on being a woman. I didn't.'

'That's entirely different.'

'Use your head, Frankie. You're supposed to be a journalist. Who has the resourcefulness, the weapons, the opportunity and the militancy to do away with someone getting in their way?'

Frankie carefully put down her gin glass on the bedside table and looked shiftily at Milly.

Twinkle rolled her whole head, swaying the turban precariously. 'Where do seamstresses meet showgirls? Buckingham Palace?' She gave another of her weary sighs, reached into her bedside table and grunted as she rooted around, coming back with a pair of pince-nez and a stack of papers.

'They're in here somewhere.' She rumpled through a heap of newspapers, tossing some of them aside. The cat looked as if it was thinking about making a play for them but either it knew where its bread was buttered or considered the effort too great. Eventually she found what she was after.

'Yes. Here. Isabel Kelley, broke into Kinnaird Hall, Dundee, via a skylight. 1909. Wonder where Miss Diamond acquired her Albert Hall idea. Emily Wilding Davison – she's one to watch out for – broke into Big Ben on the night of the census. A government building, Puss. Where they have guards on standby to watch out for those dynamite-wielding Irish like your little friend out there.'

'He's . . .'

Twinkle cut her off. 'Alice Paul, hid on the roof of St Andrew's hall in freezing rain. Miss Philips, broke into an organ, two of them hid on top of Bingley Hall in Birmingham and hacked slates off the roof to throw at Asquith. These are dangerous women, Puss. They have money, they have resources, they have wherewithal. To kill. To kidnap. To make someone disappear.'

Milly breathed in, and when she breathed out she said the word that was on all their tongues, soft and quiet as if it were a betrayal even to whisper it. 'Suffragettes?'

'But why?' said Frankie. 'Why would they murder one of their own members?'

'I don't know. They're not going to embroider it on a banner, are they?'

Frankie didn't answer, thinking instead of the altercation at the Brook Street crossroads, her dressing down from Ebony Diamond, the cartoon. Coming to blows with the women's movement again; but this time it wasn't just mockery, it was accusation. Murder, bumping off and kidnapping dissenters. Once she jumped down that rabbit hole there was no going back. And they would string her up like a mutinous sailor if she was wrong.

They sipped their gin in silence for a few moments. Milly asked whether she might be directed to a bathroom. Frankie watched her leave, feeling the gin sinking to her stomach and wondering if she should drink some water. When the door closed she turned back to Twinkle. 'But the corset shop,' she began again. 'I know there's . . .'

Twinkle cut her off with a croak that had none of her high drama in it. 'The Barclay-Evanses.'

Frankie frowned. 'Pardon?'

'The Barclay-Evanses. They'll be able to help.'

'Who are they?'

'He's Evans, an ex-colonel, and she's Barclay, a law graduate who can't practise.'

'And what have they got to do with anything?'

Twinkle stared at her like she was simple. 'They're suffragettes. Or they were until this week. There's been some kind of split in the ranks; you can ask them about it when we get there. And before you open your mouth again, don't ask how I know them. Just don't. Clear?' She fumbled among the mass of trinkets on her bedside table until she came to a little bell. 'Right, what is that new girl's name again? I've forgotten already. I'll get her to send a telegram.'

Twenty-One

The front door had been deadlocked from the inside. Primrose felt for his key with a pang of hurt. It was true there were burglaries from time to time in the neighbourhood, but there was a latch. Surely Clara didn't feel threatened enough in her own home to deadlock the door? She must have done it on purpose. Swallowing the sting in his throat, he unlocked it, pushing it open with as much enthusiasm as he could manage.

'Darling. Clara, I'm back.'

There was no answer. The hall was dark, the gaslights off. The grandfather clock chimed quarter past eleven as he shut the door. The air was cold, there was no delicious scent of cooking. He gingerly turned the doorknob to the small parlour.

She sat in a rocking chair by the fire, her head drooped against her chest, a pair of knitting needles on her knee lolling down to a ball of blue wool that rested against her ankles. A little bonnet, far too small for a newborn baby, was taking shape on her lap. Laid out on the armrest were other minuscule items of clothing; little white knitted gowns and stockings as slim as first carrots. Primrose swallowed looking at them.

The room was thick with warmth compared to the hall, but the fire had died down to a mass of black ash and jewelled embers. He dropped his briefcase and crossed to the coal scuttle, scooping up a handful of lumps to toss around the bright ash.

Clara sat up with a start and looked blankly around the room, then down at the little bonnet on her lap. Seeing Primrose she frowned, confused.

'Freddie.' He loved her voice, the softness of it. Though it could be sharp too when she wanted it to be.

'Yes, I do come home sometimes.' He forced a woeful smile.

'I must have fallen asleep.'

He took off his overcoat and reached out a hand, trying not to look at the knitting. She took it between both of her small palms, warm as kittens. Her mouth opened into a yawn. He wanted to grasp her, nestle his cold head against her warm shoulder but she looked so peaceful.

'They've put me on a murder case.'

Clara looked puzzled rather than surprised. 'Oh? I thought you'd changed division.'

'Well, it's connected to a suffragette. It might be. Complicated really.'

She nodded and yawned again. He hitched up his trousers and sat on the small couch facing the fire. He wanted to talk about something other than work, but it seemed there was nothing left in his head to think of; all had been drowned in case files and arson and window-smashing the past month.

'Chief's been looking for a way into them for ages. Now it seems he has his chance. If only he wasn't so brazen about it. I don't know what to say to the men.'

'What do they think?'

'Oh, they realise. They must do. Most of them are from Special.'

'Would I know any of them?'

He rubbed his forehead. 'Probably not. I shouldn't really be talking about it. I'm just cautious—' he let the words die out in his mouth. Her watching eyes rekindled them. 'Stirring up trouble with a group who already have volatile feelings towards us. If this woman was some kind of liability, some kind of deserter . . . Perhaps. I don't know.'

'You could try asking them yourself.' She cocked her head as if searching for a way into his thoughts. 'Take a trip to their headquarters. A peaceful one, mind. See what they know.'

'We have surveillance.'

Clara rolled her eyes. 'Because that's the way to make them cooperate?' She watched him. He tried not to give anything away, but could tell she saw through his expression. Trying to get an idea like that past Stuttlegate, who preferred to go in barrels ablaze, would be like trying to get a crooked sixpence past an expert minter.

'There is this man,' he began, 'in Pentonville, that the Chief thinks might be able to help.'

Clara narrowed one eye. 'A man?'

'He's a suffragette supporter.'

She shook her head, then stretched out her legs and got up from the chair, folding away her knitting. 'I'll fetch a plate for you.'

He clasped her waist as she passed him. 'No, don't. Stay a while.' He tugged her gently onto his knee. The shawl round her shoulders smelled of the kitchen.

'You're going to interview a man before you go to suffragette headquarters because you think he'll be more likely to play turncoat?'

'I shouldn't be talking about it.' Primrose clamped shut his mouth and looked away.

'Have you eaten?'

'The usual rubbish.'

'I can tell. Cockles, was it?' She retreated from his breath.

They sat for a while with an awkwardness Primrose had not felt since their wedding, when they first bought the small house in Camberwell. He cast his eye round the room, the neat clean collection of furniture, the humble bureau and the stiff couch, a gift from his family. His gaze landed on the knitting on the armrest and she caught him, the too-small bonnet and stockings. 'It's for the parish.'

'I know.'

'They need it as much as the ones that live. You can't go to God without a stitch on.'

He said nothing.

She stood up. 'I'll fetch your plate.'

As she reached the door jamb she paused, hanging the door half open. A rush of the hall's cold air flooded in like an unwelcome guest. 'It was a boy, you know.'

Primrose looked up sharply.

'My sister's. I didn't think you'd ask.' She smiled a little sadly. 'She had a baby boy. Healthy and bonny.'

Twenty-Two

Frankie hunkered her shoulders into her jacket as the carriage rattled towards Maida Vale. Under her bottom she was aware of the raffia pressure of a nosebag, while up above, Liam's heels rhythmically kicked the roof of the cabin in protest at being made to ride on top with the cabbie and the wind. She looked jealously at Milly who had borrowed a mink coat from Twinkle's slaughterhouse collection, hanging with paws and tails. On the other side of her, crammed into the open-fronted carriage sat Twinkle, her feet bound by a pair of Russian boots and a skirt that hobbled her legs together. The fog was so thick they could barely see beyond the length of their own arms; streetlamps were balls of orange mist in a moonless night. The horse crept carefully, placing one hoof after the other.

The cabbie stopped short and called the name of the street down to them. Twinkle grunted and thrust a fistful of coins up over the roof, at the same time making a great fuss of stepping onto the pavement. Liam jumped down, landing nimbly on both feet.

'Come on, haven't got all night.' Twinkle waddled them to the front door like a goose. It was only the second time Frankie had seen her outside her boudoir. She looked faintly ridiculous in outdoor clothing, the way a pet might look dressed as a human.

The Barclay-Evanses lived on the ground floor of a block of flats identical to Twinkle's in all but the garish colour. A maid, nonplussed at being called to duty so late in the evening, showed them to a parlour where a fire sputtered behind an embroidered screen. The room was furnished with fine-legged settees and trinkets from the east; fans, elephant tusks and a Turkish water pipe, with tubes coiled around its glass dome like snakes. Frankie saw Milly eyeing it up, while Twinkle busied herself depositing Liam into the custody of the maid. She had tried to insist he use the tradesman's entrance but he doggedly refused. For the first time Frankie saw behind his eyes a wounded look underneath the bravado. 'He's taking notes—' she began.

He held up his chin and winked. 'I'll keep guard outside. Don't you worry about me.'

In the bay window of the lounge a man with a solid figure was waiting, his belly thrust proudly in front of him. Though he was only wearing tweeds he carried the look of someone in uniform. His wife, standing by the fire, matched him in height. They both shared the same kind of soft face, flesh in their cheeks and chins that had grown plump and rosy with age, noses and eyes that had sharpened.

They made their introductions and invited the trio to sit while the maid poured black tea. 'Don't mind our little habits.' Mrs Barclay-Evans gave a half-hearted stab at humility. 'We've travelled around a bit.'

Twinkle beamed. Frankie tried not to think of how the three might know each other.

An awkward silence spread as they sipped the strong brew and Frankie only then began to realise how tired she was, the strangeness of the night before closing in. Her head felt steeped in treacle, her brain all clogged. She found the Major's low voice far too soporific and had to shake herself to concentrate as he gently probed, 'Do you know if your girl is Peth or Pank?'

Frankie and Milly cast glances at each other.

'Don't look at me,' said Twinkle, stirring sugar through her tea while not very subtly scanning the room for a liquor cabinet.

Mrs Barclay-Evans explained. 'When the WSPU split last week, they divided themselves into Pankhurst supporters and Pethick-Lawrences. We're Peth, by the way.'

The name stirred in Frankie's head. She remembered seeing the name in the newspapers but had never paid it much attention.

'The Pethick-Lawrences were kicked out of the organisation this week – Panks might dispute "kicked out", but that's the size of it – for refusing to go along with the new militancy.'

Milly, who had been discreetly picking the sides of her

fingernails, stopped suddenly and leaned forward. 'The "new" militancy? What was wrong with the old militancy?'

'Not violent enough.' The Major picked up his cup. Silence hung and he went on. 'Christabel Pankhurst – I don't know if you know, but she's hiding in Paris under an arrest warrant at the moment – well, she snuck back to London last week to a meeting to unveil new plans, now the Conciliation Bill's officially kaput.' He paused to slurp his tea.

'What were the new plans?' Milly asked, a note of impatience hovering in her tone.

He hesitated. 'Not something we could approve.'

'Window smashing?' asked Frankie.

'Arson.' Mrs Barclay-Evans, noticing Frankie fumbling in her pockets, passed her a sleek fountain pen.

'Arson?' The word hovered.

'Do you want to start at the beginning?' Frankie asked. 'We'd like to know as much as we can about the suffragettes.'

The Major and his wife exchanged a glance. At last Mrs Barclay-Evans said, 'It depends how far back you want to go?'

'Anything that can help us make sense of what Ebony Diamond might be running from.'

'It's hard to pinpoint exactly when the beginning was.' Mrs Barclay-Evans eased herself down onto a chaise longue in the window. 'I suppose John Stuart Mill and Richard Pankhurst were important once. Ironic really, those men, back in the day. Well, I mean you could trace it back to Mary

Wollstonecraft. Oh dear, you don't recognise any of these names, do you?'

Frankie shook her head politely, though her insides prickled.

'It doesn't matter, really. There have been official branches campaigning for women's suffrage since before you were born. Before I was born. Not Nigel though,' she added with a teasing smile. No one laughed and she coughed, embarrassed. 'But the militancy, the violent action, started with the Women's Social and Political Union, the WSPU. You know that, don't you?' She could see Frankie nodding and went on, encouraged.

'They started out travelling round street corners and fairgrounds, speaking, handing out pamphlets. That could have been where they met Miss Diamond. They disrupted the odd meeting but nothing notable. A couple of years passed like this, then Christabel and a woman called Annie Kenney decided to get themselves thrown in prison.'

'For the publicity,' her husband added.

'Not just the publicity. They wanted people, they still want people, to know how serious they are, that being voteless is so thoroughly intolerable you might as well be incarcerated. Disrupting a meeting wasn't enough to end up in gaol back then. Christabel had to spit at a police officer. I had to slap the cheek of one once; I did it lightly, mind. He asked for my lapel badge as a souvenir.' She smiled. 'They started in Manchester but came to London about six years ago . . . But you're not interested in that, are you? You want to know what might have gone wrong. Well, the first split in the union came just after that London move.'

Frankie stopped scribbling. 'What are the government doing all this time?'

Major Barclay-Evans raised an eyebrow. 'Standing firm. Asquith didn't come to power until a couple of years ago, but the party have always toed the same line. Do you know, he says he will resign if women are given votes?'

Mrs Barclay-Evans put her spoon down. 'So on we went, meetings, rallies. I remember once the crowd threw live mice at Christabel. We'd march in deputations to Parliament, rush to the lobby. We'd get arrested for this, of course. That was the point.'

'Arrested for lobbying Parliament.' Twinkle raised an eyebrow. 'And to think, it's not that difficult really to get close to a politician.' The corners of her mouth curled into a smile. Frankie shot her a look. Mrs Barclay-Evans shifted stiffly and Frankie wondered again what had brought them to know one another.

'So, the first split,' Frankie scuffed the nib of the pen against her pad.

'Yes,' Mrs Barclay-Evans blinked, aware she was dawdling. 'Bills were being raised by the government and talked out. We were busy chaining ourselves to the ladies' gallery, hiding in cupboards, getting arrested. But then in the middle of this came the suggestion that we should have a conference. Vote for a new committee. Well, Christabel and her mother, Mrs Pankhurst, will tell you that they didn't like this idea because they didn't want to waste time canvassing for votes from their peers when they could be fighting the cause. But whether you believe them or just think they wanted to keep control over the movement,' she shrugged, 'they set up as autocrats. And at the time, I really think the majority of us believed that was the best solution. But a group of women objected and broke away to form the Women's Freedom League, that's Teresa Billington-Grieg's organisation by the way, they are non-violent militants.'

'Are these the suffragists?' Milly asked.

Frankie shook her head. 'They're all suffragists. It just means campaigning for a vote. But back a bit, are they autocrats, the Pankhursts, do they essentially control the suffragettes, undemocratically?'

'Yes.'

Milly cut in. 'Isn't the problem here,' she asked pushing aside her finished teacup, 'that there are so many factions fighting for the same end that they end up squabbling with each other?'

Mrs Barclay-Evans looked at them in turn. 'You could say that. You could also say that different people have different ideas on what they are willing to do to make themselves heard. Should they have to fight in a way they don't believe is ethical, or not fight the cause at all? There should be a method of protest and an organisation for everyone.'

Frankie gestured with her pen for her to go on.

'Well, what next?' She removed a strand of hair from her crinkled face and tucked it behind her ear. 'Hunger striking, that was next. Mrs Wallace Dunlop rushed parliament one day, made it through the police lines and managed to stencil on the walls of the lobby, "It is the right of the subject to petition the king and all prosecutions for such petitioning are illegal".'

'Might I guess,' said Twinkle, 'that she was put in prison for it?'

'Second division.'

'Where the proper criminals are kept.' Frankie remembered sitting in on trials for the *Tottenham Evening News*. You could wait all day for something juicy to come along, if it ever did, meanwhile line after line of sad drunk women were tossed into second division for pickpocketing, begging or soliciting.

'So she went on hunger strike to protest,' Mrs Barclay-Evans said. 'Not so much about being sent to prison but about being given second division. After the others followed suit, the force-feeding began. It was about this time Constance Lytton decided to make a stand about the way privileged women were being treated compared to the working classes.'

Frankie looked up sharply. 'Why do I know that name? What did she do?'

Mrs Barclay-Evans took a large breath. 'She's a suffragette, an aristocrat by birth, with I believe, a somewhat frail constitution, as every Lady should have.'

Frankie noticed Milly wince.

'When she was imprisoned first time round the doctors checked her heart and decided she was too weak to be force-fed. So she was discharged. She was indignant about this but the Home Secretary insisted it was medical practice, there had been no favourable treatment given. Lady Constance was not convinced. She believed the government were letting poor women waste away in prison and keeping the wealthy ones safe for the sake of the headlines. So she travelled to Newcastle, cut off her hair and forged herself some fake documents under the name of Jane Warton, Jane for Joan of Arc, Warton, I believe, was a corruption of an old family name, and she posed as a seamstress.'

'She was arrested for vandalism,' the Major interrupted.

'You can be arrested with a false name?' Frankie tilted her head. 'Didn't they cotton on to who she was when they had her lined up?'

'My dear, you can tell them anything you want. You could say you were me, or your friend here, or the daughter of a beggar from France. The police of this country may think they are sophisticated, but compared to the continent their methods for logging prisoners haven't advanced since the Domesday Book.'

Frankie sat back.

'And so this time when the doctors came to do the feeding, they took a stethoscope to her chest and announced her heart was "ripping splendid".' Mrs Barclay-Evans's teacup rattled in her hand. 'The horrors you will see in gaol are unimaginable. When you are left alone with your own thoughts and only a copy of the Bible and that dratted *Englishwoman's House and Home* book that they leave in our cells, you begin to think that there is no mercy, that Christ has left the souls of these men and women who hold you down and look at you as though you are an animal when you are sick on them. To spend the night with vomit in your hair . . .' She had turned greenish pale and made a little inarticulate groan, then sat her head back up fresh. 'Silly to be so affected. There were women who went back again and again. Like your Miss Diamond.' Her eye was drawn to the little gold carriage clock on the mantelpiece. 'Time's getting on. I should tell you where we are now. I hope it's helpful. You'll want to write this down, I'll try to speak slowly.'

She sighed. 'Ironically, the background to the new militancy started with a truce. Two years ago. It looked as if it was going to be a year for change. Lloyd George's People's Budget, the promise of reducing the powers of the House of Lords. The government set up the Conciliation Committee, and it looked like we might be getting somewhere. Women came from all over the country to march peacefully. I remember it well because we marched the same day the National Vigilance Association marched on the Lords issue and some of our lot ended up in their parade and vice versa and—'

Milly squinted. 'What were the NVA doing marching about the Lords? What's it got to do with closing down theatres?'

'Die-hard aristocrats, the lot of them,' the Major said. 'Ferociously scared of change. That Thorne woman, the one whose father shot himself years ago – she'd march on the opening of a new brand of soap.'

'Anyway,' Mrs Barclay-Evans said, looking at her husband, 'she's a silly woman, always in and out of Biarritz curing spas, and they didn't spoil our day. It could hardly have been better, in fact. The newspapers praised us for the first time. People began to speak of the philosophy behind giving us the vote, rather than simply calling us hooligans. So many of the MPs are behind us – Lansbury, Lloyd George, Lord Lytton – which makes it all the more infuriating that devil of a man Asquith . . .' Her fingers scratched the knee of her wool skirt. 'The truce lasted until November when arguments over reducing power in the House of Lords meant Parliament had to be dissolved. Well, that's when Black Friday happened. November. Two years ago.' She didn't elaborate. Frankie could remember reading the headlines: women mauled and assaulted in alleyways, knocked sideways, left for dead. Winston Churchill, the then Home Secretary had been blamed by the suffragettes but never brought to task for it. Frankie exchanged a glance with Milly and wondered if she should mention the two deaths and the cocaine on Ebony's mouth strap, or Jojo's claim that cabinet ministers came to his shows.

Mrs Barclay-Evans looked about to go on when something caught her eye outside. Startled, she jumped out of her seat. 'Did you see that?'

Twinkle's head, which had been beginning to droop, sprang back up. Frankie leapt to her feet and crossed to the window. The panes gave off a chill air against her nose. The fog outside was still thick, the streetlamps casting dirty yellow shadows onto the pavement and shrubs.

'Lot of feral cats round here,' the Major said.

'Perhaps.' His wife sounded unconvinced. 'But it looked larger than that. More like someone on horseback.'

'Or a bicycle?' Frankie offered.

'Strange to be riding around at this time of night.' Mrs Barclay-Evans looked unnerved, but they settled back down onto their couches. Twinkle, Frankie noticed, immediately slumped down again and looked ready to fall asleep.

'Would anybody like me to ring for more tea?' Mrs Barclay-Evans asked.

They all shook their heads. 'Very well. Where was I?' She gave her head a little shake and remembered. 'At the start of this year the government were still promising but dallying. It was always the next session that it would be debated. Then the one after that.'

'Votes tomorrow, votes yesterday but never votes today,' said the Major softly.

'Now listen to this, if you're looking for a reason for increased militancy.' Mrs Barclay-Evans leant forward, hands on her knees, her eyes earnest. 'Asquith received a visit from a gentleman, complaining of the inadequacies of male suffrage. That not enough men had yet been granted this privilege. And do you know what he did?'

'I can hazard a guess,' Twinkle said drowsily.

'Extension of the male franchise. I wish I were joking but I'm not. The very next session a Bill was drawn up. No demands, no uprising. One lone man, one crusading hero just had to rap at the door of Downing Street.' She looked darkly towards the cracking fire as if she could see right through the tapestry screen. '"Awake, for morning in the bowl of night, has flung the stone that puts the stars to flight".'

Milly snorted in recognition. 'Omar Khayyam. My father gave me a copy.'

'And mine too,' Mrs Barclay-Evans said, returning her gaze. 'Violence upped its force that night. Window-breaking. The stone put the stars to flight. MPs like Charles Hobhouse, who dared to say too that not enough has been shown to demonstrate our passion for the cause, found themselves with war declared. The West End smash in April. Ebony at the Albert Hall. When Asquith went to Dublin in June, one woman set fire to the theatre, another dropped a hatchet into his carriage. But the war we had declared, it was war on property, not a war on human life. Bandstands, buildings. No one could be hurt, that was the rule.'

The Major had begun to pace in front of the fire. Frankie watched his stride, his footfalls vibrating through the legs of the chairs they sat on. 'You're a military man though. Don't you think that there's no point threatening violence if you won't see it through?'

He stopped and stared at her. The pupils of his eyes were huge in the light and seemed to travel back deep in his head. 'There is a grave difference between war when your life is in danger and war when it is not.'

'So what is this arson, then?' Milly coolly met his gaze. 'This increased violence that the Pethick-Lawrences cannot approve?'

There was silence.

'You mean you don't know?' Milly asked.

The Major shifted. 'There was never any exact knowing at Clement's Inn. It was only ever planning.'

'That's not the point, I mean the Pankhursts must have said something to upset the Pethick-Lawrences. There must have been some specific arson plan they couldn't approve.' Frankie stood, slotting the fountain pen Mrs Barclay-Evans had given her between her front teeth, rattling it up and down. Mrs Barclay-Evans's brow knotted into a disapproving frown. Frankie was halfway to taking the pen out and wiping it down on her jacket when the black sheet of window behind her sang out a high note, and shattered.

Shards of glass spewed into the room; everyone slammed to the floor. Twinkle shrieked and clung to her hat as she flattened out prone. Frankie dived, smacking her ear off the mantelpiece. The sound of uneven hooves rattling off stone echoed away through the window's smashed hole.

Silence settled, along with a biting draught. The parlour door flung back and the maid came dashing through with her white hands clutched to her cap.

'It's all right. We're all right.' Mrs Barclay-Evans stood up, joining her husband who had risen to his feet and was fumbling around the fireplace. He pulled out a tarnished antique rifle, took aim at the window, then lowered the gun and shook his head.

'Can't see a damn thing in the fog.'

Frankie thought of Liam and leant her head carefully

through the treacherous hole to see if she could spot him. The street outside was misty and dim, the noises from the main road rumbling in muffled waves. 'I think we'd better leave,' she said, keeping her voice level.

Milly was on her knees with her hand raised, grasping something about the size of a fist. She stretched her arm out. Frankie took it from her, feeling the sudden weight. It was a stone, with flecks of glass still stuck to its surface, shining. Around it was wrapped a page of newspaper. Gradually Frankie unfolded it, tamping down the creases, until they could all see plain the paper's title: *The Suffragette*.

The second the front door had closed, Twinkle scraped up her hobble skirt into one hand and retrieved a hipflask of gin from where it was strapped to her thigh. She raised it to her lips and took it hungrily like milk from a nipple.

'Oi, save us some of that.' Frankie reached out and grabbed the flat pewter bottle. 'God strike me,' she downed a burning gulp. 'Well, that settles something at least. We're staying at yours tonight.'

'What?'

'It will make things easier in the morning.'

'Puss, you just saw what thuggery passed in there. You were followed, plain and simple and I won't put my reputation or my life at risk.' She looked away, her neck stiff and bristling, and Frankie wondered briefly which of the two was more important to her. Curiosity caught Twinkle up and she turned back. 'Why? What do you think's happening in the morning?'

Frankie passed the flask to Milly. 'Miss Barton here is going to infiltrate the suffragettes.'

Milly had tilted the gin bottle towards her lips but now her jaw slackened and a dribble of gin spilled to the ground. 'I beg your pardon?'

'Well, *I* can't do it, I'll never get past the front door.'

'What do you mean?'

'Oh yes,' Twinkle said slyly. 'The cartoon. Does Miss Barton know about the cartoon?'

'What cartoon?'

'Never mind,' Frankie said hotly.

Milly took another slug of gin. 'Hang on here. Apart from the obvious dangers, what exactly am I to do with the suffragettes?'

'Pretend to be one. Twinkle's sure to have a schoolmistress costume lying around, you can wear that.'

'How dare you!' Twinkle spat.

But Frankie wasn't listening. She was already wandering up the street to where Liam was loitering against a lamppost, playing with a box of Vestas, lighting one, burning it down then tossing it. It took her a moment to realise he was trying to keep warm. The wind had begun to howl and the street was empty with no carriages to be seen. She called over, 'Oi dozy, did you clock who went past? Just now.'

Liam stretched his back against the post. Frankie heard his neck bones crack. He shrugged. 'An old dustbin man or woman with a wee barrow on the back.' He looked at her frown, a smirk brewing on his face.

Frankie's tone stopped it short. 'Didn't you see that stone that went through the window?'

The blood drained from his face, and for a second Frankie felt a prick of guilt at allowing a boy so young to dive into something she knew was dangerous. But then his defences sprang back up and his lips hardened. 'It's hard to see in the fog, what – do you expect I've got eyes on every fingertip?'

'Well, didn't you hear it?'

He shrugged. 'Maybe I heard breaking, but I thought it was the wind blowing about the milk bottles. I was trying to keep warm, you know.'

Frankie frowned. 'What did you mean just now, when you said man or woman?'

'What?'

'Man or woman, you said dustbin man or woman.'

'I don't know, the face was all bundled up in rags for the cold.' He scowled and pulled the lapels of his coat tighter over his shivering shoulders, stabbing Frankie with a pointed look.

The gesture was lost. She tutted, irritated. 'Go and get us a cab, will you?'

Liam stared at her.

'Please,' she said flatly.

He skulked off towards the main road. Milly was on her heels. 'Frankie, what do you mean Twinkle's got a school-mistress costume? You want to dress me up as a suffragette? Are you mad?'

Frankie turned. 'You saw what was wrapped around that

stone. It was a warning. What if Ebony had uncovered a suffragette plot she didn't like the sound of? What if she had threatened to out the ringleaders, go to the press, tell the police where Christabel was hiding? She might have thought she could spill the beans.'

Milly set her chin firm. 'Anyone could wrap up a stone in a copy of *The Suffragette*. It doesn't mean a thing. Weren't you listening? If anyone has reason to be after Ebony Diamond, it's the government. Jojo told us this evening he had Cabinet Ministers come to his shows. You said they might have tried to murder Ebony if she had something on them.'

'I know what I said. But unless you've got a bright idea of how to wheedle our way into Downing Street and casually put it to Asquith whether he and his Cabinet have been a-murdering, I'd suggest we start where we might be able to get some answers.'

Twinkle had caught up to them both now and was surveying Frankie with a scowl. She held out her hand for the gin bottle. Milly passed it to her and she rucked up her skirt to strap it back into place. She looked both shaken and doubtful as she wriggled her outfit back down, smoothing the creases. After a moment her face softened and she closed in on Frankie, easing the wrinkled roots of her hands up onto Frankie's lapels to flatten them. 'Actually, I rather think Puss has a point. Infiltrating the suffragettes could be just the path to follow. And you know you're always very welcome to bed down chez Twinkle. I'll make it as comfortable as I can.

Being on the top floor at least you'll be safer. That'll be my bit towards your . . . investigation, shall it?'

With one hand clutching her skirt, she waddled ahead into the fog. 'Of course,' she called back, nodding towards the main road where Liam had two fingers in his mouth whistling for cabs, 'he can't stay.'

Twenty-Three

4 November 1912

Mist was steaming up in lazy swirls from the dung and muck in the middle of Caledonian Road as Primrose rounded the corner. Half-way down Wheelwright Street Wilson sniffed the air like a connoisseur, then made Primrose pause, one eye on his pocket-watch, while he ducked along a side lane beside a public house. He re-emerged with a wink, a shining eye and half a pint of ale.

'Go on, have a slug.'

Primrose eyed him warily, wondering about this chipper mood, and whether he had been informed about the report on him. He was, however, parched, and slightly headachey from the gritty coffee he had bought at Vauxhall railway station so he took a sip.

'Old boy loves us. Always leaves us a half out.'

'I shall remember that.'

'You never do that when you was based at the rat-house?'

Primrose winced. The rat-house was the Section House he had lived in before marrying Clara. He had heard about the practice of leaving out ale for constables but never taken advantage of it. It always seemed easier to forge relationships with innkeepers if you had a London accent.

Wilson plonked the glass back at the mouth of the alley and they walked on towards the entrance to Pentonville Prison. On the crisp air Primrose could smell chemical soap on laundered cotton, horses, and something almost like food. He looked up at the cold stone walls of Pentonville, the so-called model prison, now pressing in upon them among the rising fog. Behind him on the freezing street Sunday costermongers were setting up pitches, and omnibus drivers slapped their ponies to wake up. Taking their lead he blinked and clenched his hands to try and wake himself up. He still felt a churn of scepticism at the Chief's logic. Who knew if this man was even acquainted with Ebony Diamond, and who or what he would know? His wife was right, they should have been at suffragette headquarters, trying to get an identification of the murdered woman.

The black iron horseshoe gates loomed ahead and Primrose gave a last minute squeeze to the knot of his necktie. The thought of Clara lying curled and warm in bed, her knitting dropping from her hands where she had nodded off, crossed his mind and he felt a twist of melancholy. Prison visits made him distinctly uncomfortable. He always thought in the back of his mind that but for the grace of God he could be on the other side. A distant family member had been hauled off to Lancaster prison a generation back, for stealing milk from one of the landowner's cows, and it had brought such shame on the family that his mother winced if she heard the man's Christian name, even on someone else. He had always been filled with the dreadful sense that life was a precarious tight-rope between morality and punishment, that the penal system was there, hovering with its jaws open, braced to swallow you if your concentration slipped for a second.

And yet here he was, about to question a man who had smashed a window and insulted a judge defending, as he put it, the basic rights of his mother and his wife. He looked side-ways at Wilson to see if he could guess what he might be thinking. Wilson belched quietly into his balled-up fist and straightened his own necktie.

'You been in here before?' Wilson asked.

Primrose nodded. 'Striking bargains.'

A cloud travelled over the gate in the opposite direction as they passed through it.

The duty officer signed them in and led them down a dirty corridor, past the chapel where the scent of dead incense and sweet wood drifted, and into the main chamber, the palm of Pentonville's model 'hand'. From the centre, four long corri-dors marked A to D splayed off. It was said that in theory an officer could stand and see perfectly down each in turn just by rotating 180 degrees. In reality, the multiple levels, the spiral staircases and the traffic constantly going on down each of the halls – washing of floors, slopping out of excrement – meant that unless it was the dead of night it was difficult to discern what was legitimate activity and what was troublemaking.

As soon as they entered the airy chamber the smell hit Primrose: sickly bread, boiled potatoes, milk and urine, lots of it, sharp and savoury. He noted with a churn of his gut that they were heading down B Hall, the corridor ending in the condemned cells and execution chamber. He had unpleasant memories of being summoned a few years back to hear a man's final desperate confession in one of those cells. The man, once a respectable Smithfields butcher, had hoped that by telling the police where he had hidden the missing digits of his victim, he could bargain his life back. Primrose's superior had noted down the particulars in a leather-bound book before the prisoner was hauled off by four warders, screaming all the way to the noose.

'The doctor's with him at the moment,' the officer said, a freckly youth who wore his hat with absolute symmetry. The further they moved down the corridor the noisier it grew; prisoners tapping out messages to one another on the hot water pipes, the echoing of water on bathhouse tiles. 'You've actually come at rather an inconvenient time.'

'What do you mean?' Primrose smarted slightly from the man's bluntness. He had heard in the past that CID were not well liked anywhere other than Scotland Yard, but didn't know if it was true or a rumour started by someone with a chip on their shoulder, like Stuttlegate.

The man looked at Primrose squarely. 'He's on hunger strike.'

Primrose moved aside as a warder with a chamber pot full of vomit passed. 'He's what?'

'He's on hunger strike. Sympathy with the women. And protest at being put in second division.'

'It is a little harsh to put him on B with the condemned men.'

The officer shrugged. 'Only place we had a solitary cell.'

Wilson was smirking. 'So he's given up his meat and two over votes for the ladies?'

The officer looked tentatively between them, trying to work out whether it would be prudent to laugh. 'We've had one in before who did the same. Frederick Pethick-Lawrence.'

Primrose nodded. 'Name rings a bell.'

They passed a row of closed doors with the observation flaps shut and the buzz of movement seemed to die down. Primrose noticed with a stab of sympathy that they were almost parallel with the execution chamber outside. The man would have a prime view of it through the bars of his window.

'What's his name again?' Wilson whispered.

'Reynolds. William.'

Outside a painted grey metal door, peering through the observation flap, stood a man in a white coat with grey hair bushing around his ears and temples. A stethoscope dangled round his neck; shiny gold wire glasses clung to his neat face. He snapped the flap shut when he saw them and stuck out his hand.

'Dr Fairwater. Very pleased to meet you. I'm the Senior Medical Officer.' He looked back over his shoulder towards the cell. 'It's a slightly inopportune time, but if you do want to get anything out of him, my presence may be a good motivator, shall we say?'

Wilson nodded. 'Feeding time?'

Primrose noticed the contraption in the man's hands, a funnel attached to a long tube that glistened even in the gloomy light, as if it had been rubbed with petroleum or some other lubricant. Perched at the door was a jug filled with lumpy yellow liquid – the appearance of beaten eggs, but the scent of brandy.

Primrose's stomach rolled a clumsy somersault. 'If it's an inopportune time then of course we can . . .'

'No, no,' the doctor seemed oddly cheerful. Primrose realised with a sickening tug that perhaps there was some kind of novelty in the task, trying out a new technique on a live specimen for the first time. 'Just have to wait for the warders. Or you want to question him first?'

'If you wouldn't mind.'

The medical officer stood aside, offering them the door. The young officer unlocked it with great care then scraped it back.

Aside from being run down, cream paint flaking on the lower half of the wall, the cell looked clean. The small barred window high on the far wall was open, letting in a foggy breeze. On the wall above his concrete truckle bed the words were etched, 'Under a Government which imprisons any unjustly, the true place of a just man (or woman) is also a prison.' A shiny black jug and cup made from gutta-percha lay on the floor. The whole room had a rubbery tang to it, underneath a festering scent.

Reynolds was a pitiful sight, lying on his side, his spine curled against the cold wall, barely covered by two brown wool blankets. His high cheekbones and fine plump lips had faded to a mustard yellow, and under his eyes the skin was purple and shiny.

Primrose coughed, feeling sudden embarrassment to be privy to the man's indignity. Were it not for the circumstances, he may have passed the same man in a first-class train carriage, in the doorway of a club, stood aside for him in a restaurant, or called him 'Sir' when taking a statement about a pickpocket who had thieved his wallet. Reynolds stirred a lazy blue eye up to them, then took in a big breath of fetid air and let it out slowly.

'Mr Reynolds?'

'Yes.' Even under the croakiness there was a clipped politeness.

'I'm Inspector Primrose, I work with the suffragette division at Special Branch. Can I ask you some questions?'

'Blimey, they have a whole division now, do they?'

Primrose looked for somewhere to sit but there was nowhere except the bed. He stood awkwardly, shifting his weight from one leg to the next. Wilson paced gently along the wall with the window, inspecting things that caught his eye.

'This is Sergeant Wilson. Would you care to sit up?'

'Not particularly. I haven't eaten for three days.'

'And why is that?'

'Because you brutes put me in second division and that's what suffragettes do when not given the privileges of political prisoners.' He kept one sleepy eye on Primrose.

'You consider yourself a suffragette?'

'I'm a member of the Men's League for Women's Suffrage.'

Primrose eyed the door. Voices were gathering there; he wondered if the warders were ready. 'I'm not here to talk about politics.' He nodded at the quote on the wall. 'Did you know a woman called Ebony Diamond?'

Reynolds raised an eyebrow at the inspector and stared. Primrose waited. Behind him he could detect a smile developing on Wilson's face.

'Do you know anyone who might want to harm any members of the suffragettes?'

Reynolds snorted into his horsehair pillow. 'There's two of them standing outside the door right now. Have you tried the Houses of Parliament?'

To Primrose's faint horror Wilson dropped to his haunches. 'Listen up, son, don't get smart with us. You see what that doctor's got in his hands out there? We can put a stop to that.' He looked shiftily towards Primrose. 'But you'd better give us some useful information first.' He creaked back up and nodded to Primrose.

Primrose swallowed, bristling with being shown up by the sergeant, but continued. 'A woman thought to be Ebony Diamond was found murdered just off Tottenham Court Road three nights ago. You might be familiar with one of these?' He fished in his pocket and pulled out a little paper bag, then dropped the portcullis pin into his palm and held it out.

'Holloway degree,' Reynolds said softly. 'It means the girl's been inside.'

'That's right. It was found on her body.'

'Well, that narrows it down. There are about five hundred of those floating around London. Have you asked at Lincoln's Inn?' He was quick enough to see the look that passed between the two officers. 'You haven't been to Lincoln's Inn, have you?'

Primrose coughed again. Wilson's shoes creaked as he rocked back and forth.

Reynolds strained up onto his elbows. 'You haven't been to Lincoln's Inn because you thought you could trust a man to rat on those old girls before you went after them yourselves? Oh dear.' He rolled over to face the wall. 'Oh dear,' he repeated.

'We know the woman is not Ebony Diamond,' Primrose raised his voice, 'But we want to know why she was dressed like her and more importantly who she was. You've heard of Ebony Diamond?'

The man kept his sunken eyes pointed upwards. 'Have you heard of the sinking of the *Titanic*?'

Primrose held his slippery nerve. He didn't like this man, his cut-glass vowels and his high morals. He took his hand out of his pocket and clenched it a couple of times, feeling the sensation calm him. 'Miss Diamond was performing at the Coliseum last night. But she never finished her act. She's gone missing now. We believe that this might be connected to the death of the unknown woman. You don't know anyone who would be after Miss Diamond? Not just any suffragette but her particularly.'

William Reynolds tilted his head round and gave Primrose a good hard stare. He raised a weak hand from the blanket and scratched his temple. 'There is one man; his name is on the tip of my tongue. You might know of him. Asquith? Do you want a list of Cabinet Members? My memory goes a little sketchy when I get past Home Secretary. Although he would be a good place to start.'

Wilson stopped pacing. 'Do you think the doctor might trigger your memory?'

At that moment the Senior Medical Officer poked his head into the room. The door scraped back and Primrose glimpsed the small army that had gathered outside: four warders, the officer who had shown them through the hall and a freckled female nurse, whose cold eyes matched her grey uniform. 'Ready?' the doctor asked.

Primrose stood back. He wished to turn aside but a compelling terror congealed with professional pride and morbid curiosity made him press his back against the chalky wall and keep his eyes on Reynolds. The nurse went over first, her sleeves rolled up, coaxing him to sit up. He flashed her a game smile and Primrose despised him a little bit more.

'Come on,' she said.

'You can't be serious.'

'I am, sunshine.'

'You are. You are like sunshine. Your hair's a very pretty shade of red.'

'Oh, I've heard it all before. Soldiers in the Boer, every line and trick in the book. Sit up, let me take the covers off.'

'I refuse passively.'

Primrose watched the doctor who watched the nurse. The warders had brought up a chair and were hovering with it in the doorway.

'Have you got false teeth?' She tried to poke a finger into his mouth but he craned his neck out of her reach. 'If you do, you should take them out now because it's going to hurt.'

The doctor stepped a little further into the room and held out the instruments in his hand as if he were offering the gentleman a selection of quality neckties. He drew the prisoner's attention to the glistening pipe. 'This is a stomach tube. If you don't comply, I'll feed you through the nose.'

Primrose watched Reynolds's expression calcify; horror concealed beneath the crisp shell.

The doctor looped the tube over his arm and gestured to his other hand. He held braced between his fingers a small carved block of wood and a larger metal block that chimed against the signet ring on his pinky. 'I have a wooden gag or a steel one. I should warn you that the steel one will hurt more, so I would advise you to choose the wooden one. Please do not force me to use the steel gag. I must warn you that women have had their teeth cracked by forcing medical officers in Holloway to use it and our dental facilities here are limited.' He waited for a minute or two then when Reynolds said nothing, stepped back to let the warders pass inside. As they hauled the man's fragile body, heavy with hunger, from his hard bed, the doctor conversed quietly with the nurse who nodded and kept pressing her sleeves back. Once in the chair, she took the sheet from his bed and wrapped it around his throat and shoulders, taking his slim neck in her hands and easing his head back.

'I shall cease to resist this,' he said, fluttering a brittle smile, 'when the country's legislators have enfranchised women.' He flashed a glance loaded with betrayal at the nurse. She did something to him that made him flinch. Seeing one of the warders leave the room and return with the brandied egg mixture, he looked sobered; his smile faded. But the nurse had not yet recovered from the look and gazed down at him with her own chilly smile. 'I can look after myself, but thank you for your concern.'

The doctor glared at her as if to say that the discussion had gone far enough, and she raised her gaze and looked straight ahead, keeping his head in her hands like a stone she was about to throw.

Two warders took his legs and two his arms. The doctor moved between his knees, leaning in to pinch his nose, trying to prise open his lips. 'I really would advise you to take out any false teeth. This will press into your gums in the most horrible way.' He grunted as he worked. Primrose looked down to see that his own knuckles were white and he suddenly wished he had drunk more of that ale. It was embarrassing to have his nerves so flagrantly on display in front of the brawny warders, the efficient doctor and the red-haired nurse. He chanced a glance at Wilson who seemed engrossed but not affected.

'All right,' the doctor said, tossing the wooden gag onto the bed. 'But I did warn you.' He cried out as Reynolds's tooth caught his finger, then slapped him in retaliation.

'I'm sorry I didn't mean . . .' Reynolds started to say, but the doctor was fast and knew every trick, and used the opening of the prisoner's mouth to wedge his fingers in, followed by the steel gag. It knocked his teeth with a horrible crunch. Reynolds began to make the impotent strains of dry retching, continuing as the doctor unwound the glycerine-slick tube from his arm and began to feed it down his throat, inch by careful inch. The red-headed nurse took the pulse in his neck and nodded.

Reynolds choked and twitched. His chest and shoulders shook. The doctor attached the funnel to the top end of the tube and poured the liquid in. The prisoner tried to double over. The warders prised him back in the chair. Vomit spurted from his nose in a fine mist. A spray of yellow landed on the doctor's coat, another dripped down onto the nurse's fingers.

The doctor took William Reynolds's stubbly chin in one hand and waited until he had his gaze. 'You do that again and I will feed you twice.'

Primrose felt cold sweat congeal on his back, gluing him to the wall. His heart was beating irregularly. He felt, underneath the horror, a deep well of depression, the same depression that always returned to him, a depression for everything on earth that was wrong. Underneath the stained bedsheet, with his back turned and his eyes closed, the man could have been anyone, he could have been any number of women, he could have been Clara.

The doctor wiped his hands on a rag and the warders let Reynolds go. Finally he was free to bend over, panting.

'We'll be back tomorrow. In the meantime, I'd clean yourself up.' He pointed at the gutta-percha jug, then made eye contact with Primrose and bowed politely. Primrose worked to keep his face neutral and thought he had succeeded, but once the doctor had left the room he saw that the red-haired nurse was regarding him curiously.

She peeled the sheet off Reynolds, then in a moment of pity or regret suddenly took up the rag the doctor had left behind on the bed and wiped his mouth clean. 'I'm afraid I can't get you a change until tomorrow,' she said gently. 'It's not laundry day for this wing.' Reynolds coughed into his fist and nodded. He looked around for a place to wipe his hand but there was nowhere. She folded the sheet loosely and placed it back on his bed. The warders hung about for a few moments then dispersed slowly back to their duties.

'Lucky you didn't get any on the floor,' the nurse said. Then she stopped and her head turned as if she had only just noticed Primrose and Wilson still standing there. 'Do you have more questions?'

Primrose looked briefly to Wilson then cleared his throat.

'Still know nothing about Ebony Diamond?' he tried hard to keep his voice steady.

William Reynolds looked down at his vomit-covered breast and coldly back up. 'If I did, do you think I would kowtow to torture?'

'Withholding information is a criminal offence.'

'And this isn't?'

Primrose held his gaze. He could feel Wilson's weight shift behind him.

'Inspector,' Reynolds continued, 'it's possible I could tell you things that would turn that shocked complexion of yours even whiter. But until you come back here with an order to stop force-feeding in His Majesty's Prisons, not just me, but all suffrage prisoners, it's possible you'll never know.'

'Be careful. We could have your sentence extended,' Wilson said.

Reynolds looked at his feet then coughed up a scrap of yellow mixture and spat it onto the floor.

Primrose breathed out, adjusted his coat. He gestured to the nurse. 'It's probably best if your patient . . . prisoner can rest.'

William Reynolds looked back up, his gold-crusted mouth breaking into a fragile smile again. 'Yes, I am a very patient prisoner,' he said. 'I have all the time in the world.'

Primrose didn't smile back.

Out in the icy air again, Primrose felt the blood return to his cheeks. Wilson lit a cigarette and offered him one, which he took gratefully. To their left, prison vans were just beginning to arrive with the day's cargo. They watched a procession of boys, who could only have been fifteen or less, led in handcuffs across the courtyard, their breath puffing out as much steam as the horses that led the wagons.

Wilson sucked his cigarette like a humbug. 'Wonder what the old dutch makes of it all.'

Primrose looked at him strangely. He still sometimes felt like all the London-born peelers talked in a foreign tongue.

'Duchess of Fife – wife.' Wilson did a little sing-song dance. But Primrose wasn't paying attention any more. He was racking his brains back to something he had read in the man's file. There was a wife in there somewhere. He thumbed his briefcase for the manila folder, his cigarette dangling from his lips and dropping ash everywhere. Wilson watched him, a smile tickling his mouth.

There it was. Wife, Louisa Reynolds, not a known member of the WSPU. No suffragette affiliations, no suffragette-associated offences, no offences whatsoever.

'So why would he . . .' he murmured aloud.

'Are you all right there, Inspector? You need to stay off the booze first thing in the morning?' Wilson wheezed at his own joke, but Primrose didn't hear him. He was too busy puzzling over the mystery of a man who would sacrifice himself for a woman's cause in a way his own wife would not.

Twenty-Four

Frankie rose with backache and a bleary head. It took a few seconds for her to register where she was. She blinked and picked the crust from her eyelashes, taking in the heaped fabrics, the devoré, the birdcage with two speckled budgerigars pecking at each other inside. A lump of cloth on the sofa moaned, and she remembered everything from the night before.

'Milly?'

'What time is it?'

The bells from a nearby church were striking on the wind.

'Don't know. Late already. It's Sunday, mind.'

'Oh, the old girl plied me with the gin last night. I've got a thrashing head on.' She sat up and Frankie couldn't help but let loose a snort of laughter at her golden hair tangled round her head in a Medusa nest. The kohl had smudged her eyes to hollows.

'I'd get the fright of my life if I bumped into you in a churchyard.'

'Don't.' Milly fiddled with the covers. Her face grew grave. 'I'm still thinking about that stone.' They both jumped as the door handle turned.

The maid, Alice, brought in tea and toast and clucked her tongue quietly as she set the tray down, catching sight of the state of them. Doubtless, thought Frankie, she was used to a more civilised madam. Twinkle's rose-petal jam was so sweet it made her teeth sting but Milly didn't seem to mind, bolting it down as though she had never seen food before.

When they had washed and dressed they stood by the front door. Twinkle had still not stirred from her bed. In her schoolteacher costume, pinned and bunched in to fit, Milly looked eerily like the lay mistress at Frankie's convent school, the one who kept the birch pickling in water to keep it smart.

'Are you comfortable in that get-up?' Frankie cast her eye over it, trying not to think of where and why its last airing might have taken place.

'Do I have much choice?' Milly's face had a glimmer of stubbornness. 'She offered me a leather strap too. I declined.' She pinched down her collar and her eyes grew serious. 'If they wouldn't tell Mrs B-E. about the arson plans, what makes you think they will tell me?'

'Because you'll make them trust you.'

'Will I?' The amusement picked back up in her face. She looked tired from the night before but there was a gloss in her pupils. 'Might need that strap after all.' She did a final twirl.

Frankie looked at her, spinning in the woollen contraption, an ankle length skirt exposing the top of sturdy boots and a matching jacket, with cream blouse poking out at the collar and cuffs. She looked so like the stereotype, the Mrs Ought-to-be-spanked-first who appeared on seaside post-cards and propaganda, that she couldn't help smile. Guiltily she thought of her cartoon. 'Go on, you'll fit right in.'

The air outside was damp but bright, the fog washed away by the rising sun and Frankie felt her head begin to clear. The streets were empty, except for the odd family scrambling along, late for church. It had crossed their minds that there would be no one at suffragette headquarters on a Sunday, but Milly knew from the rhythms of Ebony's disappearances over the past months that Sundays were one of their busiest days. The working women could come along, fathers were free to take care of children and houses quiet enough to justify sneaking out for a few hours. Besides, the growing numbers of Darwinists had left the churches emptier now than when Frankie was a child.

They chatted idly as they walked. A burning curiosity itched at Frankie about Milly's family, but she didn't dare ask. As they reached the corner onto Kingsway a few doors down from Lincoln's Inn, something occurred to her.

'How many people knew she did that tiger trick before?'

Milly thought for a second. 'It was well known in circus circles. She didn't do it at Jojo's because she didn't have the space to keep a cat. But everyone who knew her even vaguely knew she kept an eye on the tigers at the zoo whenever she could, watching the way they moved, keeping up her practice.'

'Would anyone be able to mimic it?'

Milly laughed incredulously. 'You think she might have been done in after all? There's no one who could do what she did. Foucaud even looks like a buffoon. He only gets away with it because the timeframe is so tight when he's in the costume, no one has the chance to notice the tiger is moving like a pantomime cow.'

Frankie chewed this over. 'So it can only have been her.'

Milly opened her plush lips slowly. 'I wouldn't stake my life on it . . . But I should say so.'

They both looked up at the huge columns of Lincoln's Inn House emerging from the pavement like tree trunks. It had a high imposing façade, Greek lines and classical edges striking an odd note with the houses on either side. It was a fine headquarters indeed. There must have been supporters with bottomless pockets.

Milly took a couple of breaths and fiddled with her cuffs. 'I could murder a cigarette.'

Frankie raised an eyebrow at the phrase, then fumbled in her jacket catching the fruity whiff of herself. She would have to change her cotton shirt soon. She held out a pack of Matinees. Milly waved a hand. 'It's all right. Best not in front of here anyway. Blow my cover.'

'Smoking? It's emancipation.'

Milly raised an eyebrow. 'Is that what you think?' She brushed down her skirt. 'Right.' Her lips curled tentatively into a smile. 'Where are you off to anyway?'

'The morgue.'

Her smile disappeared. 'Why?'

Frankie stared at her. 'That Turkish Delight jam rot your brain did it? The body of Mr Smythe, Inspector Millicent. Where d'you go when there's a body?'

Milly's lips sulked down. 'I was only asking.'

'Besides, I got my contacts,' Frankie said smartly, watching Milly's slim back weave a few paces away from her. Just before Milly reached the door, she turned. 'Frankie, where shall I meet you next?'

'Lyon's tea room, Piccadilly, six o'clock?'

'I'll be there,' she paused. 'Have fun with your cadavers, Constable Frankie.' Moving like a roe deer, she hopped up onto the doorstep and had her hand brandishing the knocker in an instant.

Frankie watched a motor bus puff past the building then turned back up Kingsway towards Covent Garden. She reflected that it had not been twenty-four hours since she had first learned Millicent's real name, and yet she was trusting her in a way she wouldn't have trusted any of the staffers from Stonecutter Street. Before last night she had just been one of the exotic West End figures Frankie would pass from time to time on shady streets, dolled up in curious costume. Artists' models, mannequins, girls whose jobs you didn't know, but who insisted on making their own living. How had her fleet, fragile, perfectly crafted feet ended up on Jojo's doorstep? 'I wasn't born a showgirl,' she had said. So did Milly, unlike Ebony, have a safety net she could escape into if someone was on her heels?

Frankie walked on carefully, feeling the burden of what she had set out to do creeping up onto her shoulders. She had wanted this. She had pictured herself time and again in sharp tweeds working her way through London on an investigative piece, had scoffed at Teddy Hawkins's shoddy reporting, known she could do better. She convinced herself when there was a murder in the papers that she could slot the facts together silky and quick, not like the lead-headed coppers and dozy reporters covering it, if only she was given the chance. But the flip side of that was that undeniably, most things Frankie had done up until now hadn't turned out quite the way she'd expected them to. Being a society columnist wasn't champagne and sparkling ideas, it was gin and Twinkle's bizarre whims. Being a cartoonist wasn't coffee houses and satire, it was sketching to please others without thinking about the consequences.

She tried to shake off her fermenting self-doubt as she stopped outside the Endell Street Hospital, and looked up and down the street. There was a back entrance where the undertakers' carts pulled up out of sight of the main road. She hopped the fence and passed down an alleyway alongside a high wall. From a couple of the open windows the sounds of the hospital drifted outside; quiet feet padding on wood floors, the scraping of gurneys being moved. Someone inside moaned, low and guttural.

The entrance to the morgue was discreetly screened from view by a patch of shrubs, but she didn't get that far before she felt the hands: one slapped straight across her eyes, the other smothering her mouth and nose with the thick taste of something chemical.

She bit down on a set of fat fingers. The voice behind her let out a shrill cry. 'Ow! You've got teeth like a bleedin' wolf.'

She jabbed her elbow behind her and wrenched herself free. 'You think I don't know the stink of your fingers, John Bridewell? You should be locked up, creeping around hospitals, frightening young women.' Though she was scowling, her voice was shaky. He had caught her off guard.

The fat boy in the white apron shook his hand up and down furiously, a sheepish smile pushing into his heavy cheeks. He hadn't changed a bit, not in the two years since she had seen him last, except for putting on even more weight around his hips and belly. He'd always been one for sinister pranks, whenever she'd been sent to him by the *Tottenham Evening News* editor, to sniff out dirt on a gruesome death or suicide. It seemed he was still a crafty little bastard. He extended a hand. Frankie took it reluctantly. 'You're lucky I didn't bite it off.' She spat the nasty taste onto the ground. 'Formaldehyde. You're a sick boy.'

'That's what they all say.' He chuckled, loud and ribald.

They stood for a few seconds eyeing one another up like cats not knowing whether they were about to fight. 'You've grown taller I think,' he said after a while. 'Must be the Fleet Street ale.'

'It's perspective. Maybe you've shrunk.' She forced a grin. 'I never thought I'd see you again. Aren't you too busy writing about the colour of the Queen's knickers?' He laughed again but there was a note of nervousness in it. 'What's the matter? You told them she didn't wear none so they kicked you off back to the morgues to write about people who can't sue?'

'I need a bit of help, John. You got much work on just now?'

'Few waiting to be picked up.'

'It's someone important.'

He narrowed his puffy eyes.

'Olivier Smythe.' She watched him but his face gave nothing away. 'I think he was murdered.'

'Your paper went with "accident" on that.'

'So you do read it then?' she smiled.

He stiffened. 'If it's lying around.'

Frankie ran her fingers through her hair, taking a few seconds to let his surprise attack wash off her. In his apron, stained with thin smears of yellow fat and brownish red there was something singularly unsettling about him. His nose had a proud little turn up and his skin was always ruddy and mottled, the way dead flesh looked. It was a pity; he was a nice boy who had been unlucky enough to be in the wrong place when there was a job going spare as a mortician's assistant. Even after all the times he had bailed her out, broken the rules to let her have a glimpse of a corpse, or gone through with her the exact mechanisms of the body of a person who had drowned or suffered a heart attack, she still felt her skin recoiling slightly at the sight of him. It was his soft round belly more than anything. How could a man who did his job have such an appetite?

'He was collected this morning, there's nothing to see.'

'Who by?'

'Solicitor's arrangements.' He looked around at the small yard. From the street came the sound of a cab passing. 'Look, if you're coming in you'd better do it now. Master's had to nip up to the office for a minute. But,' he held up a chubby finger. 'It's going to cost you, Frankie.'

'I don't have any money.'

He smiled. 'I don't mean money.'

A quick wave of nausea passed over her. She wasn't swift enough to hide it and she saw John Bridewell's cheeks stiffen and felt ashamed.

'Come on, Frankie, I don't mean that and you know it,' he said quietly. An awkward livid blush spread over his face and she felt even worse. 'I'm applying for the university. He said he'll cover the costs for me to study anatomy. Don't want to be a trolley boy all my life and I know the organs, I've got good cutting skills.' She stifled a shiver. 'Can you read over my letter?' There was a note of defence in his voice, hurt pride.

'Of course, John,' Frankie said too quickly.

'You was always good with letters.' He nodded softly, then inclined his head to the green painted door. 'Come on.'

It was startling how quickly the smell came back to her, and with it waves of memories, a different life, handwriting by paraffin lamp, stories of the dead people who lay like soapstone on the morgue shelves. She thought of the man who was savaged by a pig, the woman who bleached her stomach. *Tottenham Evening News* had gone to town on that one. Page two with an illustration. She had felt proud at first, until one of the leader writers told her that the reason they asked her was that no one else wanted to do it. Then she had felt ashamed, like she was only one step up from the body snatchers of the last century. Wait until I'm on Fleet Street, she had thought. I'll show you. And now she was back at the morgue, fighting Teddy Hawkins for the privilege. It flashed across her mind how strangely the world worked.

There was a dripping sound coming from somewhere and the air was cold but sweet. John Bridewell moved efficiently through the cluttered space, clearing one empty trolley out of the way, moving instruments onto a wooden table scattered with an assortment of knives and hooks. Two naked bodies lay in the far corner, wizened at the necks, swollen at the wrists. Frankie tried not to look but it was hard not to and her gaze ended up falling on a row of pickled body parts, ears, fingers and tumours in large jars.

'What's this for, Frankie?' His question caught her off guard. 'Is this personal? Because I know your paper's covered it already, I spoke to Teddy Hawkins.'

'You spoke to Teddy Hawkins?' She could barely conceal the jealousy in her voice.

'Yes.'

'And it was you that told him it was an accident?'

'I said nothing of the sort. I said you get all kinds of

corset-related deaths. Typically when they say accident, they mean over a period of time.' He shifted his hand on the corner of a trolley.

Frankie looked around and her eyes fell on a pile of clothes soaking up the damp around a drain in one corner. 'You worked on him?'

He puffed out his cheeks. 'I thought I was going to be sick. Haven't felt that way since I took my first turn with a scalpel.'

'So what really happened? Was it progressive? Or had he just laced himself in too tight?'

'Tight? When we took the corset off him, you could see his shape, the ribs went in, right in, like they'd been stunted, dug up to his lungs. His arse was an upside-down heart. His liver was dented. Boss says he must have been wearing one since before his bones hardened. Call himself a man.' He looked away. 'I don't know what happened. You can guess what happened, I don't need to know.'

Frankie tried to hold his darting gaze. 'John.'

John Bridewell shifted uncomfortably. 'No one wants to read about that over their toast and marmalade. Perhaps . . .' he pushed back his hair, 'you paper folk like this stuff but . . . Frankie, perhaps there's some things that should be left alone. For the dignity of everyone.' He wouldn't meet her eye. He was holding something back.

'What time did he die?'

'Not certain.'

'But he was found in the morning?'

'It was during the night. Rigor mortis was full. One of the girls worked for him found him.' He chewed on his lip.

'Spit it out, John.'

'Frankie.'

'I'm serious.'

'I don't see what relevance it has. The man had funny leanings.'

'So he liked to wear corsets. So what? Come on, God knows what people say about me. Or you.'

The blood rose rapidly in his cheeks. His eyes flicked to the door. 'You ought to watch your tongue.'

'You're not telling me the whole story are you?'

He sighed deeply. 'You heard of Toxicodendron radicans?'

'Yes, I had some with my morning coffee. What do you think?'

'Poison ivy. You get it in botanical houses. It's an exotic plant, from America.' He shifted his weight anxiously. Frankie stared at him. He let his breath out and his eyes lowered. 'All right. There was a rash on his body, the torso, underneath the corset. I think, well, boss thinks – although he wouldn't commit to it – that was what made him swell. He bloated up inside the corset, you know like when you get stung by a bee, and it suffocated him. It was front opening so he could have put it on, then when his body reacted, it expanded, strangled him. Whoever put the poison on, *if that was the case,* wouldn't have needed to be there.'

'Have you tested it?'

251

'Frankie, there's some things should be left alone. Don't put that picture in people's minds. You'll be put on trial for . . . well, you know he made corsets for the royals.'

She cut him off. 'He was murdered. He deserves justice.'

'If you knew that already, why did you come here?'

She sighed deeply, thinking of Mr Stark's words. 'Because I need facts.' A noise from outside whipped both their heads up sharply. Frankie looked at the door. John Bridewell saw her skittish eyes.

'It's cats, Frankie. They're everywhere in the yard. I've never seen you like this before. Anyone would think someone was out to murder you.' He laughed his nervous laugh but there was a questioning edge in his eyes.

Frankie let her breath out again slowly, resisting the urge to steady her heart with her hand. She realised her whole body had tensed, bracing just in case another stone came flying through the window. 'I went to Smythe's corset shop to interview that acrobat, Ebony Diamond, for the paper the day before she went missing. You must have heard about her going missing.'

He nodded uncertainly.

'Well, you want to talk about skittish? She was bloody skittish about something. I saw her again at his shop, the day they found him, and she was even worse.' She breathed out. 'I know something's going on, John, something I don't understand. It's not like them suicides I used to write about for the *Tottenham*.'

John looked shiftily at the pile of clothes in the corner.

'Look, there was something else,' he said slowly. 'It came in with the body. I haven't given it to the police yet.' He headed over to a short cabinet in the far corner of the room, near a high window with panes dripping yellow-tinted condensation. From the third drawer he withdrew a small silvery object and flicked it into his hand.

'A gift from a lover?' He held it out to her. It was a brooch, a small silver brooch, long and thin, with a bronze or gold picture carved into the front, a shield with a trio of lions heads surrounded by vines.

'Boss said it looks like a family crest. But it wasn't his. Wasn't the crest of the shop.'

Frankie shook her head, not understanding. 'It was on his body?'

'He had it in his hand. Tightly gripped. Police couldn't even prise it out, we had to wait overnight for the rigor mortis to subside. Don't know if it means anything. Most likely a token. But it's always the lovers that drive folk over the edge, isn't it?' He gave a cheerless smile.

'Always the lovers,' Frankie repeated quietly.

It was an odd lover's gift, a family crest. Surely the gift a husband would give, not a lover. And why would he have been clutching it? Why would he have clutched hold of anything if his corset was strangling him? She turned the brooch over in her hands. If he knew there was nothing to be done, he would know that he was going to be found. He would know that eventually someone would peel his hand open. Suddenly she remembered Smythe's words to his seamstress: 'I'll try it myself.' They had been talking about a costume the girl was stitching for Ebony. Was it possible that was the very garment he had died in? That whoever had laid the trap had meant it for . . . ?

She pulled her thoughts back. 'Can I keep this?'

John Bridewell looked doubtful. 'It should go to the police really.'

'Even if it was all just a nasty accident?'

John looked uneasily at the clock.

An idea struck her. She quickly took out her notebook and the one blunt pencil she had left in her jacket. Sliding the brooch between the pages she took a hasty rubbing. The carving of the lions didn't come through but it was enough to see that it was heads and leaves. As she was finishing, John began to snap his fingers. She withdrew the brooch and tossed it back to him. He placed a fleshy index finger to his lips. Just as the door began to creak open he managed to slip it back into the drawer and extract from the top of the cabinet a sheaf of papers. He tucked them close to his body, using his other arm to usher her quickly to the outer door. She didn't look behind her until they were back in the yard. John was sweaty-faced and panicked. 'He don't like journalists.'

'I know,' Frankie said, tucking her notebook back into her jacket. 'Thank you.' She met his puffy blue eyes for a second then looked back towards the door of the morgue. It waved in the wind and closed with a nasty creak. 'You don't still have the corset?'

He shook his head. 'Took a sample for the laboratory and we burned the rest. Safety.'

She narrowed her eyes.

'Safety from your Fleet Street lot. You're the second one come asking for it.'

'What?'

'Yeah,' he scratched his head. 'Woman came by the day we got him in, said she worked for him. Horrible-looking woman. If I was a cynical man, which I'm not, I would have said she was one of yours in disguise.' He chuckled stiffly.

Frankie shook her head fast. 'What do you mean?'

He tilted his head. 'Come on, Frankie, you know all the Fleet Street tricks. Who gets the story first? What do you call it, milking, when you steal someone else's newspaper story . . .' Frankie continued to stare at him. 'Well, you know, she had her face all bundled up. With a scarf. All filthy, like. Worked for him, my eye. If she did, I'd not have let her out in public. What's that thing they get at the match factories?'

Frankie frowned. 'Phossy jaw?'

'Yeah. Phossy jaw. Awful.'

Frankie said quietly, 'She does work for him.'

John Bridewell shrugged. 'Oh well, goes to show what I know. Anyway, I didn't give it to her.' He looked down and rummaged in the manila folder then pulled some papers free. 'Now about this letter.'

Frankie took a second to snap back out of her thoughts.

Then she smiled weakly and took the paper from John's outstretched hand.

The Lyons tea room was at the tail end of its opening hours when Frankie arrived. She was shown to a plush table big enough for four, decked out in velvet. A brass chandelier was reflected in the gilt mirror on the wall in front of her.

It was only end of the day food left. Scones were off, éclairs were off, tarts were finished, profiteroles done for. There was no cucumber left for sandwiches. Just meat paste and tuna fish.

'We have toast and cream fingers,' a waitress in a Lyons' pinny offered with her notepad poised in flushed hands.

Frankie ordered cream fingers and tea for two and waited for Milly, slowly flicking through the pages of her notepad, trying to decipher her own shorthand. She had decided what it was they would do next, whether Milly would join her or not.

At quarter past six she saw a figure dashing past the window, blurred by the steamed-up panes and the hazy streetlight. She didn't wait to be shown to the table, bustling her way past pairs of ladies in wide hats with Fortnum's bags at their feet.

Milly sat down with a thump and exhaled in one long breath until her cheeks were sucked flat. She clumsily took off her hat, leaving strands of her hair pricked up with static electricity in the wake of the felt.

'Calm down. You look as if you've seen a ghost.'

She met Frankie's eye with a cold look of disbelief. 'I feel like I have. Ebony's.'

Twenty-Five

They waited for the waitress to pour the tea. Frankie could feel Milly's leg hovering and twitching under the table, counting the seconds for the girl to leave.

'That's quite an operation they have in there,' she said when they were alone. Her eyes were fixed on the plate of cream fingers. Impulsively she reached out for one and crammed it between her lips. 'I'm famished. They gave us tea at four but it was shared between about sixty of us. Their stomachs must have all shrunk, being in Holloway. Where's the boy?'

Frankie shrugged. 'Haven't seen him since yesterday.'

Milly spoke with her mouth full of cream. 'They're planning something. There's a closed office upstairs, no one's allowed in but the committee.'

'So?'

'So I spent most of the day in the press room writing letters to prisoners. If you can write you get to do that. If not, it's banner-stitching or making trinkets for the next bazaar. They tried to send me out on the streets to hawk papers but I resisted. First time, you see, I had a good excuse.'

'What about Ebony? What did you mean about her ghost?'

She wiped her mouth with a napkin. 'I got talking to an old woman called Mrs Dale. We bonded. We both left our husbands.'

She dropped it in as casually as if she were talking about hats. Frankie frowned but didn't dare interrupt.

'By the time I arrived, there had already been one meeting. There's a couple of women coming out of Holloway tomorrow so they're organising a deputation. They'll put on a feast and, bizarrely enough, a bagpiper because one of the women is Scottish. Flora Drummond, she's the one they call "The General", she's arranging that.' She took a mouthful of tea. 'That's better. It's icy cold out there.'

Frankie looked down at her own clothes. She couldn't bear winters, and wasn't looking forward to getting back to her room and the meagre pile of coal Mrs Gibbons considered a fire. 'So what happened when you arrived? What did the building look like inside?'

'Be patient and I'll tell you.' Milly looked for a second at the plate of cream fingers then took another one, nibbling it more delicately this time. 'There's a hallway where you go in, and that's where the noticeboard is. They have all sorts up, notices for bazaars, calls for demonstrations, a register of political meetings that you can put your name down to attend in secret and they'll sort you out with some help. And then there's the pictures and postcards, morale boosters; there's one by Bovril that says, "After having my Bovril now they need six officers to arrest me rather than one", that sort of thing.'

Frankie raised a smile.

'Downstairs is the press room, that's where Mrs Dale sent me first. There were a few new ladies today, she said, and I ended up sitting next to quite a singular girl called Roberta. I wasn't sure whether I liked her; she was one of those boyish women, quite cold. I didn't mean—' She looked at Frankie's suit jacket and her fingers flew to her mouth.

'Don't worry.'

'Well, you know what I mean. She had strong cheek-bones, that sort of thing. Maybe I'm just jealous, her clothes hung off her the way they do off models these days. And I was thinking to myself, I suppose this must be what suffragettes look like. Then I started to wonder what they must have thought of me. Anyway, we wrote letters to prisoners all morning, mostly to women in the north-east, congratulating them on their effort, telling them about the fight. The press room was used for the journalists who worked on *Votes for Women*, but that's changed now they've launched *The Suffragette*. They have a few typewriters set up, two telephones. Mrs Dale said the police are always trying to cut them off. And there are three very stern looking women who wear navy blue and do the sub-editing.'

'Sounds about right.'

'Pardon?'

'Nothing, go on.'

'Well, then there's the office, where the treasurer and secretary sit. It looks like it was once the study of the house. It's the only room with a decent fire. And I suppose they take charge of donations and funding for all the costs of publishing pamphlets and zooming women around the country on trains. And in what I suppose would have been the parlour or dining room, there were women boxing up little posies of lavender and designing brooches to sell in the next bazaar. Did you know,' she frowned, 'that they are encouraged to melt down their jewellery and have it re-set in the suffragette colours, amethyst, emeralds, pearls. There's some of the most expensive jewels you ever saw on some of their throats. Family heirlooms, gone,' she flicked open her hand, 'just like that. Would you do that to your jewellery?'

'Do I look like I own jewellery?'

Milly blushed. 'No, well, neither do I. I sold mine to pay for my passage back to England.' She hesitated, breaking gaze with Frankie. Once again Frankie burned with the urge to ask her about her past, but before she could open her mouth, Milly suddenly said, 'This skirt is so itchy, you know.' She reached down under her blouse and, as discreetly as she could, gave her waist a good scratch. A bulbous-eyed woman at the next table glared.

Frankie sighed and tried to keep focus. 'So what about Ebony?'

Milly's eyes darkened and she looked up slowly. 'She hadn't attended a meeting there for nearly a month. No one had seen her after her last time in Holloway. And do you want to know something else? No one missed her.' She shook her head.

Frankie sat forward, nearly toppling her teacup as she caught the edge of the tablecloth. 'What?'

'Not a soul. I'd say if she hadn't abandoned them, she'd have been kicked out before too long. Funny thing was, this girl, this boyish little Roberta, Miss Jenkins, she wanted to know all about it too. Like she was some kind of crazed fanatic who'd gone along just to find out about her.'

'She might have thought the same about you.'

Milly nodded thoughtfully. 'She might.'

'So who told you this, about Ebony?'

'Well, like I said, at four o'clock we broke for tea. There's a kitchen at the back of the house and some of the older women, by that I mean the ones who had been there for a while, went to prepare bread and dripping, and pots of tea. So naturally I offered to help. So did Roberta Jenkins. She was the one who first asked about Ebony.'

'Did you ask how she knew Ebony?'

'She didn't. She said she had read about her. She was there at the Albert Hall that night, so she said. And Mrs Dale stopped stirring the jam pot, cold, and she said, "I wouldn't go bandying that name about here if you want to stay on folks' good sides." She was perfectly serious. Her face was as sour as I saw it that day, because she really was a very nice amiable woman. But the mention of Ebony . . .'

Milly took some of her tea and kept the warm cup in her

hands. 'And so I pretended I knew very little about her. And I asked what it was she had done. Frankie, it was like a fisherman opening a bag of maggots and watching them spill out all over the table. The things Ebony wanted them to do, the plans she made. July this year, you remember Mrs Barclay-Evans said they called a truce. Ebony had grown very agitated at this, according to Mrs Dale and had begun making all sorts of schemes. Instead of flying a hot air balloon over parliament and throwing pamphlets overboard she wanted to throw pebbles. She didn't understand until one of the women who has a bachelor of science degree explained to her that from that height a pebble could kill someone. She wanted to ambush the Prime Minister at his country home, to take him hostage. She wanted to throw him tied to a trapeze off Big Ben. And this one you'll like.' Milly dropped her voice. 'She wanted to release the tigers from London Zoo and set them loose on the streets with a note round their neck saying "Deeds Not Words".'

Frankie swallowed uncomfortably. Suddenly all the cream and tea in her stomach was making her feel sick. Could it be that the woman she had seen at the corset shop, on stage that night, had not been frightened at all, she had simply been unhinged? Was her agitation the twitchings of a woman who belonged in the Bedlam? 'It's all talk though.'

'She said they had drawings on file, no written plans, Ebony could barely write her own name, let alone spell. They wanted rid of her. Her stunts, they said, were getting out of hand.'

'But what about the militancy? The arson, what the

Barclay-Evanses said about the split? They said militancy was on the up anyway.'

'Not like this. They're very strict about not harming anyone.'

'And you think she's a liability? That someone wants rid of her for good?'

'I don't know what to think. Mrs Dale swore blind that she hadn't seen her since the last time in Holloway. She was in for window-smashing I think, or she might have thrown a stone at a cabinet minister's car.'

'And was it universal? I mean did everyone hate her or was anyone behind her?'

'She had one friend in the movement. A girl she met when she first joined. They were thick as thieves, Mrs Dale said. She helped her rig the trapeze at the Albert Hall and they'd been in Holloway together a couple of times. She was working as a parlourmaid but she lost her job for some reason a few weeks before the last time they ended up in prison. Ebony helped her find a new job, somewhere, and then after they came out of Holloway they left the WSPU. That is to say, no one saw either of them again.'

'And her name?' Frankie asked softly.

'It was Annie. Annie Evans. It was her. The girl in the papers, the one that was killed on Tottenham Court Road. I saw a photograph of them both at a rally.'

Frankie put her face in her hands and ran her fingers through her hair. 'One down, one to go. Maybe they weren't after Ebony that night after all, they wanted both of them.'

Milly nodded gently. 'I couldn't write anything down, of course, I was trying to take it all in.' She took a long blink. 'I don't know what to think of Ebony now. What was she thinking? Could she have gone through with her plans? I just don't want to think.'

Frankie watched her carefully. Without her hat, her hair looked scruffy and wild and in the plain brown suit she could from a distance have passed for any ordinary governess or working woman. But there was still something in her face, the way the muscles round her mouth moved when she talked, something in her lips and vowels. After a while her shoulders fell back in the chair, exhausted. 'Anyway, how did you get on at the morgue?'

Frankie filled her in quickly. The poison in the corset; the brooch found on Smythe; the woman who had come for his clothes. She took out her notebook and passed the rubbing across to Milly. 'Did you ever see Ebony with that?'

Milly looked at the sketch for a long time. Her eyes roamed its rough lines from the top to the point at the base. After a while she looked away and rubbed at her eyelids. 'It's hard to make out what it is.'

'Looks like a family crest.'

'I've never seen it before.'

'Did she have a lover? An admirer who came to the club? You know Jojo talked about cabinet ministers.'

Milly was looking sceptically at her. 'I've never seen any cabinet ministers. He talks himself big, Jojo.' She sighed. 'If Ebony had a lover she was as clandestine with him as she was with everything else. Like where she was going for the past month when we thought she was at suffragette meetings.'

Frankie thought for a moment or two then looked Milly in the eye as she took back her notebook. 'I have a hunch about that. But we won't find out about it until tonight.'

Milly cast her eyes down at the scrappy remnants of their tea. Her brow became creased with rows of little lines. 'I'm tired, Frankie. And I have to work tonight. Club's open again.'

'So we go afterwards.'

'Go where?'

'Smythe's. The corset shop.'

Twenty-Six

Annie Evans. The name sat on the tip of Primrose's tongue as he strode down the mucky road the omnibus had deposited him on, back towards Pentonville Prison. Robert Jenkins had telegraphed the office with the information that afternoon, and now Primrose had in his pocket a Judge's order for William Reynolds's discharge, if, and only if, he could be of reasonable use to a police investigation. It had been procured during Mr Justice Curtis Watkins's medicinal nap, taken after Sunday lunch and, as Stuttlegate continued to remind him, at great inconvenience. But as the prisoner was male, and therefore more likely to make rational decisions when issuing blackmail threats, Stuttlegate did not have a problem signing off the telegram.

There had been no dental records to verify the identity, but a strong-stomached suffragette had agreed to view the body. Photographs were sourced from the Holloway files. Doubt was erased. The methods they had set Jenkins up with for gathering his information may have been unorthodox, but the facts were correct. It was Annie Evans.

Primrose's nerves jangled in his great skeleton as he walked, still dizzy-headed from his own interrupted afternoon nap that he had managed to snatch in his office, his clothes creased and pulled from their usual shape, his limbs warm in some places, cold in others.

A guard pulled open the front entrance gate. The yard was empty of horses now; the shells of Black Marias lay shining in the crisp cold sunlight. Reception was busy: visiting afternoon. Primrose wedged past the crowds of wives, brothers, sons and mothers, scrubbed, combed and in their Sunday best, and approached the front desk.

There was a different officer on, who all but sneered as Primrose displayed his warrant card.

'CID? It's Sunday.'

'It's extremely urgent. I have a court order, and I need to speak to the Senior Medical Officer.'

'You're having a laugh.'

'I beg your pardon.'

The man bared a set of rusty old teeth in a frosty smile. 'He's at afternoon tea.'

'Afternoon tea? In Pentonville?'

The officer gestured to the crowd. 'Stand aside please, we're very busy.'

Primrose turned to see a woman behind him, dabbing at her eyes with a threadbare handkerchief, and a creep of dread swam over him, not anchored to anything in particular. He turned back to the officer. 'I'm afraid I'm going to need to be dealt with before these people.'

The officer scratched his freckled chin and ran his finger down the ledger book, humming a ditty. 'What's the prisoner's name you're after?'

'Reynolds. You'll know him, he's the suffrage man.'

The officer looked puzzled for a second, then nodded. 'Yeah, I do.' He didn't offer any more, just continued to peruse his italic scribblings in the ledger. Just as Primrose felt a jostle in his back, the officer snapped his head up. 'He ain't here.'

'What? That's preposterous, I visited him this morning, he's here.'

'Well, he ain't.' The man shrugged. 'You're the second person come looking for him just now.'

'Well what do you mean ain't'?

'Isn't.'

Primrose stemmed a well of vitriol. He looked into the man's blue eyes and slowly clawed back his temper. 'Men don't just disappear from prison.'

'No, they don't,' the man said, enjoying himself. 'He was discharged.'

Primrose reached a heavy hand across the desk. 'Let me see that ledger.'

The man stiffened but let him take it, aware of the boundaries he could push. CID men were the bane of his existence, swanning in with their thick coats and fancy hats, flapping their warrant cards.

'Can I speak with the Governor?'

'Governor's at afternoon tea,' the man said levelly.

Primrose scanned down the slick pattern of handwriting until he found the name. In the 'admitted' column the date was 2 November, two days ago. The convictions were vandalism of property and contempt of court. Then in the discharge column, beside the governor's signature, a set of initials had been scrawled. 'CH.'

'Who's CH?' Primrose demanded.

The man was chewing the flesh of his cheek. 'Yeah, his wife was in again just half an hour ago. She come in earlier today as well, but they hadn't told her neither. Not that there's any reason they would but for a transfer of this kind . . . Of this nature, I mean.'

'Dammit, what do you mean?'

The officer looked shocked, then affronted, then reproachful. Primrose looked around to see that the people beside him had fallen silent. Blood swam to his cheeks. He leant towards the officer, close enough to smell the man's soap. 'Tell me where the prisoner has been taken. I have a murder investigation dependent on it and a warrant for his release.'

'Release?' the man snorted. 'That's a laugh. You'll have a fine time trying to get him out of there.'

'Out of where?'

The man squared Primrose in the eye. 'Colney Hatch. Lunatic Asylum. Governor signed the warrant just after lunch. Should have seen his wife's face, she was almost as hysterical as you, Inspector.' He coughed quietly.

Primrose said nothing but as his hand slammed into the officer's desk he startled even himself.

Twenty-Seven

Jojo's was dark and cavernous, the only light coming from candles shielded in hurricane lamps or jugs, giving off a warm oily smell and a glow like dirty moonlight. Frankie had spent the last few hours in a Turkish coffee shop round the corner, drinking a thick brew that Milly had ordered for her, and trying to separate in her heavily caffeinated mind each of the facts she had learned.

Someone had attacked and killed Annie Evans on Thursday night. The same evening, a black corset was laced with poison ivy, and Olivier Smythe had tried it on. Ebony Diamond's equipment had been booby-trapped at the Coliseum on Friday and she had second-guessed it and escaped. She knew that Ebony was afraid Annie had been mistaken for her, but could it be possible that Ebony was the only target for both deaths? That phrase she had used, sitting outside on the pavement, 'nine lives'. Did she already know that two were gone?

Then there were the poisons. Cocaine drops could be

easily sourced from a druggists, but poison ivy, John Bridewell had said, was a rare botanical. So that meant someone with a hothouse or access to an exotic garden. But the murderer would also have needed access to Olivier's corset shop and the Coliseum. And she couldn't for the life of her see how a cabinet minister could have either. A suffragette on the other hand . . .

And then the brooch. One image had been permeating Frankie's thoughts for the past while. Ebony holding up a brooch in the gaslight before hurling it at Smythe. She had yelled something too, but Frankie couldn't remember what. There were too many open questions, and she was certain now of where the answers had to lie.

She was grateful to Milly when a waiter came over and slapped a plate of chops down in front of her. They were grizzled little things, more fat than meat, but they soaked up the gravy and she hadn't had a proper meal for two days. She bent her head and tucked in. Halfway through, she felt eyes on her, looked up and jumped. Liam had silently taken the other seat at the table and looked like he had been staring at her for some time.

'Can I have one of those?' He pointed to the remaining chop.

An emptiness tugged at Frankie's stomach but she looked into his pasty freckled face and nodded. He pulled the plate towards him and picked the chop up by the bone, rubbing it in the leftover gravy, concentrating on peeling every fibre of meat off with his front teeth. She was about to open her mouth to ask where he had been, when a compère in a top hat and tailcoat threw back the turquoise curtains with his cane and the audience began to applaud.

The show got off to a sorry start. There were some fire jugglers and a man who talked in rhyme. The patrons knew when to laugh and when to coo and were mostly men grouped at tables clutching mugs of ale. A few had bored-looking women seated on their laps, fondling the men's hair. Cups of cocoa laced with whisky, gin and absinthe were being offered for a ha'penny, and the monkey capered around with an upturned hat collecting donations.

Next came a contortionist who claimed to play the piano with her feet but made a bad job of simulating Strauss on a pianola, and a woman with a talking raven, that looked suspiciously like a parrot inked black, and that she'd taught to say 'Fanny Fairbrass fucked a Frenchman'. They brought out a man who had allegedly been fasting for thirty-four days. He staggered onto the stage, the hollows of his eyes gazing outwards.

Frankie was beginning to grow anxious, and withdrew her pocket-watch from her jacket, but the candlelight at her table was too dark for her see the face. She was about to poke Liam and ask him the time when there came a crackle from beyond the wings and the floor filled with the sickly choke of incense. The footlights flickered to black. Two tiny glows became visible in the mist. From a gramophone in the corner a hard nasal drone struck up and down, jogging and scratching as the record settled. Drumbeats joined in, crisp and fast. It was like nothing Frankie had heard before. As the footlights slowly came back up she could see Milly shrouded in a long translucent purple veil, clutching in each hand a candle in a small glass like a milk bottle. The men stopped their carousing. Laughter faded.

Milly swayed from side to side, snaking her arms out until the veil dropped away and the candles in her hands seemed to stretch far from her. Her belly was naked – except for a small chain of tumbling bells that rang in time to the music – and looked as supple and soft as pale clay. Trinkets and pearls dripped from her hair. Clasping her hips tight were a selection of scarves – some fringed, some with shells or pearls dangling and running towards the pantaloons that puffed round her feet in the light breeze of her movement. Her breasts were enclosed in a top of rippling silk that ran the length of her arms and floated to points beneath her wrists. In and out of the smoky light her face ebbed, and when she paused to place down her candles Frankie saw the expression on it, her brows set firm, her soft proud cheeks calcified with a determination that extended into her pale eyes. She looked almost frightening.

A boy emerged with a basket and Frankie's nerves began to prickle. She looked around the room and saw Jojo staring at Milly, concentrating.

Slowly Milly reached down and pulled from the basket her snake, wrapping it first round her waist while she tilted her hips, then letting it weave up her arms until its face found her throat. The licking of its forked tongue was enough to give Frankie the horrors; she fancied she could see its black eyes catch the light even from a distance. The compère spoke up. 'And now, Miss Salome from Cairo, Egypt, will swallow her serpent.'

'Where on earth did you learn to do that?'

'I told you, Cairo.' Milly was still dressed in harem pants but had thrown on top of them a silk gown and a periwinkle cloak. Her greasepaint had been taken off in haste and she still smelled faintly of cold cream.

'Yes, but not everybody who goes to Cairo comes back swallowing snakes and dancing the hoochie-coochie. I could come back from France and I wouldn't know how to make Swiss cheese.'

'Swiss cheese is Swiss,' Liam said.

'You shut it,' Frankie spun to him. 'What have you been doing all day, anyway? Apart from brushing up your cheese knowledge.' She watched his little twig of a hand prise open the greasy pocket of his wool jacket, then withdraw from it a fragile wisp of paper folded into quarters. He paused under a streetlight and with great ceremony untucked the paper and smoothed it into his palm. Frankie bent over him, breathing in his sour odour. The paper was a playbill capped by inch-thick letters and a swirling ribbon. 'Englebert Fink, Travelling Curitorium and Big Top.'

She took a step back. 'Oh. Enjoy yourself, did you? Don't suppose you won me a little tweeting bird in a cage? While I was off at the morgue and she was taking tea with Boadicea's barmy-army, you were having a nice time up Hampstead Heath, were you?'

Liam waited until she had finished and he had her in his needling eye. Then he pointed to a picture of a man on the flyer, grossly overweight, with rolls of fat waterfalling down to his knees. 'That's her Da.'

Frankie peered at the drawing, remembering the postcard propped against Ebony's dressing table, the strong man in the leotard. 'I thought her dad was a strong man.'

'He was. Attila the Hungarian. Not any more.'

She looked closer. Underneath the picture of the man was written the word 'FATTILA'.

'So what?' she said. 'You find her?'

'Not this time. But she's there.'

'What makes you so sure?'

He shrugged. 'I don't know for certain. But it was better than following you around for the abuse you give me. I should report you to Dr Barnardo.'

Frankie blew spittle between her lips. Liam folded the paper again and they resumed walking. 'I thought she cut her ties with the circus,' she said.

Liam threw up his hands. 'There's a lot of circuses. They don't blacklist you just because you ditch one. Besides, I told you, her Da is there.'

They reached a crossing and stopped to let a pirate bus amble past. Frankie turned back to Milly. 'Anyway, you still haven't told me where you learned – that.' Milly sighed and picked up pace as the traffic cleared.

'You don't really believe I swallow it, do you? You saw the silk top I wear. There's a pocket that runs up to my throat. It's a trick of the light. It's so dark in there and the men are so drunk they wouldn't know the difference. I'm not so cheap I'll risk my life for the money he pays.'

'What about the dancing?'

'Nobody dances with snakes in Egypt. They're as petrified of them as you are. But that's not what Jojo's idiots want to believe.'

'But where did you learn?'

'You wouldn't believe me.'

'I've heard enough far-fetched tales these past few days I'll believe anything.'

'A hammam.'

'A what?'

'A Turkish bath.'

Frankie blinked, thinking of the contraption in Twinkle's room.

'I told you you wouldn't believe me. The women would dance in the baths. It's very sociable. We're alone, it's the chance to gossip. Sometimes they have sweets, pipes.'

'You learned to dance in a bath?'

'It's not like a gem-wood cabinet. It's a bath house. Anyway that's only half of it. The rest's too long a story. Are we going to walk the whole way to this damned corset shop?' She stopped again, puffing her cheeks out.

'It's not far. Come on, it's late, they might already be gone.'

'Who?' Liam asked.

'You'll see.'

It took a quarter of an hour to reach New Bond Street. The streets were busy, despite it being Sunday. Revellers spilled out of the Music Halls as they drew closer to Oxford Street. Down Regent Street a muted glow came from the restaurant rooms in the hotels, and doormen in livery stood rubbing their hands, watching cold breath drift from their mouths. As they walked through Hanover Square the shops and hotels gave way to fashionable townhouses and the streets grew dark and quiet, drapes drawn in first-floor parlours.

Frankie halted on the corner of Brook Street. She pointed at Liam. 'You're going to be look-out. Me and her are going in. Understand?'

Liam blew out smoke from a cigarette he had acquired en route. 'No.'

'Don't argue. There's . . .' She stopped as footsteps behind them drew heavy and close. A low melancholy whistling and the bulky outline of a policeman crossed their paths. He paused, surveyed the trio and tipped his hat at Milly. 'Mister, Miss.' He glanced at Liam, then kept walking.

Frankie let her breath out. 'God, we could almost pass for a respectable couple if it wasn't for Fagan's valet.'

Liam fired the cigarette at Frankie's shoe, showering it in sparks.

Milly was looking across the street. 'What are you hoping we'll find in there?' Her voice clouded on the cold air.

Frankie followed her gaze. She could just make out the lines of the shop front, the curved window with its dainty square panes and the discreet 'Closed until further notice' sign hanging in front of a black drape inside the door. She thought of the last time she had ventured inside, the smell of linen and Mr Smythe's eyes on her thick waist. 'I don't know. But we won't find it looking in from the outside.'

Frankie glanced to her left where the painted doors of the Maid in the Moon were padlocked shut. She turned to Liam. 'If you stay over there, we'll shout if we need you.'

Liam jammed his hands into his jacket pocket, and pulled his cap low on his head. As they started across the street he whistled. Frankie turned.

'Hey, want me to dip any pockets for you while I'm waiting?' He saw the alarm in her eyes and burst out laughing.

A fresh needle of irritation pricked her but she brushed it off and walked on, trembling inside, heart thumping. Bond Street was near empty, but further down a few of the hotels had their lobby lights on and carriages idled outside. A clock chimed half past eleven and was answered shortly by another from the opposite direction.

Frankie looked up at the windows on the first floor. The curtains were drawn but there was a very faint bronze glow slicing the middle. They could hear sounds of muted conversation coming from upstairs. Frankie raised a brow at Milly.

As they approached the front door Frankie touched Milly's wrist and pointed with her chin towards Lancashire Court. Passing the shop window, they caught a glimpse of the inside.

Corsets hung in uneven rows from the ceiling, like dismembered torsos in a butcher's shop.

The alleyway was wet and dark but they found the back door easily. Frankie wrapped her palm round the brass handle. It was icy cold and creaked as she turned it. It stalled. She gestured to Milly to stand behind her and angled her shoulder to the door in preparation to force it.

'No,' Milly hissed, pulling her back. She began fumbling in the pile of fine gold hair under her hat and pulled out a hairpin. 'This is surveillance, not an ambush.' Bending towards the lock she wiggled the pin until they heard a small snap like a twig breaking. 'Need another,' she mumbled reaching up into her hair again. She pulled out a second pin and jammed the first one up, wriggling the other until she heard the click she was looking for. Turning, her lips spread into a wicked grin. 'My nanny used to lock me in the attic if I was bad.'

Frankie grunted and moved past her to open the door. Immediately, the smell of dust and fabrics drifted out, sweet cotton on musty air. Frankie recognised the back passage of the shop from before, a pitch-black lobby, the feel of a velvet curtain on one side and a staircase on the other. Gently, Milly touched aside the curtain and a wedge of streetlight from beyond the windows lit up the front chamber of the shop. She ran her eyes down the rows of hanging corsets, braced open with wooden pegs and wire frames and gave a shudder.

'Good lord, I'm glad my nanny didn't know about this place. She used to lace me up like she was stuffing a divan.'

Frankie peered into the space beyond the curtain. Suddenly something touched her wrist, silky, almost alive in texture. She jumped and looked round to see a padded mannequin, headless, its midriff covered in a dark turquoise bodice piped with French lace. Her hand reached out curiously to caress the silk. It felt like oil under her fingertips. Milly flicked the hard, brittle catch of whalebones with a fingernail.

'I will never understand Ebony's passion for stays. I burned all mine.'

They pushed the mannequin out of the way and moved towards the stairs, a jute carpet underfoot absorbing the sound of their tread. Overhead they could hear the irregular lilt of trodden floorboards. The staircase had a high Dutch feel to it, almost vertical in its steepness as if it would reach right up into the attics of the building. They had reached halfway when a loose board made a pitching groan as Frankie's weight bore down on it. She felt her breath seize. Milly's cool fingers wrapped round her wrist. No one stirred on the upper floor and they continued on.

At the top, light was coming from a keyhole on the left and from under the doorframe on the right. Voices carried from both sides; laughter and the gentle chinking of ice or teaspoons on saucers.

With her fingertips in front of her, hearing the seashell thrashing of blood in her brain, Frankie moved towards the keyhole. A fine ghostly finger of light extended towards her. She could feel Milly's breath on the back of her neck. As she drew closer she crouched to the keyhole's level, braced her hand against the wood and put her eye down low to the gap. A small portion of the room came into focus. She let her eye adjust to the light, and her mouth gaped.

At first it looked like a plain storage room, bare wooden floorboards, brick walls painted in a thin coating of white lime. A curtain hung unevenly over the window. Beside it a candle flickered in a hurricane lamp, firing shadows up the walls. To the left stood a rack of flesh-coloured corsets, thick with buckles and rivets, more like surgical braces. Over on the right stood a tailor's dummy, pale wood at the belly revealing where it had been gouged to narrow the waist. A garment of beaten metal was strapped to it, a lattice of worn steel tightly clasping the wooden bosom. Squinting at it Frankie saw that it wasn't only the shape that held it to the wood but each join in the lattice had a sharp stiletto protruding inwards, making a deep wound in the dummy's chest. It reminded her of something she had read about in a book passed behind the privies at school, an iron maiden. Only snugger, tailor-made. Her gaze rose to see hanging above the dummy something that looked like a trapeze, fixed on both sides by thin lengths of rope, immobilising it so that it couldn't swing. Frankie had seen one of those before too at her convent school. A lacing bar. The wearer would stand with their arms aloft while someone else laced them in, the stretch allowing for a tighter pinch.

Without warning, a black cloud passed across her vision, too close. Someone had walked in front of the keyhole. The floorboards groaned.

'What is it?' Milly whispered.

Light returned and Frankie saw sitting at eye level on a plain stool the back of a slim woman chatting quietly to a maid who stood above her. She lifted a leg and rolled on a sheer stocking, pulling a sheaf of pale green petticoats out of the way. When she tucked them back down and stood up, Frankie saw the full length of her outfit; frothing underskirts, a white camisole covered at the arm with a black band, and a long dark green corset. The maid was decked out in a black smock under a white pinny, with the same mourning band.

The woman in green stretched her arms until they cracked lightly. Gently, her maid eased her down until she was prone on the dusty floor. Frankie heard a short sniff, then what she saw sent her heart up into her throat.

The maid lifted the woman's underskirts to the side, and with the flat of her foot, stamped on her back, pressing the small of it so hard that her own face contorted. She reached for the corset laces and pulled them up, using her weight to lever them as tight as the flesh would allow. The woman let out a long moan then blew out her breath. She took a few moments before standing up.

Frankie felt a creeping sickness at the memory of Ebony hanging on the trapeze, the light and her corset so black she looked split in two, at the vision of Smythe's flesh rupturing out of his stays. But underlying it there was something else, a thick channel of fascination, for what on God's earth were they doing, violently lacing themselves in at this time of night in a room above the shop?

She was so puzzled by it all that she didn't feel the first blow. Suddenly she was astonished to find herself on the floor looking up at the ceiling, without pain but with a cloying fuzziness in her vision. Someone was screaming. Milly. She heard a second blow. Her head bounced to one side. Then she felt the third blow and the lights went clean out.

Twenty-Eight

'Visitors?' the enormous pink-faced matron in the grey smock said. 'At this hour? They compromise the dignity of the patient at the best of times.' She glowered at Primrose as if he had come up with the very concept of visiting patients in lunatic asylums himself. It was true it was late. The paperboys by the side of the road had been strapped into their sandwich boards, peddling the first edition of tomorrow's news as he hurried off his tram in sleek black rain and up the great drive-way of Colney Hatch Asylum. But then he had also been made to wait for almost two hours in the asylum lobby. He wondered whether it would be prudent to point this out to the matron and decided against it.

They were standing in the entrance, a high airy hall with a faint institutional smell and a floor that conducted bright echoes of every noise that came into contact with it: foot-steps, dropped pencils, the lick of a mop. It was a gloomy night and beyond the front door a wide sprawl of clipped hedges and gardens were soaking up the fierce rain. Weather and time of night aside, Colney Hatch seemed a peaceful place, more docile than its forbidding name; and more docile than its Matron, Miss Large, who was now chewing the flesh of her lips as if she couldn't quite make up her mind whether to sedate Primrose or not. He noticed with a flash of discomfort that she carried a thin metal syringe in her breast pocket.

He held out the Judge's order. Travelling back and forth between Bow Street, Pentonville Prison and the Embankment had creased it somewhat.

'Let me see that.' She unfolded it and scrutinized the print with marble-hard eyes. Primrose felt his chest wilt looking at her, memories stirring of schoolteachers and formidable dairy-farming aunts. She passed it back.

'You won't get anything out of him. He's been doped with opium and hyoscine. Can barely talk.'

'Do you know why he was moved here?'

'The report that came in to us said there had been an incident at Pentonville.'

Primrose flushed. 'Well yes, I saw that they were force-feeding him.'

She shook her head. 'No, no. It was following a visit from his wife earlier today.' She looked at him to emphasise her point again about visitors.

'Do you think I could speak to him?' Primrose tried to relax and not show fear.

The matron rolled her sleeves further up her salmon-pink arms. 'It's very late and it doesn't do to cause a patient stress.'

'It's a murder investigation.'

'Besides you can't always be certain that what is coming out of their mouths is true.'

'Perhaps there's a viewing flap?'

She hesitated, then sighed noisily through loose nostrils. 'The first sign of distress and I'll have you escorted from the premises, CID or not.'

Primrose acquiesced politely. He looked around him as they passed through the corridor and thought that perhaps Matron Large might be right. If he ever had the misfortune to be locked in such a place, he probably wouldn't want visitors.

The layout was so vast he could have been walking through a small village, different streets leading off from junctions and crossroads, all painted a bright detergent-scented white. In the parlour near the lobby a few patients idled with late-night needlework and packs of cards. They turned through another corridor and passed through a wing of eighty or more beds, all filled. Matron Large watched Primrose from the corner of her eye. He tried not to stare.

'I shouldn't really be taking you through here,' she said to him as if it were his fault she had brought him this way. 'It's the women's wing.'

His face coloured and he tried his best to look straight ahead.

They rounded a few more corners, passing through empty corridors with secure doors lining them.

'He's a suffragette, you know,' Primrose offered by way of conversation.

The matron looked startled as if she couldn't think to whom he was referring, then curtly said, 'Yes, I know. I'm not trying to protect him.'

It was Primrose's turn to feel uncomfortable. Their exchange of words felt like a particularly nasty game of chess, although he didn't mean it to be so. He decided to keep his mouth shut until they reached Reynolds. But the matron had been piqued. 'I have no truck with them you know. It's not an organisation for working women. We don't have time for the At Homes; can't afford to spend time in prison either. Fat lot of good it will do us, fighting for property owners to win the vote. Do you think I own property, Inspector, what was your name?'

'Primrose.'

'Primrose.'

'It's not my job to say . . .'

'Do you think I will be any better off with the voices of ten thousand Tory-voting well-to-do women representing my opinions than I am with the voices of men? No one is trying to win me a vote, Inspector. I do my job. That's my only concern – my patient.'

Primrose had it on the tip of his tongue to contradict her, he wanted to spit out something about Sylvia Pankhurst's new East London Federation for working women that some of his colleagues were monitoring closely, or the Lancashire mill girls. But the words stuck and he reflected that it was not his job to go recruiting extra suffragettes.

They passed a small dispensary where men and women in

laboratory coats were measuring out powders and tinctures. His eyes fell on the breast-pocket syringe again.

'Has he had any other visitors?'

'His wife.' She stopped for a fraction of a second, and it came again, the flash of something, words unsaid, put back on the shelf. Graciously, with gritted jaw, Primrose held open the door for her.

'His wife visited him here already?'

'As far as she could. He had to be sedated.' She stopped fully now. They were in a corridor of secure metal doors. 'We're not sure but we think there might have been a bereavement. Something he didn't know about before his wife visited him in prison, that caused him to break down.' She sighed again and touched her chin. 'He seems to not even want the sight of her now. He became very agitated when she came here to visit. But then, Inspector, that's visitors.'

At that moment a bell rang out, high and clear, carrying on the corridor's arched ceiling. 'Excuse me,' the matron said and ran at a trot down the corridor to a room in the far corner where the door had already been flung back. Primrose could just make out a dim wailing from within, hollow, like the cry of a fox. There was an attendant in blue overalls in the doorway already; a straggle of others quickly joined. As the door opened wider, the sound of punches and knocks echoed into the corridor.

'Wet sheets. Cold wrap,' an attendant was ordering.

The matron's voice replied. 'No, I'm giving him extra

opium; there now, let's have your arm.' Her feet echoed an irregular tattoo inside the cell as she moved about, scurrying for purchase on a flitting body. 'Keep him in a lock.' The patient uttered something and the nurse replied, 'No one's coming for you.'

Primrose, with a shudder to his nerves suddenly recognised the timbre of the voice, the enunciated vowels. He dared to step closer to the cell's open door. Reynolds was lying prone, dribbling onto a cotton pillow, an attendant holding him by the wrists while Matron Large bent over him and inserted a needle into his already track-marked arm.

'Don't you see?' he was saying. 'They killed her.'

'There, there.' The matron dabbed at the sweat on his head.

'They killed her and they'll kill again.'

'No one's killing anyone. Not while you're safe in here. You have to learn to talk back to those voices or we'll never get anywhere.'

'Who did they kill?' Primrose took a step forward then froze as the matron locked him in cold admonishment. The attendants fell silent.

Reynolds twisted his head enough to see Primrose. A blur of recognition floated in his eyes, then disappeared again, replaced by sedative.

'Who's been killed?'

The matron stood forward. 'I told you, you weren't to stress my patient.'

'Annie,' Primrose said, 'Annie Evans, is that who?' He

took a step closer, dropping to his knees so he was eye level with Reynolds.

'Patients feel very unsettled when they come in here, voices, paranoid notions. Now if you put ideas in there . . .'

'It was Annie, wasn't it? You knew Annie Evans, didn't you? Who killed Annie?'

The matron began backing Primrose out of the room with her powerful frame. He resisted but was loath to lay a finger on her. Reynolds's smeary face looked up from his pillow. Lucidity swam into his eyes again and he looked helpless as a boy for a few seconds. He nodded.

'Who killed Annie?' Primrose repeated, feeling his arms now being yanked back by spare attendants, dragging him from the room into the corridor. He ground them away, startling the men with his strength. They had not banked on a man who had learned the craft of cow-wrestling at a young age. By the time he fought his way back into the cell, Reynolds's eyes were gone again. He dropped his neck, gave up the fight. Tears collected in his pinked eyes. He murmured two words into his pillow. 'Remember. Remember.'

Back in the corridor the matron pinched Primrose's arm into a medical grip. 'You didn't tell me it was *that* murder investigation. I could have saved you the hassle and my patient the abuse.'

Primrose looked confused.

She marched him over to a side table and directed his gaze down to a newspaper. The date was printed at the top, one of the very early editions of tomorrow's. 'Don't your men communicate?'

'What?' Primrose reached for the paper. 'Who?'

She puffed her breath out again, tucking the syringe back into her pocket. Primrose continued to rifle through the paper, then realised it was on the front page.

'Suffragette Murder: Unexpected turn! Police Raid WSPU HQ.'

Twenty-Nine

Frankie felt the world turn a fast somersault before it came back to her. First in her ears, a clattering like dogs' feet on flagstones. Then water on her face, cold on the ground. She realised it was raining and she was flat on her back. Next to her Milly moaned. Frankie felt sick to her gut. The back of her head throbbed. She opened her eyes and saw the silhouette of a figure peering over her, a cloth cap on oily hair that glowed red in the streetlamp.

'Still happy I'm just the look-out boy?' Liam spat. Frankie wriggled her shoulder, and spat out a bad taste of her own: blood. She coughed a couple of times and tried to focus. Whether it was the dark or her dizziness he looked a little blurred.

'You could be a gentleman.' She stuck out her hand.

Liam looked both amused and affronted by the suggestion. He grabbed her by the forearm and yanked her to her feet. Milly rolled to sit up, picking up her silk dress where it had clung to the ground. 'What just happened?'

Liam ran his eyes over her filthy blue cloak and smeared make-up. He put a finger to his lips and pointed up at the first floor window of the corset shop. The curtains twitched, then the slice of marmalade light was gone.

'See, they're watching you,' he whispered. 'Come away and we'll go down there.' He pointed to Haunch of Venison Yard, helped Milly up and led the way.

The yard was sheathed in tar-coloured mist but Frankie could just make out a ruby graze on Milly's temple. The back of her neck felt like it had snapped. She rubbed it, trying to squeeze out the pain. Liam found some shelter underneath an awning for them.

'Yous hadn't been in there five minutes when I heard a scream.' He looked at Milly.

'Someone hit us from behind.' She blushed.

'Well, I didn't hear none of that,' Liam went on, 'but they brought you downstairs over one of their shoulders. Took two of them to carry you,' he nodded at Frankie.

'Who's they?' Frankie asked.

Liam's eyes were blank hollows. 'I don't know. They were dressed like maids. Three lassies wearing black. White bonnets,' he drew a ring round his head. A memory rippled across Frankie's mind. She had knelt down, peeped through the keyhole, and she had seen . . .

Liam turned to the mouth of the yard as a noise echoed towards them. It was a couple out strolling, hurrying under the gentleman's coat, loud footsteps and laughter carrying behind them. He shook his head. 'They put something in your pocket.'

'Mine?' Frankie's hands began to root around her trouser pockets.

'Top pocket.'

Gingerly she raised her arm, wincing at a pain in her shoulder that extended from her neck muscles. Her fingers dipped carefully into the fabric, as if what lurked in there might be laced with poison or razor-sharp. Instead she found a card, a heavy embossed card with eggshell finish on it and a pearly sheen. It looked blank on both sides, but someone had scrawled a note in an uncertain, jerky hand. 'Invitation only.'

Frankie turned it over in her palms, seeing nothing but the scribble, when she began to detect underneath her fingers a slight denting of the paper in parts, a textured valley under her thumbs. She moved towards the mouth of the yard.

'Be careful,' Milly croaked.

In the weak streetlight, misted with rain, she could just make out the outline of an imprint, deep in the card, pressed by the heavy metal hand of a machine: an hourglass.

There was nothing else on it, no address, no post office box, not even a telephone number. The scribbled ink began to run, smearing the finish to a charcoal grey. Milly's voice came from the pitch dark of the alley. 'Frankie? You saw something through the keyhole. I heard you gasp.'

Frankie tried to snatch back the memory. It was bent out of shape, the edges blurred, the way dreams were when she woke up. She remembered a woman rolling on a stocking, and that steel thing braced on the wooden dummy. A woman lying on the floor while another pulled in her laces. But she wasn't quite sure she hadn't dreamt it while she was unconscious. The only real things she had were the card in her hand and the pain. She sniffed; her nose was threatening to run in the cold. 'That old witch fobbed me off twice, and what have we got to show for it but boiled eggs on the back of our heads? Come on, last time I promise.'

Milly and Liam both looked at her. 'Where now?' Liam asked.

'Twinkle's.'

The rain kept up its assault all the way. Milly huddled close under Frankie's jacket for shelter, their feet trotting in quickstep. Once or twice a cab passed them, spewing fountains of water from the street onto their ankles.

Twinkle's new maid answered the door with a finger on her lips. Frankie pushed past her, sliding the coat off her head and squeezing water from the soaked edges onto the doormat. Milly tossed her hair, shedding drips onto the wall.

'Sorry about that,' Liam said gently, fixing the maid in his gaze and removing his hat.

Frankie knocked once then smartly opened the boudoir doors.

From the chaise longue Twinkle sprang up straight-backed at the waist, as if rising from the dead. In her hands she held open the pink pages of an evening newspaper. When she saw who it was she released her breath and her expression darkened for a second, then the gauze went back up like a stage curtain and she beamed enthusiastically.

'What opportune timing. I was just reading about a mistress

who stabbed her secretary with a pair of curling irons. Can you believe it? How did you fare with the old insufferables? Finger a murderess yet? Any newspaper headlines imminent? Hmm?'

Frankie reached into her pocket and flicked the card across the room. Twinkle held her gaze as it spun through the air then floated down onto the chaise. It sat for a second before she bent to pick it up. She held it delicately in her stiff hand and her smile vanished. After a few seconds she rubbed her lips together. The room grew chilly; Liam's and Alice's voices drifting in from the parlour died away.

Twinkle sat back. 'Pleased with yourself?'

'I don't know yet.' Frankie scanned the furs on the bed then took a tentative seat on the edge. Milly hovered by the door.

'They're not what you think.'

'And what is it I think?'

'You tell me, Puss.'

Frankie didn't answer. After a moment, Twinkle reached a finger to the base of her neck and gave it a quick scratch. 'Can I have some gin, please?'

'What are they?'

'Gin.'

Milly began rummaging in the bedside cabinet.

'What are they?'

Twinkle rolled her mouth as if she was savouring wine. Then, as if it had turned bitter on her tongue she stopped and spat the word out: 'Fetishists.'

'Fetishists?'

Twinkle's chins wobbled as she nodded. 'People who like a certain thing.'

'What kind of fetishists?'

'Oh, Puss.'

Milly was making a symphony of clinks and knocks in the cabinet. Frankie scowled across at her. 'So they get their thrills watching women dress up in clothes they can't breathe in? A club for men who like to see women in pain? Charming.' She raised a hand to her sore neck again and noticed to her distaste her fingers already smelled of the furs of the bed.

Twinkle leaned forward and beckoned closer the gin glass Milly was offering. 'What exactly did you see, Puss?'

Frankie tried to quell a blush as she described the scene through the keyhole, from the wooden dummy with the gouged waist to the woman on the ground being laced. As she spoke, she remembered a story John Bridewell had told her about a girl whose liver had been split in two after lacing her corset up too tight; 'tightlacing' they called it. The warning articles that used to appear in *Titbits* and the *News of the World* came flooding back. Was that what Ebony Diamond was up to, instead of going to suffragette meetings, taking part in some terrible ritual, parading herself in front of a line of wealthy men? Was that what Olivier Smythe Parisian Corsetier did to his workers, made them into a freak show for the pleasure of his clients, siphoning him money for their titillation?

Twinkle was staring at her. 'Of course, it's not the women

who are the tightlacers. The Hourglass Club is for tightlacing men.'

'Pardon?' Milly dropped the glass. Twinkle sighed wearily, and twitched the satin edges of her gown out of the way of the sticky spiky mess.

'Oh, you pair. Think you know everything, don't you? You're worse prudes than the Victorians. Which is, of course, why places like The Hourglass Club exist in the first place. You saw Olivier Smythe, in the flesh, didn't you?'

Frankie contemplated this. 'I thought he was a one-off.'

'Oh, Puss.' Twinkle looked bitterly disappointed, as though Frankie had just admitted to abstinence from gin or a passion for owls. 'There's no such thing as a one-off.' She ran her eyes along Frankie's trousers and up to her waist. 'Don't you remember the adverts for Madame Dowding's creations when you were a child? Military corsets for military men.'

Frankie shook her head.

'The corset letters from men in the *Englishwoman's Domestic Magazine*?'

'I'm too young for that,' Frankie said testily. She watched Milly from the corner of her eye. The graze on her head looked bad. She would have to see to that soon. 'But what about the woman I saw in the dress?'

Twinkle arched an eyebrow, staring at Frankie's trousers.

'That was a man?' Frankie sat back. 'Small relief, at least.'

Twinkle narrowed her eyes. 'What do you mean? It's all right as long as it's the men in the unbreathables? Really, Puss.'

Frankie's shoulders prickled.

Twinkle leaned her head to concede. 'A few women come to lace if it pleases them. Like Ebony. And I daresay it's still fashionable among a certain type of girl. But most of the women there are maids. To lace the men. And the men—'

Frankie snorted. 'I don't want to know.'

Twinkle locked a reproachful eye on her. 'The men . . . do whatever they want. Play bridge and drink tea. They're about as deviant as an At Home in Hampstead.'

Frankie took a glass of gin from the bedside table, where Milly had just poured a fresh round, and looked away.

Twinkle threw up her hands and landed them in her lap. 'Well, that just proves my point, doesn't it? If someone like you reacts like that, try telling it to their peers and colleagues.' She waited until she had Frankie's attention again. 'The club was started by a colonel back in, let me think, 1870 or so. There were rumours he had been at one of those figure train-ing schools, you know, that you used to read about in penny dreadfuls, where the governess makes them wear steel belts and keeps the key round her waist. He had been in the Raj and then perhaps his wife followed the local fashions and refused to wear one.' Her eyes fell very quickly onto Milly's uncorseted waist, then she moved them away, embarrassed to be have been caught looking. 'But they have quite a follow-ing. A wealthy one. *And* a powerful one at that,' she added.

Frankie thought back to those high-stepping horses outside the shop.

Twinkle kicked the broken glass at her feet, making it

crunch like ice. 'Stranger things happen at sea.' She chewed her lip. 'And I should know. I've accompanied a few Grand Tours.' A brief smile flashed on her face then, as she saw that neither of the others were amused, it vanished. 'I thought they only met once a week but perhaps it's twice now. Wednesdays were their originals.'

'They were wearing black armbands.'

'Ah, perhaps a memorial for Mr Smythe.' Her gay smile flashed again but her eyes were melancholy.

A cloudy silence settled. Milly eventually spoke. 'But what does it have to do with Ebony going missing? Or that girl Annie?'

'She worked there,' Frankie said. 'She'll have known the lot of them.'

'And Smythe?'

'It would be easy as pie for one of them to smear poison on a corset. Especially if it was meant for Ebony and not him. And the cocaine at the theatre; money, contacts.'

'So Ebs was about to go public?' Milly said. 'There must be a list somewhere in there of their names and addresses. A club secretary. And someone didn't like it.'

Twinkle was shaking her head vigorously. 'No. No, they wouldn't do that. Not to that girl, not to one of their own and certainly not two, not Olivier,' she said firmly. 'He was their darling.'

'Oh come on, Twinkle. How can you be so blinkered?'

'But they wouldn't. They simply wouldn't.'

'Is this why you sent us chasing after bloody suffragettes?'

Frankie's temper flared. 'Protecting a mob of your old cronies. We could have had them by now. How could you?' She pinched the bridge of her nose.

Twinkle stared at her. 'They're gentlemen.'

'She'd have created a scandal. Besides it's against the law.'

'Oh pooh, the law.' Twinkle snorted and a fizz of gin came through her nostrils triggering a coughing fit. Milly slapped her awkwardly on the back until she raised a hand. They waited until she had finished spluttering. 'Do you really think, Puss, that they would still be meeting in the very place they had murdered their patron?'

Frankie pushed her hand through her hair. It felt greasy and dirty like a mop. 'I don't know what to think.' A sudden wave of frustration hit her and she felt like lashing out at Twinkle, at whoever had hit her on the back of the head, at all of them. 'Well, at least I have a story to run with if we don't get to the bottom of it. That'll be worth a few bob.'

Twinkle looked at her with deep disgust. 'You wouldn't, Puss.'

'Why not? Mr Stark would go for it, I'm sure. And if not him then someone else. *The Star*, *Titbits*, *News of the World*. They love all that stuff. Tightlacers, perversions. If you can't beat 'em join 'em, I say.'

There was an embarrassing silence that lasted a minute or so during which Frankie felt a hot current of regret rising in her. She wished that now like so many times before, she had kept her mouth shut.

Twinkle spoke at last, her throat frogged over. 'You would

land a man in jail for the sake of a scoop, would you? Is that the sort of woman you are, Puss? Is it? You might think that because you have the guts to go around dressed the way you do that it's easy for everyone. Twenty years ago, before Vesta Tilley and Ella Shields dressed like that on stage, before Mrs Bloomer invented the bicycling trouser, you'd have been lynched. You know, they burned Joan of Arc alive for wearing trousers. Would you like that? Can you imagine any one of those men in a Pentonville cell?'

Frankie avoided Twinkle's eyes though she could feel them burning on her.

'Puss, you might think it's fancy—'

'But they are deviants.'

Twinkle had fire in her eyes now. 'What do you think you are, Frankie George?'

Silence settled again. The noises of chatter and laughter from the parlour ceased. Twinkle swallowed, caught off guard at her own rage. She began settling the thin folds of her gown around her, looking down and playing with the lace. 'It's never the deviants who are the problem, Puss. Don't forget that. It's people who won't open their minds that are dangerous.'

Thirty

Frankie got up off the bed and went to the window. Down below, a couple were climbing out of a hansom cab and heading into the next building. She paid attention to the woman's waist, trying to see under her coat if she too was a tightlacer. This new knowledge, that the practice hadn't died out but was thriving above a shop on Bond Street, by monied men with chauffeurs and maids, had thrown her.

She turned back to Twinkle, feeling her face burning with bashfulness. Milly knocked back the last of her gin and poured another round.

'What about the maids? Are they forced to tightlace? Is it part of the job?'

Twinkle pursed her lips and smoothed out a fur on the bed. 'It wasn't in my day.'

'What do you mean, your day?'

She swallowed. 'I was honorary. Like Ebony Diamond.

Only for a very short period, when I was on the payroll of a member.'

'So they're not . . . ?'

Twinkle began to look weary again. 'Puss, it has nothing to do with whether you prefer ladies or gents. Whether you like to wear it with a shirt or a frock. It's about the corset. The corset itself provides gratification. The pain makes you dizzy, delirious. You feel cut in half. Without religion – and let's face it, who wants to sit and listen to a man wearing purple? – it's the closest we come to transcendence. Mysticism, a natural drug.'

'And those maids believe that too?'

She paused, tilted her head again and sipped her gin, swilling it round her mouth.

Milly spoke up softly. 'So it's not about wanting to be a freak?'

Twinkle rolled her eyes. 'It's about sensation.' She glanced at Frankie, who suddenly felt self-conscious of her boyish figure. 'If you read any of these treatises against tightlacing from the past century, they are all attacking women for indulging in an activity perceived as sexual. Women who tightlace don't belong in the home, they don't make good mothers, good floor-scrubbers, good cooks. They're enjoying the feeling of being laced. Men can feel that too.'

'But can't it induce hysteria?' Frankie said.

'Only in its critics,' Twinkle said pointedly.

Frankie sat back on the bed twiddling the stem of her glass between her fingers. She could feel Milly breathing gently behind her, waiting for her to say the thing that was on both of their minds.

'Then why did they hit us? We just got attacked by a gang of enlightened women who work for a club of male corset fetishists.'

'It would seem that way.'

'I understand that we were intruders,' Frankie said, 'and that we weren't invited. And,' she said, waving her glass about, 'that they need to preserve their anonymity.'

'Quite,' said Twinkle.

'But what makes you so certain that they have nothing to do with Ebony's disappearance? She's scared, that's if she's still alive, and it seems too coincidental that everyone involved has connections to this club, this place.'

'Puss, I don't have all the answers, and even if I did, I thought you were the reporter. But I know those men, and the ones I know wouldn't commit murder.' She tilted her head, hesitating for a moment, then put her glass down. 'You asked me a minute ago if those maids agree with the club's philosophy. I said I know the men. The tightlacers. I don't know any of these maids, whether they lace or not. Whether they do it because they believe in it or,' she sighed, 'for the money.' Her lips narrowed again. 'Or whether they are quite as enlightened as one might like to think.'

'We'll go back when it's empty.' Frankie strode with such force Milly had to skip to keep up with her. She was tired and cold and all she could think of was a hot coal fire and a bed that wasn't covered in fur.

'You're not going back in there without protection,' Liam said.

'Oh shove off.' She felt guilty as soon as she had said it. Liam stopped walking and hung back under a streetlamp. The light caught the fragile gnarls of his cheekbones. They had come to the crossroads between Pentonville and Gray's Inn Road. After walking the length of Euston Road Frankie's legs were beginning to ache.

'Don't you think we should sleep on it?' Milly asked. She puffed her cheeks and stopped too.

'Nothing to sleep on. What's the first rule of a murder investigation? Mary Ann Cotton, Crippen, the Chocolate Cream poisoner. You start with the people they know, the people they saw last. Only place I saw that girl, Annie Evans, was in that shop. They're guilty. Someone in there's guilty.' Frankie checked for traffic and was about to cross the street when she saw Liam still waiting under the streetlamp. 'Oh come on, I didn't mean it. I'm tired. You're right, we do need – look, you can sleep on the floor by the hearth, though I can't promise it will be warm.'

He had turned away from her. The gold light caught the tufts of his unruly mane sticking out from under his wool hat. His ears were a grimy brown. He shook his head. 'I have things to do.'

'At this time of night?'

He gestured towards King's Cross Station. Despite the

hour the public houses were still glowing, women spilling out of their dresses, gents in sharp cut top hats holding umbrellas over their heads.

'Best hour for work.' His face flashed a grin of bravado.

'Work?' Realisation dawned on Frankie. 'You really are a dipper?'

He didn't answer, just tucked his bony hand back in his pocket. He was almost out of the light and into the station shadows when he turned his head back. 'Don't you think the best way to find out what she was up to, is to ask her yourself?'

'Oh brilliant idea. Brain of Charles Darwin there. Don't you think I would have done that – if we could find her?'

But it was too late. He had slunk into a group of men circled round a creosote barrel of fire and become invisible among torn tweed jackets and woollen caps.

Frankie led Milly the few hundred yards further in silence until they reached Percy Circus. Her key jammed in the latch; she wiggled it until it gave. The house was pitch black and they scrambled gently past the sideboard in the hall and up the stairs. Frankie ushered Milly ahead into the bedroom and switched on the gaslight.

The room was bare.

Her papers and the Blickensderfer were gone from the desk. The fire was empty, save for a few scraps of dead coal trailing across the hearth. There were no blankets on the bed. In one corner, her clothes had been dumped in a heap, piled to a peak and capped by the lavender-tinted unopened letter from her mother. Her few books, a copy of W. T. Stead's *Government by Journalism*, a dictionary and an illustrated edition of *Alice in Wonderland,* were stacked nearby. The tin of Colman's mustard had been swiped.

Milly's mouth hung gently open. Frankie crossed to the desk where a single sheet of paper flapped up and down with the draught through the cracked windowpane.

'Typewriter taken in lieu of owed rent.' There was a receipt clipped to it from a pawn shop.

Frankie groaned under her breath. She knew Mrs Gibbons was tight-fisted but had never imagined she could be so cruel. Her hand clenched the paper into a ball, then she thought better of it and smoothed it out, folded it and stuck it in her inside pocket. Milly sat down on the bed.

Frankie gave a short laugh. 'It's normally a lot more cosy. Coal in the fire, blankets on the bed, I even have a washstand, wouldn't you know it.' She looked at the empty corner by the window.

'Don't worry, you can come to mine.'

Frankie said nothing. Her fingers trailed the cracked edge of the desk.

'My flat-mate's seldom there. She poses for a man up in Mayfair most evenings and doesn't tend to come home.' She nodded to the pile of clothes in the corner. 'Do you want to collect some things to wear?'

After a few seconds Frankie sunk her hands into the pile of clothes and pulled out a pair of trousers, a waistcoat and a tie her father had given her. As an afterthought she picked up the letter on top. Milly had stood and was pacing the cold room.

'Won't be a second.'

She tore open the seal and took out the crisp paper inside. The smell was familiar, the special notepaper her mother had been given over ten years ago by a lady who lived in Hampstead Garden Suburb. She kept it in a drawer in the parlour and it had taken on the whiff of mothballs. Once upon a time it was scented with lavender. She only used it on special occasions; thank you letters, birthdays, congratulations. Frankie picked through the Italian, skimming the grammar. It was a notice of a wedding. Harry Tripe had met a second cousin of his on a visit to the country and proposed to her last month. Between the lines of joy and excitement there was a very sharp message: it should have been you.

She was surprised to find her heart sinking a little. She tried to shake it off. His family were brassy, he was unappealing and she would have done anything rather than become a Tottenham butcher's wife. But because it was dark and it was late and her room had been scalped by her landlady and there were no foreseeable ways of buying back her beloved typewriter, her only source of income, she felt the emotion rising in her throat.

Milly seemed to sense that the letter was bad news for she stood up and wrapped her cold fragile fingers round the back of Frankie's hand. 'Come on,' she said, 'I'll show you how to hop a bus fare.'

* * *

The inside of Milly's lodgings on Talgarth Road looked like a Parisian boutique dumped on the floor of a shed. The boards were bare and dusty except for two rugs; one a Persian carpet in red and gold, the other the skin of a lion with its mangy head still attached. Piles of silk gowns in pastel colours were scattered in various corners, draped over lampshades and hung on the backs of chairs. There were brassieres on coathooks, furs on tables and beaded scarves hooked over the corner of canvases leaning against the wall. A bookshelf was piled full, almost to toppling. Frankie cast her eye discreetly at the volumes. A picture book on Toulouse-Lautrec, a torn copy of *Anna Karenina*. A volume of Sophia Poole's *An Englishwoman in Egypt* lay on its side, and placed reverently on top of the case, a copy of the Qu'ran. Anywhere there wasn't a picture or piece of furniture there was a mirror, either hanging or standing, echoing repetitions of the room. Cold air rippled in great tingling waves through a wall of lead-framed windows overlooking the street and beyond where London stretched out in a labyrinth of bronze and gold dots.

'It's to maximise the light,' Milly said, nodding first at the mirrors and then at the wall of windows. 'She's an artist.' She whipped the cloth off a huge canvas that was braced against the wall. 'Boo.' The picture was a full-length likeness of herself, naked in the pose of Botticelli's Venus, her hair unloosed, looking down at a snake wrapped round her waist. Frankie cast her eyes round the room with sudden nerves.

'It's not here. I keep it at Jojo's. And it's had its teeth pulled anyway. They do that to all the snakes over there.'

Frankie breathed out and Milly smiled cautiously. 'They're not actually the best dance partners, you know. I'd get rid of it if I could. They can be very stiff, very clumsy, I don't know if you noticed when I was holding it. They form shapes of their own, you have to copy them, they won't copy you. And you spend the whole time worrying they're going to throw up on your costume. But I don't think Jojo would have taken me without one.'

She gave a huge satisfied sigh, contented to finally be in her den, and looked around at the selection of chairs and couches before taking one, clearing the clothes off it into a crumpled ball.

'There you go. I'll get the fire on.'

Frankie perched on the edge of the velveteen divan at first, but after a few seconds she felt herself sinking into it and couldn't help but lean back, letting the stuffing take the weight of the day off her. Her eyes wandered lazily round the room, watching Milly on her knees scrabbling with the coal scuttle, unfazed about the dust muddying the front of her dress. By the window lay a strange pair of drums, an Arab tea set balanced on a leather pouffe, and next to it the same kind of water pipe she had seen at the Barclay-Evanses.

'I could put a record on. Or do you just want to rest?'

'I don't mind.' Frankie watched the fire slowly grow from a red shivering line on the kindling paper into a hissing, scratching glow, eating each coal slowly in turn.

'If you're fine there, I'll stay here.' Milly pulled the lion rug over the hearth. 'You can join me if you want.'

Frankie smiled stiffly.

'I know. It's comfortable that divan.' She watched the fire for a few minutes, following wisps of smoke up with her eyes. Abruptly she turned. 'How did you meet Twinkle?'

'She knows the paper. It was chance. Luck, misfortune, black magic. I was looking for work, sending articles here and there, cartoons, bits of satire.'

'You can draw?'

'A bit.' Frankie said, squirming under the scrutiny for reasons she didn't quite know. 'They published a cartoon of mine and I suppose Mr Stark, he's editor there, I suppose he was looking for someone with the right temperament to work with her.' She gave a small snort of laughter. 'Not that I have; I could poison her gin some days.'

Milly coughed and looked at her hands.

'I didn't mean – I'm not being flippant. About poison.'

'No, it's all right. You're right about Twinkle. I mean, about the poison.'

They settled into silence for a while, the sounds of the street coasting through the window. The heat of the fire warmed the room quickly. Milly got up from the rug and wedged a record onto a dusty gramophone with an enamel green and cream horn. Everything about the place stank of luxury. But a careful selection of chosen luxury and a disregard for all else. There were no electric lights, no comfortable carpets, no polished furniture. No polished anything and no maid to polish. But there were expensive trinkets, goodies gathered from travels, family heirlooms in shrouds of dust.

A quiet opera crackled round the room. Milly flopped down by the fire again, tucking her legs under her, and played with the lion's fur in her long white fingers. 'So what, did you just send your pieces in, in little brown envelopes? How did you start?' She flashed her eyes wide.

Frankie snorted. She had never told the truth about how she became interested in newspapers to anyone at all and didn't know if she should now.

'Come out with it, you're hiding something, are you going to tell me a lie?'

'I was an apprentice in the foundry, for a printer. Used to pour lead casts for the rolling cylinders. Man used to come to my father's veg barrow.'

'That sounds like a boy's job.'

'That's what he said.' She tugged her fingers through her hair. 'He cut my plaits off on my first day.'

Milly rolled onto her stomach. The silk at her ankles rode up a little revealing a few inches of flesh-coloured grubby stocking. 'That's not the truth though, Frankie George. Printers are mechanics. I know a little about the press. My father's–', she hesitated, '– he sort of dabbles in it. You don't jump from being a foundry apprentice to being a newspaper-girl. Your mouth is twitching, you're itching to tell me.' She leaned off the rug and grabbed a small copper jug. 'Would you like some sherbet?'

Frankie peered across. 'I suppose. Is it legal?'

Milly grinned wickedly. 'Is that what worries you, what's legal and what's not? It's what they serve in the harems. The fancy ones.' She collected a couple of short thin glasses and blew the dust off them, then wiped her fragile finger round the rims. 'But don't let's change the subject. Why did you decide to be a journalist? What brought Frankie George to the *London Evening Gazette*? What created that fine marriage?' She laughed, a gentle tickling sound.

Frankie prickled again, feeling as if she was somehow being put to a test in this bohemian den, as if she might be found out for a fraud any second and sent packing. But she was too exhausted to make up a lie. 'I don't suppose you had an outdoor lavvy when you were little?'

It was Milly's turn to blush. 'No, we didn't.'

'Well, I did. And my father, or next-door's, they would cut up newspaper to put in there. Bumf. Bum fodder.'

Milly tilted her head to the side curiously as she poured the pinkish liquid.

'There were all kinds of stories in there. Mrs McGunnery's divorce goes all the way to the High Court as she battles to out her husband as a white slave trafficker. A woman in Bristol gives birth to three brown rabbits. Dairy cow learns to tell the time.'

'*Tit-Bits* common in your street was it?'

'I think that one was *News of the World*. And then the theatre reviews. The West End, Shaftesbury Avenue, The Strand. Shows my family never could have afforded to go and see. But you could read about it while you were spending a penny.'

Milly handed her a glass. It smelled like Turkish delight.

'You are joking, Frankie George. You decided to be a journalist because you fell in love with newspapers while in the privies?'

Frankie shrugged. 'Believe it or not.' There was a pause while they sipped their drinks. The sherbet was sweet like lemonade but more pungent, strong with rose water. Frankie sighed looking round the room. She had heard of women like Milly but never thought they really existed. She thought of her dancing in the baths in Cairo the way she had danced at Jojo's, thought of her and Ebony backstage at Jojo's, eyeing up each other's talent.

Milly was stretching her back out on the rug. It cracked musically and she winced.

'So go on then, if we're sharing secrets: do you ever miss Cairo? Do you ever wish you were back there?'

Frankie watched her tip the dregs of her sherbet into her mouth.

'Miss it, yes, but I would never go back. I took everything I wanted with me.'

'What was that?'

She rubbed her lips together and put the glass down on the hearth. 'I know what you're thinking. Why you're looking at me like that. You've read about the harems, you think women are kept under lock and key. Well, they are in a sense. But you will never know freedom until you have travelled down the street in a riding cloak, veiled from head to toe. Even your hands. You could be anyone underneath it. No one to judge who you are, what class you come from, how high your cheekbones, how thin your waist. It is the most exquisite disguise.'

'But don't you take . . .'

'My clothes off when I dance? Is that what you were going to ask?'

Frankie shrugged. 'It didn't seem like much of a disguise tonight.'

Milly took a few moments to answer and Frankie thought for a minute she had said too much. Then she cracked her neck to both sides and stared frankly at her. 'Well, you would think that. But something comes over me when I dance and I'm damned if I can explain it. When I start up, when I hear that particular kind of drumbeat, it feels, don't laugh, but it feels like I'm being uncrumpled. Like paper has been curled inside me for a long time. And it slowly unfurls and straightens out as the drumbeat goes on and on until it's tingling every nerve of me, and the more it tingles the more like myself I feel than I have ever felt before. I feel happy. There aren't many things that have ever made me that happy.'

'I should try it.'

'Everything is funny to you.'

'Well, it's just that you don't look happy when you dance.'

'Don't I?' Her gaze was more than a question, it was a challenge.

'No, you look fierce.'

She looked at the fire. 'Perhaps I'm concentrating.'

Frankie let her bristling subside and felt guilty for saying anything. But Milly seemed to brush it off quickly. 'Doesn't anything make you feel like that, like you have been lying asleep and someone has suddenly woken you up?'

Frankie's eyes shifted from the fire to Milly's curled legs, which she was now hugging close to her, and back again. She shrugged.

The fire had calmed down a little and Milly reached for a cashmere shawl by the hearth. She wriggled her feet out of their slippers so they could be closer to the glow. 'I was given this on my wedding day by a woman who lived opposite us. She was a lay judge. People would come to her to solve their disputes. And she would stay behind her latticed windows and whatever judgement she made had to be stuck to. People respected her. She was a spinster. Do you think anyone in this country respects a spinster?'

Frankie was silent for a moment, feeling her untravelled unworldliness creeping in on her, making her feel both insecure and defensive. 'Who knows how people feel respected? Everyone has their own ideas. Is it having your own money, not being tied to a husband, not having to scrub floors for a living, scrubbing floors to make your own living?' She shrugged. 'Having the vote. That's certainly what Ebony thinks.'

Milly was quiet for a moment. She began to play with the lion's scrappy mane between her toes. Wrapped up in the shawl she looked somehow wise, like the old woman in a fairy tale, the light picking out the lines curling round her mouth and across her brow. 'I think Ebony wants people to respect her. All the girls who have a trade in the circus are independent, and they're stronger than half the men. Some of them could lift a donkey. But when you come to a city like London and you suddenly find you don't have equal rights to the men, the wages are unequal, mothers don't have rights to their children, I mean you can't even drink port in the dining room after a meal or whatnot, what can you do?' She tilted her head. 'Is that why you're so interested in what's happened to Ebony? You want to get involved in the votes movement?'

'I'm interested because a woman and a man died and another might be in danger.'

Milly looked taken aback and Frankie realised her tone had been spiky. She sighed. 'But yes, perhaps I ought to become more involved. Afterwards.'

'You certainly look like a suffragette.'

'What, these?' Frankie gestured to her trousers. Despite her usual feelings about that statement there was something innocent in Milly's tone. 'They're comfortable. I don't know,' she shrugged. 'You get involved with who you fall in with, don't you? Pick your battles. I ended up busying myself making my own way on Fleet Street.'

'But you agree that it's important?'

Frankie bit her lower lip. 'I used to think you just had to look after yourself and if everyone did that we'd all be hunky-dory. But I'm learning.' She met Milly's eyes and sunk back into the divan. Her hand went unconsciously to the back of her head, where the ache was. She peered into the bottom of the sherbet glass and saw that the mixture had formed a lump.

Milly looked across. 'Would you like a spoon?'

Frankie stared down into her glass.

'For the bottom. It's the best bit.' She began rummaging in a copper pan by the fire and pulled out a little silver ship with engravings carved all over its hull. Small thin-handled pieces of cutlery were strung from the rigging on hooks. She extracted a spoon and tossed it through the air. Frankie caught it and began to churn up the clogged sugar. There was a few minutes awkward silence, then she said, 'So what about this marriage? Who was he? An Egyptian?'

Milly watched the fire, her lips poised to curl either way, into a smile or a frown. When she looked back at Frankie her eyes were drained, the crease on her brow had deepened. 'A Frenchman. An archaeologist. Dr Frederic Barton. I daresay you would have heard of him if you moved in those kinds of circles. I was in the middle of a world tour by ship and he took me to see Heliopolis, just outside of Cairo. The old city of the sun. We'd docked for a few days to give us the chance to see the citadel and the pyramids, but I didn't fancy the pyramids. I'm claustrophobic; I think Doctor Freud would say it probably stems from that evil nanny. Anyway, along comes a handsome Frenchman speaking perfect Turkish and Arabic and whisks me away.'

'And you stayed.'

'To the horror of my family. Yes I did. I think the tour was supposed to iron out my wayward tendencies. My terrible latchkey girl ideas.'

Frankie swallowed the last of the syrup. Her thumb moved

comfortingly back and forth over the pattern on the spoon's fine handle. Another family heirloom, she thought to herself.

'What went wrong?'

'My husband.' Milly picked at a thread on the shawl with her slender fingers. Fingers meant to wear rings and droop languorously around a necklace or lace collar, or a well-groomed hound. 'You're looking at me in that way you do. Your face is creased up at the eyes. Trying not to judge.'

'I'm just concentrating.'

'I don't really have a problem with infidelity. People think that children don't know what goes on in their own houses. When I was little I knew fine enough when the room-swapping was going on overnight. At breakfast time it didn't make a difference. It happens, Frankie, maybe not in your world, but it happens in mine.'

Frankie felt a prickle but she bit her tongue. She was watching Milly carefully, observing the fresh violence in her voice. Her shoulders propped the shawl round her, her jaw was set, her mouth moved in a little pout. She looked as defensive as Ebony had when she doused perfume on the camera and set it alight. Frankie played with the handle of the spoon, sticking it between her fingers. She had managed to lick most of the residue off but there was still a little stickiness. Annoyed, she looked down to see if she could pick off the sticky patch and when she saw the pattern on the handle she started.

'Are you all right?'

'Yes,' she said quickly. 'So what did go wrong?'

'Bad luck comes in threes.' Milly didn't elaborate at first, going back to stroking the lion's head. Then she leant back, opening out her torso and propping herself up with her elbows. 'As well as being a cheat, he was selling artefacts to the British Museum, creeping into certain kinds of bath houses, that sort of thing.'

Frankie swallowed. 'Did you divorce him?'

'No. I left in the night. I packed quietly, caught a boat to Alexandria and the next merchant ship to Dover. And on the boat there was a man with a basket of toothless snakes.'

'So you bought one?'

'To remind me. Better to share your life with a snake than with Frederic Barton.'

Silence settled in the air between them. The opera had come to an end and the record was clicking round the turntable. Milly reached across and slipped it off. Frankie didn't know how she was expected to react and no words came naturally to her so she said nothing. The noises of the street had died down, the gaslamps beginning to fade out. It was late. She thought of the day ahead of them tomorrow and wondered whether Liam had gone back to Jojo's to sleep.

Milly dragged herself to her feet and rummaged in the open trunk. She pulled out another cashmere shawl and tossed it at Frankie. 'I hope the fire stays warm enough.'

'I'll load it with coal if it goes out.'

'Usually I'm on the divan too but I suppose if Lilian's not here—'

Frankie looked at her empty face. She didn't know how she was meant to reply so she just nodded. 'All right.'

'Right. I'll use her room.' Milly scratched her head through her bundle of hair. 'You'll wake up with the sun. Through those windows.'

'I'm sure I will.'

'Wake me if I'm not through.'

Frankie tugged her jacket off and laid it across her. She dragged the blanket to her chin.

Milly paused in the doorway, her hands carrying a tin bowl full of coal, the red shawl hanging off her shoulders. 'I don't give up on people. I want you to know that, Frankie. I'm not just dogging you because I told Jojo I would. I left Frederic because I had to.'

Frankie nodded quickly, perhaps, she thought to herself afterwards, a little too quickly. She hunkered down into the blanket, already starting to gather a layer of her own cosy body warmth. Underneath it, clutched close to her chest, her thumbs still worked away curiously at the pattern she had spotted on the handle of the spoon.

Thirty-One

Kingsway's wide thoroughfare was scattered with carelessly parked vehicles, police wagons and press cars. Some had beetled up onto the kerb, others were discarded diagonally to the oncoming traffic, causing swerves and hoots. A crowd of newspapermen moved in an uneven throng along the street, cat-calling, shoving, pausing only to load up flash tubes. The air was smoked with magnesium, the pops came blinding fast.

'Freddie!' A hand stuck out from the grand door of Lincoln's Inn House, beckoning Primrose through the police line. As he squeezed past he noticed the uniformed officers had shotguns slung idle across their forearms. It was like the Sidney Street siege all over again.

The stout hand grabbed his collar just as a knot of reporters tried to force their way through the line in his wake.

Stuttlegate pulled him inside, slamming the door on a journalist's fingers.

'Freddie, glad you could come. Red hot out there, isn't it?'

'Actually, sir, I wasn't thrilled at finding out through the
newspapers. I was under the impression this was my
investiga—'

'Never mind, you're here now.' He slapped him between
the shoulder blades.

'Chief, if you don't mind my asking, what brought this
about? I read a headline or two, but I know what rot these
men come up with.' He looked around. The atrium of the
building was packed with policemen, cuffing and searching
women, leaning against the Greek columns scribbling in
notebooks, tossing piles of paperwork into heaps on the floor.
He swallowed, and found he could still taste the decaying
pork pie he had grabbed outside Colney Hatch Station and
sank on the underground.

Stuttlegate's response was to shove into his hand a brown
file with a mass of papers haphazardly piled in it. Some of the
notes were Wilson's writing; some were labelled at the top of
the flimsy with Robert Jenkins's name. Pinned to the top was
a typed copy of a cable that had been intercepted earlier in
the day, a simple message from Christabel Pankhurst to
Suffragette HQ: 'Please burn down Nottingham Castle.'
Primrose understood the symbolism; Nottingham Castle had
been scorched to the ground at the time of the men's suffrage
uprising. He had seen the telegram already, late in the afternoon before leaving for Pentonville and dismissed it as a

hoax, too bald, too convenient. And that word 'please'. It reminded him of the decoys of herself she sent leading them a dance all over London when the fancy took her.

Underneath were some more notes on Ebony Diamond and a conclusive 'report' from Wilson based on Jenkins's information that both 'Diamond' and 'Evans' had been about to spill the beans on a mastermind suffragette plan.

'Forgive me, sir, but this seems like scant evidence for . . .' He looked at the hallway drawers being tumbled out, the furniture tossed over. 'If it's top secret that they're planning to torch Nottingham Castle, why send an uncoded message from Paris? Jenkins heard nothing this afternoon to corroborate that's what they're up to.'

'Doesn't matter why we ordered it. Point is, Freddie, now's the chance to wrap it up. Get her for double murder and you'll sink 'em all.'

'Get who for murder?'

Stuttlegate's eyes danced. 'How'd you like your name to be up in the hall of fame? The man who broke the suffragettes.'

'But you can't be suggesting—'

'Annie Evans, Ebony Diamond. Look it's all in there.'

Primrose looked down at the file, noting how big his hands were against its slim brown card. Big and useless and clumsy. He squeezed the bridge of his nose. 'Get who exactly for what murder?'

Stuttlegate came close. 'I've got Mrs Pankhurst in one of the rooms up there.' He pointed to the top of the stairs where a policeman was trying to wrestle a safe box from a woman. His eyes were alight. He waited, anticipating admiration, but it wasn't forthcoming so he went on. 'Now madam's not under arrest. Yet. But you can have a crack at her. If you want. First jipper.'

'What am I supposed to say to her?'

Stuttlegate brought his face devilishly close. 'I don't care, Freddie. I really don't care what you say. So long as you leave the wheels off her bath chair this time.' Before Primrose had cottoned on to what Stuttlegate had said, the Chief was wading out into the lobby, sticking his fat hands out again, directing the black insectile forms of the uniformed officers as they burrowed about their growing evidence piles.

Primrose felt his teeth clenching together. Bath chair indeed? So it was Stuttlegate who had left that article on his desk the other day, the one about May Billinghurst and her bath chair with the love heart round it. It had to have been. The whole point of giving him the investigation, while continuing to meddle in it from afar seemed to become suddenly clear. It was a test; the gloves were off and he was being tested right here, right this minute, as a suffragette sympathiser.

He flinched as he turned to see Wilson's lanky shadow on the column beside him.

'Sorry, sir. Didn't mean to startle you.' He paused. 'Did he mention who was upstairs?'

'Yes. Is she being held against her will?'

'Not yet. Becoming ratty though. Saying she might not

cooperate without a solicitor, so if we're going to get anything out of her . . .'

Primrose disliked that 'we' but was too tired to argue. 'Do you know which room she's in?'

Wilson gallantly held out his arm to usher the Inspector forward. Primrose, as he mounted the stairs, felt a growing sense of dread. If indeed he was standing on the cusp of a landmark moment in the fight against the women's movement, why hadn't his superior elected to take the interview? At the back of his mind, alongside sleep and indigestion, was the groggy hope that he wasn't right now being led into some kind of professional trap.

Tussles were breaking out on the stairs. One woman had managed to get a young blond constable into a ju jitsu lock, but released him when Primrose and Wilson passed. On a side table in the upper landing, Primrose noticed a small shiny pistol tossed into a police evidence box, along with a packet of blanks and a brace of scratched wooden Indian clubs. The whine of the electric lift, sending box after box of seized goods down to the lobby, blended into the background.

They continued along the corridor until they came to a gallery with a door leading off to the left. Above them a domed skylight let in the bleary violet night.

Wilson didn't bother to knock but cranked the handle open to let Primrose pass. Inside a woman sat with her back to them, facing the windowless wall, still wearing her outdoor hat: a white creation tied with a wisp of silk under her chin.

She was perched upright and proper on the near side of an oak table covered with ledgers, pamphlets for rallies and copies of the day's newspapers. Strewn carelessly atop them and labelled with an orange police evidence tag lay a dog-whip; a hard black handle stiffly tapering into a tongue of yellow leather.

Mrs Pankhurst didn't turn around. Primrose headed behind the desk for the second chair, then thought better of it and pulled it around to her side. Wilson closed the door and leant against it. Primrose introduced them both and muttered a weak thank you to her for agreeing to help.

She took a moment to look at him. Her eyes carefully roamed his features, taking in his throat and shoulders as if she might be assessing a cow at market. 'I didn't have much choice, Inspector. Your men don't respond well to reasoning when handcuffs and rubber bats do the job so nicely.'

'They're just doing what we have asked them to do.'

'Look at this place. Did you see, on the way up? They've taken records, lost the order for filed documents. Nothing we are doing, right now, in here is illegal.'

Primrose's eye fell upon the dog-whip. Her gaze followed.

'How can I assist you?' she asked. Her face, he noticed, was drawn, much more so than the photographs made out. She had high cheekbones and large round hooded eyes that cast down to her lap every so often. Her skin was so fragile that fine blue veins were visible beneath its surface, mirroring the flat sea-blue of her eyes. She made him feel like a boy, like she had seen better and more terrifying men than him countless times before.

'Your daughter Christabel—' he cleared his throat.

'It is hard enough,' she interrupted, 'keeping tabs on my daughter for my own purposes without having to worry about keeping track of her for yours.'

Primrose shifted. The upholstery on the seat was uneven, sloping on one side. He wondered if this one was reserved for unwelcome visitors. 'Are you proud of her?'

'I'm proud of all of my children, alive and with God. If you're asking if I approve of her evading conspiracy charges while the rest of us went to prison, I approve of her cause. Sometimes that's enough to justify the methods.'

'Methods. That is why we are here after all.'

'Your tone doesn't become you. It makes you seem even more nervous than you are.'

Primrose took a sharp breath, steadying his hands. 'Violence is a WSPU method.'

'We prefer militancy. Militancy means war. And this,' she jabbed a finger towards the ground, indicating downstairs, 'is a war, Inspector. We didn't mean it to be but it has become one.'

'And in war people get hurt. Murdered.'

'In your wars perhaps but not in ours. The only recklessness the suffragettes have ever shown has been about their own lives, not the lives of others. You obviously haven't been put on surveillance duties at enough of our rallies.' She nodded at the dog whip. 'See who is violent to whom then.

It has never been, and will never be, the policy of the Women's Social and Political Union to endanger human life. We leave that to the enemy. We leave that to the men in their warfare.'

Primrose caught Wilson's eye but the sergeant's expression was unreadable. He put the brown file on the table and opened it. Mrs Pankhurst watched his hands carefully.

'I want to ask you about a woman called Ebony Diamond. Know her?'

She didn't blink. 'Of course.'

'When did you meet her?'

'I think she came to us almost a year ago. She had met some pamphleteers at a country fair. That's what our ladies do. Go to country fairs, spread the word. You wouldn't like to believe most of the things we do are peaceful.'

'Doesn't matter what I'd like to believe. Violence speaks for itself.'

She waited until he looked at her again. 'Violence frequently attaches itself to reform. Without it no law would be passed. We would still be waiting for the corn laws, or common man's suffrage. You, I dare say, Inspector,' she looked him up and down, resting her eyes on his broad labourer's shoulders, 'would likely not be allowed to vote.'

It was too much. Primrose felt his exposed neck beginning to boil. Being yanked in here, disorientated, unprepared, dumped in chaos on his own investigation. He would not be humiliated in front of an inferior by this cool-throated woman. He thought of Stuttlegate waiting in the lobby rubbing his ginger chops, and felt suddenly helpless, as if to punish the woman in front of him would be to play right into the Chief's hands. But to let her goad him would be something worse. 'Violence is one thing, but murder is quite another. What if I told you that all this, all this here tonight had nothing to do with your pamphlets and your rallies and your silly hammers. What if I told you that you and your daughter weren't wanted for conspiracy any more, you're wanted for murder. Would you still fob me off with nonsense riddles about the past?'

'I still wouldn't tell you where Christabel is. That's a mother speaking, Inspector.'

'Then you're more stupid than I took you for.'

'What are you driving at? I'm getting very close to not cooperating until I see a solicitor.' Her voice finally tightened. 'Arrest me or release me.'

'Annie Evans.' He watched for a reaction but she gave none. 'Found with her throat cut last Thursday night, the night of your window smash. Tempers were high that night.'

'Tempers against the government.'

'And any dissenters who didn't want to toe the line on your plans?'

She said nothing. He tried a different tack. 'Christabel was in town. Miss Evans was found with a portcullis suffragette badge on her.' Still no reaction. 'Ebony Diamond. Would you care to comment on where she might be?'

'I have no idea, Inspector. They both left the WSPU weeks ago. We can't keep track of every girl who comes and goes.'

'There's been no black drapes in the window for Annie, no mention of her in your newspaper. No talk of her in here.'

She opened her mouth in shock then closed it quickly, as if chastising herself for her own surprise at being under their surveillance.

'What did you think of Ebony?' Primrose asked. 'Did you like her?'

'Like most women who come to us, we find comfort in each other. We find hope in the thought that we are doing something to change the world.' She chewed her lower lip. 'The truth is I was very sorry when Miss Diamond and Miss Evans stopped coming to meetings. But we don't have time to dwell on the whys. Perhaps she couldn't afford to be associated with us once she was engaged at the Coliseum.'

'What about Miss Evans?'

'Annie and Ebony were very close.'

'So you think Miss Diamond left because of her career? And Annie followed.'

'I would like to think,' she said slowly, 'that if it came to it, Ebony Diamond would rather use herself to gain publicity for the movement than the other way round. But then I am an optimist, Inspector. Suffragettes can't really afford not to be.'

Primrose scratched his head. The uneven cushion was bothering him. He stood up to stretch his legs, and Mrs Pankhurst looked quietly aghast at such ungentlemanly behaviour. Her husky-dog eyes followed him as he paced.

He could feel Stuttlegate's shadow hanging in the corner of the room, waiting for him to make the stab, the kill, slurp up first jippers or whatever he had said. Defeat knotted in his stomach as he stretched out his back and realised Mrs Pankhurst was still watching him.

'Was there anyone who might have been afraid that Ebony Diamond was about to ruin some grand plan of theirs? That out of spite, because her ideas had been rejected, that she might threaten to leak some great event, sabotage some piece of destruction, like burning down Nottingham Castle?'

Mrs Pankhurst didn't flinch but she scraped back her chair, then put her hands on the table, inches from the dog-whip. 'Inspector, I'll forgive you if you're confused. Perhaps you weren't listening earlier. But the suffragettes do not put people's lives in danger. When the men burned Nottingham Castle two people died. Two people were murdered so you could have the franchise. That telegram my daughter sent was destined for your eyes. She wanted to make a point. And by God,' she gestured at the door where the beating of footsteps and thump of papers hitting floorboards filtered in, 'she's had you busy.'

He opened his mouth but she hadn't finished.

'It's the militancy of men, Inspector, that has drenched the world with blood, and for these deeds of horror men have been rewarded with monuments, songs, epics. The militancy of women will continue to harm no human life save the lives of those who want to fight the battle in their own way. Time will reveal what is rewarded to them. I would suggest,

Inspector,' she said, letting her gaze settle back on the dog-whip, 'that if you are looking for those with blood on their hands I would try looking a little further towards the government.'

It was only in the lobby, warmed by the bodies of men at work, that Primrose realised how cold the interview room had been. He pumped the blood back into his fingers, while Wilson stood staring at him. Behind them at a distance Mrs Pankhurst leant over the gallery rail, looking down at the ransacked office.

'You're letting her go?' Wilson said softly.

'You don't believe what she said?'

Wilson shrugged. 'You can't trust them. Look what happened with her daughter.'

Primrose pushed his hand up through the greased parting of his hair and let his breath out.

'She makes you uneasy.' There was a goading smile on Wilson's face.

Primrose felt the chill in him curdle quickly into a hot anger and began walking towards the stairs. 'What makes me uneasy is that there's a murderer on the loose and all we seem to be concerned about is using it as an excuse to spy on suffragettes. Suffragettes here, suffragettes there, the only place we're bloody looking is suffragettes. It wouldn't make such a damned difference if it wasn't murder. It's that girl's funeral tomorrow.'

The smile faded from Wilson's eyes.

'She's right. We're looking in the wrong place.'

'If you want to go doing this palaver inside government offices you're going to have to—'

'To hell with government.' Primrose waved a hand. 'Ebony Diamond left the suffragettes after her last bout in Holloway, didn't she?' Wilson nodded his big-eared head cautiously.

'There must be a reason for that. Take a car to Embankment. Not tomorrow, *now*. Have Bain brought in to look out prison shots of everyone she was in Holloway with. If any of them are matched to suffragettes, discard them. It's the ones who aren't we want.'

Thirty-Two

Frankie woke early to the sound of motor traffic spluttering along Talgarth Road on its way into the capital. A waterfall of bright gold light was pouring through the studio windows, heating the cashmere shawl lying over her. She was already warm in the heat from the coal fire's residue. Careful of waking Milly, she crept out from under the covers, and reviewed the room in its dancing kaleidoscope of illuminated dust. What she wanted to do would be easier now, and she needed to do it in private.

Avoiding the litter trail of last night's crusty sherbet glasses she made her way over to the fireplace. She scraped the gramophone out of the way and saw what she was after wedged behind the coal scuttle, its beaten silver sails catching the sunlight: the cutlery ship.

As she reached for it, a shatter pierced the daylight haze and the whole thing collapsed, spilling its metal cargo around the hearth. Panic struck Frankie as she scrabbled to collect the fallen spoons, knives and forks. A voice behind stopped her.

'What *are* you doing?'

She hadn't heard Milly enter. Hastily she hung back up some of the cutlery and righted the ship. Milly crossed to join her, answering her own question as she went. 'Don't let's make coffee here. The stuff I have is horrid. Let's get some from the man at Baron's Court station. He doesn't use chicory or anything.'

She was wearing a fresh dress, another Paul Poiret creation, a blue silk tunic on top of harem pants, a crimson velvet cummerbund strapping her ribcage. The sleeves hung loose and smelled faintly of cinnamon as she flapped them about, re-assembling the ship.

'Is that yours or Lilian's?'

Milly looked at it with a puzzled expression, staring for a few seconds at its curved solid sails. 'Mine, I think. Yes, of course it's mine. Horrid, isn't it?' She snapped a smile and stood up. 'Listen, I don't know what the plans are today, but I've remembered I have to do something at Jojo's; would you mind awfully if we went there first?'

Frankie wasn't quite sure either but heading into Soho might just give her the opportunity she was after. With a last glance at the cutlery ship she said, 'Suits me just fine. So long as I can have some coffee.'

Milly groaned. 'Oh I know, can't function without it. And with that head.' She rubbed her graze. 'Brutal, horrible women, how dare they?' She stopped herself, Frankie supposed, remembering that they weren't the worst off.

Frankie stood up and dusted off her trousers. Her body felt

sticky underneath the cotton and she realised she hadn't even loosened her collar to sleep. The pile of spare clothes lay crumpled at the foot of the sofa. 'What is it you have to do at Jojo's?' she asked casually as Milly picked up her hat.

'Oh,' Milly raised a breezy hand and smiled wickedly. 'Just feed my snake.'

Frankie sat with her fingers wedged between the pages of her notebook as the Piccadilly Railway train slithered towards Covent Garden. She had no talent for braille and her writing wasn't firm enough to emboss anyway, but somehow she felt as if it kept her mind on the problem. Why had she given so much of herself away last night? Milly had scrutinised her like a frog in science class, and now it felt as if she held bits of her, secrets, floating in little formaldehyde jars. She swallowed her nerves and kept hold of the notebook.

At Covent Garden station she was horrified when Milly hopped down onto the tracks after the train, squatted like she was about to piddle and coaxed a rat from one of the sleeper holes with a lump of sugar. As they rose in the lift, she tried to keep as far as possible from Milly's squirming pocket.

'It has to be fresh,' she said.

'I don't want to know.'

They found the door to Jojo's unlocked and were greeted by the monkey in chattering hysterics. Milly hoisted him onto her shoulder until they reached the inner doors to the club, then picked him delicately by the scruff of the neck and deposited him into the ticket booth.

'Strange that the door was open. Jojo's not usually up at this time.'

'Maybe the monkey unlocked it,' Frankie murmured. As soon as they opened the double doors into the club however, it was clear all was not right.

The tables and chairs were neatly arranged as they had been two days ago when Frankie had first ventured inside, the extra chairs stacked in heaps. The sticky floor smelled faintly chemical. Tables had been wiped and wax candles and salt pots placed side by side. Electric lights illuminated the ghoulish artefacts around the walls, and once again glared off the cracked and chipped cornicing. But the stage curtains were open, peeled back in threadbare folds.

From the shadows by the door a familiar voice echoed through the space. 'She's been in.'

Frankie spun to see Liam leaning against the flaking door jamb. He looked rested but there was an air of worry underneath his expression that he was trying to conceal by chewing on a toothpick.

He walked towards Frankie and pointed at the stage. Frankie had already seen it. The trapeze was hanging down dead centre, rippling vaguely in a breeze. A shining hook had been attached to it in place of Ebony Diamond's leather mouthstrap, a meat hook impaling a small piece of paper.

Milly moved swiftly over to the stage.

'Careful,' Frankie shouted. 'How do you know it's not a warning like that stone?'

'Look at it.'

Frankie joined her, taking the three steps at once, feeling the strain in her knees. The stiff piece of dangling paper batted towards her and she saw that it was a playing card in a suit she didn't recognise. The bottom edge had been skewered, pinning the image upside down; a queen on a throne with flowing black hair. In her right hand she carried aloft a pointed sword, with a tip sharpened to a diamond point. Her left was open-palmed.

'It's a threat.' Milly touched the hook's steel tip. 'This is what they'll do to her if she comes back.'

Liam's voice cut through the open space of the cabaret. 'The door was unlocked. Ebony kept a key. It must have been her what left it.'

Frankie flicked the card, making the trapeze swing lightly. 'But what's it supposed to show, then? What's she doing?'

'What makes you think it's supposed to be her in the picture?' Liam asked from below.

'Look at it,' Frankie traced a finger down the face of the card. 'Long black hair, diamond point.'

'You don't know much about the Tarot, do you?'

Biting a retort she looked back at the card and realised it wasn't a playing card at all, but one of the Major Arcana, or was it Minor Arcana, she could never remember. She had come across a Tarot reader once at a fair but her mother wouldn't let her go near her and made the sign of the cross as they passed. It was the kind of thing girls were put in the 'box' for at school.

Milly was stroking the card's edges, frowning, concentrating. Suddenly the rat in her pocket squeaked. Irritated, she let out a sigh. 'I have to go and feed Hatshepsut. Won't be a second.'

Frankie shuddered as Milly disappeared into the wings of the stage. She turned back to Liam. 'So what do you know about Tarot?'

'Not much.' He bit down on the toothpick. 'But I know what elephant shit smells like.' Frankie stared at him, waiting for him to elaborate. He spat on the ground instead, then nudged with his head. 'Come on.'

She knew she wasn't going to prise anything out of him without dancing to his tune so reluctantly let herself be led back down the hallway towards the entrance. Just before they reached the doormat he pointed down. 'That.' There was a smudge of muddy footprint, not enough to even see what kind of shoe it had come off or whether it was a male or female one, just a small sticky clod, trodden into the shiny floorboard. Frankie could smell it now, a scent like horse dung but more pungent and earthier.

'Right,' she said, bringing her collar to cover her nose.

Liam moved a couple of steps forward and opened the front door. Halfway down the gloss red paint was a blemish the size of a fingerprint. Frankie leaned closer. The light was bad but she could see that a few black threads were clinging to something sticky.

'Lick it,' she heard Liam say.

She recoiled. 'No, you lick it.'

'I already have.' He kept staring at her. She stayed at the juncture between doing what he said and losing face for a few seconds, then finally leaned towards the door, poking the tip of her tongue out until it made contact with the fuzzy threads. At first all she could taste was bitter silk but after a second she got it.

'Sweet,' she straightened back up.

'American Fluffy Stuff,' said Liam, biting his toothpick. He raised both his scrawny eyebrows. 'Told you she was at the circus.'

Frankie straightened her jacket. 'Smug little Sherlock, aren't you? All right, but we still haven't found her. And what's she doing there?'

'It's safe,' he said, pinning open the door back into the cabaret, blocking the path of the skitting monkey. 'You stay outside,' he told it with a stern finger. 'At least we know she's alive.'

Frankie hopped back up onto the stage and pulled the trapeze towards her. 'Well, we still don't know what this means.'

She heard Milly's voice from the wings. After a few seconds Milly herself appeared, brushing down her hands. 'Actually, I have a pretty good idea.'

The dressing room was barely big enough to swing a cat, let alone for three of them to cram in alongside the aquarium that housed Miss Salome's snake. Frankie made sure Liam was wedged between herself and the tank.

Along the ring of naked bulbs that framed the mirror, postcards had been jammed. One of Ebony Diamond stood out, her arm draped casually around a tiger's neck, her waist pinched in to the width of its paw. Milly saw her staring and gave an embarrassed laugh. 'It's an old one. Touched up. She was never that thin.'

To the right of the mirror, next to a cluster of bottles, powders, brushes and unguents spilling their contents onto the counter, sat a small row of books. It was from here that Milly withdrew a slim volume, its shiny new cover painted in the Art Nouveau style with florals and maidens with unloosed hair. 'The Key to the Tarot' was written across the top in red. She flipped it open and began leafing through the pages. It was beautifully illustrated, small descriptions of each card beside pencil sketches. The sections were divided into suits. Wands, cups, swords and finally pentacles. Milly flicked a heap of pages over in a small thud and began scrambling through the chapter on swords. Frankie heard a tapping sound behind her and turned to see to her horror Liam flicking the glass of the snake tank, making the little serpent rear its head.

'Stop that.'

'What's it going to do, crawl up your legs? It's behind glass.'

'The Queen,' Milly was musing to herself. 'In reverse. I thought so.' She drew Frankie's attention to the illustration on the page, the same picture as the card, only black and white. It looked like Boadicea or Joan of Arc, with an eerie resemblance to the suffragettes when they dressed up for parades. Milly pointed at the introduction. Frankie murmured aloud to herself. 'Her right hand raises the weapon vertically . . . the left hand is extended . . . countenance severe but chastened; it suggests familiarity with sorrow. It does not represent mercy. Sounds like Ebony,' she snorted. She read on to the section below. 'In reverse the Queen of Swords can portend to deceit, malice, bigotry, artifice, prudery; a woman who has become bitter due to loss or sorrow. It is commonly used to illustrate a mask, someone hiding something, someone who is not who they say they are.'

Frankie straightened up. 'Someone who is not who they say they are.' It chimed in her head. She knew she had heard that somewhere over the last two days but couldn't for the life of her think where. Milly was looking grave.

'You know who that is, don't you?'

Frankie shook her head. Then it hit her like a clod. The story Mrs Barclay-Evans had told. A woman who disguised herself as a seamstress to expose the double standards of the prison system. 'Lady Constance Lytton,' she blurted out. 'She wasn't who she said she was. She disguised herself as Jane Warton and . . .' Frankie trailed off as the thought ran dry.

Milly was staring at her with knitted brows. 'What are you talking about? I heard that story and as far as I heard Lady Constance Lytton did nothing but good for the movement. She's a suffragette anyway, she's stayed a suffragette ever since. We're looking for someone with malice.'

'But . . .' Frankie breathed out. 'Then who?'

Milly leant closer, her porcelain features hardening in the bright light. 'That girl, Annie Evans. She was wearing Ebony's jacket and hat the night she died. Maybe she stole them. Disguised herself as Ebony for some malicious reason. Some early editions of the morning papers even reported the name as

345

Ebony Diamond.' Milly held up a finger. 'If Ebony's been laying low at the circus, especially if she's been following the newspaper reports, as far as she is concerned no one has made the connection between Olivier dying and Annie being murdered. His death was reported as an accident and hers was a Ripper-type random attack. She wants Jojo to know it starts with Annie.'

Frankie followed Milly as she wedged her way out of the tiny dressing room, peeling aside a curtain of jangling costumes. 'Well, why didn't she write it down?' Frankie asked.

'She can't write. Besides, too dangerous. She obviously thinks the killer, whoever they are, won't be able to read Tarot.' Milly pulled the trapeze towards them and picked off the speared card. Frankie could see the woman's face now, side-on, impassive, warrior-like. 'She wants to deliver a message that this is about mistaken identity. That girl, Annie. The corset, on Olivier.'

'But we knew that anyway.'

'She doesn't know that.'

Frankie pressed her hands back through her hair, feeling how unkempt and oily it had become over the past few days. Liam was lingering at the edge of the stage, mashing his toothpick to a pulp.

Milly continued. 'Annie either stole or borrowed her clothes that night. She must have had a reason.'

'They were friends,' Frankie countered.

'But I don't lend my friends my clothes willy-nilly.'

'Wouldn't want to borrow yours now I know what you've got stowed inside those pockets.'

346

Milly ignored her. 'She was outside the Rising Sun, by herself, dressed up in a fancy jacket and hat. Is that normal behaviour for a seamstress on a Thursday night?'

Frankie cottoned on. 'She was meeting someone.'

Milly's china-pale face lit up. 'Someone special.'

Frankie chewed on this for a minute. 'And either they didn't show, or they came and left. So they might have been the last person to see her alive.'

'Or worse, they killed her.' Milly looked sharp now, her eyes glimmering with the challenge. 'Her family. She must have had sisters she talked to.'

'But how to get her home address?'

Milly puzzled for a while.

Then Liam's Irish accent cut through the silence from the wings, distorted slightly by the toothpick. 'Thought yous two were suppose to be the clever ones.'

Two faces glared at him sourly. He idled for a moment, savouring the knowledge, until Frankie looked like she might rip the toothpick from him and his brown teeth along with it. 'There's a very easy way I think you'll find.'

The woman in the treasury office at Lincoln's Inn wouldn't budge an inch. There were rules. There was privacy. What if they had been sent by the police? Didn't she see what the police had done to the place?

'Do I look like I've been sent by the police?' Frankie leant across the desk, directing the woman's gaze to her wrinkled shirt, her dishevelled tie, the grime on her collar and hair.

The woman peered intently at her for a few seconds then pointed a finger. 'I know you,' she bobbed the finger up and down. 'You're the one that drew that cartoon.'

'Oh, for the love of God.'

Milly stepped in. 'Could we please just give you our word that—'

'Absolutely not.'

Frankie kicked the corner of the table. The sting ran up her leg.

'I'm going to ask you kindly to leave.'

'Yes, I did a bloody cartoon. And you know what? I wish I had a copy with me, I'd roll it up and stick it up your nose.'

'Frankie!' Milly's hand went to her forehead.

'Out. Both of you. Now.'

Frankie whipped a finger of her own to the woman's face. 'I'm doing this because a girl who was one of yours was killed. And where are you? Sitting behind a desk like the queen in the counting house. How do you think the papers would like that? Lend credence to your cause, would it? Make you all look like the martyrs you want to be. You lot don't give a donkey's.'

The woman paused for a moment, looking down the barrel of Frankie's finger. Then she dropped her eyes to the ground. She made her way behind the desk and pulled out an address book from the top drawer. 'Once only.'

Milly glared at Frankie.

'Thank you,' said Frankie. And tried to sound as if she meant it.

Thirty-Three

Down by the wharf at Bermondsey, the winkle-sellers were calling out 'all alive-o' and men were rolling barrels of creosote onto horses and carts. The murky tar smell hit Frankie as soon as she stepped off the tram; the scent of the Thames riverbed and an unpleasant tang coming from a tannery where pigeon shit was curing leather. It was already eleven and Liam had been instructed to meet them outside the corset shop at noon sharp.

As they walked down the cobbles, children with bare feet came running up to them, their arms full of sticks, noticing Milly's fine gown, regarding Frankie curiously as if they were an odd sort to be man and wife.

'Penny for kindling.'

'Piss off,' Frankie said.

Milly reached into her pocket and squeezed sixpence into the child's warty hand. Her hollow eyes didn't even light up. Frankie felt suddenly embarrassed as the little girl put her thumb to her nose and blew a raspberry at her.

They counted off the streets. Down one of them some children were pushing a slumped scarecrow, dressed in a man's old suit, around in a barrow. A browning carrot hung off its face for a nose. When they saw Frankie and Milly they came charging towards them. 'Penny for the guy.'

'Remember remember,' Frankie muttered to herself, 'the fifth of November.' How could she have forgotten? It was Guy Fawkes night. And she wasn't even going to a bonfire. She thought briefly of the bonfires she and Harry Tripe had used to light in the back square. Once they had thrown an old damp pack of cards onto the pyre only for them to explode and Harry's father to angrily explain that playing cards had gunpowder in their ink that would go off when wet. It became a secret tradition after that, she and Harry dousing the cards, hiding them somewhere in the kindling and waiting for them to go boom. She dug in her pocket, mindful of Milly's earlier charity, and found a filthy penny. Holding it up she said, 'Right, whichever one of you can tell me where Mill Street is gets the penny.'

An older boy had a sneer on his face. 'You're on it, nincompoop.' He grabbed the coin out of her hand. The children guffawed, then seized up the barrow and began skipping back down the street.

Frankie looked round at the row of red brick houses, the shabby corner shops and market sellers parked up. The curtains were all drawn, the street, apart from the children tearing up and down, was silent. At the opposite end a public house on the corner had a black sash draped across the doors.

Outside it a man was dismantling a greying horse from a splintered gun carriage.

'Her funeral,' Milly said quietly.

'Shit,' Frankie murmured. She blew air up into her hair and turned slowly around, taking in the street, then pulled her pocket-watch out and looked at the time.

'What do you want to do?' Milly asked. Frankie looked back up the street.

'What number was her house?'

Milly pulled the note out of her pocket. 'Nine. It's that one,' she pointed at a broken door, skewed on its hinges, the wood warped in the doorjamb.

'They'll all be in there, won't they?' Frankie nodded towards the public house. Gentle sea shanties and tempered laughter were spilling out from behind the doors. She began walking directly to number nine.

Milly gathered her skirts and hurried after her. 'That's intrusive.'

Frankie dropped her voice and pulled out the Queen of Swords. 'Who was she meeting that night again?'

Milly pouted.

'You're coming with me, like it or not.'

'What if there's someone in there? Her mother, her sister?'

'We came to pay our respects.'

Milly let out her breath. 'Fine. But tact, Frankie. Tact.'

Frankie dropped open her mouth, then closed it again. 'When have you seen me not . . . ? Fine, tact.'

The rickety door to number nine was so splintered Frankie

had to wrap her handkerchief round her hand to protect it. She knocked a couple of times then called gently through the gap. 'Hello?'

There was no response, only the quiet of the street and the creaking and cracking of an old salt-battered house. Frankie pulled the door, gently at first, then firmer until it scraped open just enough for a person to slip through. From inside came a mild fishy scent, dinner cooked the night before. She wedged herself sideways into the hall, and heard the threads of Milly's silk dress catch behind her followed by a gentle curse.

Off the hall lay a small parlour where a mean fire hissed charcoal smoke behind a metal grate. At the window end, looking onto the street, an empty rocking chair moved gently in the suck of air from the chimney. Frankie heard a noise, the dry pull of breath, and turned to see a box bed at the other end, with a girl sitting on it whose black curls were the spit of Annie Evans's. She was bent over, bawling quiet sobs into her fists. Sensing the intrusion she snapped her head up and her rich brown eyes focused.

Frankie raised two palms. 'It's all right. We're only come to pay our respects. I'm Frankie George. I knew Annie.'

The salty white straps running down the girl's blotched cheeks made her feel a slap of guilt for the lie. But hearing Annie's name seemed to soften the girl. She blew her nose into her soggy sleeve. Her tears quickly ceased, she dried herself up, buttoned herself back in again, a hasty return to form and propriety, the sorrow stowed. She had the same luxurious hair, the same handsome brow as Annie, though from her movements she seemed much younger. Not yet packed off to service or seamstressing. She moved her eyes over their clothing, Frankie's suit and Milly's gown.

'They're making up songs about her. Annie Evans, danced with the devil, Jack the Ripper cut her up.' She shook her head, making her curls sway. 'She never did nothing to no one.'

'I know,' Frankie said.

The girl leaned forward and stood up. 'I forget my manners.'

'That's all right.'

'I'm Beth Evans.'

'Frankie George,' Frankie said again. 'This is Milly Barton.'

Beth Evans looked at Milly and her mouth pursed. 'Friends of Annie's?'

Milly looked hesitantly at Frankie then said, 'Suffragettes. We were with Annie in prison.'

Frankie felt the guilt left over from the first lie harden.

'It was prison that did for her,' Beth Evans sniffed. 'She weren't happy after that last time. Weren't happy at all.'

She sat back down and gestured to a small settee and a box by the fire. Frankie took the box. After a few moments her attention was slowly caught by a strange smell, smoked and perfumed. She looked over at the snivelling fire and saw to her curiosity that someone had stuffed a new bouquet of flowers between the coals. The fresh white petals of the lilies had just begun to smoulder, the edges singeing to a brown crisp. It was a strange place for an offering to end up. Beth noticed her staring at it.

'My Mam would offer you tea if she was here,' she said suddenly, drawing Frankie's attention back. 'But I can't do anything at the moment. My legs is just so heavy.' She started to cry again and Frankie thought about venturing closer but considered it a deceit too far.

'She was at the window smash that night?' Frankie said. 'I thought I saw her.'

'No, she didn't do the windows no more. She said no more, after last time in prison. And she got thrown out of service.'

'She was in service?'

Milly nodded pointedly.

'Of course,' Frankie said, remembering what the suffragettes had told Milly. 'I remember now. I mean she didn't mention she'd been thrown out. She just said she'd left service. Got new work.'

Beth gazed at Frankie with an unnervingly cool stare. Frankie couldn't work out whether she had been suddenly rumbled or whether the girl was moved by the insensitive line of conversation. She looked away, at the curling daguerreotypes on the wall, the framed verse from the Bible, and those peculiar lilies, still smouldering away.

Eventually Beth said in a weak voice, 'It's all his fault.' She pointed to the fire in the grate. 'You think anyone goes to be a seamstress when they been a parlourmaid? And her, mistress, the cheek to send flowers, once she chucked her out.'

Frankie peered closer into the fire. The ribbon was tucked between two lumps of unlit coal; attached to it was a card, but she couldn't make out the name. She sat back again. 'The family Annie worked for, they let her go because they didn't like her going to prison for the suffragettes?'

Beth almost smiled. Her shoulders shook bitterly. 'No. He bloomin' encouraged it. Master of the house. She came home one Sunday for supper, told us she spent all day in the garden with him, telling him all about suffragettes and he said he'd give her Tuesdays off for meetings. He were so excited, he were even going to get involved hisself.'

Frankie frowned, thinking she had misheard. 'Sorry, the master said this or the mistress?'

'Master,' Beth croaked into her sleeve then coughed. 'Mistress were a vixen. Mistress were what let her go. Mind you, who can blame her. Master takes an eye for you. But it weren't Annie's fault. She's got a pretty face is all.' Beth's eyes filled up again. 'She had a pretty face.'

The tear gates opened and a fresh stream rolled down until it dripped from her chin. Milly leaned across and placed a hand on the girl's knee. Beth looked at the hand and Milly withdrew it gently.

'What you do about it? She told me she were in love with him.' She leaned on the greasy wall and her voice started to rise. 'She were soft for him. He took a curl of her hair, she kept his handkerchief. I said, "He's never going to marry you, Annie Evans. You see." But she thought she would one day be in the big house, and they'd both have a vote, and all them smashes they did together, they'd be worth it.'

Frankie sat up. 'What did you say? Smashes they did together?' Her eyes darted to the fireplace. The flames were spreading now, catching the coals either side of the ribbon in tendrils of smoke. She moved closer, tilting her head until she could just make out the writing on the card. 'Reynolds.'

'Reynolds.' Beth spat. 'Mr Reynolds. He were her sweetheart. But it were Mrs Reynolds put her out. And had the cheek to send them flowers.' Beth looked at the fire for a few seconds. 'Still, better to bleed your fingers in a clothing factory than have the mistress try to trip up your every move.'

Frankie's memory stirred. She knew that name. It swam around for a second, like a fish, then snapped at her. The day in court, the suffragette man that had ended up in Pentonville.

'Did she still see Mr Reynolds?' Milly probed quietly.

Beth nodded and rubbed her eyes. 'Tried not to but she were soft on him.'

'She dress up nice when she went to see him?' Frankie asked.

Beth looked confused and peered out of the window. The noises from the street grew momentarily louder. They heard the swinging of doors and a surge of tin whistle. Voices filtered out from the public house.

'Was she meeting Mr Reynolds on Thursday?' Frankie asked urgently.

But Beth wasn't listening. Her eyes had drifted beyond them to the road outside. 'She shouldn't have been walking

the streets by herself that time of night. Is that what a gentleman does? Leaves a woman by herself.' She looked at her
guests in turn, suddenly aware of the humiliation of having
strangers in perfectly tailored clothing sitting in her unwashed
parlour asking questions about the sister she had just buried.

Frankie glanced around the room at the orange walls and
smoke stains from the paraffin lamps. Her mind was working.
She had seen Reynolds in the dock that afternoon for
window-smashing, so he couldn't have turned up to meet
Annie. He must have stood her up, leaving her to walk the
streets alone. That eliminated him, but didn't bring them any
closer to who might have killed her. Frankie looked back at
Beth. 'The factory Annie went to work in, was it on New
Bond Street?'

Beth nodded.

'What did she make?'

'It was seamstress work. Corsets. You only had to look at
her fingers. All made to order, fancy stuff.' Her eyes fell onto
Milly's silk patterned skirt. She didn't need to say the rest of
the sentence. The look was in her eyes. For people like you.
'That's what beauty gets you. Everyone always said Annie's
face was her ticket.' She heaved a huge breath in. The sigh
that came out was quiet and controlled.

'And she worked every day at this corset shop?'

'Every waking minute.'

'Who got her the job there?'

Beth's eyes thinned into narrow black pools. 'Who are
you?'

357

Frankie hesitated, swallowing. 'I told you. We're suffragettes.'

'You don't look like suffragettes. Where's your green, white, purple? What do you want to know so much about Annie for?'

Frankie let the girl stare at her for a moment, shadows of betrayal moving through her stomach. Sitting in Beth's family home, wondering who had murdered her sister while she prised gentle answers out of her. 'Who got her the job at the corset shop?'

Beth bowed her head. 'It was a friend she knew from the suffragettes. A famous girl. She came by the house one time, with another of the seamstresses that worked there. An old lady with her face all bandaged up. Annie said she'd had an accident or disease. But you couldn't catch it.' She picked at a sore on the side of her lip. 'They didn't come in. Sat outside in a hackney waiting for Annie.'

'Phossy jaw,' Frankie murmured. Beth looked up sharp. Frankie leaned forward. 'Did it have a name, this corset shop?'

Beth picked at her lip again. Then a look of languid scorn came into her eyes. She snorted with laughter and shook her head. 'It had a nickname all right. On account of what they were making in there. She said they called it "The Hourglass Factory".'

Thirty-Four

'No, Frankie George. No. Not again. Not this time.'

'I think you know it's necessary. Anyway, Liam's meeting us there.'

'Well, he can be your dirty partner in crime. I'm not getting whacked on the head again. Not for the sake of your bloody scoop.'

'But the answer to it all has to be in there. Twinkle said it. Those maids, not as enlightened as you'd like to think. How would you feel if you spent your days with bleeding fingers, lacing in rich men with fancies? They're up to something.'

They were standing at the side of the pavement, waiting for the next tram. Frankie had a cigarette hanging from her lips like a long growth. She was scribbling fast in her notebook, ash soiling the pages like grey snowflakes.

Milly put a hand to her forehead. 'Well, in that case, isn't it about time we went to the police?'

'Hang the police.' Frankie suddenly became aware her

voice had risen and took a few breaths to stop herself sounding hysterical. 'Don't you ever have a hunch?'

Milly looked at her as if she had just sprouted wings. 'A hunch?'

'A feeling. I know that the answer to whatever happened to Ebony and Olivier and Annie is in that shop, and we aren't going to get anywhere at night.' She smoked the rest of the cigarette quickly, aware that Milly was watching her and that manners dictated she should really offer Milly one. 'The shop's closed just now; it's the only chance we'll get. That woman she mentioned, the one with phossy jaw. I saw her. Did you ever see a woman with her face bundled up with Ebony, at the club?'

Milly said something quietly in the direction of the traffic. The wind muffled her voice.

'Pardon?'

'I said I think you should leave it to the police. You've got enough to write up a piece, just put a bit of intrigue into it. Didn't you say the *Evening Gazette* make most of it up anyway?'

Frankie fixed her eyes on Milly in disbelief. Her features had become repugnant all of a sudden. She resented the high large nose, the perfectly cut cheekbones, the aristocratic brow. 'Is that what people of your world do, leave it to the police?'

'Oh Frankie, for God's sake.'

The tram approached with a heavy rattle and Milly made towards it. Frankie flinched as her notebook fluttered out of her hand and with it a couple of loose leaves of paper, scraps she had stuffed in. She almost lost her balance as she reached to stop them spilling into the road. Milly had already boarded and Frankie followed her up to the open top deck. There was a woman at the back reading a copy of *The Suffragette*, who watched them as they took the front seat.

'I saw you flinch when I said that last night. I didn't mean anything by it, just that we're different.'

'You don't have to work for your living. I do.'

Milly locked her eyes on her. 'I work for my living good and proper. I enjoy what I do, but that doesn't mean it isn't work and there aren't nights when I wouldn't rather be curled up in a nice big house with hot water bottles and maids to turn down my bed. I ran away. I didn't want to live that way even though I could have.'

'And I suppose that makes you more righteous than poor jugginses who don't have a choice.'

Milly looked straight ahead at the streets branching off each side of the thoroughfare's bony spine. 'Spare me the match girl act. You have a choice, Frankie.'

'This or scrubbing floors.'

'You're not like that girl in there, that Beth. Or Annie.'

'Annie's not in there. She's dead.'

Milly shook her head, irritated. 'Why don't you trust the police? You just hate everyone, don't you? Suffragettes, Twinkle . . . you most likely hate all women by the way you dress. You'd hate Ebony too, if she gave you the chance.'

Frankie looked down at her black trousers. Milly's words

stung and the trousers suddenly felt ostentatious on her, foolish and provocative rather than practical.

'I want to get to the bottom of it. I thought that was what you wanted too.' She let the words stew in her mouth for a few seconds and then came out with it. 'This doesn't have anything to do with your brooch being found on Smythe's body, does it? Care to tell me about that?'

Milly's shoulders froze. She kept staring at the road disappearing under them. The electric whine of the tram suddenly seemed unbearably loud.

'You should be more careful what spoons you hand out to guests. Family crest, is it? Beautiful. You should see mine. Got a leg of mutton on it, a bar of carbolic soap, barrow wheel.'

Milly held up her hand. 'All right.'

Frankie waited patiently for her to speak.

'Frankie, I don't know how he got that brooch. I didn't even know I had it.'

'Ebony had it on her, at the corset shop.'

Milly's cheeks stiffened, her eyes widened for a split-second. She recovered quickly and said, 'Well, she must have stolen it. Maybe she was going to sell it or something. I have noticed things go missing sometimes in that dressing room, I thought it was Lizzy but perhaps—'

'Why didn't you mention it when you saw the rubbing?'

'Because it's not relevant. I thought it would just complicate . . . You might not trust . . . I don't know. I was tired when you showed me the rubbing, I didn't even know what I was looking at.'

'Curious.'

Milly turned her head to face Frankie. There again was that downward scoop of her lashes, the scorn sliding down her nose. 'You think I'm behind this. I would come after a show-girl in a basement supper club because she stole a brooch of mine? You think I care about family crests and heirlooms? More than people's lives?'

They rode in silence for a while. As the tram curved round towards Oxford Street, Milly reached to pull the bell.

'Where are you going?'

Her mouth was set in a solid pout and she looked at Frankie for a couple of seconds as if contemplating long and hard whether to share what was on the tip of her tongue. Then she leant close enough for Frankie to smell the frank-incense on her collar and the faint tang of orange blossom on her breath, and whispered, 'If we're going in there, I want to be armed.'

'You what?'

She rubbed her lips together. 'I want a gun. A pistol. It's dangerous. That's two people they've murdered. And my head's still sore from last night.'

Frankie looked confused. 'Where are you going to get a gun from? Do you just have a stash of them at the club in case you want to go pigeon-shooting in Hyde Park, taking pot shots at peasant girls down Frith Street?'

Her jaw was still tight. 'I'm going home.'

Frankie tilted her head back in the direction they had come from. 'But Talgarth Road's—'

'I'm not talking about Talgarth Road. I'm talking about *home*. Belgravia.'

She started to descend the winding stairs of the tram when it pulled to a halt sending them both knocking into the sides of the staircase. Once again Frankie cursed as the loose papers came fluttering out of her notebook. She stumbled to retrieve them all from the sticky stairs of the tram, then stuffed them back in with one hand, swinging herself off onto the street with the other. By the time the tram moved off with a jerk she saw that Milly was already crossing the street, dodging horse-drawn hansom cabs and black motor cars. Tucking her notebook away, she hopped the few steps to catch up, thanking her stars as a horse and cart whizzed past at a full trot, just missing her.

Frankie did as she was told and waited on the street outside the scoop of stairs and the columned portico, feeling like a petulant footman who had spoken out of turn to his mistress. It was an impressive house, right enough: five floors including a basement and a balustrade at the top. The street was wide, with a green square on one side, and so full of quiet air it seemed as if a muffler had been placed between it and the rest of London. There were no newspaper boys crying their pitch, no shopgirls or clerks, no drunks. Only a few purring motorcars and the occasional carriage. At the next house along, a lady in a long string of pearls with streaked iron-grey hair was twitching her first-floor curtain.

Frankie stuffed her hands in her pockets and whistled for a

while, still shaking off her sulk. What Milly had said about her hating everyone wasn't true. It was only a temper, only her shooting her mouth off without thinking. Some people seemed to always find time to think about what they wanted to say; for Frankie, those extra minutes and seconds didn't exist, she didn't know where they were found.

She scuffed the dirt on the path with her foot and looked up as she heard the rattle of a carriage approaching. The horses drew closer, the vehicle began to slow and she saw that it was bound for where she stood. She hopped back a few paces to give them room. The door of the carriage opened, a foot in a squeezed brown kidskin boot stepped onto the path. Just as it made contact with the crunch of dirt, Frankie heard a crash behind her: the sound of a slamming door. Milly came charging down the steps. Then Frankie saw her freeze.

The rest of the figure appeared from the carriage.

Frankie saw the stack of pamphlets in the woman's hand first. Bold printed, some smeared, the smell of burnt ink and paper coming off them, the words 'This way to the gates of hell'. They bore the stamp of the National Vigilance Association in the bottom corner. The woman adjusted the cloak on her shoulders and Frankie saw before her a curtain lifting so vividly it made her want to laugh in shock. The features were the same. Why hadn't she seen it? The high nose, the proud cheeks, the fine ice blue of the eyes. Granted there was far more skin round the old woman's jowls but it was unmistakable. Milly was the daughter of Lady Thorne.

Lady Thorne took a few heavy, unsettled breaths and

adjusted the stack of pamphlets in her hand. Her eyes fell to the pavement. Frankie thought back to the exchange on the street outside Jojo's. She should have made the connection. She had put it down to the spitting familiarity of a showgirl troubled by her nemesis, nothing more.

Lady Thorne's daughter dancing with a snake round her waist! Frankie's first thoughts were on the scoop. How delicious to have walked blindfolded into an exposé on the licentious life of London's most notorious moral guardian's daughter? She tried to keep the smile from her eyes. It vanished properly when she saw the coldness on Milly's face. Her lips were drained of their colour. The lines on her cheeks fissured deeper. It sent a chill through the back of Frankie's neck. She had never seen a look so loveless between a mother and daughter.

Milly grabbed Frankie's wrist like a walking stick. 'Come with me.' She led her roughly off the path and down onto the road, speeding up until she had broken them both into a run.

When Frankie dared to turn her head back, she could see Lady Thorne staring after them with a distanced look in her eyes, a carefree gaze that was enough to make her shudder.

At the end of the street she yanked them both to a halt, feeling the burn in her lungs. 'I'm not made for this.' She watched Milly splutter and pant, refusing to meet Frankie's eye. 'Did you get the gun?'

Milly nodded.

'Why didn't you tell me?'

Milly could hear the smile in her voice. 'Don't.'

'It's nothing to be ashamed of. It's—'

'It's what, Frankie? The scoop of the century? National Vigilance Association daughter dances like prostitute in Soho? It's none of anyone's business is what it is. She made her living by marrying. You don't think that's prostitution? You ever heard of a debutantes' ball? You don't think that's prostitution? Arranged marriages, parents plotting behind your back. At least I'm only letting the men look at me.' There was a sour downturn in her mouth. Frankie was astonished to see her spit phlegm onto the pavement, as if she could rid herself of a bitter taste. She touched the silk of Milly's arm.

Milly shook her head and wrenched her arm away. 'Let's just get on with it, shall we?'

They arrived at Bond Street to find it bustling with shoppers and pleasure-strollers wrapped up in furs taking arm-in-arm turns. A short nimble man in brown pinstripes was handing out flyers for a show in the West End.

Outside the Maid in the Moon, Tommy Dawber was watering a trough of winter seedlings, weedy looking holly and ivy. Frankie closed in on him quietly, making him jump and choke on his own saliva.

'Stone the crows, Frankie.'

'I'm sorry, Tommy.'

He made a pantomime of clutching at his chest. Then his eyes, like everyone's seemed to have in the past two days, fell on Milly. He straightened up and adjusted his tie. 'What's brings you here? You on another newspaper job?'

Frankie glanced across the street to see if she could spy Liam. It wasn't quick enough for Tommy to miss.

'Leave it. I saw you here the other day. Let a man have some dignity in death. I've had nothing but questions, questions, questions from everyone. I'm doing better than that drinking-hole in Whitechapel after the Ripper business.' He shifted his shoulders uncomfortably and set down the watering can. 'It wouldn't be so bad if . . . don't give me that look, Frankie. You know as well as anyone, it's not right . . . what he wore.'

'I don't care what colour knickerbockers he wore. I just want to know, has anyone been in there? Anyone you've seen?'

Tommy's teeth hovered threateningly over his bottom lip. 'The police a couple of times, on the morning it happened.'

'No one else?'

His eyes dangled on Milly for a second, fishing for an introduction. She was fiddling in her deep silk pockets, pretending to watch a woman down the street heaving two giant poodles from a carriage into a hotel lobby.

'I've got my nose in a brewer's tap half the time, Frankie. You know that. I haven't been watching.'

Frankie fought the urge to scowl. 'Well, can you watch now, just for a second. Give us a whistle if anyone does come?'

'Frankie.' His face turned down.

'Come on, Tommy. One for the Spurs.'

'You had your one for the Spurs off me, couple of nights ago.'

Frankie discreetly wiped a fleck of his spittle from her lapel. He noticed. 'Just once. But if any police come sniffing round, wondering what two,' he hesitated, 'ladies were doing in that shop when it's supposed to be locked off, private property.'

'Then you tell them, both short, fat, corset-wearing types, one of them had a glass eye and a Scottish accent, the other one walked with a limp, like she had a peg leg. Thanks, Tommy, keep an eye out. Both ways, mind.' She gestured in both directions up the road as they moved to cross it. She could hear Tommy tutting loudly under his breath.

'Where the hell is that boy? Only time we could bloody use him.' Apart from not being able to see Liam anywhere, Frankie was relieved to find Lancashire Court empty. Milly made a careful check that no one was around then very casually drew a silver pistol from her pocket, monogrammed and engraved with elaborate patterns. A thrill of revulsion swelled through Frankie. 'What does he use that for?'

'Who?'

'Your father.'

She frowned. 'This is mine.'

'You can shoot?'

'Keep your voice down. Of course I can shoot.'

'But I thought women . . .' she trailed off, seeing the scornful triumph in Milly's eyes.

'Don't shoot? Of course not. That would almost be as bad as them writing the news.' Milly busied herself picking away at the lock with fixed concentration.

'What's taking so long?'

'It's stiffer this time. Not just the latch. It's been twisted twice, deadlocked.'

'Well, that's good, isn't it, it means there's no one in there?'

Milly looked at her with an eyebrow raised. She had started to say, 'I think you're going to have to smash it,' when there came the familiar tiny snap, and the lock slid across. She eased the handle with the tips of her fingers and they both stepped inside.

The place seemed dustier in the blue haze of day, murky streams of sun picking out particles floating in the air. There was the same smell of linen and cotton but it was fustier, warmer and ranker, as if damp was already setting in with no door blowing open and closed, no customers to air the garments out.

They crept up the high stairs, feeling for the creaks in advance until they were on the tiny landing between the two rooms. Frankie pointed to the one she had peeped through the night before.

'Hold it out. In front of you.'

Milly's brow creased.

'The pistol.'

'I don't want to use it, Frankie.'

'Better you than me.'

'Don't joke.'

'I'm not. I can't even piddle straight let alone shoot.' Frankie dropped to her knee, wincing from the pain still there from the night before, and peered through the keyhole. It was harder to see now. The curtains blocked out most of the day's light, filtering it to a dirty emerald. She could see the iron corset on the carved dummy once again and shuddered. 'Drink tea and play bridge,' she muttered.

Feeling like she was about to jump into iced water, she gave the handle a sharp twist. It jammed and she waited. No noises came from inside. 'You're going to have to pick this.'

'I'm not going to have any pins left to hold my hair up.'

Milly carelessly dropped the gun into Frankie's hands, catching Frankie off guard with the weight of it, still warm from her grasp, the polished metal smooth. The engravings gripped Frankie's palm and she shivered, feeling the dread immediacy of the weapon, the heavy possibility of her finger slipping and killing someone faster than she could blink. Her hand felt too large for it, the gun dainty like a lady's comb, shiny against the grime under her fingernails.

Milly scraped and scrabbled for a few seconds then came the prise and click. Frankie shoved the gun back at her and inched the door open.

'Be gentle with it. It's not an ornament.'

The room was in two parts, a small white-washed warehouse stuffed with gaudy embellished designs, and a splintered mezzanine which stretched halfway across the length of the space, accessed by a thin wooden ladder. Underneath it, more rows of antiquated corsets hung, gathering dust; crushed moth wings and beetle droppings. A rack was tucked separately from the rest, with conspicuously larger bodices lined in a neat row, cleaner, worn more recently, and each pinned with a piece of paper identifying it by a nickname: 'Jess', 'Bobby', 'Alfie'. On the mezzanine a row of seven neat Singer pedal sewing machines sat, lovingly polished.

'Careful,' Milly warned, as Frankie placed a foot on the pale ladder. They climbed to the top and found themselves in a clean, well-kept workshop space. Reams of silk and linen were stacked tidily in one corner, the floor had been recently swept and the boards, though sticking with the odd nail and splinter, were in good condition. Patterns had been arranged in little bundles tied with ribbon on a shelf. By the edge of the platform next to a gas lamp sat a box filled to the brim with bobbins of cotton in various colours – whites, golds, peaches – then next to it a casket of lace trimmings; spidery French lace, strips of Chantilly, some thicker Finnish lace Frankie recognised from a bedcover in Twinkle's boudoir. The organisation was spotless, a factory as neat and boutique as the shop below it. It was not at all what Frankie had expected from Beth Evans's description of bleeding fingertips and merciless hours. But then, appearances were deceptive. A boiling laundry house looked clean and calm at the end of a shift.

Milly began picking over the piles of cloth with her eyes. The gloom silhouetted the shape of her gown, billowing round her body in the draught from below. Frankie tugged a loose floorboard. It came up half-way and she peered into the dirty gap underneath, sniffed, then replaced it.

'You'd better keep an eye on the door and have that thing ready.'

'I'm only using it as a threat. There are no bullets in it.'

'What?'

'There are no bullets in it. I don't intend to use it.'

'But you were the one wanted to be armed.'

'As a threat,' she said firmly, then sat on the platform, tucking her legs underneath her, flicking her eyes between the room below and the door.

There were a few ledger books on the shelf. Frankie opened them, wishing she knew how to decipher sums and figures. They looked like her father's accounts from the vegetable stall. She ran her eyes down the notes, looking for a name, an order placed, something that might chime with anything she had heard before. She scraped the flaps at each side of the book, where the paper was glued to the blue pasteboard, to see if they would give, but they were stuck firmly and running her palm along them revealed that nothing was wedged between the book and its casing. When she replaced it, she noticed that on the same shelf, underneath the account log, lay a little black address book. With her heart giving the tweak of a jig she creaked open the leather, hoping to see the names and addresses of Lords and MPs, members of The Hourglass Club. It was only clients though, the names of some suppliers of fabrics and seamstresses for outsourcing specialised labour. She gave a sigh, looking back at the row of sewing machines. After a few seconds of staring at the black wood cases she heard Milly's breath hiss, a sound like gas escaping a valve.

'What?' A wave of fright trickled down her spine. She braced herself for a confrontation. But Milly wasn't staring at the door. She was staring at something below the platform on the clothing rail, a white and black rectangle stuck to a moth-eaten black lace veil.

'What is it?'

Milly didn't answer. Frankie scrambled towards the wooden ladder but couldn't see clearly through the slats. She made to descend.

'No, don't. I'll get it.'

'You sit there, watch the door.'

'No Frankie, I'll get it.' Milly gingerly prised herself off her knees and clambered down the ladder backwards, pointing the gun to the ground. She reached forward, straining into the rack of corsets. From above, the object looked like a palm-sized photograph with holes cut into its border. The seconds stretched as Milly stared at it, then she climbed back up, clasping it to her throat.

'What is it?'

It took Milly a moment to prise her tight fingers off it, then she held it out, watching all the time as if she could change the face of it by staring.

Frankie squinted in the green light. At first it just looked like a nude on a penny playing card, a woman posing with one arm loosely braced behind her head. Then Frankie clocked the snake and her lips moved into a tight 'o' to whistle.

Milly cut her off. 'It was when I'd just got back. I was

feeling very, very rebellious.' Her voice fractured. 'Like I wanted to liberate myself or something. Be naked after what had happened. I did it in one of Lillian's friend's studios. A greasy little man who works off the Aldwych. Lillian had told me it was empowering, posing for men. Oh, she loves to take her clothes off. Thinks it's revolutionary, like she's a courtesan in the Belle Époque. A bit different when it's an oil painting to a penny pack of cards.'

'Hold on a second, what's that?' Frankie was peering beyond her, to the ground. She wedged past Milly, hopped onto the ladder and dipped down. Dress hangers smacked together as she pushed the clothing rail aside. Nestled underneath it was a sack, the top lip just draping open revealing another playing card with a picture of Milly on it, nude and pouting. Again the suit markers in each corner had been torn out. Frankie dragged the bag towards her and it tipped, spilling masses of the same cards all over the dusty floor.

She picked one up and ran her hand along the edge, then dropped down and fumbled through the rest. The corners of the hearts and diamonds cards had been gouged, leaving ragged gaps in their place. The black suits, the spades and clubs, had been left alone.

'What are the holes for?' she wondered quietly.

'That's what I don't know. Although they would have been where the red suits are. Hearts, Diamonds.'

'Diamonds,' Frankie muttered gently.

Milly looked down at her.

'Did Ebony have a pack of these?' Frankie asked.

'Not that I knew of.'

Frankie thumbed the hole carefully.

'What did you mean, "diamonds", Frankie?'

'Nothing. Just that it's Ebony's name and it's a coincidence that the Diamonds were—' Her throat went tight. She could feel her eyes jam in her head.

'What?'

A memory stirred. Harry Tripe out in the communal yard at the back. Bonfire night. Throwing playing cards onto the blaze. Guy Fawkes night. Tonight.

'Oh Milly, Lordy.' Frankie scraped her hair off her forehead as she began to sweat. She moved her arms around in front of her, scattering the cards about, trying to divine what she was looking for.

'What?' Milly snapped. 'What have you thought of? I wish you would share what goes on in that head of yours.'

'We have to find them.' She scrambled to her feet and climbed back up the ladder, scrabbled at boxes of cotton and linen, tipping over rolls of silk, sending bobbins tumbling onto the floor.

'Frankie, tell me what you are looking for.' Milly climbed to her feet, stepping out of the way as Frankie toppled a ream of cotton.

She stopped for a second, biting her lip. 'Gunpowder.'

'What?'

'The red dye on packs of cards is – it's gunpowder, it's got gunpowder in it. Nitro-something or other. You add liquid and a spark to it and it will blow up. What night is it tonight?'

'Monday?'

Frankie shook her head, irritated. 'Guy Fawkes night.' She stared with hollow eyes at Milly. 'They're building a bomb.'

Even in the swampy half-light Frankie could see the blood drain from Milly's face.

'Playing cards with me on them.'

'Doesn't matter who's on them, it will be whatever was lying around.' Frankie was back on her hands and knees now, pulling up another floorboard. Outside in the distance she could vaguely hear Tommy's distinctive voice shouting 'Oi' at someone in the street and then the slapping of hands on backs. She wondered again where the devil Liam had got to.

She lifted the floorboard but there was nothing there. The other room, she thought, it will be in the other room, across the hall. Sitting back on her haunches she leaned against one of the sewing machines. It rattled as her weight fell on it.

Milly snapped her head up with frightened eyes. She wobbled the sewing machine behind Frankie's back with her hand. It rattled again.

Carefully they eased off the painted wooden lid. It was heavy, the metal machine underneath giving off a rich smell of oil and polish. The base of the machine was three inches thick, like a small table. Frankie knocked it with her fingers. It was hollow and something light rattled inside.

'Check the others.'

Milly ran her hand quickly across the two machines within her reach while Frankie did the same on the other side. All had hollow tables underneath them. All rattled when they were knocked.

'How to get inside,' Frankie murmured. She tapped her fingers against the smooth metal, feeling for loose screws or sections that could be pulled off. At last, on the base under the needle she found a penny-sized circle of metal that popped away when she tugged it. She heaved the whole table to a tilt and a scroll of paper slipped out. Frankie hesitated as she bent to pick it up. Was that a creak on the stair?

Milly craned towards her as she flattened out the paper, her neck so close Frankie could smell the spice on her again. It was a newspaper article, more than twenty years old.

'It's from an archive. British Museum. Do you see the faint stamp?'

The headline ran 'Walsall Anarchists: What They Planned'. Beneath it was a thin line diagram, shaped like a pear. The diagram showed arrows pointing to the stalk and text pointing out a detonator, two soft metal cogs that would spark when the protrusion was pressed against them, while the cup was filled with gunpowder.

'Who prints this? A guide to bomb-making. I mean they worry about the Irish throwing bombs, but look at this.'

They both looked at the title running along the top. In familiar circus style lettering, alongside the date, 1892, were the words '*London Evening Gazette*'.

Turning back to the machine, Frankie stuffed her finger further into the hollow cavity, retrieving more pieces of paper. The first was an instruction manual to a student chemistry set from Gamages, then there were a couple more rogue cards with the suits cut out and finally two tightly rolled sheets of paper, gnarled so small they could have been wads of chewed tobacco cast away.

Her head shot up as there came another creak outside the door. She thought it could just be the building settling as the temperature changed from cold to hot and back, and looked anxiously towards the window. The sun had dipped behind a cloud. But there were no more sounds. Milly tapped a finger to her lips and slowly fumbled along the floor until she found the gun.

They unravelled the papers carefully, trying not to tear the delicate sheets. They were line drawings, the edges torn; both wore the stamp of the British Museum.

'Did Ebony Diamond have a reader's ticket for the Museum?' Frankie whispered. 'I don't even have a reader's ticket.'

Milly's head was shaking to and fro over the diagrams. One was long and thin and rectangular with boxes branching out from other boxes, architectural patterns filling in the details. The other was a closer diagram of a large chamber, with benches running down two sides and a gallery above. Distances had been measured and recorded in pencil and arrows drawn. It looked almost like a dressmaker's pattern, neat, calm and dainty. Frankie flicked between them and looked at the titles. One was a general diagram of the Houses of Parliament Westminster complex. The other was the House of Commons. Her heart suddenly plunged. Images flickered and reeled through her head. She tried to picture what had been in Ebony's mind, go back, probe through what she had been thinking when she started that fight with Frankie in the street. Had she really stood there, blurting out her heart about the suffragettes, chastising Frankie, fearlessly igniting a camera in public while all the while knowing that bombs were going to be set off inside the Houses of Parliament?

Frankie's face was scanning the room, stricken. Milly was holding up a bony finger. 'You don't know anything for certain.'

'I've got a damned good idea.'

Frankie had her hand inside her breast pocket, reaching for her notebook when the door swung back with a bang.

Both hands flew onto the gun but Milly's reactions were quicker and she caught it, raised it to shoulder height, and whether she intended it to or not, a deafening round cracked out of it scorching the air with hot smoke. Someone in dark clothing ducked, there was a man's cry and two pink hands covered the face and dark hat of the intruder. Frankie couldn't help a stiff yelp escape her mouth.

The bullet sent a waterfall of plaster cascading down the wall.

'You said it wasn't loaded,' Frankie cried.

'I was lying. I didn't want you to panic.'

The man stood up and a second entered behind. It took Frankie a second to clock their identical dress.

'Police. Stay absolutely still. Put the pistol where I can see it.'

The first constable blew his whistle and a shrill unbearable noise filled the small room. Only when it stopped did Frankie hear the noise below of Tommy's spitting tongue. 'Frankie, you still up there? There's coppers on their way in.'

Thirty-Five

Primrose leaned his head a little too harshly against the cold wall of the officer's room at Bow Street, enjoying the ache that spread out between his brows. He heard the door open and hurriedly rolled down his sleeves.

'Possible breakthrough.' He was dismayed to hear Wilson's voice, animated and buoyant and clearly relishing the case. Primrose could see it in him every time they passed in the corridor, the flush in the sergeant's cheeks, the perky twitch of his huge nose and ears. He had begun to imagine the team whispering about his leadership qualities, that they had no purpose or direction, that they didn't know what they were looking for. Certainly Jenkins was starting to get impatient about how long he would be required to maintain his 'surveillance'. He'd had little guidance on his role since the night raid, and that morning's messages from Lincoln's Inn showed he was starting to wonder what exactly he should be doing there. Primrose felt his large head very heavy on his shoulders for a moment, then nodded at Wilson to go on.

'We've pulled in a couple of cats from that corset shop on Bond Street, where the bloke . . .'

'Yes, I know.'

'A shopgirl on Bond Street told one of the beat constables that she thought she saw two women with a gun breaking into the locked-up shop. I recognise one of them, think she's a reporter.'

'Sorry, Wilson, I might be lost but I don't understand the breakthrough.'

Wilson cast his eyes deferentially at the inspector's chin, but there was a sly contempt underlying the look. 'Annie Evans used to work as a seamstress in that shop. Now the girls are kicking and screaming blue murder something about bombs being found in there, or plans for bombs or something. I think we might have our foiled plot. If Ebony and Annie both knew about it. Boom.'

Primrose tugged the hair at his browline. 'Right! Get down there as quick as you can. Take Mathers. Telephone the Yard and get fingerprints to come. I'm sure they can spare someone. Where are the two girls?'

'In the cells. That cross-dresser's got some tongue on her. The driver said he'd never heard such language, not even from a sailor.'

'Where did they get the gun?'

Wilson screwed up his face. 'One of them's a bit of a set type, says she borrowed it from the family home. It tallies. We checked.'

Primrose fixed his lips. 'All right.'

'Oh, Inspector, one other thing.' Wilson had one hand round the doorframe so his head was craning diagonally now, giving him an irritating jaunty appearance. 'There was a telephone call from your house. Seems your wife wants to speak to you. She's had a bit of a turn or something.' He waited for the words to sink in and was gratified as Primrose glared at him with renewed seriousness.

'What sort of turn?'

Wilson shrugged. 'Don't know. Funny turn?'

'Did they say if it was serious?'

'A faint, I think. I've already asked Chief Stuttlegate to take over those interviews . . .'

'That won't be necessary. Prioritise getting a team down to that shop.'

'What about Jenkins?'

Primrose shook his head, irritated. 'What about him?'

'If it's bombs, then shouldn't we have a sapper?'

'Fine, take Jenkins.'

'But he's on surveillance.'

'Pull him off.'

'That will take a while.'

'Dammit, isn't there another bomb expert you can use then?'

Primrose reached across to the chair where his jacket was slung and picked it up. It had the smell of coal on it. He tried to battle the sickness growing in him. The thought of a telephone call from Clara was filling him with an ugly combination of guilt and anxiety.

'And if the Chief's looking for you?'

He held the door open deferentially for Primrose to pass.

'Tell him . . . Tell him I'll be here in the station. In here or in the interview room with those girls.'

'Very good, sir.'

The corridor seemed to stretch past Primrose, as if it was spreading longer the further he walked down it. Time stretched too; his feet wouldn't move at an adequate pace to reach the telephone. When he did get there he was irritated to find the desk sergeant glued to the earpiece, taking orders like a military man. Primrose waited impatiently, conjuring up all manner of scenarios in his head. She had taken laudanum, she had fainted in loneliness, his mind ran morbid. And then another thought struck him, deep and terrifying and warm at the same time. Could it be possible? A faint was no sure sign of – he didn't dare think it aloud – but Clara wasn't a woman to take unwell despite the shopping and the weather and the smells inside the butcher's shop. She had been so lonely for two years. If it was – no, he would not think the word aloud in his head – if she was to have company in the house from now on . . . A person to nurture. He let the thought run its course for a few minutes. Sherry would be broken out at the farm, topsides would be roasted. His father would play the tin whistle. And would he in some way vindicate himself from this guilt, this sense that he was keeping a woman prisoner in his life?

At last the desk sergeant handed him the receiver, still warm from his hand. Thoughts of interviews fell away as

Primrose steadied himself to lift the earpiece. Just before he did, the telephone rang shrill; he jumped and flinched out of the way as the sergeant reached for it again. After a few seconds the man snapped his fingers at Primrose and handed back the phone.

'Clara?'

The voice was distant and crackling. 'No, this is Dr Windermere, Medical Officer at Colney Hatch Asylum.'

Primrose felt a wave of embarrassment and waited for the man to go on.

'We have a patient in our care whom I believe you visited last night.'

'I did.' He braced himself, he wasn't quite sure why.

'You are in charge of the investigation into the death of a suffragette and any connected . . .' a small pause, 'incidents?'

'Yes.'

'This man claims he knows something. I don't know whether he's off his chump or on the straight but he's been making quite a racket about some bomb plot or other and the Medical Officer in charge of him seems to think I should pass it on. There's a name keeps cropping up. Annie Evans.' He let it dangle.

Primrose was already beckoning one of the constables from the reception desk over with his fingers. 'Give him whatever he wants. Put him up at the Savoy and give him caviar if necessary. And keep him off those damned drugs. I'll be over in a car as soon as I can.' He shoved the receiver back in place and snapped his fingers at the approaching constable.

'I need a motor car and I need someone who can drive it. Straight away.'

'Right, sir, where's it headed?'

'Colney Hatch. On the double.'

'No, you don't.' The voice came momentarily before the hand, clutching Primrose from behind, round his collarbone, the way he himself used to collar unruly calves if they tried to shy. He didn't need to see or smell his superior to know it was him.

'Freddie, interviews! Wilson was lucky to catch me before I left.'

'Those girls will have to wait. There's a . . .'

'Oh no no, Inspector, I'm not leaving this for you to mulch up later. I heard about your shenanigans with old Mother Pankhurst. Now those two girls are hot out of the wagon. You're coming with me.'

'But Colney Hatch. I just had a telephone call about that man there, the . . .'

'He can wait. Freddie, I know you're third rank up the ladder but there's a few things I've not been happy with on this case. I don't care how things were in your last squad. You work for me now.'

'But . . .'

'No arguments.' Stuttlegate flexed his shoulders, curled his finger and beckoned Primrose. 'It's time for you to watch and learn how a proper interview is done.'

Thirty-Six

Frankie stared at the porridge that had been placed in front of her. Porridge was too grand a word; it was more like sloppy gruel. Her cell-mate, an old woman who reeked of wine and eggs, saw she was not going to eat it and pointed.

'Can I have that?' she crackled.

Frankie pushed it towards her. The woman, who had been singing ballads about London cats since she arrived, slurped at the filthy brown liquor until she began to choke and splutter.

Frankie banged the back of her head gently against the wall of the cell and tried not to breathe in too deeply. The air was rancid with mushroom spores. Her arms were bruised where the constable had frog-marched her and Milly into the van and stowed them each in a compartment, an upright coffin, caged with wire on all sides. They had rattled like cargo over the cobbles towards Bow Street. It was the most miserable and undignified way to travel and she thought with a sting of shame about the women who had made their journey to Holloway in the back of those vans.

The police hadn't cared a jot about their protestations, the pieces of paper they brandished with the bomb diagram or the floor plans. Both peelers had a look in their eye, casual but determined, practical and practised. They had seen it all before. Strange vagrants pillaging a locked shop's contents, high as two kites on mescal or Limehouse opium, squawking about the end of the world or the end of something-or-other. Frankie was exhausted from the pleading and the protests; her mouth was too tired to force any more words out, her brain too tired to form them.

Still a ball of dread bounced around inside her.

She had questions. How did the bombers plan on getting into Parliament? Since the Fenian Brotherhood had set off dynamite in the Crypt, there were legions of guards at every entrance. The suffragettes had made it in a few times, once in a tradesman's van armed with paint and pamphlets; another time, during the census, inside Big Ben. But on both occasions they had broken in before nightfall, either during regular traffic or as tourists, and hidden in the vaults and crannies, or taken their chances and used brazenness as disguise. A horrible thought struck her. What if the Hourglass Factory women were in there already? What if that was where Ebony was now?

And then another image floated into view. A woman's face made featureless in straw and paper, with stuffing ill-fitted to her body, broom-handle legs and a witch's hat, feet smouldering on a bonfire while children squealed and hot wine was passed round.

> *The fifth of November, since I can remember,*
> *Was Guy Faux, Poke him in the eye,*
> *Shove him up the chimney-pot, and there let him die.*

They would burn their effigies, just like Guy Fawkes, for centuries to come. Any of them, women who were part of it, women who weren't. Emmeline Pankhurst, Christabel. No matter that the WSPU had nothing to do with it. They would blame all women's organisations and they would burn them like they were witches dredged up from a dark past that had already killed thousands and haunted millions. Frankie had listened enough to her convent school education to know what had happened to Catholics when Guy Fawkes tried to blow up Westminster Palace. A persecuted group already, made into pariahs ripe for execution and exile.

> *A stick and a stake, for King George's sake,*
> *If you don't give me one, I'll take two,*
> *The better for me, and the worse for you,*

Frankie shivered. Her cell-mate noticed and took the shawl from her shoulders. 'Would you like to huddle for warmth?'

'I'm fine, thank you.' She squeezed her arms in close to her body and jammed her hands in her pockets, and then she felt a prick on the corners of her fingertips and pulled out the calling card that Liam had found in Ebony's dressing room.

What had Ebony thought she was doing in the first place, leaving the suffragettes for that group? Had she not realised they were planning destruction on a mass scale? Did it not occur to her that rather than furthering the cause, an act that devastating would soon solder the idea that women were every bit as dangerous and unstable as Asquith wanted to make out? Worse still, they were working women, seam-stresses. How could she not have realised the long-term danger of what she was involved in? Then the truth caught up with Frankie: *she did. Just a little too late.*

But it still didn't make sense. If Ebony had raised her doubts to the Hourglass Factory, surely it would have given them the chance to back out. Take better action, reconsider the implications of what they had planned. If the goal was to show the government that they were serious about obtaining votes for women, they would want to do it right. It was almost as if—

Frankie stopped herself and wriggled up straighter. The thought threaded through her mind and wound ahead of itself. She pulled it back and tried to get a firm grip of where she was going.

The picture Ebony Diamond had left. She had wanted to speak in code, to hide the meaning. She had meant it as a cry for help. The Queen of Swords, upside down. A woman who wasn't who she said she was. A woman grown bitter by sorrow. A bigot, a prude. Artifice. They had assumed it meant

Annie Evans, mistaken for Ebony Diamond by her murderer and the police.

The thoughts came fast and tangled now.

A woman who wasn't who she said she was? But Annie had never professed to be anyone else. She had only dressed in Ebony's finery to impress her lover, and had been mistaken by others.

Frankie pulled out her notebook and looked at the fountain pen notes she had taken at the Barclay-Evanses. She came back once again to the story of Constance Lytton. A Lady who disguised herself as a seamstress to expose the prison authorities for abusing poorer women. What was it Milly had said? She was a force of good for the suffragettes, a crusader showing the duplicity of the government. But what if her goodwill, her noble idea could have been copied? Taken by someone else and used for darker gains? What was it Twinkle had said about people without open minds being dangerous?

Someone was not who they said they were.

Someone who knew that if they could harness a group of desperate, raging women to perform an act of reckless violence, they could have groups like them shut down and suppressed forever. Preserve the status quo, play into the enemies' hands.

Someone who knew the power of stunts that backfire.

Someone who didn't stand for women's rights at all but who hated political progress, freedom, and the way the world was emerging from a dark historical hierarchy to a terrifying free-for-all meritocracy.

Someone who would hate the way a showgirl could square up to a politician, a woman from Tottenham write in the newspapers, or a Lady find herself living off scraps in Baron's Court as she struggled to make her own independent living.

A reactionary in the guise of a seamstress.

It came quick and fast now. The brooch, the spoon, the old lady with her face bundled up; in the Hourglass Factory, at the morgue, outside Annie Evans's. Milly's face on the playing cards; the woman with phossy jaw. Frankie knew she had seen those eyes before. She scrambled to her feet, kicking over the bowl of unfinished porridge, spilling a slippery mess over the floor of the cell. She grabbed the bars of the viewing hatch at the top of the cell door and rattled the aching weight of the metal as hard as she could, crying 'Help!' She needed to get to Milly.

Primrose stood awkwardly in the corner of the charge room, trying to keep his fingers static, not sure whether his blood was still up from the ticking-off or his anxiety over Clara. Stuttlegate meanwhile was busying his hands like the clock had stopped and they hadn't all just been told minutes ago about a bomb threat. He ruffled his papers, sorted his copy reports from photographs, lined his pencils up tight on the desk as if he was preparing a magic trick. Every so often he checked to see that Primrose was watching him. He paid scant attention to the prisoner, who was seated on the other side of the table, except to nod at her and say to Primrose, 'Get the niceties out of the way, will you?'

Primrose thought the prisoner a very curious wispy little woman – gothic pale but oddly fierce – although right now her beauty was interrupted by a small smear of beef tea to the side of her lip, which she kept trying to lick away. He pulled out his notebook. 'Can you confirm your name for the record please?'

'Millicent . . . Milly Barton.'

'What is that, Miss or Mrs?'

She eyed him coldly. 'The Honourable Ms.'

Primrose felt a twinge of something – annoyance, embarrassment – but he wrote it down and stood back against the wall.

Stuttlegate had by now finished meddling, and was greasing up his hands, rubbing them first in his hair, then palms together. Primrose watched him as he paced the room, scratched his ginger whiskers with the flat of his hand, then slammed it onto the table. 'How long have you been supplying weapons to the suffragettes?'

Caught off guard, Primrose swallowed a yelp.

'Excuse me . . .' Milly Barton frowned.

'How long have you been their go-to girl for guns?'

'I don't know what you're talking about.'

'Horse-whips, dog whips, pistols.' He bent over the table turning over a few of his evidence reports. 'If you don't tell the truth . . .'

'You'll do what?'

Stuttlegate stopped turning the papers. 'How many other headquarters are there then, miss, that we don't know about?'

'If you'll listen, sir,' she said, then when she had his

attention added, 'And please don't call me "miss".' She stared at Stuttlegate. 'We had a tip-off. My friend is a reporter for the *London Evening Gazette*.'

'That pappy rag,' Stuttlegate snarled.

'We were investigating the tip-off.'

'The *London Evening Gazette* investigate tip-offs with guns?' As he passed by on one of his pacing rounds, Primrose caught the scent of eel pie on his collar.

'That gun is registered under my name. At least it was.'

The Chief's pig eyes held her for a second. He took a step back and sniffed. Finally he turned to his puzzle of manila files on the table. As he shifted the pile of photographs, the markings on the backs became visible, the Special Branch ordering stamp. The Honourable Ms Barton waited patiently. Primrose felt too ashamed to look at her. He wondered what she must be thinking; perhaps that being made a Chief Inspector was a game of chance, as arbitrary as choosing nude girls for the *tableaux vivants* at a supper room. He dared not look at his watch.

'Are you going to let me see them?' She pointed at the pictures.

'This tip-off.'

'Yes?'

The Chief said nothing but continued to stare at her.

'Yes? . . .' Still he said nothing. Milly looked up at Primrose. 'Oh, for goodness' sake,' she said. 'It came from the family of a girl called Annie Evans. I think you know who she is.'

The Chief pounced like she had delivered him a peck of

treasure. 'She was a suffragette! One of yours. And that friend of yours, Ebony Diamond.' Now Stuttlegate looked at Primrose, his eyes gleaming.

'They left the suffragettes.'

'But a leopard never changes its stripes.'

Milly sighed. 'Spots.'

'Don't take that tone with me. I've locked up men with higher titles than you before. I had a duke in here once.'

'There are bombs in that workshop, I told you that, and all you've done is insult me and talk about suffragettes.'

Primrose stepped forward, then lost his nerve and retreated. He thought he could feel his watch in his chest pocket ticking through his shirt, and wondered how much longer this would take. Stuttlegate stared the girl down, making a peculiar little humming sound between clenched lips. He began flipping over the scattered photographs at random. 'You want to talk about suffragettes? Fine.'

'No, I don't want to talk about suffragettes. I want you to . . .'

'Chief, should we . . . ?'

'Let me take care of this.' Stuttlegate turned his dog-taming stare on Primrose, then went back to flipping.

'This one. Know her?' He flipped more and more until it became a parody of a manic parlour game. A prison mug shot of a woman's profile came up and he pointed. Wild black hair covered her ears above a ragged coat.

'Why would I know her, Chief Inspector, and what has it to do with anything?'

'Not her. How about this one then?'

'Are you doing anything about the bombs?'

'Not her? Fine, this one then.'

He flipped over another image. This one was a surveillance shot of a prison yard. The image had been taken with a long lens; the woman had her head turned slightly but even so it was possible to recognise the distinctive shape of her waist and her tar-black hair. She wore stays even under her Holloway uniform.

Milly looked up at Stuttlegate.

'Well?'

'That's Ebony Diamond.'

'That's more like it.'

'You know I know Ebony, you just said we were friends.'

'Suffragette friends?'

'Working friends.'

He pulled his nose back into a little sneering snout. 'Why would I believe that an Honourable Ms –' he buzzed the word with his teeth clenched '– would be working with a performing tart like that?'

'Because I'm a performing tart too,' she spat. 'Next.'

He pushed another photograph under her nose. 'What about this one?'

'No, never seen her.'

'This one.'

'No.'

'How about this, recognise her?' Another surveillance shot from the prison yard.

'That's Annie Evans.'

'I see we're developing a pattern here.'

Milly Barton looked contemptuously at the Chief from beneath hooded black-lined eyelids. When she looked back down he had placed another photograph under her nose. Primrose spotted the recognition in her eyes even before Stuttlegate spoke. 'Another suffragette friend?'

'No, I know her from . . .' she cut herself off.

'Where?'

'Lincoln's Inn House.'

It was as if a gavel had come down in a music hall. He leaned back, cocked his head and bellowed. 'Oh, really, Lincoln's Inn House, remind me, I can't quite remember what that is; it's the headquarters of some organisation. My memory, my wife says, is terrible.' He slapped himself about the head. 'You know I put the butter in the game pantry the other day? No wait, I don't have a game pantry, there're for honourable ladies like you, aren't they? Lincoln's Inn House. That's . . .'

'Oh for goodness' sake, look at yourself!'

'All right, Chief, perhaps we can just . . .' Primrose stepped forward but Stuttlegate was in full swing.

'Headquarters of the suffragettes!' He slammed the table; the smack made the woman jump. 'No, you look at yourself. You're lying to protect that coven of witches. Right. Next.'

He flipped over a photograph. Milly's hand went to her mouth.

He watched her for a moment then said quietly, 'We are

particularly interested to trace this woman. However we have hit a dead end. She gave her occupation as seamstress on the Holloway register, and we have reason to believe she also gave us a false name. It's not on last year's census.' He pointed gently at the spectacles on the woman's nose. 'These might be false as well, and I know it's hard to see her face through the bandages, so think carefully. At Lincoln's Inn they say they have no record of her, no record of any woman with phossy jaw. They're not your sisters, Lady Millicent. If you tell me lies . . .'

She shook her head.

'You don't know her. How about this one?' He pushed a picture under her nose and this time there was no mistaking it. She was linking arms in a prison yard with Annie Evans and Ebony Diamond. Ebony's waist formed the centrepiece of the picture. She and Annie were laughing into one another while the third woman looked coldly at the camera. Her hair this time was blown back by the wind, and although she still wore the large horn-rimmed spectacles, her eyes cut through the glass as clear and chill as if she had the second sight and could look straight through the photograph into the eyes of the beholder. Across her mouth, a rag was drawn, almost obscuring her whole face except for the terrible eyes. 'She's an ugly piece of work. Must have been a match girl back in the day. One of the few phossy-jaw survivors. Our photographer says she nearly broke the lens, but that's why they do it, don't they? No man's going to touch that. And they know it. It turns their insides cancerous. Makes them lash out, makes them bitter, because when it comes down to it, that's what this is about, this voting nonsense. Jealousy, bitterness that the men have what you want, and because you can't have what you want, because you're a silly little woman, a silly woman with silly smears of greasepaint on your face and lips and the brain of a rabbit and—'

'Enough! Chief Inspector, enough!'

Primrose felt the room detach very quickly from his consciousness. His hands flashed with a mind of their own as they lifted, and it took a great effort, a great effort in concentration to bring them back to his sides. His face tingled, and he thought that both people in the room must now be staring at him; Stuttlegate with hatred, and the woman with hatred too for wading in like a coward, too late, and implying he could somehow protect her from this farmyard beast. Stuttlegate looked to him, in that moment, like a creature he had seen painted on the inside of his mother's Bible, a creature from a bestiary.

But Milly wasn't staring at him at all.

She was looking at the photograph. Threads of blood had begun to shoot through her eyes. She clutched her head at the ears and looked as if she might be sick on the table.

'She went away earlier in the year,' she said. 'She said she was going to Biarritz to rest. Very fine lie, but why? Why?' It was Stuttlegate who caught her arm as she scraped back the chair from the table.

'Don't you dare close ranks on me. I swear I'll arrest the lot of you. You suffragettes . . .'

Primrose made to move the table out of the woman's way, to stop her from hitting her head as she sank towards it. 'Inspector Primrose,' Stuttlegate intercepted him with a flat hand. 'I think you've done enough here. Don't you think it's about time you buggered off to Colney Hatch?'

The Honourable Ms Millicent Barton was clutching the edge of the table. 'That is no suffragette,' she said coldly, halfway to the ground. 'That is my mother.'

Thirty-Seven

'Somebody shut that bitch up! Can't hear my own breath.'

The prisoners in the other cells were starting to turn on Frankie, but she wouldn't let up. Twice a guard had come down. Once he had slapped the hatch shut on her fingers. She banged again on the door. 'Let me out! I know who it is. They're going to blow up the Houses of Parliament.'

'And let me guess, you're Mary Queen of Scots.'

She lashed the wall with her arms. The old woman in the corner was curled into a foetal position holding her head. Frankie slid back down the cold wall until her bottom came to rest on the floor, and listened to the sounds of the Bow Street cells filling her head until she was bunged up. The scrapings of bowls, the shuffling of feet. Three different songs from different cells and a whistler from a fourth. For a second she saw herself in Stark's office, pictured herself telling him no thank you, she'd have a write-up of the Wimbledon quoits on his desk by noon the next day. If she had never clapped eyes on Ebony Diamond she wouldn't be sitting in a Bow Street cell howling like the child who wanted the moon.

The cell flap snapped open and she felt a cold jolt of shock.

'Frankie George?'

'Yes, sir.' Her shoes slipped as she stood up, traces of wet gruel still forming a dangerous layer on the stone.

'Someone's asking for you.'

'Hold on,' came a cry from down the hall. ''Ow do you know I'm not Frankie George?'

Frankie waited, feeling her heart speed up, as the constable fumbled and squeaked and scraped until the lock opened. A menacing dissent had started in the cells and she heard spittle hit the ground behind her as she followed the constable down the corridor. 'That's right, send 'er to the funny farm.'

'Don't bring her back, officer. She's got a tongue like cow-hide. Needs a good spanking.'

Brandied steam curled up from the cup in Milly's hands as she lifted her head. Her eyes took a second to focus and for a moment Frankie, standing in the doorway, thought she might be one of those people who become lost forever, for whom something just disconnects in their head like a jigsaw piece fallen out of place and down the back of the table never to be found again. Then all of a sudden her pale eyes were lucid.

'Nerves steadier?' Frankie nodded at the cup. It smelled metallic: black tea and brandy.

Milly looked patiently towards the officer at the door as he cast his eyes between her and Frankie. 'Five minutes,' he murmured and retreated back into the corridor, locking the door behind him. When the clink of his keys had faded, Milly dropped her voice.

'We have to break out of here.'

Frankie crossed to the hard little bed and sat down next to her, looking at Milly's bone-white wrists holding the hot cup. She thought for a second she might touch her, but a heaviness kept her own hands in her lap.

'The police are looking after it now. You're in shock, you're not in a state to—'

'I'm not the one who was in a state, from what I heard. Could have heard you in Covent Garden, so they said. Sailors with cleaner tongues.' She stiffened and took another little sip of the spiked tea. 'How did you know?'

'That card. Queen of Swords reversed. What you said before, about malice and bigotry. Deceit. Annie wasn't deceiving anyone. So why would Ebony have meant her? Then there was that brooch, your family brooch. But most of all,' she breathed out and looked at the cup's pool instead of Milly's face, 'it was those bombs.' Milly looked down at the cup too, paying attention to the ribbons of steam that rose and vanished. 'No one would be stupid enough to think that would do their cause any good. What would violence like that bring? People declare war on you. They fight against you. And then I knew we weren't looking for someone who wanted change, but someone who wanted to preserve things the way they are. Someone who wants the authorities to turn on their supposed cause. Someone who believes that even theatre is a vice that opens people's minds too far.'

'Silly Ebony,' Milly said quietly. 'Why didn't she just say?'

'Would you have believed her? She might not even have known who Lady Thorne was. She just had that brooch to go on.'

Milly looked at her lap for a long time, rubbing her fingers over the silk threads of her gown. 'So you have your scoop,' she said after a while. 'All neatly bundled.'

'I'd say the only thing that matters is that they're stopped.'

Milly shook with a bitter laugh. 'Well, that wouldn't be such a good story, would it?' She raised her hand to her face and pinched the skin above her brows. Then she turned and looked Frankie in the eye and Frankie was struck the same way she was the first time she saw her, by the absolute clarity of her gaze. Like blue quartz. She put the cup down on the hard ground and began re-fixing the pins in her hair. 'When I was a little girl, she told me I must grow up to marry the king. Or a prince, at least. I think a duke was the worst-case scenario. That was what she pinned her hopes on, her only hope because I had no brothers or sisters. She took a dislike to my father, and that was that.'

Milly took a high gulp of air and Frankie's hand went to steady her, to make its way round her back or onto her leg. Milly saw the movement from the corner of her eye and flinched away, then looked up at the tiny window cut into the wall of the cell.

'I dreamed of the boys that came to the house. Not the

greasy little fops her friends would bring round who never knew how to play properly. How to make nests in the wood, or carve a spoon out of a branch, and smelled of wood or car oil or earth. I would like to say I fell in love but there were too many of them. A valet, a gardener's boy, a delivery boy. She only caught me once and only because the silly woman wanted to pick her own raspberries. Can you imagine! Lady Thorne lifting a finger! I was at the very bottom of the garden, completely out of sight. And I had my hand . . .' She shook her head and looked down through the tangled lace of her long eyelashes at her skirt. 'I'm so ashamed, Frankie. I wasn't then but I am now.'

Frankie felt her lips clamp up. She longed to say something but the words wouldn't make the short journey between her brain and her mouth. After a silence she managed, 'There's nothing to be ashamed of. Boys get away with those things, why shouldn't we?'

'Giving birth to a hussy, with an appetite, who runs away to Cairo?' The poison on Milly's voice took her by surprise. 'You don't know what she is capable of. Nobody does, except those seamstress girls she has lied to.'

'So what are we going to do?'

Milly put her cup down on the stone floor and reaching out, smothered the palms of Frankie's hands with her own, still warm from the cup. 'You're going to do what you set out to.'

'But . . .'

'If my mother can find a way to dupe vulnerable women into dynamiting parliament, we can find a way out of here.'

'But we don't have to be there. I know enough now to write about it. The police can take over. You don't have to be there.'

'I do.' Her blue eyes had softened now; the resolve in them was perfect, alarmingly calm. 'I'm the only one who can bargain with my mother in the dark.'

The high window in the wall of the cell hung open like a question mark, moving back and forth in the slow breeze. There was no way either of them were going to fit through. Even if Milly's slim hips had managed to wedge through, there were bars on the other side, and there was no chance Frankie would even make it that far.

Milly had tried with her hairgrips in the keyhole but it was a more sophisticated bar system than household locks and she couldn't even get the wedge placed well enough to click it. Frankie was pacing the square cell, aware that their time was fast draining from them.

'What about when the guard comes back? I could punch him – he won't expect that.'

Milly raised a sluggish eyebrow at Frankie. 'They'll raise the alarm within seconds. Besides, did you see the size of him?'

'Faint? They'll have to take you to hospital.'

'With my hand cuffed to a stretcher. And what about you? They won't fall for that one twice.'

Frankie chewed her lip. Her stomach was beginning to grumble and she half wished she hadn't given away her gruel. Milly pressed her hands back through her knotted hair.

'Just tell them the truth,' Frankie said. 'Tell them we need out so we can help them.'

'They'll let a reporter come along for the fun of it? A female one? That horror of a man who interviewed me wouldn't even trust a woman to button his collar.' She wrinkled her mouth.

Frankie sat back down on the bed, pulling up her trousers from the ankles. Her bottom had no sooner sunk into the coarse grain of the mattress than they heard the rattle of the key in the lock. They looked at each other. Frankie saw in Milly's face what she felt in her own chest: it was over. Five minutes were up. They had failed.

The door juddered across the hard stone floor, catching the uneven texture with a horrible scrape. Frankie breathed in and sighed. She looked up, and she squinted.

The silhouette in the doorway was much larger than the man who had shown her in, with shadows of lace spouting in stiff arcs from the neck and wrists. A raised hand dangled a set of prison keys insouciantly. Frankie's eyes hadn't yet adjusted to the light coming in from the corridor when the familiar voice emerged.

'Tut. Tut. Tut.' The enormous hatted head shook slowly. 'The shame. Oh, Puss, the shame. Dragging a respectable woman down to the Bow Street clink to fish you out. I can barely look at you. And yet to my credit, benevolence has always been a part of my soul that will not shake, no matter how hard it is pushed.' On the last word, the two steel tips of her eyes focused on Frankie.

'Twinkle!' Milly cried.

'Well,' Twinkle replied drily, 'are you both enjoying the thrill of underbelly life so much you're just going to just sit there like the knaves who stole the jam tarts? Or are you going to say thank you and come with me?'

'How did you . . . ?' Frankie began.

Twinkle held up a palm that crunched with thick metal jewellery. 'Hush, Puss. Questions later. Suffice to say that a certain Police Commissioner is an old acquaintance of mine who may – or may not, as the official line is – have needed a little companionship in his youth.' She put the hand with the dangling keys to her lips. 'Now just shut up and follow me, it's embarrassing enough being seen with you in public anyway, never mind down here.'

Frankie knew better than to answer back and for once was grateful to do as she was told.

They kept their heads bowed as they moved, casually effi-cient, through the corridors of the police station. Twinkle winked at the police sergeant holding the main gate to the cells and fuddled a crumpled pound note into his breast pocket, patting it for good measure as he swung open the door. The corridors sprawled out like channels in a labyrinth, each one coloured pale green by a fine coat of shiny new paint that had left its smell lingering in the air.

'Now,' said Twinkle, as they ascended a set of stairs, 'that Sergeant has given us three minutes before he's going to ring the cell bell. So you'd all better run like the three little blind mice as soon as we get out of here.'

'What do you mean three?' Frankie said. 'Who's the third?'

Twinkle held a finger to her lips. They passed interview rooms and offices with closed doors, and several times courted sly looks from uniformed constables. Frankie found herself pondering once more upon the dark web of Twinkle's client list. As they pushed open a set of double doors into reception she saw a young boy's back, loitering over by the reception fireplace, picking at a stain on his jacket. He looked up as they entered and tipped his hat with a sour wink at Frankie. 'You're very welcome.'

'Liam! You went and fetched her?' Frankie asked.

Twinkle pinched her in the back. 'Don't speak to him. They might think we're associated.' It was too late. The duty sergeant, who had been watching Liam like a buzzard from behind his desk, now hopped out to greet them. 'This young man with you, madam?'

'Oh, bravo Puss,' Twinkle hissed. 'Yes, officer,' she smiled. 'Indeedio.'

The man ran his eyes across the winking gemstones slung about Twinkle's throat, then looked suspiciously down at Liam's threadbare cap.

Twinkle hesitated. 'I've adopted an urchin. You see, benevolence has always been a part of my—'

He interrupted. 'What about those two?'

'Oh, bailing out my wayward . . . um . . . daughters. Again. Well, girls will be what they are, Sergeant. Anyway, must dash. Keep up the sterling work.' She grabbed Liam's wrist like he was a fur that had fallen off her shoulder and made for the front double doors.

As Milly reached to open them, they swung back and she almost collided with the wiry, large-eared detective who had booked them in when they first arrived. Sergeant Wilson stumbled in from the cold, coming to a halt, an icy layer of air on his coat. Somewhere behind them, down in the cells, a bell had begun ringing. Wilson looked at Frankie with a creased brow, as if he knew he had seen her somewhere before, perhaps behind a bread cart or serving coffee from a stall earlier that day.

Learning quickly from Twinkle's exchange with the duty officer, Frankie fixed a jolly smile on her face as she said, 'Afternoon, sir. Ooh, there's a chill out there, that's for certain. Remember, remember the fifth of November. Glad we could be of use and thank you for releasing us back to our mother so quickly. Come on Milly, Liam, there's a bonfire up Hampstead Heath. Be warm as toast, I'll bet you.'

They held their heads high as bridled horses as they stepped out into the pebble grey fog, leaving Sergeant Wilson agog at the strangest family he had ever seen.

Then they ran.

Wilson, who was still puzzled as to why the two prisoners had been set free, and who that woman and boy with them were, couldn't be certain if it was the cell bell he was hearing over the noise of the reception. He was startled out of his thoughts by Stuttlegate who appeared, twitching his neck and rubbing his hands like a limbering boxer.

'What did you find at the corset shop?'

Wilson tried to peer past him. 'Primrose about?'

'Never mind Freddie, he's off chasing a madman. What did you find?'

Wilson pursed his lips and shrugged wearily. 'Either they were lying or the place was frisked before we got near it. Not a sausage. Definitely no gunpowder. Plenty of chopped up playing cards, and a Gamages student chemistry set. Very strange.'

Stuttlegate growled and slapped a hand up to his chin. Those whiskers, thought Wilson, must itch him something awful the way he always picked and worried at them.

'Right. Let's get to Lincoln's Inn.'

'But you did hear the girls? The ones you let go. Said it wasn't suffragettes, it was a separate cell.'

Stuttlegate worked the flesh of his lower lip with his teeth. 'Until Freddie comes back from his gallivanting I'm not taking any chances. You want to be the one who leaves that stone unturned? The one with all the lice wriggling about under it?'

'No, sir.'

'Well come on, get your togs together. Chop chop.' Stuttlegate was passing back towards the double doors when he stopped. 'What did you say about those girls being let go?'

'I passed them just now in reception, sir. Burlington Bertie and the flash one. They were with their mother.'

'Their mother?'

'That's what she said. A woman wearing rather a lot of jewellery, and a boy, a ginger boy of about fifteen.'

They stared at each other plain. And now Wilson heard it. It was the cell bell ringing. Slow and steady, like a death knell. Like someone's hand was weary from ringing it for so long.

'Oh Christ.' Stuttlegate suddenly looked like he might crush his fist into the doorway. His face crumpled, his fingers clenched. With some effort he gathered his wits and snapped his fingers at the two constables by the door. 'You two, on the double, after those two cats that just went out. Don't stand on it, go!' He roared into the air and ran in the direction of the cell bell.

Wilson waited for the chaos to pass before he crossed behind the desk to the telephone. The duty sergeant had his neck craned over a ledger; the rest of the reception had emptied.

He picked up the receiver and quietly requested a private number. The operator was new and she took two attempts to connect him. Then a voice came over the line.

Wilson cleared his throat. 'Mr Hawkins, please. Newsroom.'

He waited for a few seconds for another voice to crackle into the earpiece. 'Teddy? Yes I know, good to speak to you too. Listen Teddy, I think you'll want to be outside the Houses of Parliament tonight. Don't ask, just be there.'

Thirty-Eight

Frankie and Liam skidded to a halt inside Covent Garden Jubilee Market, dodging a donkey cart laden down with pears. The stall owner swiped at Liam's ear, but he ducked. The sun was already sinking and desperate flower girls were beginning to harass anyone within ten yards for cut-price damask roses and boxes of Pugsby's garden fireworks. Frankie thought she could smell bonfire smoke on the wet fog. In the far corner of the market, sellers were cracking empty crates over their knees and chucking them into a heap for firewood.

They looked back in the direction they had run from, waiting for Milly and Twinkle to catch up. After a few seconds Twinkle appeared round the corner, clutching the swinging mass of her jewellery in one hand and the froth of her underskirts in the other as she hurried along.

'She's gone into a soapmaker's with a telephone kiosk to place a call to Belgravia,' she puffed, coming to a halt.

Moments later Milly's silken shape appeared in the crowd, striding towards them, her cheeks a pallid mushroom colour.

'She wasn't there.'

'What about your father?' Frankie asked.

Milly shook her head. 'He goes to his club most afternoons.'

Frankie sat down on an empty apple barrel and bowed her head. Twinkle gazed round her with a frown at the quantity of aproned workers within touching distance of her, clearing up their pitches. She scratched underneath her hat. 'Would somebody care to illuminate me on what exactly you pair are up to? It's that missing trapeze girl, isn't it? You're obsessed. I told you she was a bad apple.'

Milly was about to open her mouth when Frankie interrupted. 'I think if all goes to plan, Twinkle, you might read about it in tomorrow's early edition.'

Twinkle puckered up her mouth. Frankie could see the tentacles of gossip-detection itching to reach out from her, doing battle with her desire to remain irritated at being called to their rescue.

At length she gave a little grunt. 'Very well. If you can manage not to go for any more jollies with the constables, I might be able to make my Harley Street doctor's appointment after all.' She extracted a watch from the valley of her bosom and looked at it. She gave a little nod of satisfaction and began looking around for cabs. 'Now whatever you do,' she raised a finger, 'I was never at the police station. Understand?'

'Harley Street,' Frankie said. 'You're not unwell are you, Twinkle?'

'No, no, the very opposite. I am in rude health, as they say. But the doctors on Harley Street give such excellent pelvic massages. Preventative for all sorts of ailments.'

Before Frankie could cotton on to her meaning she was air-kissing Milly goodbye and waggling her finger at Frankie, muttering warnings about journalists and criminal records, then tottering back into the crowd, waving manically at a motor cab driver who had stopped outside the flower market. 'Thank you,' Frankie yelled. Twinkle raised her arm without looking back. They watched her bundle herself into the rear of the car and instruct the driver as he rumbled off into the traffic.

Frankie swallowed and looked at Liam. 'So, Scarlet Pimpernel. How d'you think to go fetch her?'

Liam scowled. 'Oh that's a fine thank you.' He thinned his weedy eyes. 'You think I've cloth for brains, don't you? I'm not the one went and got myself arrested. Jojo's women are all the same. Can't look after yourselves.'

The heat rose quickly in Frankie. 'I'm not Jojo's woman. And where were you, anyway? Wouldn't have been arrested if you'd been where I told you to be.'

'I was outside watching when they dragged yous away. Listen, I couldn't give a donkey's if you two go getting yourselves banged up. I'm doing this . . .'

'Because Jojo's paying you, I know. You mentioned it. Nice to see that's the conscience of the Irish.'

Frankie saw his cherubic cheeks flash an angry red and she felt regretful that her tongue had lashed too quickly. A few market traders turned round, dangling their baskets, watching. She suddenly noticed Milly staring at the donkey cart full of conference pears they had passed by. She remembered the diagram, the pear shape of the bombs, and a sickly taste grew in her mouth. 'Are you all right?'

Milly nodded gently.

'Listen, I've got an idea. Think you can get us into Lincoln's Inn? It's just that I think if anyone knows how to break into the Houses, it might be the suffragettes. Heard on the grapevine that was something they were good at.'

Milly's drained face told Frankie she wasn't in the mood to laugh. She looked across to the flower market, watching the bonfire outside take further shape. Then she looked up Exeter Street.

'If we go via the Aldwych we'll be less likely to run into anyone from Bow Street.'

'I'd say we were the least of their worries at the moment,' Frankie offered.

'Aye but they don't think that way,' Liam said. 'That's what you have to be careful about with peelers.'

Milly raised her head slowly. 'So now we have two sets of lunatics to worry about catching us.'

As they set off, they were glad for once of the brewing gloom. Streetlamps were beginning to be lit by the lamplighters, creating little beacons to mark out the path. Once Frankie thought she heard a barrage of footsteps behind them as they turned a corner but the noise took another route and faded. What she certainly didn't hear were the quieter footsteps much closer behind, carefully measuring the distance between the electric streetlamps and sticking to the shadows, so that the owner of the two quick-moving feet, the owner of the tightly armoured black waist would never be seen.

Thirty-Nine

'Why can't we just let them go ahead with it?' one woman asked, crammed into the crowd of chairs round the long table.

'If they burn the building to a crisp it'll teach them a lesson.'

'And,' said a third woman, 'weren't us. Not on our watch. Nothing to do with us. There's two birds killed with one stone.' She raised her hands into a little fluttering dove diving towards the table. A few of the others laughed nervously.

Frankie and Milly waited for it to die down. There were almost fifty members of the WSPU wedged into the press room of Lincoln's Inn. Some of them had hissed and whispered when they saw Frankie, but they recognised Milly and the sickly pallor of her silenced any mutinous jeers. Liam had been made to wait outside again. Frankie had donated him the last of her cigarettes out of guilt.

There was an electric charge in the air; the women were tense and curious as to why Mrs Dale had pulled them all off their posts so late in the afternoon for an emergency meeting; tables were strewn with galley proofs for the latest edition of *The Suffragette*. Abandoned typewriters sat in orderly rows and Frankie thought with a prick of sadness about her Blickensderfer sitting in a pawn shop.

A small-boned woman with a twitching nose was speaking. 'We must be allowed to continue protesting. Stopping these girls sets a dangerous precedent.'

Frankie laid her palms flat on the table. 'They are not protesters, they're murderers. Whether they set the bombs off tonight or tomorrow, there will be people in there. People will perish.'

'Christabel once said,' the woman replied, 'that if we broke into the Houses and seized the mace we would be the Cromwells of the twentieth century.' There were a few taps on tables and 'hear hears'.

Then a throaty voice sounded at the back of the room. 'Ay, but blow up the Houses and you'll be the Guy Fawkes of the twentieth century.' The ladies all fell silent and bowed their heads or fidgeted with their jewellery. There was an uncomfortable sense of duplicity in the air. 'Do you want people to think we're as brutish as the police?' the throaty woman went on. 'That we care as little about people's lives as they do?'

A current of dissent and murmurs surged round the room.

'And you're quite certain they're going to do this?' Mrs Dale asked, turning to Milly.

Milly turned her head to look at her.

Mrs Dale nodded. 'All right. But what if they blow it up with you inside?'

Frankie wasn't quick enough to disguise the look that came across her face. It belied her, it said that they didn't quite know either. Voices rose. Mrs Dale watched the women settle. Eventually she said, 'And how exactly are we supposed to help you?'

'You have floor plans of the entrances and exits to Parliament, don't you?'

She raised a weak smile.

'If they're handy, can you get them out?'

'It's not as easy as you think. They've increased the guards on the gates. Commons' door is still the best but you have to pass through a central gate to get to it. The Fenians did for us when they set those bombs off. We only got inside once and only by making a Trojan horse of a furniture delivery van. You won't be doing that tonight.'

'How are the others going to get in? How was Ebony going to get in?' The question came from the back of the room.

Milly stiffened and Frankie opened her mouth to answer when she felt a pinch on her wrist. She caught Milly's eye. 'Because one of them,' said Milly, 'is the wife of a Lord.'

There were cries; a Scottish voice called 'God save us.' 'Is this what it's come to?' cried another.

Mrs Dale was raising her finger to beckon over a girl in a shabby grey dress. She had a young smooth-skinned face, though when she spoke her voice was much older than Frankie expected. 'There's a guard on the west door. Back entrance. He's on shift every night and they don't rotate them.'

'How do you know?'

'Because he's my brother.' She hesitated for a second then spoke firmly. 'I'll come with you.'

Mrs Dale had bent down to a cupboard next to the window and was rooting through a sheaf of papers when a shattering of fists on wood below made them all jump. She sprang up, startled for a moment, then rolled her eyes even before they heard the voices outside. 'Police! Open the door now.'

A collective groan rose. 'Not again.'

The girl who had volunteered to show them into Parliament prodded Frankie in the back with a finger and spoke quickly and urgently. 'Out the garden way. You'll be into the back green but I'm sure it's not the first time you've had to hop a fence or climb a tree.' She yanked Frankie with one arm and Milly with the other and led them down the stairs and through the kitchen to a back door. The shadows of two constables reared in the door's glass panel and they stopped dead.

'The cellar,' the girl said quickly. The sounds of gathering police were growing, drummings of noisy footsteps and the shifting of bodies. Someone was roaring out orders, dividing the men into packs. The girl took a kitchen knife from the draining board and prised open a hatch in the kitchen floor. A splintered ladder led down into darkness. The smell of coal and dirt rose in a gust. Frankie thought of rats.

'Go now.' The girl shoved her roughly in the back.

'What about you?'

Another tattoo of fists erupted down the hall.

'Don't worry about me. I ain't done nothing wrong. They got nothing to pin on me.'

Frankie started to say, 'But how will we—' but the girl had already shut the hatch on their heads.

Milly was coughing and Frankie reluctantly clamped a hand over her mouth to quiet her. Milly took the message and shook her head when she was done. 'Your fingers stink of porridge.'

Frankie's breathing relaxed. She found Milly's cold dry hand in the dark and raised their tangled fingers towards a dim patch of violet on the wall, a window leading out onto the twilit garden behind the house.

They shuffled towards the light, Frankie privately terrified of the strange dark objects that touched her legs, bracing herself for something that might topple and clatter or worse, something soft, furred and warm. Eventually she felt her palm make contact with brick and realised they were beneath the window. She tried not to think of the hairy winter spiders in the outdoor privy at home as she prised open the clasp, soft with cobwebs. It was shoulder height. Milly vaulted up first. Frankie heard a little grunt and the soft crunch of feet on gravel.

'It's fine,' she whispered. 'It's not high.'

With the window open onto the air they could hear noises from inside the house. Flesh hitting wood. Men's shouts and women's cries.

'Give us a pull.' Frankie thought for a moment her arms might come away from her like a marionette as she was yanked up. Scraping her feet against the brickwork she eventually managed to haul herself through the window and land just off kilter on the path. Pain shot through to her knees. She winced and bent to rub them but Milly's eyes were wide and beckoning so she swallowed the pain and scuffled along the pathway to an untidy vegetable patch backing onto the yard of the house next door.

They prised through fences and shimmied over two walls until they found themselves back on the corner of Kingsway. The sun had sunk; the air was thick and purple with a velvety damp to it, and painfully cold to breathe. Windows glowed in houses and shops along the road. They took a few minutes to gather their breath.

'Unexpected detour,' Frankie grumbled, bent double and finally able to rub her stinging knee.

The footsteps that came round the corner came sharp and sudden, before either of them saw movement through the fog. The long needles of a human shadow cast onto the street, mist obscuring the face, neck and shoulders of the figure. Instinctively Frankie moved to dodge out of the way, then she heard Liam's voice. 'I'd say that's not the direction you want to go in. You two and peelers, you're inseparable.'

She turned startled, then saw he wasn't alone. There was someone standing beside him, concealed in the mist. Their body was all but invisible. But the shadow on the ground was unmistakable.

'I'd say, in fact, it's time we banged our heads together.'

The pockets of fog cleared and Frankie blinked. She blinked three times. Standing next to him was Ebony Diamond.

Forty

Primrose had instructed the driver to make haste, but the traffic down Finchley Road was clogged with omnibuses and traders' wagons leaving their pitches early to prepare for the fireworks. When he hit Baker Street, the sludge of cars grew even heavier, four-wheelers trotting at a stately pace and lined up outside large houses where gentlemen dressed in smart wool frock coats and gloves emerged with women in enormous furs. Clara had asked if he had wanted to go to a bonfire on Clapham Common tonight but he had suspected all along he would be working, and she wouldn't go alone. He felt a stab of guilt that he had not yet telephoned her.

His head was reeling with the things William Reynolds had told him. The detailed plans of the Hourglass Factory, the secret meetings Annie had snuck off to, the careful cutting up of cards for gunpowder, the mysterious old woman she met in prison who claimed to be a seamstress but whom they had never actually seen sew, the sourness of Ebony Diamond after her plans were rejected by the suffragettes. Annie Evans had been loose-tongued and trusting with her lover, the man she believed would marry her one day. And the sad thing was that Reynolds had believed it too; he had believed in a world where men could divorce the women they had married too soon, too young, too influenced by parents, and join the woman they loved now, regardless of birth or class. Deep down, Primrose reflected, they both must have known it would never happen. When hopes were frustrated and had nowhere to go, violence crystallised.

Bow Street loomed ahead, and he ordered the car to stop so that he could run. He had telephoned Scotland Yard for back-up but Stuttlegate was nowhere to be found. Hoping he was still at Bow Street, Primrose hurried along past the rows of wagons and took the steps two at a time until he was in the warmth of the station.

It was eerily quiet inside. The desk sergeant was typing something behind the counter, punching the keys in staccato beats.

'Where is everyone?'

The typing stopped. Ribbon shunted back to its starting position and the sergeant stood up, pulling up his waistband. 'Don't you know? Out raiding Lincoln's Inn. The lot of them.'

'Again? But that's preposterous. It's not suffragettes we're after. Who ordered that?'

He didn't have to wait for the sergeant's response. Even as the word formed in the other man's mouth Primrose could feel it take shape in his own. 'Stuttlegate.'

Forty-One

She was there, in black and white it seemed, her dark body standing out against the fog. And yet Frankie couldn't quite fathom it. She felt as if she were looking at a ghost. All this time she had known Ebony was alive, but part of her hadn't really grasped the notion that she had ever been real in the first place. She couldn't quite believe that the body in front of her was flesh and blood; flesh and blood armoured in whalebone and black silk.

She was pulled in tight from hips to bosom, her neck sweeping upwards in a high collar protecting her china throat. Her hair, though flecked with straw and pungent with the scent of the outdoors, was piled neatly on top of her head, clasped by a tiny top hat. She looked straight-backed, jut-nosed, black-eyed, red-lipped. Ready for a fight.

When she finally spoke, her voice was rough. 'Evening, Miss George. I'm sorry I couldn't keep our appointment outside the Coliseum. I believe you've been looking for me. I've been staying at the circus with my father.'

'Told you,' Liam murmured. Ebony pierced him with a look.

Not for the first time that day, Frankie's tongue stopped fast in her mouth. The mist was beginning to permeate her clothes and make her cold and damp.

Milly looked at them each in turn, then rushed forward and embraced Ebony loosely by the neck. Ebony flinched but accepted the hug, though her fingers only made a tentative clutch on the small of Milly's back. 'We were worried about you.'

'I can look after myself,' she said quietly.

Ebony turned her eyes on Frankie and cleared her throat. 'I'll not say a word here.' She raised her hand and flicked open a tarnished ring on one finger of her glove revealing a tiny ticking watch, then nodded to a public house, where bronze light glowed behind a set of double saloon doors. 'Come on in quickly and I'll fill you in.'

Inside the pub, cabbies and tradesmen were drinking pints of ale out of greasy glasses; pink evening newspapers with scandalous headlines were spread all over the tables. The floor was patchy with clumps of sawdust. Ebony slid into a corner table while Liam ordered a round of porter for them all. Frankie threw her last few coins onto the table for the pot.

They waited for Liam to come back with the cups. Ebony slurped up half of hers in a couple of gulps. 'I'm sorry,' she wiped her mouth with a gloved hand, smearing only slightly the rouge on her lips.

Frankie watched her put her glass back down. 'When did you know who she was?'

Ebony's eyes flicked round the room. 'I was never sure about her from the start. I can say that now. She wasn't right. Even in Holloway, she was a strange one. Didn't hunger strike, didn't seem to know anyone.' She glanced at Milly. 'Don't take offence by what I say.'

Milly shrugged.

Frankie put her hand across the table. 'Start from the beginning. Holloway, was that where you met her?'

Ebony nodded. 'Of course I knew about the National Vigilance Association, I'd seen her handing out her devil pamphlets, but she wasn't playing herself in Holloway. She was in her fancy dress from the start.' Ebony gestured to her mouth, drawing a scarf about her lips and chin in the air. 'Why would I have recognised her with that phossy jaw get-up on her face? Damned insult. I knew women who'd worked for the match factories.' She sat back. 'We'd ended up in the same Black Maria van on the way to prison. She'd obviously had her eye on the suffragette window smash I was on that night, because as soon as we'd been arrested and took off, the van stopped, and in came this bent-backed drunk woman, bundled up in her face, filthy and stinking of sherry.'

Frankie nodded to Ebony to go on.

'She was in second division for stealing, so I heard. She approached me in the exercise yard one day. Why would I have known her? Filthy woman, she had cotton tufting out her mouth. I thought then it was for the disease but it must have been to disguise her voice.'

Milly spoke. 'We had a gardener once when I was little whose mother had been at the match factories. She came to visit.' Her eyes darted between the tabletop and Ebony.

'Well, anyway she did a good impression. She didn't miss a trick, though it looked like she didn't change that bandage cloth the whole time we were inside.'

'What did she say?' asked Frankie.

'She asked me if I was happy with the suffragettes, and whether I thought their violence was the right way to win votes. I said I didn't see how else we was going to do it seeing as what had happened when Mrs Pankhurst tried to be peaceful in the truce and that. She said, well in that case, don't you think the violence needs to be upped? This I remember; "Vitriol," she said, "and hammers are like stones in a lake, only so effective when poured and dropped. If you want to make that splash, if you want the waters to rise up, you have to throw them hard."'

'Oh words. Words she'd got from somewhere. She kept talking about the men's uprising and how the MPs were saying that the women hadn't done anything half so violent, seeing as how no one had died yet for the women's vote, and the men killed at least two when they burned Nottingham Castle. I was swept up, I was furious.' She paused to scrape the hair off her forehead. Her voice was tight and defensive. 'You have no idea how long it took to rig that Albert Hall stunt. The reccies we did, the ropes. And at any moment I could have fallen and broken my head. And for what? Nothing. Taken from the front pages by a ship that sank because it was badly built by men. I wanted to do something. The suffragettes, they had their limits, but I wanted to do *something big*. I said I knew a man could help us; some girls who'd want in. When we got out, me and Annie, we took her to the Hourglass Factory.'

'All right,' said Frankie, 'so you made your plans. You built the bombs. And then you found her brooch.'

'How do you know about that?'

'I saw you throw it at Mr Smythe.'

Ebony swallowed. 'It had dropped out from under her skirts. I wouldn't have been half so interested, would have thought it was one of her petty thefts, but I knew the pattern. She's got the same design,' she nodded towards Milly, 'on the clasp of the wicker picnic hamper she keeps her snake in. So I started to remember. Confrontations you'd had outside Jojo's some nights with that Vigilance Association woman. Oh, there was rumours going about for months that you were her daughter. But it all just started to fall into place with the brooch.'

'Mr Smythe had it on him when he died,' Frankie said tentatively. She didn't elaborate but Ebony caught her look.

'Ollie.' She rolled a nugget of foam round her beer cup. 'Smart boy. Must have kept it when I threw it at him.'

'Did he know?'

Ebony shook her head vigorously. 'He knew I wanted out

at the end. I got him into the mess. He offered up his shop so we could meet. Ollie was a gent that way. He never asked questions. He was good on privacy, was Ollie.' She sighed and her red mouth hung open. 'Even I didn't know what the full plan was, until the day I met you.'

'What *is* the full plan?'

Ebony sat still and silent.

Frankie leaned across the table and said more firmly, 'Miss Diamond, what is the full plan?'

Ebony swallowed again. She looked as if her collar was giving her some trouble. 'They're going to stitch the bombs inside the leather benches so they detonate when sat on. They don't just want to blow the houses. They want to blow the politicians.'

Frankie felt her stomach turn. She looked sidelong at Milly who was staring into her beer glass.

'As soon as I knew that, I said I wanted out. I never wanted to murder no one, just do some damage, raise our voice. She knows and I know that murder's too far, not only that but it'll turn folk against you. I think she knew that if I spoke out I'd take the women with me.' Ebony's eyes darted nervously to the clock above the bar. Quarter to five. The sun had sunk already, dimming the light outside to mauve. Parliament would be winding down soon, the politicians returning to their offices and the terrace where they took their drinks. The women would wait until they were all away home for the night. And then . . .

'But why didn't the other girls want out too? When they knew? She must have told them by now.'

'Those women? You don't know what they've been through. They'll do anything.'

'What do you mean? Were they suffragettes?'

Ebony shook her head hurriedly. 'Suffragettes? No, no, never. They didn't have time to be suffragettes. They worked all hours God gave, and then with children, some of them in the double figures, men that had buggered off. I'm not making excuses. There's plenty good folk rage, but some just hate . . . There's so much anger in that shop. You get the right people, given the wrong chance. They don't stop to think . . .'

'We know about the men. I mean what goes on at the Hourglass Factory after hours,' Frankie said quietly.

Ebony looked sharply at her, colouring slightly. 'You mean The Hourglass Club? The tightlacing? They're not involved, got nothing to do with them. The seamstresses just do that for the money. But anyway,' she bowed her head, 'that corset on Ollie was meant for me. It was me that had said he should try it on. And it wasn't the seamstress girls who poisoned it. She must have dabbled with it after I left that night.' Ebony was trying very deliberately not to look at Milly. 'Same as what happened to Annie was meant for me, I know it. Annie'd only said she wanted to borrow my jacket and hat cos she wanted to look nice for her gent.' Her voice dropped. 'Annie.' She put her forehead in her palms and rubbed. 'God couldn't have made a better girl than Annie.'

Ebony's lips twisted and her eyes grew grave. 'I did mean to meet you that night. I really did. But she was there, back-stage at the Coliseum, and I lost my bottle. Would you have stuck around after two of your closest friends were murdered, both dressed as you? Circus was the only safe place. No one going to touch you when you're sleeping next to a tiger's cage.'

'What about going to the police?' Frankie asked impatiently.

'And have them do to me the bonnie job they did on you pair? Policemen love to believe a dirty deviant woman with a far-fetched story, don't they?'

Milly shifted. 'The suffragettes told me you wanted to set tigers free from the zoo.'

'That would have been a stunt,' Ebony said quickly.

'People could have been killed.'

'They wouldn't have been.'

Milly opened her mouth to protest but thought better of it. The image of Ebony calmly wrangling a live tiger through the streets of London flashed on Frankie's mind.

Ebony drained her drink. 'She's dangerous, you know.'

'You don't say. She followed us.' Frankie told her about the stone through the Barclay-Evans's window.

Ebony pursed her lips. 'Sounds about right. She'll have guessed that sending you to Lincoln's Inn would keep you away from Smythe's for a while.' She sat up and smoothed her hands tightly down over her bodice. 'But your turn now, tell me what you know.'

Frankie looked at Liam, who was watching them from beneath the hood of his wool cap. 'What did you tell her?'

'Nothing.'

She pushed the beer cups to one side and pulled out her notebook where she had sketched from memory some of the pear-shaped diagrams from the *Evening Gazette*'s spread.

'That's them.' Ebony nodded queasily.

Frankie filled her in quickly on what they knew, Ebony occasionally stopping her to ask for more detail or clear up a question. When Frankie had finished, Ebony sat back against the grimy wall of the public house. Milly was leaning her chin on her hands. Liam dipped his fingers in his empty beer cup to scrape up the foam.

Frankie turned to Ebony. 'How much money have you got on you?'

'Some.'

She looked at Milly. 'You?'

Milly rattled her pockets; the sound of coins made a small chinking.

'There's a chemist's on High Holborn, down that way.' Frankie jerked her head then drew out her pocket-watch and looked at the time. It was creeping closer to five. 'Buy me two shillings worth of Muller's flashpowder, would you? Don't ask, just do it. Please.'

'What are you going to do?' Milly's voice wavered.

'I have to fetch something from Gray's Inn Road. But I'll meet you in Parliament Square in an hour.'

Liam eyed her with suspicion. 'I'm not letting yous out of my sight. I've already bailed you out once today.'

'Shut your mouth,' Ebony said softly. He twitched and sat up straighter. 'Where are you going, Miss George?'

Milly was also looking at her with thinned eyes. 'Yes, where are you going, Frankie?'

Frankie looked back at them, Milly's calm, pale and serious face, Ebony bristling under the surface of her powdered skin with a tension that threatened to erupt. 'Trust me this once,' she said. 'Milly, you stick with Liam, and don't let him talk you out of it. Miss Diamond –' she ran a grimy finger down her pocket-watch's face. Her hands, she realised, were filthy with the dirt of the day. '– Miss Diamond comes with me. We can pick up some rope on the way.'

Ebony looked doubtful. She hardened her black eyes at Frankie and clasped her gloved palms on the dusty tabletop. 'I'd rather know what you expect me to do before we leave this saloon.'

Frankie looked back down at her grandfather's watch. The years of scratches had faded into a haze on the surface of the glass. 'Trust me this once', that was what she had said to them. And her father had asked for her trust too when he gave her the watch. She clenched her hand round it until it pinched, then, looking through the window, measured the distance in her head between the corner of the street and the little Italian repair man on Gray's Inn Road. 'We're going to need a good vantage point.'

'For what, Frankie?' Milly sounded irate now.

'You think we can stop those women from setting the bombs?' Frankie asked.

Ebony turned her palms upwards. 'I don't know how.'

'Well, I don't either. But we can make sure they're caught before they go off, and we can make sure everyone knows exactly who set them. I'm going to get my camera back.'

Forty-Two

The sun had disappeared, the streets were smothered in pillows of mist. Carried on its cold wet fronds came the sweet smell of wood smoke and bitter smouldering junk. From the corner of Gray's Inn Road Frankie could hear the pop of fireworks going off in domestic gardens and children squealing nearby. Somehow the children's voices made her feel even sicker and more choked than the smoke. She had in her hand the camera she had carried so carefully on her back to Bond Street a few days ago, traded with the man in the repair shop for her grandfather's watch until she could stump up the money. The man had managed to straighten out the bent clasps and polish up the leather but it still bore the grazes of its adventure, scorchmarks and a burnt musky smell. The wind probed through Frankie's jacket as she peered into the dark of the street.

'Got you,' came a whisper from behind. Frankie's heart leapt.

'Don't jump, I'm sorry.'

She spun to see Ebony carrying a large red and gold carpet bag. In her slick black crepe dress she looked no different from a respectable woman about to take an evening journey, a governess on her way out. Her hat rested at an angle, her black eyes were alight; there was a flush on her face from the cold. Frankie breathed out.

'Got my camera,' she said patting it. 'Listen, if you don't want to help with this—' she began.

In response, Ebony started walking smartly down the street ahead of her. Frankie inhaled another gush of cold, smoked air and followed.

Traffic was backed up and from down each street came the impatient snorting of horses and catcalls from the cabbies stuck behind omnibuses and trams. Behind the smoke and fog the moon was a rheumy unblinking eye. Halfway down The Strand, Frankie turned to Ebony.

'How did you know about the cocaine?'

Ebony tilted her head. 'Cocaine?'

'That's why you ran away. From the theatre.'

Ebony sighed and switched the carpet bag into her other hand. 'I knew she was planning something. That backstage boy that always follows me around let slip there was a new dresser for the chorus girls. Someone with phossy jaw. She was stupid to think that people inside a theatre wouldn't notice that and talk.'

Frankie shuddered, thinking of her backstage tour with

Stoll's clerk and how close she may have come to brushing against Lady Thorne.

'I didn't have to know what it was she had planned. I checked all my own knots and did my own rigging, but I knew I wasn't coming out of that theatre through the front door. Not as myself anyway.'

'There must have been an easier way to escape.'

Ebony stopped and looked at her square, and Frankie caught the prickle of whatever it was she had felt at their first meeting. She could feel herself shrink back in her skin and wished she had kept her mouth shut. But Ebony simply said, 'I thought it was easy. I let the hatch before the act began. It was hanging open all the time I was in the air, but folk don't notice that, do they? That's the whole point about magic and diversions. I'd already shoved around some hay bales to land on. Closing the hatch quietly was the tricky bit but Old Fouc-up or whatever his name is has a pole to keep the tiger at bay so I used that. He was stupid enough to leave his costume lying around at the interval while he was leching over the chorus girls, so I'd already nicked it and put it waiting by the cage. And that tiger was a charm. Dopey old thing only had three teeth left anyway. I don't know what all the fuss was about. I can't stand the way they treat tigers in theatres. Give me a zoo or menagerie any day. A circus even. But a theatre? I wish it hadn't been caught.' She blinked a couple of times, shifted the bag to the other hand and upped their walking pace.

When they reached Parliament Square Frankie was

surprised to see a small bonfire smoking in the centre. She picked out Milly and Liam in the spiked shadows of Victoria Tower and hurried over.

Liam spotted her and took a few steps away from the pyre's licking flames. The heat was immense despite the fire's size. Some people were dancing and drinking beer from tin cups, others were still and quiet, trying to let the warmth melt their frozen flesh. The smoke had already started to make both Milly's and Liam's eyes red and raw.

'Did you get the flash powder?'

Liam reached into his pocket and held out a tiny glass bottle with a rubber bung and a matchbox of guncotton. In a thin paper packet was a bundle of brittle fuse papers.

'Good. Keep hold of them for now.'

She turned to address Ebony but Ebony had disappeared.

Frankie spun a circle, trying to pick her out on the grass among the revellers. Eventually she spotted her idling close to a railing, in the dark patch between two street lamps. She hurried over. 'Where did you . . . ?'

Ebony held her finger to her red mouth then pointed. It seemed at first as if she were pointing towards Milly and Liam who were making their way over to them. Then Frankie followed the line of her glove to the fire where three or four tramps were cavorting. 'I didn't think you were allowed fires on Parliament Square,' she said.

Frankie squinted closer. A noise had started up behind her in the distance, a heavy but familiar thumping sound. She turned to see Parliament Guards pounding across the frozen lawn in navy blue uniforms, their warm boots throwing up powder puffs of white air. Some of the revellers held off dancing and began to scatter.

'Scarper!' a cry rang out. The mob dispersed like cattle struck by lightning.

Frankie suddenly realised the one thing that was not being watched. 'Clever little witches.'

Ebony nodded grimly. 'Start a fire on Parliament Square. Get the guards to abandon the palace gates. Come on.'

Two guards were careering towards them; they dodged outstretched arms just before the men crashed into the railings. Ducking to the right, they ran parallel to the length of Westminster Abbey.

'Liam!' Frankie suddenly realised and turned.

'No time,' Ebony shot back over her shoulder.

'But he's got the flash powder. We won't be able to get a clear shot without it.'

She heard a thump behind her and peeped over her shoulder, trying at the same time to keep pace with Ebony who was surefooted in the mud. Milly had slipped and fallen and was sliding around on her knees in wet muck. She was trying to get purchase on her hands but it was too late. A guard reached for her waist and toppled her again, wriggling a pair of handcuffs from his waistband with his spare hand. 'Got ya!' Frankie heard him cry. 'You behave yourself and you've got nothing to worry about.'

The guards were going berserk, grabbing anyone they could lay their hands on, knocking them to the ground with truncheons, jamming them in headlocks and armlocks until they could be cuffed.

As they reached the corner of the square and ran into the traffic Frankie saw that Liam had managed to dodge them all and was barrelling towards the public entrance to Westminster Palace. She did a quick check around her and saw that there were guards stationed on every corner. So the police had taken them seriously. She wondered if anyone was watching the Peers' door. They stopped in the shadow of another lamppost and Frankie ducked to her haunches. Ebony joined her.

'How's he going to get in?' Ebony jerked her head towards Liam who, a hundred yards off, was hanging back beside the public gates to Westminster Palace, where the majority of the guards had run from. Frankie looked and saw him poke his head out of the shadows, scanning the street. Suddenly a white hot spark flared and a sharp cry rang out. Liam, his fox-tail hair flaming under his hat, threw a flash of guncotton and magnesium in the face of a guard. Frankie couldn't see clearly but suspected from the swaying of the guard's body and the shape around him that Liam's fingers were working his pockets for keys like a squirrel, while he was blinded. A second later the guard hit the ground; the fox tail was gone.

'That's how,' she murmured. Liam was in. 'Fat lot of good it does us, though.'

Frankie turned back to Ebony and found her staring into the distance towards the Thames. After a few seconds she pulled Frankie close. 'If we follow parallel to the river we'll come to the Peers' carriage court. There's an entrance there.'

'Yes but . . .'

'Will you grab the bag?' She pushed the rough carpet bag into Frankie's arms. Frankie took the camera off her neck and slipped it inside. They rose and began to hurry in the foggy direction of the river. They hadn't made it fifty yards when a black shadow swelled up ahead of them.

A guard stepped from the hollows of New Palace Yard straight into their path, his boots crunching on the icy ground. Frankie's breath froze.

'Stop.' He raised his palm.

Without warning Ebony suddenly swooned towards Frankie, throwing her full weight on Frankie's shoulder and chest. Startled, Frankie caught her just in time with a groan. The guard's hand flew out to grab Ebony's spare arm.

'I'm sorry, I don't feel well at all,' Ebony gasped. 'I'm . . . I'm . . .' She clutched her belly.

The officer took a moment to absorb her meaning, then ran his eyes up and down her corseted form and flashed Frankie a filthy look. 'You let your wife go about dressed like that in her state?'

Frankie felt temporarily affronted and defensive, the shock of Ebony's improvised plan, the sudden weight of five foot six of muscular acrobat bearing down on her, and the guard's admonishment stopping her tongue. Ebony seized the advantage. 'Oh, I'm fine really,' she said, making a pained show of the opposite. 'I just need a little water, a little warmth, ow, a telephone to call our chauffeur, you wouldn't have . . .' She looked past his shoulder to the gate where a wooden security hut glowed in the weak glare of a bullseye lantern. 'No, I don't suppose. It's just that we have to get back to Hampshire tonight, and I know our chauffeur is in the club. He's very easily reached, he's nearby on Whitehall, I could give you the number, I just don't know if I can . . .'

Frankie marvelled at the stream of sudden and convincing drivel trailing effortlessly from Ebony's mouth. Seeing the guard's hesitation, she dropped the timbre of her own voice. It came out not quite as low as she had hoped, more like an effeminate Harry Tripe than a man whose chauffeur visited clubs on Whitehall. 'Darling, don't let's trouble this man. You've taken turns before.'

The guard's head wavered, then turned towards his hut for a second. Then he said, 'Come on inside, there's an office. One of the sergeants will be happy to telephone on your behalf. What name should I . . . ?' He pulled Ebony's upper arm a little too forcefully away from Frankie and began leading them past the Westminster Palace entrance.

'Hawkins,' Frankie said quickly, noticing that cries and heavy footfall were coming from inside the courtyard, where Liam had stolen the guard's keys. 'Mr and Mrs Theodore Hawkins.'

The guard glanced over at his colleagues bustling round the gates. 'Very well.' With breathless efficiency he marched them out of New Palace Yard and along the length of the narrow gothic building. Ebony took the liberty of peeking over her shoulder at Frankie, who had been subtly manhandled to the rear of the party. They turned a corner signposting the Sergeant-at-Arms's residence, passing another security hut where a guard quickly tucked away a newspaper as they approached. They filed through a concealed unlocked door straight into the building.

'We've been having a bit of trouble tonight,' he apologised as they walked an echoing corridor. 'Some nonsense about women and bombs. I told them, there's no chance anyone's getting in here that doesn't belong, we've got as many guards as there are politicians. Still, we have to be on alert.' He paused as they approached a cubby office. From underneath the wooden door came a thin streak of gold light. He knocked twice and the door opened inwards smartly. Still loosely clasping Ebony's arm the guard poked his head inside and said, 'Here governor, I've got a woman in a – delicate condition, taken a funny turn. I don't suppose . . .' He didn't finish his non-supposition.

Ebony stuck her hand into the room, grabbed the man's waist and pulled on his keys so hard the fabric of his breeches ripped. His hands dashed to his belt.

'Bag,' Ebony blurted.

Frankie whipped it open. Ebony shouldered the man into the little cubby and slammed the door by its brass handle, leaning her full weight away from it, her muscles bulging through the silk of her dress. She slicked the key into the lock and turned it. 'Rope,' she barked.

Frankie up-ended the bag and a long snake of rope tumbled to the ground. She picked it up and watched Ebony thread it round the bulbous handle and across the short corridor they stood in, until it reached the handle of the door opposite. She looped it across both handles twice, weathering the tugs and bangs from within the cubby, then bit her gloves off one by one, and worked the ends into a knot with mechanical speed. She was breathing heavily now with the exertion. Frankie stood by, her eyes bulging.

'There's a knife in that bag, pass me it, will you.'

Frankie dipped her hand into the bag and scrabbled at the bottom until she came upon a small hard bone handle. She tossed it to Ebony who trimmed the ends off the rope quickly. Ebony squeezed her hands over the knots, nodded and breathed out, then tucked the knife into her waistband.

Frankie realised her heart had shot up to a gallop. She tried to control her breathing. The door of the cubby thumped and rattled but each time the two men inside pulled on it, they tautened their rope.

'Come on, let's find Liam,' Ebony moved off into the darkness of the marble-floored corridor, frowning as a fresh set of violent jolts shot through the door and onto her cat's cradle prison.

Forty-Three

Lady Thorne had selected red for the occasion. It was no use hiding it from the girls any more, not since the embarrassment of Ebony Diamond's discovery, and not since she had set her mind that the best disguise for their purpose was to waltz in, in full view of the guards. A full red cloak of the nicest, most luxurious wool. And 'red for the workers'. She had managed a wink at the girls in the carriage parked on Victoria Embankment when she said that.

Now she wished they would watch their feet on the carpet outside the Lords' chamber. It was a plush pile and had been there since Victoria's early days on the throne. She could remember standing on it as a girl, her palm in her father's, fascinated by the patterns on it that looked like goblin's faces. She had stood there many times since too.

A known opponent of the women's movement.

A known figure of the utmost propriety.

A known warrior against vice and intemperance.

A devoted wife picking up some papers from her husband's office.

The sergeant on the door to the House of Lords had slammed the door in her face at first. Orders to be on the look-out for suffragettes. Then as if she was Black Rod himself he had peered through the hatch and let her in, apologising and 'yes ma'aming' and keening his head like a whelp that had piddled in the parlour.

The fact that she had not one but four of her ladies-in-waiting (sorry-looking courtiers though they were) only served to emphasise the importance of her mission at this late hour, and her dedication as Lord Thorne's wife. And besides, she wanted to show the poor wide-eyed lambs inside the House. A charitable woman of the utmost propriety.

Her hand hardened its clutch on the bag, partly to stop the ceramic cases from chinking against one another, partly to remind her why she was here, in the presence of four creatures who disgusted her. In the high gold-leafed corridor leading to the Lords' chamber she took stock of their faces like a grocer counting his cabbages on the shelves. Tilly Westcott, a fat furious little woman with poxed skin and blistered fingers who had worked in the match factories at the time of the strikes and still carried a terrible sulphurous smell about her. Victoria, 'Vicky' Crook, a keen snub-nosed willow who had started out fighting off black-leg labour on behalf of the trade unions and ended up fighting anyone she could get her fists on. Sue Milkfield, a brainless, breathless desperate sheep in curls and rags. And Danielle Boyd, a girl who had bullied her way through every workhouse in London and who hated the world with a bitterness that Lady Thorne found admirable.

She had given them ways to channel their anger, beyond any of their dreams.

She found herself thoroughly relieved that the two disenchanted suffragettes Annie Evans and Ebony Diamond had been disposed of. They had mouths on them. They asked too many questions. They wanted answers for their actions, political ends. They did not simply hate.

And Lady Thorne knew how deeply hate could run in your veins and how powerfully it could stamp on every nerve in you if you let it. That look on her wretched daughter's face, that awful creature, half-man half-woman who stood before her outside her own house today cemented it: as if she needed any more reminders that the blood in her, the blood that had come from her had turned to muck in a single generation. Her heart, which had already spread over with a leather crust, turned as hard as marrow and, like a marrow, began to rot from the inside.

Millicent might have thought it was a joke to humiliate her family by marrying in Egypt, and then to twist the knife further by casting herself as meat in a vice-show. Millicent might have thought it was funny that girls disobeyed their mother's orders and ran off to London and had their own latchkeys and squandered their fortunes and, worst of all, befriended the wretched new-monied Americans who had been flooding London for the past decade. Millicent had thought it amusing to put her fingers in the groin of a vegetable boy. But she hadn't witnessed her grandfather, Lady Thorne's own father, put a rifle in his mouth in the garden shed after the land redistribution acts, death duties and new land taxes lost him half his estate, half his workers. She hadn't heard the awful sound of gunmetal on teeth, and then the blowing of the whole world to bits. That was what happened when the classes mixed, when you gave the workers an inch of power and they took a mile.

Twenty years ago to the day. But the hour for commemoration, the time for anniversaries, churchyard vigils, was past.

What they would do tonight would be so horrific it would stitch a fear as thick as catgut into the soul of England, so that no suffragists, trade unionists, no women or collective workers would ever be allowed such free rein again to meet, to plot or even to exist. The Lords would take back what was theirs by birth. And she would use the workers to do it.

Frankie caught pace with Ebony quickly in the gloomy corridor. As they walked, Ebony surveyed the leftover rope in her hands. 'I hope there's enough.' She lengthened her stride and Frankie found herself puffing to keep up. They passed ornate doorways leading to libraries and offices, tapestries and sculptures. Every shadow on the wall, every wood or marble carving made Frankie start, her heart quiver. Just as the corridor was beginning to look as if it would never end, Ebony turned sharply into a side lobby.

In front of them stood a pair of glass-panelled doors. Frankie raised herself to her tip-toes and peered through. Beyond the doors lay a sumptuous lobby, illuminated in weak electric lighting. Benches lined the walls, statues protruded from the floor, carved from chalk-white marble, their curves glowing faintly in the light. Quickly trying to orient herself from the plans and the direction they had walked in, she deduced that they were outside the famous octagonal lobby, the Central Hall, Peers entrance on one side, Commons on the other.

She turned back to see that Ebony had begun taking off her skirts, and felt a blush rise. Ebony noticed and scoffed a laugh. 'Convent school, was it?' Her small scarlet mouth wove into a wicked smile.

Frankie didn't know where to look so made herself useful, taking the rope off Ebony as she stashed her mound of under-skirts behind a cabinet. Her legs were clad in black stockings, the upper parts covered by loose black bloomers. She discarded her hat and tightened her hairpins. 'Are you ready for this, because you're going to have to hold tight, you see? If you want to get close enough for the shot.'

Frankie nodded and swallowed a trickle of nerves. She peered through the glass pane again and thought she saw a shadow moving behind one of the doors.

'Ebony,' she murmured, 'look.'

Ebony had to stand on tiptoes to see through the window and Frankie only then realised she had taken off her heeled shoes. Her frame was suddenly miniature without them.

'If they're coming in, it'll be through the Peers entrance, through there, won't it?'

Ebony squinted then dropped to her heels. 'Don't want them to see us before we catch them.'

'But we need to find Liam. If he came in via Westminster Palace . . .' Frankie pulled out her notebook and looked at the skew-lined sketch she had made, then tried to fit it back into the plan she had seen. 'Come on, I think I know a way.'

Doubling back on themselves, they moved further along the stone-floored corridor. Footsteps rained down from somewhere but they kept going until they reached a crossroads. Ebony, only wearing stockings, barely made a sound and Frankie wondered if this was how she had clambered into the rafters of the Albert Hall, all those months ago.

Frankie gestured ahead. 'I think we're going to come out at a cloister.'

'Won't there be guards? Or locked doors?'

She let out her breath. 'Shit.'

'If we go left here, we'll end up back . . .'

'Oi, suffragettes.' A whisper in the dark sent a shock though Frankie's skin. Then she noted the accent and slowly turned.

Liam was grinning like a wolf, a Swan Vesta held up to light his freckled nose and cheeks. Frankie snatched it from his hand and stamped on it. 'Don't waste those or we'll have none for the flash. Where is it?' She raised a discreet hand to still the thudding in her chest while Liam rooted in his pockets, pulling out the corked bottle and cardboard box.

'You see what happened to Milly?' she asked quietly.

'Aye, they took her.'

'Probably for the best,' Frankie murmured.

Ebony had already pulled open the gilded door ahead of them, leading to another holding corridor. She clicked her fingers for the carpet bag. Frankie tossed it to her. Carefully, she withdrew the rope and wooden beam of her trapeze and began checking over the knots, threading them closer, joining them up with the spare rope she had cut earlier. Frankie took the bag back and rooted for her camera, slung it across her shoulder and slid it round her back. She withdrew the metal flash pan from her pocket and held it loosely in her hand. It had a strange forbidding smell, burnt metal and chemicals.

Liam swung the door quietly behind them and they traipsed along the corridor, a thinner one than before, darker, until they reached a set of stairs. 'Can we get all the way round from here?' Frankie asked.

'We want the Ladies' Gallery.' Ebony wedged a measure of rope into her mouth and looped the rest round her shoulders.

Frankie stopped. 'Why the ladies'?'

'Has the grate.'

She shook her head. 'No, no, they took that away. Suffragettes chained themselves to it.'

Ebony pulled the rope from her teeth momentarily. 'They put it back. We can rope to it, it's the safest way. It'll hold.' She spread her mouth into a smile, one that crept for the first time into her eyes. 'It'll be fine. You just have to hang on.'

Frankie followed her up the stairs, watching the curvature of her form underneath the black clothing. When they reached the top landing she gestured to Liam for the bottle and the box of guncotton.

'Guncotton first.' He opened the box and Frankie reached across and teased out a small measure. 'Magnesium.'

He grunted and took the bung from the bottle with his teeth.

'Can you have a match handy, not struck, just ready with a surface to strike it on, so when I need it it's there?'

'Peck, peck peck. Can you just trust me?'

'All right, don't start an argument now.'

'I'm not arguing, you'd argue with a crocodile you would.'

'Well just as well you're not . . .' She stopped when she saw that Ebony had pinned open the upper staircase door with her foot and was waiting for them. The light was even bleaker; Frankie could only just make out Ebony's silhouette six feet away. She suddenly flashed back to the sight of her on stage, spiralling through the air, hanging from her perch, and felt a wave of vertigo, a longing more than anything to make their mission a success, to prove she too could do something right. She dropped the camera case and hopped the last few steps to join Ebony.

'You'll want to take off your shoes,' Ebony whispered. 'You'll need all the grip you can get.'

They had found themselves in a corridor, where a carved finger pointed them to the Ladies' Gallery.

'Go down to the Reporters' benches, it's along and down a couple of those steps. I'm going to rig this from inside and I'll join you.'

Frankie obeyed and led Liam along to a sign that guided them to the press entrance. As soon as she pulled open the door, the scent of leather and furniture polish drifted up from the chamber below, and another smell lurking beneath it, pomade perhaps, or tobacco. The chamber was completely black, the air chilled and stifling, all warmth sucked into the hardwood reporter's seats. She wondered briefly if Teddy Hawkins had ever sat his bottom on one of those seats. Behind them, she could just make out the weaving gothic lattices of the Ladies' Gallery grille, the shape of a rope being fed through it. She quickly moved to the grille and took the ends of the ropes until they were through.

Though there was still no light, she thought she could detect a sound below, a scratching like mice, and waved at Liam to get down.

Without warning a naked hand landed cold on her shoulder. She flinched and just caught the gasp that tried to escape her, then breathed in *poudre d'amour* and found herself looking up at Ebony's white round face. Ebony had taken off her gloves. A puff of powder flew off her fingers and Frankie was hit by the smell again.

At that moment came a clatter and hiss, the striking of a match in the chamber below. A hurricane lamp swelled into a glow in the distance down behind the Speaker's chair. A portion of the green parliamentary benches lit up, and the sight Frankie beheld sent ice into her veins.

She had expected chaos. Women with their eyes ablaze, mad with passion, tossing pear-shaped bombs about like zookeepers flinging meat to lions. She had expected demons and hell. What she saw instead was three women, so hard at work, so concentrated on the intimacy of the task they were completing, they had barely noticed the light of the fourth go on. The scratching Frankie took for mice was the rip and pierce of leather, as each woman took a pair of tiny thread scissors and neatly sliced a line into the centre of a green bench. With quiet diligence she saw each of them take from their knapsacks a plump bomb, insert it into the slice, with the detonator pointing ceilingwards, and stitch it closed with a hard twine needle. Frankie's eyes raked the room for Lady Thorne; she saw Ebony do the same, but neither could see her. Then the shrill scrape of a door on a wooden floor underneath made them sit up. Ebony clutched Frankie's arm and gestured for her to take off her jacket.

Directly below them, the back end of a blood red cape trailed into the centre of the chamber. Lady Thorne, her disguise discarded, her hypocrisy cloaking her like a totem, stood proudly surveying her colleagues. 'Good work,' she whispered. 'Good work.'

Ebony pulled Frankie towards the edge of the balcony. Frankie's fingers flicked at Liam and she mouthed the word 'match'. He kept close to them, the Vesta held between finger and thumb while they clambered onto the trapeze.

Ebony wedged herself onto the bar first, looping one wrist round the rope. With her spare arm she pulled Frankie's legs until they wrapped her waist and crossed Frankie's stockinged ankles in front of her own thighs. Frankie wriggled her shoulder out from under the camera strap and slung it instead round her neck, easing the shutter into place as quietly as she could. Lady Thorne looked up sharply, then, distracted by the sounds of stitching and cutting, began to pace, monitoring each of the chamber exits.

Frankie was pressed so close to Ebony's back she could feel the muscles around her shoulders pushing into her own flimsy breasts, and the heat from Ebony's legs through her trousers. Ebony nudged her a glance over her shoulder. Frankie nodded and looped her wrists round the rope, keeping the flash pipe tight in her left hand. They inched towards the lip of the balcony, staying low. Just before Ebony kicked them up onto the rail she reached into the pocket of her bloomers and retrieved a crinkled ribbon. In the wisps of light Frankie could make out three colours: purple, white and green, crested by the portcullis badge. She pinned it quickly to her chest and raised her eyes to the roof. For the first time in her life unbidden to do so – either by a nun or her mother – Frankie crossed herself and asked the Virgin to protect her.

They swung up onto the railing. Liam shoved the match in Frankie's right hand.

And they jumped.

Though it wasn't a high jump by Ebony's standards, Frankie felt as if her stomach had been scooped out of her and tossed behind as she plunged through the air into the heart of the House of Commons. They jolted quickly, the ropes short. Cold wind gushed through Frankie's hair, down her neck. She pressed her body forward and scraped the match head on the bar beneath them. A wisp of gold lit the air.

One by one, each of the seamstresses looked up, stricken. Some of them cowed their faces in their hands, unsure what was happening in the dim heavens above. Ebony was breathing heavily, beginning to use her force to heave the trapeze back, to take another swing forward, when one woman raised a pear-shaped bomb above her head and flung it. It missed and went smashing into a wall where the hard terracotta splintered to pieces. The detonator dropped to the ground, unspent.

Frankie loosened her right hand from the rope and, holding on tight with her thighs, dropped the match into the flash pipe. She looked for the sweep of red cape, found it, aimed, just as Lady Thorne rushed for the exit on the chamber's right. She pressed the shutter as a blinding flash spluttered white hot into her eyes. The eye of the camera snapped open and shut. Sparks flew down to the chamber floor.

It was bright enough in the residual light to manage another shot if she was quick. Frankie swung the camera round to catch the seamstresses, their tools spilled around the benches, the bombs wedged half in, half out.

Hot flecks of magnesium showered onto Ebony's neck and she squealed. The flash pan dropped to the chamber floor with a clatter. One of the women hurled another bomb at them, missing again.

'What now?' Frankie yelled at Ebony. They were hanging low into the chamber. Ebony had un-looped her hands and was starting to work her way up the rope. 'I'll climb back up and pull you over.'

A man's voice rang out in the darkness below. 'Hoy there, what the devil do you think you are doing?'

Shadowy bodies began to spill into the room, first against one wall, then the other. 'Who's up there? Police. Look sharp, move aside.' A cavalry of footsteps charged into the chamber. Wood on the door jambs split with cracks as the doors were flung back and men in black tunics came tumbling in from all entrances.

Frankie heard a piercing shriek somewhere.

Somewhere above her.

She angled her head up just in time to see a wash of red fabric moving up on the Reporters' Gallery, a glint of silver.

'Liam!' she cried. She heard the grunt of a struggle, the sound of teeth biting into flesh. But it was too late. As a troupe of police thundered into the House of Commons below, Lady Thorne stood above them, a knife pressed to Liam's throat.

Then the unthinkable happened.

Keeping one hand pincering Liam's neck, Lady Thorne took the knife away and sliced with careless efficiency through each of the trapeze ropes. Below and behind them another woman released the bomb in her palm. This time it didn't miss. Frankie felt it hot and slow, then cold and hard, a sensation similar to the weightless peak on a fairground swing. Her ears seemed to fill with roaring water, she plummeted on a puff of air and dust towards the ground, smashing with excruciating pain onto the front bones in her pelvis, skidding on the hard floor and stretching her arms in front to stop her before she slammed into a bench.

Sour dust filled the air and smoke spread, black miasma from the ground up. The first thing Frankie did was reach her hands up to pull her throat loose; the camera strap had twisted round her neck. Her lungs stung and itched. Behind her came the hiss and crackle of fire and a scream from a woman's gut, 'No surrender!'

Frankie raised her head and her back sang out in pain. She reached gently behind her, felt a warm sticky glue holding her shirt fast to her, and knew that a patch of her skin had melted. Each twitch she made sent cotton fibres probing deeper into the wound.

A few yards away, Ebony lay on her back, her head turned away. Her limbs were splayed into a star shape. Still on her belly, Frankie began to claw along the floorboards towards her, but even before she got there it was plain to see the ungodly twist in Ebony's collarbone. She slapped Ebony's cheeks with one hand then the next, ignoring the chaos of the four women being grabbed and collared and handcuffed by police all around her. She pinched open Ebony's eyelids, and put her ear next to her mouth. The breath was shallow and fast.

Suddenly Ebony's eyes jerked open. 'Will you get off me?'

She spluttered and a foam of spittle and blood came through her lips. 'Bloody journalists. Don't leave you alone even when your back's broken.'

The wave of relief that passed over Frankie quickly sank when her eyes fell on Ebony's far arm, wrenched backwards. Ebony saw the look on Frankie's face and inched her neck round to look. If she was shocked, she hid it well. Her eyes rolled. 'God, my mother always told me to keep my arms in. Twenty years I was working with tigers and never lost a limb.'

A line of policemen in black tunics charged past them, rifles cocked. Frankie scrambled to her feet and slammed straight into a large woollen form.

In the smoky light she caught the shape of a police warrant card.

'She needs a doctor,' she stammered.

'Detective Inspector Primrose, CID. What the hell do you think you are doing?'

'Ebony, she needs a doctor.'

'This is high treason, not an exhibition opening,' the inspector growled, stepping past her and bending down. 'What do you think the police are here for?'

'You weren't listening to us. We needed proof. We have pictures now, proof of who she is.'

'Did you get the shot?' Frankie looked down to see Ebony's black eyes roaming, unfocused. She had a deep scowl creasing her clammy forehead, a fine spray of blood on her chin and cheeks. 'Where's . . .' she paused to cough. 'Where's

Liam?' She watched Frankie's expression, then breathed out a slow moan, as if she had known all along that something like this would happen. 'Well, you have to go and get him. Jojo will kill you if anything happens to him.'

'I'm not leaving you.'

Ebony blinked. Her gaze grew limpid and she caught Frankie in her wide black pupils. 'I'll take care of the camera. Now go, and don't come back till you've got him. Don't worry about me.' She pointed her jaw down towards the singed suffragette ribbon on her chest. A smear of blood had made its way onto the white. 'Every peeler loves a suffragette. Think they're going to let me out of their sight wearing this?' Her eyes rolled backwards. Frankie wiped the hair off her brow, where it had stuck with blood. She pulled the camera strap off her own neck and placed it down next to Ebony's head.

A voice cried out behind them, 'Get down, I say.'

Another howling explosion and the short blunt shot of a gun. There came a sharp scream.

'One woman down, sir.'

Frankie made to run but Primrose snatched both of her arms behind her. 'Not so eager, my reporter friend.'

'Inspector,' she said firmly. 'You have to let me go. There's a boy came in with us. Lady Thorne took him from up there. You have to listen.'

'No, you listen to me.'

'The boy, Liam, he's only fifteen. She's taken him. I saw her drag him, put a knife to his throat. She's not safe. She's mad.'

'You're going nowhere, miss. You're going to wait with the Sergeant and we'll have you cuffed and taken to the station.'

'He's my . . . our . . . responsibility.'

The inspector scrutinised her for a moment before his eyes roved the dim chamber. The three remaining seamstresses had been wrestled to the floor and were now each raising merry hell for the six police officers anchoring them down. The two bombs had caused an unsettling amount of damage, a chunk of wood and plaster ripped from the wall, a toppled bench split in two. He looked down at the camera next to Ebony and reached for the strap. 'I'm taking this for now. We'll decide whether to confiscate it afterwards.'

Frankie looked again between him and Ebony. 'Please. There isn't much time.'

Inspector Primrose swallowed and Frankie saw a lump run down his neck. Eventually he said, 'You stick with me. You're only coming to negotiate. Do everything I say.' He called a couple of his spare men over and sent them to attend to Ebony, depositing the camera with one of them. Frankie looked back over her shoulder as she trailed him out of the chamber.

It should have been her lying there, broken boned, torn-limbed. As the two policemen bent down to Ebony's head and feet, Ebony looked straight at Frankie, full to the brim with conviction. Frankie seized hold of the look and followed the inspector out of the door.

Forty-Four

'That way.' Frankie pointed to the door that led to the octagonal lobby. They felt with outstretched hands through the choking smoke, still hearing raw screams from inside the Commons. Now there was a new noise too, loud and steady outside in the courtyard, hooves, and firemen giving orders.

The door to St Stephen's Hall had wedged itself ajar and was blowing a cool draught towards them. Primrose pushed it gently. Dim electric light glowed on the cold stone walls, muting the rich colours. Shadows stretched long and dark behind paintings and statues, twirls and ridges of intricate detail rising and latticing into the vaulted ceiling. Frankie recognised it as the old parliament from descriptions she had heard in the Cheshire Cheese. The patterned windows, the chandeliers, the frescoes that covered the walls like storytelling bedsheets. The twelve statues, and the one with the broken sword where a suffragette had chained herself three years previously and clipped the toe of his boot off when she was cut free.

They were barely into the hall when another scream rang out, high and choked. Then a grunt as if a woman had been winded in the gut. A lady's cut-glass voice filled the cold air and rattled off the stone. 'Don't come any further, Inspector, or I'll blow this boy's face to mincemeat.'

The lights sizzled off and darkness tumbled in on them. From the far end of the hall Frankie could hear feet scrambling on stone.

They moved slowly forward. After a few seconds, the door ahead swung vigorously back and forth, bringing the grand arch at the end of the hall flashing into view and out again. The inspector swallowed heavily. 'They've gone into the crypt.'

Frankie lunged ahead but he elbowed her back.

'You keep behind me, hear?'

'Of course I hear,' she snapped into the darkness.

'If she's armed . . .' He turned to Frankie, observing the stained glass shadows playing ghostly games across her handsome features. 'Setting that off in the right spot, Westminster Palace could fall. You stay behind me and you listen to what I say.'

Frankie growled an acceptance.

They moved through the swinging door into a dark stairwell, cold as a tomb, swaddling both light and sound. In the distance in front of them, Liam's voice croaked a dry protest.

Frankie opened her mouth to shout back, but the inspector was quick and landed a soft blow in her stomach. 'Keep it shut.'

As they reached the bottom of the stairs the footsteps ahead faded and a door slammed. They crept forward until they felt the sensation of a wall rising up in front of them. Primrose held his revolver out, moving it around until they heard the muzzle click against a metal door handle. He slid his hands around trying to shift it. After a couple of attempts, the latch gave. He pushed the door and a dagger of gold light cut a warm path in front of them. The smell of musty incense grew strong.

They were standing at the base of the chapel's nave in front of a long tiled aisle, surrounded on all sides by a low vaulted ceiling of elaborate curled golden designs. Two wrought iron gates before them hung open. Drifts of leftover frankincense mingled with the scent of cold wood pews.

'Don't come any further.' It was a curter pitch than Milly's voice but had the same intonation.

Lady Thorne stood with her back to them, facing the altar, her scarlet cloak spilling into a blood red cloud behind her. She had lit two creamy wax church candles, one on either side, and was using their glow to illuminate something she was fiddling with in front of her. Frankie suddenly saw two feet kick out from under the cloak on her left side, and heard a boy's high howl.

'Liam!'

'I hope you're not deaf as well as stupid, Miss George. Do as the inspector says. Authority always knows best.' There was a nasty strain in her voice. 'It won't just be your friend who is buried in this stonework.'

'What did the boy do to you?' Primrose's voice echoed round the barrel ceiling.

'Helped a nasty little gossip columnist who got above her station.'

'I have a photograph of you. It'll be on the front page of every newspaper. Do you want the world to know what you became?' Frankie reeled backwards as the inspector landed a kick on her shins. The burns in her back tweaked with pain.

Lady Thorne swung round and Frankie saw her face, as clear and memorable as it had been the first day she had seen it outside a music hall years ago, handing out flyers. The eyes, she knew them now, were the same cut crystal blue eyes she had seen on the woman with the bundled jaw. They wore the same expression now as they had then, but Frankie realised it was not zeal or anger, it was a cold brutality, an irritation with anything that disagreed with her. That night outside Jojo's when she had argued with her daughter, she hadn't come to spy or to save the souls of the punters in Soho. She had come to execute Ebony Diamond.

'Red,' she said, gesturing down her body with one hand, the other fish-hooking the struggling Liam by his mouth with an extraordinarily muscular and bony finger. 'For the Lords. I don't know if you made the connection, I doubt it,' she said looking at Frankie. 'But they are the true dynastic rulers of this country, and have been for centuries.'

Primrose raised his revolver a touch, eyeing down the barrel.

'Don't, Inspector,' Lady Thorne shook her head, tutting.

A yellow waxy light from the candles on either side of her danced on the crisp aristocratic bones in her face. She let out a weary sigh. 'Look at you. I am a shepherd leading my flock into a light they might not know they need. Just like Lloyd George thought he could lead his Welsh sheep and all the other farmyard animals we call this country into following his revolting People's Budget. What if some of us didn't want that?'

'Then you vote him out,' Frankie called. 'What the women are fighting for the power to do.'

Liam managed to land a kick in Lady Thorne's leg and she twitched. She retaliated by digging her nail further into his cheek. He gagged and choked.

'Sometimes a child doesn't know what's best for them. Does that mean you should give them what they cry for?'

'They're women, they're not children.'

'I'm not just talking about women,' Lady Thorne bellowed back hysterically. 'I'm talking about mongrels. Mongrels given status they weren't born into. Miners striking, match girls walking out. Trade Unions of railway workers squeezing their fingers up the rectum of England and pulling it down to their squalid level. Anarchist cells of broken seamstresses blowing up the Houses of Parliament. That's what happens when you give the mongrels an inch of power. We are in a hell of our own making.'

'You tricked those women. They had nothing left. You lied to them, pretended you were one of them and the one you couldn't fool any more you had killed.'

Lady Thorne's mouth twitched into a trout's grimace. 'Not quite, I got the wrong one, didn't I? It was a surprise for both of us, I think, when I saw her deathly little face. Still, Annie Evans was one of the weaker links in the chain. Her courage would have failed her anyway.'

She lowered her arm and, still staring ahead, fumbled around the altar behind her until she came upon the object she was searching for. The cloak moved and Frankie saw the whites in Liam's eyes, wild as a shying horse. Lady Thorne held up a polished shape. Its clean, lacquered sheen caught the light with horrible perfection. One of the bombs. A nail stuck straight out of it like a snake's forked tongue.

'I would ask you to consider the implications, Inspector, of trying to be a hero.'

Frankie was finding it harder and harder to breathe in the cloying air, grown hot by the candles and her own terror. She racked her brains trying to think of ways to stall. Ask her more questions. Interview subjects love to talk about themselves. 'Why destroy the structure that you stand for? If authority's what you want.'

Lady Thorne took her admiring eyes from the bomb for a second. 'You'll note I spared the House of Lords. Someone will have to pick up the mess once these anarchist women have been brought to justice. And when they're all swinging from the Holloway gallows, it will be damned certain that the rulers in charge will never let a group like that ever exist again. Workers, miners, trade unions, suffragists . . . They will shut them down. They will be despised.'

'You want to be back in the Dark Ages?' said Primrose.

Lady Thorne smiled. 'They were only ever dark for some.'

'How did you make them trust you?' asked Frankie.

'Very simple. They're idiots. At our very first meeting in that diabolical shop, we established the extent of my . . . injury,' she gestured to her jaw, waggling the bomb dangerously. 'It was easy to engage their sympathy, set the plan in motion. I even got them to put aside a third of their wages to pay for the terracotta and the chemistry set.' She shrugged. 'Well, that's egalitarian, isn't it? Ebony Diamond's anger with the suffragettes was an added bonus. I had simply planned to apprehend her in prison and offer her something better than they could. As it happened, she was only too happy to accept.'

'When she thought you weren't going to commit murder.'

Lady Thorne sighed impatiently. 'And she wonders why I didn't trust her with the full plan to begin with. No, I started them out gently,' she said, her voice very grave. 'I shared with them the simple idea of setting fire to the building, eased them in. Then it became bombs, and finally, mongrel politicians' bottoms. Ebony almost ruined the whole thing. Her and that evil deviant friend of hers.'

'An innocent man. You killed an innocent man.'

'And I'll kill more with relish.' She brandished the bomb.

A rattle of footsteps on the stairs behind them made Frankie jump. She half turned to see shadows playing on the dark stone walls beside the door's arch.

'Who's there?' Lady Thorne's sharp tongue cut the air.

'I would have thought you would know the sound of my footsteps in the dark. I at least know the sound of yours.' The long lean shadow of Milly passed into the nave. Then Milly herself appeared through the double doors, her face and hair smudged with mud. She looked like a funeral bride standing coolly at the foot of the aisle in draping silks, cuffed in irons to Sergeant Wilson by her left hand. On their other side stood a skinny boyish woman in a blue linen dress, a suffragette sash crossing her torso.

'You'd murder your own daughter?' Frankie asked quietly.

Lady Thorne's face seemed for a second as if it might melt into an expression of warmth. 'My daughter.' Then it hardened back again like stale dough. 'She murdered me.' The pear teetered in her hand. She smiled and Liam landed a small punch in her belly.

'Don't move,' the voices of Frankie and the two policemen yelled.

Lady Thorne coughed and recovered. 'My daughter started this mess in the first place. What kind of society lets a girl humiliate her family? As if my daughter hadn't proven the cancer of the age we live in by marrying an archaeologist. An archaeologist?' she shrieked. 'A French archaeologist. A man who digs up bones and feeds off snails. Did Agincourt never happen? Then she bares her breasts for photographers and her belly on stage for money.' Her eyes were suddenly empty as gun barrels. '"How sharper than a serpent's tooth it is—"'

"'To have a thankless child,'" Frankie finished the quote, and groaned as a memory dredged up; the night outside Jojo's, Lady Thorne had spat that at Milly. King Lear and his thankless daughters, she should have known.

Lady Thorne looked briefly appalled at the notion of Shakespeare in Frankie's mouth, then went on. 'You would be doing me a favour, you, whoever you are, if you were to garrotte my daughter in front of me, here in this church.' Her voice was an icy reptilian hiss.

Then, like lightning from above, hell broke loose.

Lady Thorne dropped Liam, hunched her shoulder back high over the altar and hurled her bomb with the force of a bear. It turned somersaults in the golden air, cutting a clean, spinning, clockwise path, arcing up almost to the ceiling before hurtling down again. A reeling cry of pain came sharp and deafening. A man's cry.

Inspector Primrose took the full force of the bomb as the nail tore through his shirt and split the muscle on his chest. He stumbled back against the pew; they all heard the crack of his spine on the wood as he fell. His revolver spun out of his hand and into the air where it whacked the low vaulted ceiling and pelted back down.

Frankie dived onto the icy stone, waiting for the heat and the ash and the dust. But the blast never came. She saw Liam ahead of her crawling like a lizard on his belly out of Lady Thorne's reach.

The revolver slammed the floor inches from Frankie.

'Fire it. Frankie, fire it!' It was Milly's voice.

Frankie stretched her hands for the gun, feeling the dried flesh on her back tear open again. Lady Thorne rose against the altar, reaching into her leather bag for another grenade. The smooth metal, still warm from the inspector's grip, slid into Frankie's hand. She raised the gun.

'Fire it, Frankie.' Milly's voice was desperate. Sergeant Wilson groped for his revolver on the side of his chest but his right hand was cuffed to Milly's and he struggled to get a grip on it with his left.

Frankie's fingers jammed against the trigger. 'I don't know how . . .' She ran her left hand over the top of the gun.

'The safety catch, the safety catch, left hand side.'

Metal gave way underneath her thumb and Milly screamed a bitter scream one final time, 'Just fire it!'

Frankie clenched her fingers down to the bone and pressed the trigger. Gunpowder spat back at her face, a shower of hot black pepper, and a shattering roar ripped through the chapel.

Lady Thorne, leaning against the altar, spluttered and gaped as if she had been given a nasty shock at the card table. Red foam bubbled on her lips and her mouth gave a terrible undignified belch as she slid into the pile of scarlet cape at her feet. The bomb in her hand slipped back onto the hard marble of the altar, rolled with a musical tinkling noise towards the candle and stopped silently against its wax.

The world paused for a moment. Then a powerful ringing filled Frankie's ears, the underwater feeling again. A moan rose out of the dark.

'Primrose.' Iron rattled behind her and Sergeant Wilson

dragged Milly over to the twitching body on the ground, lying between two pews.

'Don't touch,' Frankie yelled and shoved her hand back to shoo them off. She crawled over to the inspector's body and saw that his eyes were pinned wide with fear. His shirt had ripped, his jacket had fallen open and from the gash the inverted pear stuck out, its fangs wedged into his flesh. A small creeping patch of blood was growing on his shirt.

'It's going to go,' he whispered. His forehead was rinsed with sweat.

Frankie reached into her pocket and grabbed a handkerchief. An unfamiliar man's voice sounded behind her, telling everyone to move aside, and she momentarily turned. The woman in the suffragette sash was pushing Wilson and Milly out of the way and kneeling down. In her efforts she knocked the wig off her head and the mass of brown curled hair artfully arranged in French twists became a crop of fine blonde. Frankie could see it now, the male features in the face. She had taken them to be simply strong. Baffled, she let the man in the dress press her out of the way calmly as he bent on all fours over Primrose's chest.

'I'm sorry, sir, I had no time to change when Wilson called me off suffragette surveillance. We would have been here faster but that Sergeant on the lobby door wouldn't let us past. Didn't recognise me in a dress.'

Primrose managed a weak twitch of a smile. 'I told him not to let any women past.'

'I'll thank you for that later, sir. Now keep still.'

'I don't blame you if it . . .'

'I've seen one like this before and there's every chance it won't go off. It needs a spark. Now I know why you wanted me off Irish Branch. Not just a pretty face?' He kept up the trembling banter as his fingers moved over Primrose's chest prising a wider hole around the bomb. 'I'm not a doctor, mind.'

Milly, who had been staring at her mother's body on the ground, suddenly snapped from her trance and turned. 'Roberta. Roberta Jenkins. I saw you at Lincoln's Inn House. You were the new recruit, that day, you wanted to know about Ebony.'

'I prefer Robert. Or just Detective Constable.'

The inspector winced.

'Try not to breathe too deeply, sir. I need a second pair of hands but I warn you it might not work. Clear out, the rest of you. Up the stairs.'

'No,' Milly said.

'Miss . . .'

'Don't "Miss" me, Roberta.'

'I'm staying too,' Frankie murmured. She looked back over her shoulder and called, 'Liam, get out of here.'

There was a pause then a little choking voice came back. 'No.'

Jenkins rolled his eyes up to the low chapel ceiling. 'At least we're in the right place to pray for a miracle.'

'I have a message for Clara—' Primrose's finger lifted off the ground then he dropped it again and his eyes squeezed.

Frankie noticed that Wilson had discreetly taken the inspector's hand and was holding it tentatively like a dog's wounded paw.

'Make yourself useful then,' Jenkins nodded at Frankie. 'Stretch the flesh against the grain of the muscle. Horizontally, like you're stretching meat. As far as it will go. He'll cry out and howl but you just keep stretching and don't stop. All right?'

She nodded briskly feeling her heart quiver like the jelly on a pork pie, and braced her hands against Primrose's clammy shirt, trying to get a purchase on the skin. Jenkins reached into a small tool kit concealed in his dress and pulled out a tiny pair of jewellers' pliers. He snapped them a few times then jerked a nod at Frankie to keep stretching. The inspector's mouth hung open, pouring out twisted moans like a butchered animal.

Jenkins inched the pliers round the detonating wire, his tongue lolling sideways in his mouth. The detonator caught and stuck a few times, then, like a plant root loosening from the earth, the barb slid free. 'It's done, it's out.' His hand was streaked with a thin line of crimson as he cupped the ceramic pear loosely in his palm.

Frankie looked down at the wound on the inspector's chest, raw and textured, like the belly of a gutted salmon. She could feel tears conspiring behind her eyeballs for them all, for Milly and for Ebony, for everything, and she ground her jaw to will them away. She didn't deserve to cry. She would not cry.

Then an Irish voice crept up softly behind her. 'Your back looks like steak and kidney. You should get that seen to.'

Outside, the lawn was crisp with white feathers of frost. Three fire wagons had drawn up. Their horses pawed the ground. In the distance fireworks shattered luminous gold and silver into an opaque sky. The bonfire on Parliament Square had been razed to a pile of black ash.

Some of the police were standing idle, smoking cigarettes while others loosened their tunics and pushed their helmets back off their foreheads. Their faces seemed a blur to Frankie, from where she stood, at the mouth of a horse-drawn ambulance, holding Ebony Diamond's ungloved hand, a hand surprisingly small and doll-like without its sheath.

Ebony's face was smudged with soot and bomb-smoke, blood and sweat; her breathing had shrunk impossibly shallow in her chest. Someone had ripped the front of her corset open, revealing a black cotton shift underneath. Her arm had been swaddled to her side by a sheath of blankets. She tried to crane her neck off the stretcher to look at something and Frankie followed the line of her gaze to see the Black Maria with the three remaining Hourglass Factory women being loaded and chained inside. The horses leading the wagon stamped their hooves on the hard ground and tossed their manes.

Ebony took a sudden gasp of cold air and Frankie's head snapped down to her. 'I think,' she said weakly, 'they have done for me.'

'Nonsense.' Frankie held her voice carefully. 'You've . . . you've tamed cats, jumped off buildings, scared the knickers off journalists. Come on. They'll look after you at the hospital, you'll see.'

She shook her head delicately and Frankie saw then what she had seen the day they found Olivier Smythe. The other side of Ebony Diamond, the side that turned away from the crowds when she was on her trapeze, swinging outwards; the back face of the tarot card. She squeezed her own eyes tightly, swallowing a gulp of pain from her back, and held Ebony's hand tighter.

'Frankie, you have to publish those photographs. I don't want the suffragettes, the Women's Freedom League, any of those groups taking the blame. People need to know why she planted those bombs. It wasn't for us.'

'They will.'

The suffragette badge on Ebony's chest was rising and falling in a quick flutter.

On Frankie's other side, Inspector Primrose was being levered on a gurney into an ambulance, while Wilson and Jenkins made notes in their blotters. Liam was being patched up by a nurse with iodine and gauze where Lady Thorne's fingernail had pierced a hole in his cheek. Over by Westminster Palace, Milly had dropped her coat to the ground and was holding her arms in the thin silk, staring up at the knotted façade of Westminster Abbey.

'I'm sorry I didn't keep my promise, to meet you,' Ebony said.

Her words pinched inside Frankie's chest. 'I understand.'

'I was frightened,' she said, then softer, 'I'm frightened now.'

The ambulance attendants were done strapping Primrose down and came towards the stretcher where Ebony lay. Frankie suddenly found herself seized by a desperation, an absolute refusal to let go of Ebony's hand. The attendant prised it free finger by finger.

'I mean it, Frankie. Let me down over those photographs and I'll haunt you. Gypsies make for evil ghosts, did you know that? I'll come back as a house fire, finish that damned camera off.'

She reached for Frankie's arm again, and let go only as the men bundled her backwards into the van. As they closed the doors Frankie was overwhelmed with a sudden well of deep pain. She felt again the plummet they had taken from the gallery, inside her, but this time she found herself landing in cold black ice, alone. The attendant closed the ambulance door.

She waited until the horses had started up a clop, and began to walk over to where Milly stood. A glow of cigarette over by one of the police cars caught her attention and made her stop. There was a man standing slightly apart from the officers, nodding intently, scribbling in a notebook. The nose, the eyes were too familiar even smudged by distance. Then she saw the pout of the lips.

How could he possibly have known?

Teddy Hawkins caught her eye and flipped the cigarette

out of his mouth. 'Frankie,' he jogged over quickly, his polished shoes skittering a little on the icy ground. 'Cigarette?' His hand extended a pewter case as he approached.

Frankie shook her head blackly. 'Don't you dare, Teddy.'

'What?' He shrugged, a sudden bundle of innocence. His big lips pursed on the cigarette and she saw his eyes fall callously to the camera bag at her waist. They had given it back to her without question. Primrose had insisted.

'I took a trip to hell in there.'

'Sounds like a regular week with Twinkle.'

'I'm not laughing, Teddy.'

He scanned her face then flicked the cigarette onto the ground and pulled her arm confidentially towards him. 'We go halves. You tell me everything that went on in there and I'll help you write it up.'

Frankie's back was aching as if the small of it would pop out of her and onto the ground, her head swam with horror. She wanted to ball her freezing cold hand into a fist and knock it square across Teddy's ears, or draw blood from his cruel lips. 'Someone once told me that's not the way the world works.'

He saw the change in her face and tilted his chin to the clutch of police. 'See him,' he pointed out Wilson. 'He was down there with you. If I don't get it out of you I'll get it out of him. What would you prefer?'

She chewed her tongue. It felt bitter and bloody and she realised she must have cut it at some stage. Thoughts of Ebony swam in her mind, threatened to take her over. She pushed them down. Slowly she rolled a ball of spittle in her mouth and deposited it softly on Teddy Hawkins's polished shoe.

His lips hardened into a stony pout. 'Then it's a race to Stonecutter Street.' He touched his hat between two fingers and barged his way towards Wilson.

Frankie swallowed her burning pain, took the camera in two hands and ran.

Forty-Five

Mr Stark's office was lit only by a pair of wall-mounted gaslights and a paraffin lamp he kept on his formidable oak desk. The gaslamps threw stains of light up the wall and cast hollow shadows on the face of Nobby, diligently flicking his eyes to and fro over the wire tape rattling through the Reuters machine.

Stark's eyes looked even piggier and puffier than usual, brutally torn, as they had been, from his supper by telephone and summoned back to the office. He reached for the crust of his whisky glass with a ranging wandering hand, keeping his eyes on the two figures sat on the other side of his desk. Each radiated an aura of wanting to tear at the other's flesh like dogs.

Frankie gave Teddy Hawkins's soft pout a sidelong glance. He was chewing his mouth in a roundabout way, the way cattle chew cud. In his hand he held a wafting sheet of flimsy covered in type. She held in hers the stiff paper of two photographs, so freshly set from the dark room that the smell of developing chemicals was still on them. On the first photograph, the one on top, the bald eyes of Lady Thorne gaped at her from the afterlife. The flash had made a white smear of her face but the features were still distinguishable above a black swoop of cape, like a bird's wingspan, and so was the terrible expression of blind hatred. The other picture was dimmer but she had caught the faces of two of the women, twisted round from their work on the benches. The details were too dark to make out but cuts and shapes were visible on the leather.

Frankie shifted her hips, freshly aware of the pain in the small of her back, that one of the women from the ladies' page had just dressed with lavender oil while she waited for the photographs. The smell reminded her of Mrs Gibbons and of her mother's paper. In her lap her blotter shifted, and she let her brown eyes fall down, gazing through tangled lashes at her scribbled notes. She cursed the time she had spent in the developing room. Damn Teddy for being such a quickhand typist, although she suspected that he had dictated to one of the ladies on the Remington machines and she hated him even more for it.

The stalemate silence continued while Mr Stark fondled his crusty glass and Teddy chewed his invisible cud and Frankie flicked her eyes here and there and watched Nobby silently cut a length of tape from the juddering machine.

The telephone on Stark's desk rang; his hand jumped on it. He barked a staccato conversation, a pattern of pauses and short 'yes's.

Underneath, Teddy Hawkins spat in a low voice, 'I had almost garnered some respect for you, Miss George.'

'Don't worry, it would have been a one-way passage so at least you've not wasted any effort,' she spat back. She twisted and her burns stung again. Stark saw her mouth open in pain and snapped his hand into a fist to shut her up.

She leaned back on her chair, and thought of Milly standing staring at Westminster Abbey. Would anyone have taken her home? Stark slapped the receiver onto its hook and she snapped out of it.

'I don't want a word out of you pair.' His hand crept slowly to his face and he pulled his palm down from forehead to chin, as if he might stretch his skin off. Frankie noticed that he had left a little trail of whisky crust from his fingers on his cheeks. 'What happened tonight didn't happen.'

'Pardon?'

'Don't interrupt, Miss George.'

'But that's—'

'Until you hear what I have to say.'

He clicked his fingers at Nobby who understood the signal and reached for the decanter of scotch in the desk drawer. Stark poured himself a lengthy measure then fumbled under the desk and produced two cups, smeared around the rim with thumbprints of ink. He filled one up for Teddy Hawkins and handed it over. 'Miss George?'

'Yes please.'

Stark looked blankly at her for a second as if he had expected her to decline, then dripped a mean portion into the cup. The rim tasted chemical but she gulped it down gratefully and opened her mouth to let the heat wear off her throat.

'It seems the wife of our publisher, Lord Thorne, was not a well woman. I understand from the sources quoted in your piece, Teddy,' he nodded to the thin paper in Hawkins's hand, 'that there was cause to call certain members of the Special Branch police force to deal with an incident in which she became,' he averted his eyes, 'rather distressed before taking her own life.'

Frankie made to get up from her chair.

'Miss George, sit down.'

She slunk her hands back along the weathered wooden arms. Stark stared forcefully at her and in his tone and his stony twitching jaw she could tell he liked the turn of events as little as she did. 'Following a course of treatment in Biarritz—'

'She wasn't in Biarritz, she was in Holloway prison pretending to be a seamstress, rallying those girls to do unspeakable—'

'Following a course of psychoanalysis, Lady Thorne was unfortunately discharged inappropriately early—'

'You ask Annie Evans. Oh you can't, she's dead as doornails. You could ask Ebony Diamond but she's—' She broke off and couldn't finish the sentence.

'Miss George.'

'They weren't throwing those bombs about like madwomen, they weren't trying to destroy the building, you didn't see them, I did. They were stitching them into the chairs. Murderers, cold-blooded, they wanted to see politicians blown to bits through the arse. I don't think you understand—'

'Miss George, if you can't be quiet I'll have you removed from the building.'

Frankie clenched her hand and picked at a cut, hoping the distraction of the pain would help to curtail her brewing rage.

'And watch your language. Ebony Diamond had nothing to do with tonight's events and her disappearance from the Coliseum that night had nothing to do with tonight's events, as Mr Hawkins's article attests. She was in trouble with Oswald Stoll.'

Teddy Hawkins raised his hand from the chair arm and slid it in an ugly pantomime of tenderness onto Frankie's arm. 'Mr Stark has a point,' he said. She gritted her teeth to resist flinching.

Stark shook his head, wobbling his jowls. 'She wasn't at the Houses tonight.'

Frankie opened her mouth.

'She wasn't at the Houses. And neither were you.' He massaged his throat and took another swallow of whisky. 'A sick old lady became caught in the crossfire of a nasty plot. A sick old lady was picking up some papers for her loving husband and encountered a scene of violence that upset her a great deal. This paper is delighted the perpetrators have been caught and will be brought to justice,' he caught her offguard, bringing his whisky glass down on the desk so sharply she braced herself for it to shatter. 'She's nothing but a sick old lady—'

'Sick's the word.'

'Lord Thorne, this paper's owner, your boss, my boss,' he pointed a thick finger at his own chest, 'would agree. Sick is the word. And he won't have his family dragged through Fleet Street muck because of it.'

And then Frankie remembered and felt a sting of deep foolishness. Milly had mentioned her father worked in newspapers. She knew the name Thorne, and how could she not have recognised the fine nose and high cheekbones of the man she sat opposite that day in the Savage Club? She let out a short involuntary groan.

'You might well make that noise, Miss George, but I'm afraid you have to hand over the photographs.'

Frankie set her lips stubbornly. Four days, four deaths. Annie Evans, Olivier Smythe, Lady Thorne and the blunt shot she had heard in the Houses of Parliament. Her back was singing like an angry opera. And Ebony . . . it didn't bear thinking about. She sat up straight. 'I'm taking it elsewhere then. You leave us no option. Mr Hawkins and I will work together.' She turned her eyes on Teddy. He left off massaging his lips and crossed and uncrossed his legs but said nothing.

'Frankie, you can't,' Mr Stark said softly. 'Thorne owns half of Fleet Street and the bits he doesn't own he's got lawyers on like dogs. You'd be destroyed as a journalist. Just write it off.'

He could see the wildness rise in her.

'I'll give you some hard news stories, in the future. You can have your column back.'

'I saw inside the corset shop where they planned it all. We handed the plans over to the police. Parliament, the House of Commons, don't you care at all about publishing the truth, something that—' she stopped herself, seeing a look pass between the two men.

Teddy Hawkins uncrossed his legs awkwardly.

'They had a bomb factory in Olivier Smythe's corset shop. She, Lady Thorne, she went to prison, disguised as a seamstress, she copied a suffragette, Constance Lytton, only she didn't want to help working women, she wanted to trick them. I saw it and there was a diagram plan of the House of Commons with distances measured on it.' She trailed off again as a frosty blanket of silence descended over the room. The Reuters machine rattled on and Nobby quietly cut the paper.

Teddy Hawkins was gazing out of the window, his eyebrows raised. After a while he spoke. 'As I say in my report,' he gestured to the flimsy in his hand, 'Lady Thorne stumbled upon something that startled her and she committed suicide.' He pronounced 'suicide' as 'siew-icide' and it nearly toppled Frankie's anger over the edge. What was it she had thought about Ebony, Milly and Twinkle, what core of survival, what triumph ran through those women? They fought for themselves. They made the world work for them.

Teddy Hawkins let his breath out like a horse and Stark leaned forward.

Frankie cast her eyes between them both again and raised a finger at the machine in the corner. Nobby, who had been staring, quickly looked away. 'I'll take it to Reuters. Even if no paper on Fleet Street will touch the story, they'll wire it elsewhere. Overseas. I'll see Lady Thorne named, and there's nothing that you can do.'

'You can't have the plates. For the photograph. That camera belongs to me, to this newspaper.'

'How did we ever manage before photographs?' she said bitterly, standing and letting the images on her lap flop onto the floor. Teddy, startled by the sudden movement, jumped from his chair as Lady Thorne's blurred face fluttered towards him.

'Miss George. This will be the death of your career.' Stark cleared his throat heavily as if he was trying to purge his own doubt out of it. 'Lord Thorne is a powerful man.'

'It's all right.' Hawkins said. 'No one will believe her anyway. There's enough gin in her veins to drown a rat.'

'Yes they will. You forget, Teddy, I've got my own police snitches now.'

And as she slammed the door, sending a rattle through the Reuters machine that she could hear even as she went down the stairs, she thought of Ebony Diamond closing her eyes against a sky lit up and smoked with fireworks. And she thought of the man on the gurney being wheeled into an ambulance, with his chest torn open and his mouth repeating over and over the name 'Clara'. The man who had given her back her camera, as if to say that he trusted her to tell the truth.

Epilogue

Derby Day, Epsom Race Course, 4 June 1913

And there is Twinkle at the bandstand, sticking her pink arm into the air so that the lemon silk of her sleeve falls away, flapping her hand furiously. Frankie shudders and smiles and waves back, gesturing that she is making her way over. She had intended to take Milly to the races on her press card but Milly doesn't return her letters or telegrams any more and someone on the Ladies' Page of the *Pall Mall Gazette* said that she heard at a debutante's ball that the Honourable Ms Millicent has gone away to France.

That's just like Milly, Frankie thinks. Charming Paris senseless in harem pants and sequins, as if nothing more troublesome than a dinner party indiscretion had sent her packing. She imagines her from time to time, sitting on a lionskin rug in front of some Montmartre hearth, and wonders who her friends are now and how she makes her money, and what she tells them about her past.

Lord Thorne has sold up half his shares in newspapers and become a silent partner on the rest. Occasionally Frankie hears the second-hand tattle from the Savage Club when she's in the Cheshire Cheese, and knows that even though Reuters made her change the names 'on grounds of national security,' word spread sufficiently around both the peerage and parliament. The piece was wired out that night and made the next day's afternoon editions, once police sources were called in and details checked. 'Parliament attacked from within', *The Times*; 'False Flag operation planned by prominent Noble to pin blame on Suffragettes', *The Manchester Guardian*; 'Mad Aristo Dead in Guy Fawkes Plot', *The News of the World*. The headlines and the words belong to each paper, but the story is hers. Frankie is proud of the growing pile of news clippings adorning her new lodgings in Camden Town, although today she is slightly sore that she has been sent to cover the Derby for the Reuters' sports wires. True, the King's horse is running, but it is small pickings compared to Teddy Hawkins who has, if rumours are to be believed, been sent to Bristol by Mr Stark to meet a polar explorer who has just spent three years marooned off Spitzbergen living on pickled shoe leather. Once again his scoop will be front page and hers will sneak in anonymously between the back two leaves of any number of newspapers.

A flash of colour catches her side vision and she sees a woman marching across the grass, with a short flap of fabric escaping from the lining of her jacket as if it has been pinned to the inside. The bright shades stand out immediately among the pastel crowd: Green White Violet – 'Give Women Votes.' Frankie clocks her straight away for a suffragette.

Fashions are changing. Ladies' waists are growing thicker, Frankie thinks with satisfaction, and more and more of them are ditching their huge Merry Widow hats for head-clinging cloches. Twinkle, of course, is up in arms about this and has come up with a word to try and discourage its spread: mannification. She still claims she would rather die of consumption than live to see women wear trousers in public, and insists on cramming herself into hobble skirts and taxidermied hats. Today her headwear features a woodland scene with three blind mice and a small porcelain woman brandishing a carving knife.

Frankie watches the suffragette as she strides. She is a lanky beautiful Amazon, and there is such nervous determination in her march that for a second the earth crumbles beneath Frankie and she sees Ebony Diamond, clear as a mirage, her shadow materialising on the wall of Mr Smythe's corset shop, then hurling Lady Thorne's brooch at him. She hasn't thought of Ebony for a long time but she has a picture of her, secreted from an old poster at Jojo's that she keeps in a slit of silk, cut with nail scissors into the back of her Blickensderfer case.

The moment unsettles her and makes her wonder for a moment if the suffragette will cause some kind of a scene. They have been increasing their attacks again lately: acid on golf courses, paintings slashed in public galleries, sometimes bombs set off in deserted buildings.

She looks over at Twinkle, seeing her leaning against the green bandstand rail, and panic takes hold, and she feels a tweak in her back and remembers the inside of the chapel, and a residual fear she has been left with slides like cold egg yolk down the back of her throat.

But nothing will happen with the suffragette. Not today, not while there are crowds. Mrs Pankhurst has been keen to inform every newspaper on Fleet Street that suffragettes will never endanger human life except their own. Surely it can only be a matter of time before they are granted what they fight for. Frankie is certain of it, weeks, months at most.

Before Frankie reaches Twinkle, two more figures catch her attention, both making for the edge of the starting post. She recognises the brown woollen suit and stiff wide shoulders of Inspector Primrose – he had told her he would be at the races – and she sticks two fingers in her mouth to give a shrill whistle. He twitches his head a few times then locks eyes with her and as he moves to lift his hat she sees that the woman with him has a full pregnant belly pushing out through the fine linen of her pale pink dress. Frankie is embarrassed to have summoned him in such a common way in front of his wife, but she can't help crack a grin, showing the gap next to her canine tooth and he nods, albeit reservedly, and turns back to his wife, whose name Frankie can't remember although it begins with C.

And now the gunshot has ripped into the sunny sky and

the horses are off and Twinkle is impatiently snapping her fingers at Frankie to hurry up. Frankie trots the last few steps, leaping up the bandstand railings to join Twinkle, and they lean over, watching the horses fill the air with slow thunder. People are bent forward, tense, shouting out names, waving their betting cards in the air. The cavalcade pounds round the faraway loop at the end of the course, heading back towards the crowds to finish in front of the Royal Box. Suddenly, through the tremor of hooves on turf and the cries of the crowd comes another sound, a single voice so loud it's hard to tell if it comes from man or woman. A blur of green, white and purple is moving fast across the field, the tall woman clinging to her suffragette flag; first she is scurrying low under the race barrier, then striding high, then standing broad, reaching for the King's horse as its whites widen round its eyes and its hooves approach, heading straight for her, making the earth shake.

Historical Note

While *The Hourglass Factory* is set against the struggle for women's votes, it is a work of fiction, and I have frequently altered, fudged and made honest mistakes with history to suit the story.

There are however true events and people that formed the basis for particular parts of the book, and I'd like to jot a few of them down as it's my great hope that the story will pique a curiosity in some readers about this turbulent, shocking and inspiring time. Any historical mistakes made in *The Hourglass Factory* are not a reflection on the excellent sources below but are mine alone.

Ebony's Albert Hall leap was – as Twinkle notes – inspired by a suffragette named Isabel Kelley, who broke into Dundee's Kinnaird Hall via a skylight during a political meeting from which women were barred. I read about this and many more of the suffragettes' more radical activities in a book called *The Militant Suffragettes* (1973) by Antonia Raeburn. Other great suffragette reads are the Pankhurst sisters' books, *Unshackled:*

The Story of How We Won the Vote (1959) by Christabel Pankhurst, and *The Suffragette Movement* (1911) by E. Sylvia Pankhurst, which details the ghastly violence of Black Friday. Constance Lytton's diary is available online – although I was privileged to hold the original at the National Archives – and describes not only her heroic attempts to expose the prison authorities' double standards over treatment of women from different classes, but also gives a chilling verbatim account of force-feeding. Speaking of verbatim, I used several of Emmeline Pankhurst's speeches (sometimes anachronistically) when putting words into her mouth during her interview with Primrose. I hope her spirit will forgive me for taking this liberty but I wanted to convey as accurately as possible her position on violence, and this seemed to be the best way. For this I consulted period newspaper sources, but my additional suffragette research also included *Votes For Women: The Virago Book of Suffragettes* (2000) ed. Joyce Marlow, *The Suffragettes In Pictures* (1996) by Diane Atkinson, and *Vindication: A Postcard History of the Woman's Movement* (1995) by Ian McDonald, all fantastic reads.

The character of Evelina Haverfield who features briefly was indeed alleged to have led police horses 'out of their ranks' as noted in several sources. I'd like to think she did this by charming them and making them sit, however it's sadly doubtful this was the case. William Reynolds is inspired by a man named William Ball who went to prison and was force-fed for the women's cause, afterwards being transferred to Colney Hatch. The treatment of Ball was far more shocking than that of Reynolds, as is detailed in the Museum of London's online records. I completely fabricated his affair.

Twinkle, believe it or not, also has her roots in a real person, although I used only the barest facts of this woman's life. Catherine Walters aka Skittles was the last of the great Victorian courtesans. I first read about her years ago in *The Mammoth Book of Heroic and Outrageous Women* (1999) ed. Gemma Alexander, which was incidentally also the first place I came across Emmeline Pankhurst (an excellent Christmas present for a teenage girl; thank you, Auntie Ros).

For information relating to the work of Scotland Yard and the suffragettes I am grateful to the National Archives. For police history background I used the memoir *At Scotland Yard: being the experience during twenty-seven years' service by John Sweeney, late Detective Inspector, CID* (1904), *When I was at Scotland Yard* (1932) by Chief Inspector James Berrett, Joan Lock's *Scotland Yard Casebook* (1993), and *The Police Code and General Manual of the Criminal Law, Fifteenth edition* (1912), by Sir Howard Vincent (revised by the commissioner of the Police of the Metropolis). I also particularly want to acknowledge William Thomas Ewens's enthralling memoir *Thirty Years at Bow Street Police Court* (1924) from which I shamelessly poached the true story of the suffragette court riot and the egg being thrown at the clerk.

The act of a policeman dressing up as a woman to go undercover may seem ridiculous, but Joan Lock cites this as having happened during the Whitechapel investigation (though surprisingly never during the era of the suffragettes). I couldn't resist adding it in.

As for corsets, Valerie Steele's book, *The Corset: A Cultural History* (2001) was a great place to read about the history of these fascinating objects, including the man who inspired The Hourglass Club. And David Kunzle's extraordinary *Fashion & Fetishism: Corsets, Tight-Lacing and Other Forms of Body-Sculpture* (New ed 2004) was invaluable in helping me get my head round the paradoxical allure of subjugation and sexual liberation in corset fetishism.

As regards London, my deepest apologies to the denizens of the city I love so much for any inaccuracies of place or distance I might have thrown in. I spent three wonderful years living in London but for additional information on its history I am grateful to Peter Ackroyd's *London: The Biography* (2000), Stephen Inwood's *A History of London* (1998), and probably the most enjoyable read of all my research, Judith Summers's firecracker of a book, *Soho: A History of London's Most Colourful Neighbourhood* (1989).

Female journalists were not uncommon during the era, as I discovered from Elizabeth L. Banks's *Autobiography of a Newspaper Girl* (1902) and Michelle Elizabeth Tusan's *Women Making News: Gender and Journalism in Modern Britain,* (2005) (and from those indefatigable bastions of sexism, The 'Ladies Pages' in contemporary period newspapers to whose editors I must also express my gratitude). I read about the news agency tape machines and the anatomy of newspaper-making in Henry Leach's *Fleet Street from Within: The Romance and*

Mystery of the Daily Paper (1905) and about newspaper history in Dennis Griffiths's *Fleet Street: Five Hundred Years of the Press*. Other books of great use were *The Edwardians: The Remaking of British Society* (1975) by Paul Thompson, and *Edwardian Life and Leisure* (1973) by Ronald Pearsall.

Richard Anthony Baker's brilliant book *British Music Hall: An Illustrated History* (2005) introduced me to the National Vigilance Association, the history of the London Coliseum and the song 'The Daring Young Man on the Flying Trapeze', and also The Great Lafayette's remarkable stage trick, The Lion's Bride, the inspiration for Ebony's disappearing act. On the subject of outrageous tricks, the presence of nitrocellulose in the red dye on old decks of playing cards is true, and according to folklore has been used in the past to create deadly bombs. Christian de Ryck of the International Playing-Card Society was kind enough to look into this for me and confirm it.

While suffragettes were arrested and sent to prison for a wide range of arson activities in the early twentieth century, I have tried to be faithful to their ethos in presenting them as holding human life sacred. It is true that some acts of arson, such as Gladys Evans setting fire to the Dublin Theatre during a visit from Asquith in 1912, would seem to contradict this, however it is not clear whether actions such as this were sanctioned by the WSPU in advance, or merely supported retrospectively in view of the fact that no one was hurt.

The same goes for an alleged plot to assassinate the Prime Minister in 1909. Although attributed to 'suffragettes' in the media there is nothing to indicate that this was an official WSPU plan. At any rate, the line taken by Emmeline Pankhurst was that the only people in danger of harm from suffragette activities were suffragettes themselves. This was unfortunately fulfilled on several occasions, the most famous being Emily Wilding Davison's protest at the 1913 Derby.

It took fifteen more years for women to gain universal suffrage. The WSPU kept to their oath, that no human life except their own be harmed in their campaign.

On 2 July 1928 the Representation of the People (Equal Franchise) Act gave women the vote on the same grounds as men. Emmeline Pankhurst, leader of the suffragettes, had died eighteen days previously.

Acknowledgements

My deepest thanks go to the army of people bigger and more fearsome than the Hourglass Factory seamstresses who contributed to the creation of this book.

First of all I am massively grateful to Daisy Parente at Lutyens & Rubinstein for having the enthusiasm of a champion and a fantastic reader's eye that helped shape the story. Similarly, enormous thank you to Clare Hey at Simon & Schuster for her brilliant and invaluable editing, and for making the learning process fun along the way. Huge thank you also to Jane Finigan at L&R, Carla Josephson, Helen Mockridge, Leena Lane and the team at Simon & Schuster who worked on the book.

For their tireless encouragement I owe a debt of gratitude to The Scottish Book Trust, particularly Will Mackie, Claire Marchant-Collier, Caitrin Armstrong and also Helen Croney for her time and expert PR advice. The Scottish Book Trust New Writers Award I received allowed me to work on the book in the beautiful surroundings of Cove Park as well as giving me the financial support I needed to redraft it. Thank you to Beatrice Colin for her words of endorsement on the opening chapters. To receive encouragement from a writer whose work I love was a dream come true and kept me motivated.

Huge thanks to Harry Man, Araminta Whitley and Sophie Hughes for suggestions that helped shape early drafts; to Lainey Johr for reading the very first draft, Lynsey May for reading the nearly last draft and Caraigh McGregor for advice on Northern Irish accents – I'm privileged to have both their great friendship and their feedback. Rhoda MacDonald is an absolute pearl for turning her bedroom into a writer's retreat during one of my redrafts, as are Rose Filippi and Rosie Watts for being so passionate about seeing the finished book that giving up was never an option.

I conducted most of my research through books – and made a good deal of it up – but on the occasion I wanted to check a fact with a human being I was very grateful to have Evangeline Holland, of the excellent Edwardian Promenade website, patiently responding to my emails with her encyclopaedic knowledge of the era.

Finally the greatest thanks of all go to my family, Liz and Richard Ribchester for encouraging their wayward daughter, to my brother Tim, and to Chris, Keith and Lidia for the support. And for reasons too numerous and complex to describe, I thank my other half, Alex.